BLOOD BROTHERS

SOL WACHTLER
AND
DAVID GOULD

NEW MILLENNIUM PRESS
Beverly Hills

To my sons Bryan and Connor —David Gould

*To my mother Fay Wachtler in her 103rd year
of a magnificent life* —Sol Wachtler

ISBN: 1-932407-01-4

Library of Congress Cataloging-in-Publication Data Available

Design: Kerry DeAngelis, KL Design

New Millennium Press
301 North Canon Drive
Suite 214
Beverly Hills, CA 90210
www.NewMillenniumPress.com

10 9 8 7 6 5 4 3 2 1

ACKNOWLEDGMENTS

We are grateful to those who saw merit in this book when we were having some self doubts. Sol's wife Joan for her reassurance and for not telling him that he was wasting his time and David's wife Laurie for her reckless courage in reading through several drafts in order to give us helpful feedback. Gratitude also to our attorney Lauren Wachtler.

David's sisters Abby and Deborah, his brother Eric and Mel Salberg, Maxine Orocofsky, Wren Marshall, Steve Salzman, Bob Jewell, Michael Trainor and Paul Corcoran for their invaluable encouragement. Cindy who took time away from Jazzy to read the book and to Sol's brother, Morty, who swore that it was not his brotherly love which caused him to find the book compelling.

To Fred Wilpon whose unbridled enthusiasm really inspired us. To Dick Heffner who kept an open mind. To Elliot Kastner who read the book to kill time on a long flight and "loved it." To Irving Schneider who is not usually given to effusive praise, but who gave it freely to us. To the Wachtler kids, Lauren, Marjorie, Alison and Philip who although undoubtedly blinded by affection for their father, still managed to convince him that "it was really good Pop."

We both thank our publisher Michael Viner for the faith he showed in us, and Julie McCarron and Mary Aarons who very gently but unerringly helped us make our book better.

We are also grateful to Gregg Smith, and Gloria Besser for doing the copy work which was beyond our capabilities.

"The great enemy of truth is very often not the lie—deliberate, contrived and dishonest—but the myth—persistent, persuasive and unrealistic."

—JOHN F. KENNEDY.

PREFACE

Mangrove swamps are very much a part of the vast Georgia wetlands bordering rivers with strange, Indian-sounding names like Ogeechee, Ohoopee, and Oconee, and a swamp known as the Okefenokee. Not much is seen of them because they are in the backwater, snake-infested, little-traveled areas of the state.

The tendrils of the mangrove tree look like large tubular fingers dipping into the brackish water of the swamp. They seem designed as much to keep the plant out of the water as to draw nourishment from it. They do their work noiselessly—the dense heat and silence of the bog disturbed only by the drone of clouds of mosquitoes.

On this late afternoon the peace of dusk and the stillness of the water were disturbed by the lurching of a small skiff. A life-and-death struggle was taking place as three white men strained to hold a man in the bottom of the boat. The captive—Aaron Boddie, a black man—knew what fate awaited him. He was to be torched, burned alive, with his charred bones left to rot in the swamp. His struggle was so violent that it looked as though the boat would capsize.

One of his captors hoped it would. Though he had been a willing partner in the conspiracy to murder Aaron Boddie, he'd had a sudden change of heart. He was now equally determined to prevent this act of ultimate evil from taking place.

BOOK ONE

CHAPTER 1

LUKE

I loved the Augusta of my youth. Not only the wide streets and beautiful homes framed by tall trees, but also the places outside of town. The red clay hills, which in another time were harvested for the manufacturing of bricks, and the brown cornfields mixed with the green and white fields of watermelon and cotton.

And the people. By and large, they are soft-spoken and gentle, though they tend to distrust strangers. Georgia culture binds its residents close to the land and the family. Georgians are intolerant of those things, people or institutions, which could be perceived as a threat to either. They're not against change, exactly—it's just that they don't trust it or what it might bring in its wake. They seem to feel that most strangers seek to alter their regional lifestyles—not, perhaps, with the same vigor as General Sherman in his march to the sea—but even those who suggest subtle change are suspect.

This distrust is often mistaken for bigotry. Anyone who grew up in Georgia in the middle of the last century learned something about bigotry. Don't get me wrong. The people in the Georgia of my youth were not mean—in fact, for the most part I think they were really good and decent people. And don't confuse bigotry with hating. Georgia bigots didn't *hate* strangers, or blacks, or Catholics, or Jews, or Northerners, or foreign-borns—they just didn't care very much for them.

And they didn't get their likes and dislikes mixed up with strong emotions. They could like you very much without loving you, and they could dislike you an awful lot without hating you. And even if they didn't care for a person because of the color of his skin, or where he was from or what he was, they could still find him acceptable so long as he stayed "in his place."

I always knew that I was different from all my friends

because I was Jewish. There were other Jewish families in Augusta—mostly merchants who ran furniture, jewelry, and clothing stores. When they weren't tending their shops, they kept pretty much to themselves. It just seemed natural for the Jews in town to socialize with each other and not with the other citizens in our town. We had our own pool club, and the adults visited each other at night—mostly to play cards. I had no Jewish friends, and sensed that the fact that I was Jewish was best kept secret at the risk of having no friends at all.

All I learned about being Jewish I learned from my parents. They made it clear to me that being Jewish meant that I believed in God but could not accept the belief shared by Christians that Jesus was the son of God and someone to be worshiped. In fact, I was told that it was a sin to consider anyone but God as being divine. Divine meaning the person who had everything to say about what happens to you when you are alive and dead. I was led to believe that acknowledging the divinity of Jesus was a sin. When I asked my parents, flat out: "Was there a Jesus?" They said yes—that he was born a Jew, like me, and he was a teacher—but he wasn't "divine" and God is angered by the thought that anyone else would be considered as being divine.

My parents also told me that we were not really "practicing Jews." I didn't know what that meant. Did it mean that you weren't good at being Jewish if you didn't practice at it? Or did it mean that it was enough just being Jewish without having to practice it as a religion? One thing I did know was that if you weren't a "practicing Jew" you didn't go to a Jewish house of worship or observe any religious holidays. And I'm not talking only of Jewish religious holidays—about which I knew nothing—I mean any religious holidays.

In grade school religious holidays for the other kids were a big thing, and it seemed that all the holiday celebrations centered around Jesus—the person my home instruction told me I had to stay clear of. Everyone else at school seemed to spend much of his time absorbed in this powerful person whom they believed to be the son of God, conceived and born in divine mysticism. They spoke of the miracles he performed, of his death, and coming back to life in heaven. And they spoke with certainty of the fact that those who did not believe in him were blasphemers doomed to spend eternity in hell.

Of course I could not tell any of my classmates that I was one of those nonbelievers. I guessed one of the advantages of being a non-practicing Jew was that no one—at least no one that I knew—suspected that I was Jewish. The church may have been separated from the state in other parts of the country, but in the rural Georgia of my youth, they would sooner remove the inkwells from the desks than remove Jesus from the classroom.

And so when it came my turn to read from the New Testament I did so without hesitation—but when it came to reading the name of Jesus, I slurred the word or would say "Jeez" ... "And Jeez said unto them." I was fooling my teacher and classmates while at the same time not offending God.

I had other subterfuges. When we were told to bow our heads in prayer while the teacher invoked Jesus's blessings, I would keep my eyes open. I felt I wasn't really praying or committing a Jewish sin if my eyes were open. The easiest thing to get away with was the singing of hymns—I would just silently move my lips.

But it seemed that I was missing a lot by not believing in Jesus. I felt deprived when everyone else was singing Christmas carols and anticipating the receiving of gifts. I felt that my parents were denying me and themselves a joyous season because we didn't have a decorated tree and holly and wreaths that evoked all the warmth that seemed to surround Christmas. And when Easter came around I started to wonder whether my avoidance of Jesus would deprive me of "salvation" and if I might really be condemned to an eternity of damnation because I said "Jeez" and kept my eyes open during prayers.

But I let all that pass and was content with the fact that none of my friends knew I was Jewish. It was difficult enough for me to fake it here on earth without worrying so much about what was going to happen to me in eternity.

There were other times when my faith—or lack of it—was tested. Like the time the Revival Meeting came to town. The "Revival" was talked about long before it came and was a greatly anticipated and heralded event. We knew it was drawing near when they started setting up the tent on the outskirts of town, where the poor whites lived. That tent seemed huge to me. I guess it had to be, because as my friends told me, it not only had to hold a lot of people, it also had to provide a place for the "Holy Ghost," as they sometimes called Jesus. During the evening, they believed, the spirit of Jesus would pay a visit to the revival.

*   *   *

My first name was Lukash—my mother's maiden name—but everyone called me Luke. That suited me fine, because Luke was a good New Testament name. Having a New Testament name in Georgia was not only acceptable, it was desirable—particularly for a Jewish boy who didn't want anyone to know he was Jewish.

I was bigger than most boys my age and was looked up to as a sort of a leader. Part of the credentials for my role as a boyhood leader was earned by an uncle whom I never met. He'd been a hero in World War II, or so I thought at the time, and his portrait in full uniform hung in my living room. I regaled my friends with stories of the heroism of Uncle Mike (his real name was Micah). My thrilling stories of his heroism were enough to set me apart and a notch above my friends.

And my friends wanted to be with me—to follow me. Like the time I led a whole bunch of them over the Savannah River which runs between Augusta and the South Carolina state line.

Sometimes the river ran so dry you could actually walk across its muddy sandy bottom—which is what I decided to do, leading a whole pack of kids from school. We walked all the way to the outskirts of Aiken, South Carolina and back, them following me and me leading them like a general in front of an army.

"We're in Georgia, We're in Georgia, We're in Georgia," I kept repeating as we crossed the river bottom, and then when we were about halfway over I announced: "We're in South Carolina, we're in South Carolina—we've gone from one state to another!" And they all cheered—themselves for doing it, and me for leading them.

But there were others. Some smaller cliques gravitated together because they lived in the same part of town. Some of the kids from the richer part of town had their own tight circle of friends—there weren't many, but they seemed to find each other. Geography had a lot to do with who your friends were. My friends were my neighbors. The others were the kids from the poorer working-class sections of town.

These others were not my friends but they respected me. Well, respect might be too strong a word—better to say they left me and my real friends alone. They were tough kids—the kind who spent most of their days hanging out and smoking behind the gym, behind the shop building, or in the bathroom.

Their world revolved around cigarettes and Jack Demerest, one of the most ignorant, unpleasant, and nasty sonsofbitches I ever knew. Jack was never alone—he was always surrounded by his claque of "kinsmen," as he called them. They even dressed alike: dirty white undershirts sticking out of torn blue jeans, greasy black hair tied up in ponytails, and rope necklaces around their necks—probably to hide the dirt rings.

It was Jack Demerest who invited me to come to the revival. I took it as a gesture of goodwill and although I didn't like him, I appreciated his invitation.

"C'mon" he invited, "Even if you don't want to be saved,

they serve up some fine fried chicken and ribs."

The offer didn't excite me. I didn't like ribs, and I sure didn't care for Jack Demerest—but most of all I was afraid of being in the same tent with Jesus. This was the Jesus who was able to grant instant salvation or damnation. What if he couldn't be fooled by my false incantations and singled me out of the crowd for instant dispatch to hell? On the other hand, would my not going alert Demerest to the fact that I might be a Jew, thereby allowing him to condemn me to a hell on earth—or at least in the schoolyard. I reasoned that since Jesus was not really the son of God, I shouldn't fear any instant hell fire, but I did fear Demerest's mouth. And besides, I did like fried chicken.

And so I went to the revival with Demerest and some of his kinsmen. I only hoped that my parents were right about Jesus and he wouldn't show up.

CHAPTER 2

LUKE

It was a huge tent—huge and hot. So hot that I couldn't believe people would come. But they did. After milling around, eating ribs and chicken on the edges of the tent, they began to file into the canvas auditorium, which was filled with rows of metal chairs. The ground—the floor of the tent—was covered with saw-dust. Bare light bulbs hung from ropes strung between the poles supporting the tarpaulin.

On a wooden platform at the front of the tent a choir of Negroes was swaying back and forth, singing a gospel spiritual and clapping their hands in time with a piano which was playing loud chords. The piano didn't seem to be playing a melody, but was spellbinding when coupled with the spirited voices of the chorus. They wore what looked like heavy silk robes—purple with yellow collars. The revival hadn't even begun, but their faces were already covered with sweat as they sang something about Jesus being bathed in the blood of a lamb. That must be some kind of mystical allusion that I would probably never understand.

I noticed that they were the only Negroes in the tent. The others were a mixture of men who looked like farmers wearing clean overalls and women dressed as if they were going to church. As hot as it was, most of the women wore hats and long dresses with sleeves. The women all had small cardboard fans with the name of a funeral home printed on them. They fanned themselves with twitchy wrists, but I doubted that this gave them much relief from the heat.

The choir suddenly went from song to soft humming and the piano went silent. Slowly, almost deliberately, a short man walked to the middle of the platform. He was wearing a gray suit and natty tie pulled tight against his collar which seemed as wet with sweat as his face. He smiled and held up his hands for silence.

7

"My brothers and sisters," he began, "let us bow our heads."

Everyone stood up. There I was, standing right in the middle of Demerest and his kinsmen. They along with the rest of the assemblage, bowed their heads and closed their eyes. I kept mine open, certain that no one would notice because theirs were all shut. I was thinking that maybe I would get away with this after all—but then the speaker began:

"In the name of Jesus Christ our Lord and Savior, Amen."

"Uh-oh," I thought.

He continued, "We are gathered in your sight and in your name to worship Thee and sound a warning. A warning to those who blaspheme, who gamble, who smoke and drink. A warning to those who bear false witness and fall prey to the weakness of the flesh and most especially," and here he paused and opened his eyes and looked, I was certain, directly at me. "We would warn those who would deny Thee, for the wages of sin are death and those who would deny Thee are condemned to burn forever in the fires of hell. And let us all say: Amen."

And everyone said "Amen" except for me, who said, "Ahmmm."

Everyone sat down and except for the whisper of the fans which seemed to move even more twitchily, there was a hushed silence. He cleared his throat and, in a quiet, seemingly restrained voice, began again:

"There are those who speak of the "rapture" of the second coming of Christ our Lord. A silent and invisible coming which will leave the wicked alive and able to have a second chance to be converted and to serve Him. But those who believe this are mistaken."

"Yes," responded the congregation, "Amen."

"They believe," he went on, "that this 'rapture' will take place before the revelation of the Antichrist who then will bring about the tribulation. But those who believe this have not read their Bible."

"No," responded the congregation, "Amen."

"For the 'rapture' is not silent." (A louder "Amen" from the audience.) The speaker raised his voice. "The RAPTURE is not silent." (A still louder "Amen" in response.) The speaker was now shouting: "THE RAPTURE IS NOT SILENT!" A shouted "AMEN."

And now he unwound. He took off his tie and jacket, threw them to the floor and with his index finger pointing toward heaven he shouted into the microphone. "AND THE RAPTURE IS NOT INVISIBLE. Oh yes, it will be seen. It is written—" Here he picked up a Bible from his podium and waving it above his head continued his thundering:

"It is written in the book of Matthew: ALL of the angels will come with Jesus—ALL of the angels. Think about that—ALL of the angels. At His resurrection ONE lone angel appeared and the entire Roman Guard dropped to the ground as dead men."

Fervent shouts of "Amen."

"Imagine the scene—if one angel can cause the death of the entire Roman Guard, what will happen when ALL of the angels come with Jesus. No, my friends, it will not be an invisible coming. Again, from Matthew, 'For as the lightning cometh out of the east, shineth even unto the west; so shall also the coming of the Son of God be.' And from Revelations: "Behold, he cometh with clouds; and every eye shall see him.' INVISIBLE—I THINK NOT. INVISIBLE?"

Shouts of "No" and "PRAISE JESUS" from the assemblage.

He now moved from one side of the stage to the other, pounding the podium, waving the Bible above his head. Turning his back to the audience and snapping his head over his shoulder he jumped with both legs leaving the ground, kangaroo-style, all the time quoting scripture and drawing graphic word pictures of Jesus, bathed in blood, dying on the cross. The assemblage shouted along with him, swaying back and forth—hands raised toward heaven as if waiting to be lifted up—and then he suddenly stopped.

By now the speaker was soaking wet. His lower lip trembled as he intoned, "Thessalonians says it—the rapture does not leave the wicked alive. They are slain at the Lord's coming. The wicked will not have a second opportunity to be saved after the Second Coming. All sinners will be destroyed and condemned to hell's fire if they are not saved before He comes again.

"Tonight may be your last chance to be saved. Tonight may be your last chance to embrace our Lord Jesus Christ. Tonight you and I—all of us—will stand with Jesus. I know some of you may want to hold back—The Book of John tells us that the Antichrist has been active for centuries—but he fears the power of Jesus."

More shouts of "Amen."

And then he shouted into the microphone so that the very air vibrated, "Begone Satan, BEGONE SATAN, and come all of you all of you in the name of Sweet Jesus—come forward to be blessed, to be saved in the name of Christ."

At this invitation people in wheelchairs and on crutches as well as others—young and old, all with hands in the air—started moving as one toward the preacher. Arms outstretched, he held his hands facing the throngs, ready to touch and embrace them. I looked at Jack and some of his kinsmen, expecting them to be smiling at this extraordinary performance. I was surprised to see that they, too, had their hands raised and were gravitating toward the aisle. I froze. I had been undone. There was no more faking it. I either approached the preacher with the others to be "saved" or I ran. I did what anyone who feared being confused with the "Antichrist" would do. I ran and didn't stop running until the tent was well out of sight.

I feared there would be consequences. I could continue the charade by telling Jack and his friends that I'd had a heart attack or something—or I could confess to being a Jew. I would have preferred to have a heart attack. What I decided to do was to continue my deception and hope—not pray, just hope—that I would continue to get away with it.

CHAPTER 3

LUKE

I told you about the different groups of kids who seemed to gravitate to leaders. I was close to being one of those leaders—a position I enjoyed, at least until my secret was exposed. But there was one fellow who didn't follow anyone. Not me, or Demerest or anyone else. He went by the name of T.C.

He was always alone, lurking around the edges of where the rest of us were. He was bigger than me or Demerest and had a large, square-shaped head covered with blond hair. His small mouth which never seemed to smile or speak was set in a lantern-shaped jaw. His eyes also seemed too small and too close together for his large head—but they radiated a kind of primitive intelligence. Maybe when you put all of his features and everything else together you would have to say he wasn't bad-looking.

His clothes were threadbare—not to affect a style, but because he was dirt poor. He lived with his father who was drunk most of the time and did whatever odd jobs needed doing in town. They lived in the poorest part of Augusta, next to a big house called "Shiloh" which was a home for Negro orphans. I remember thinking that as bad as it was to be a Negro in Georgia in those days, being a Negro orphan must have been really tough.

Anyway, T.C. would have been called white trash if he weren't so strong-looking. You don't say anything bad about people the size of T.C.—at least not to their face or where they can hear you.

One day I decided to speak to him. Not that I needed any new friends, but I kind of felt sorry for him. No one should be alone so much of the time. He was sitting on a rail supporting a teeter-totter in a corner of the school yard looking off into space.

"Name is Lipton," I said, extending an open hand.

Without unfolding his arms or taking his eyes of the horizon he replied: "Sounds like tea."

I felt stupid. Not because of his remark, but because he left me standing there with my hand sticking out smiling at someone who wasn't even looking at me. I slowly slipped my hand into my pocket—like that was where it was heading all along—and started to tell T.C. that he could go screw himself. I even thought about saying something about his being white trash. Instead I just turned and walked away.

After that, I didn't give a damn about T.C. and would never have thought about him again if I hadn't happened to overhear Demerest and his "kinsmen" planning to ambush him. I was in the bathroom which, as usual, was filled with cigarette smoke. Demerest and his buddies were huddled together in a corner, but the only one talking was Demerest. He was telling his followers how he was going to beat up on T.C.

"I don't need any of you to help me—just want you to make sure he doesn't turn tail. What you got to do is surround him, get behind his back, and leave the rest to me." Demerest went on to say how he was going to whip and strip T.C. "buck naked" before turning him loose.

"What do you want to do that for?" I asked from outside the circle of conspirators. At first my question was greeted by blank stares, as if they thought it required an answer which they were unable to come up with. And then Demerest spoke.

"Well, well, if it isn't Lipton—what happened to you the other night? Couldn't take the heat?" And then to the others, "You know, I think Lipton here was scared by the Holy Ghost—makes me suspect that he acted just like maybe a Jew would act." Raucous laughter. And then, without pursuing the possibility of my being Jewish, "And as far as T.C. is concerned, it's none of your damn business, but if you must know that ignorant cracker is worthless white trash—keeping by himself like he does, he deserves to be whupped. Might improve his personality."

"Yeah," said another of the group," he's the kind of garbage gives whites a bad name—a real white nigger."

"That's why we want to strip him, see if he's hung like a nigger," Demerest said, again to boisterous laughter. And then to his friends, which did not include me: "Speaking of which, you know, I always considered a Jew to be a nigger turned inside out."

Ignoring his reference as if it didn't apply to me I interceded in defense of T.C, "You can't go beatin' up on someone just because you don't like him," I said, and hearing the words come out of my mouth, I knew instantly that I sounded like a teacher or a preacher—which automatically disqualified me from being a participant in this discussion. I was separating myself even further from the rest of them.

"Not likin' him don't have nothing to do with it," said one of the prospective marauders, a fellow named Wiggens, "that lump of dirt has been just asking for it. The sonofabitch insults you every time he gives you that 'down the nose—better than you are' look of his."

They were hell-bent on getting T.C.—on "whupping his ass"—and it was obvious that I wouldn't be able to talk them out of it by trying to convince them that T.C. wasn't aloof—it was just that he knew that he didn't belong, a feeling with which I could identify. He knew that he was different from the rest of them—a distinction which I had already earned by trying to stick up for him. I thought about warning T.C. But why should I? I had offered him my hand in friendship and, rather than take it, he insulted me by ignoring it. Worse, he made fun of my name. Who the hell was he to make fun of anyone else?

T.C. walked home the same way every day. Although I'd never paid much attention to it, he would always leave the schoolyard going in a different direction from the rest of us. Of course, that made sense given the fact that he lived close to "colored town"—which was what we called that part of town where the Negroes lived. It was a part of town which was alien to most of us.

The ambush occurred the day after I heard them plotting. The three o'clock bell rang and there was the usual rush to throw our books in the lockers and get away from the hot stuffy rooms and hallways that had been cooking us all day.

Demerest and a group of about five of his followers walked together out of the stucco arched doors of the schoolhouse onto the schoolyard. Instead of taking up their usual position behind the rear wall of the gym for another smoke, they started to follow T.C. who was innocently sauntering in the direction of colored town, oblivious to the menace which was stalking him.

I debated with myself. Should I follow them? If so, for what purpose? The time for warnings had passed—and I sure as hell didn't want to get mixed up in what was going to be a bad and probably bloody piece of business. I started to join my own friends and head for home, but somehow I was drawn to the drama which was about to unfold. Maybe I wanted to see T.C. messed up. The one way to avoid thinking about your own forthcoming doom was to witness someone else's.

I had never noticed it before that day, but watching him I realized that T.C. seemed to walk bent over with a kind of lumbering gait. He wore ragged overalls that were too big even for him. His slouch made his clothes look even bigger than they were, and him smaller than he was. But those of us who had seen him up close knew that he was big enough to pull a plow.

Demerest walked about ten feet behind T.C., and his five "kinsmen" followed another three or four feet behind Demerest. As a mere observer, I hung back a respectable distance.

"Look at that white trash up ahead," Demerest said, loud enough for T.C. to hear him. "Guess the trash truck didn't pick up this morning."

"Maybe they did and that lump of shit just fell off," Wiggens chimed in.

"Could be," said Demerest, "They oughtta be more careful—some respectable folks might step in it."

"No chance," said Wiggens, "They'd smell it first—time enough to step around it."

"'Cept look at the size of it," Demerest said, glancing over his shoulder and playing to his audience with a big stupid grin. "That would be hard to step around, looks like an elephant turd."

T.C. just kept walking—head down—like he didn't hear them. I couldn't see his face, but somehow I felt he wore that same indifferent mask which never seemed to show any emotion.

"I think its time to clean up the mess," Demerest said, and quickened his pace.

He was now within touching distance of T.C. He reached out and pushed T.C.'s shoulder, just hard enough to cause T.C. to stumble forward—not fall, just stumble a little. T.C. kept walking—didn't even turn around. Like nothing had happened, like nothing had been said—he just kept lumbering along.

By God, I thought, as big as he is, T.C.'s a coward. With all of his menacing presence, he's just a big coward!

"Looks like what we thought was from an elephant came out of a chicken. What'sa matter, farm boy," Demerest taunted, "you so chickenshit you can't fight?"

Demerest was now so close that T.C. must have felt his breath on his back. The kinsmen, sensing a kill, started to close in. Me, I still hung back. I felt ashamed for T.C. No person should allow himself to be humiliated this way—even someone like T.C., who must have spent his whole life living with one sort of humiliation or another.

And then suddenly, as if he was propelled by some external force, Demerest leaped forward and struck T.C. square in the back. He hit him so hard that T.C., big as he was, was thrown sprawling face down. And as quick as he hit the ground, Demerest was on top of him, his fists flailing.

T.C. cupped his hands on each side of his face as he pressed his nose against the red clay soil. Demerest's blows pounded on the back of his head as if he was trying to bury T.C.'s face deep into the dirt.

"Yeehaw!" "Hot Damn!" "Kill the Sonofabitch." Each of the kinsmen contributed to the chorus cheering Demerest's merciless pounding.

"Should I take his duds off now?" shouted Wiggens over the shouting of the others.

That did it. It was if a cattle prod had hit T.C. in his privates. He suddenly took his hands away from his face, reached over his shoulders, and grabbed Demerest by the collar of his shirt, pulling him sharply against his back. The pounding stopped as Demerest tried to brace himself to prevent being pinioned by T.C.'s strong hands onto T.C.'s wide back.

The "yeehawing" and other shouts of encouragement were still in the air when T.C. rolled over on Demerest—it happened that fast. The only thing that broke the silence was the "Whoosh" of air from Demerest as T.C. pressed his full weight on him.

There he was, still holding Demerest by his shoulders, but now it was T.C. on top. He was looking skyward, his big body completely covering the person who not a minute ago was all over him.

A muffled sound came from the red earth underneath T.C., sounding something like "Helpgethimoffame."

T.C. responded by digging both his elbows into the sides of his pinioned prey.

"Owwwohharrgh," came the anguished response.

By now the other kinsmen started to close in. They looked determined, not so much to get T.C. now, but to free Demerest before he was crushed to death.

I thought it had been unfair for Demerest, without good reason, to have jumped T.C. from behind. I hadn't done anything to stop that, but I wasn't going to just stand by and watch Demerest's five buddies try to do what their leader was unable to do.

I stepped between the kinsmen and the two prone combatants.

"Where do you all think you're going?" I asked.

"Get out the way, Lipton," said Wiggens, "this ain't your fight."

"Well, maybe I'm about to make it my fight," I told him.

No sooner did the words leave my mouth than Wiggens jumped at me, attempting a flying tackle. I sidestepped, and he went skidding, sprawled flat on his belly. I was thinking that was a pretty good move on my part when an arm suddenly wrapped itself around my windpipe and I thought for sure I was going to choke to death. I would have been if I hadn't been saved by a sharply delivered order:

"Let him go! All of you—back off! Get out of here!"

The command came from Demerest himself, who was responding to directions given him by T.C. Directions which he was bound to follow to keep himself from being broken in half by a bear hug which lifted him a good three feet off the ground.

When the kinsmen responded to the orders and started to retreat, Demerest was released from the hold. He fell to the ground like a sack of potatoes, got slowly to his feet and, straining for breath, left the field of battle. He was holding his ribs and—I don't know if I was the only one who noticed—he was definitely crying.

Without a word to me or anyone else, T.C. continued on his way home.

It must have been two or three weeks later that I saw T.C. again. I spotted him out of the corner of my eye standing near the water fountain where I was headed. I didn't say anything to him for fear of being ignored. Instead I bent down to take a swallow of the water.

"Waterin' down the tea?" It was T.C. Smiling. Making what he thought was a joke.

"Yeah," I said, "waterin' down the tea—this water is hot enough to be tea."

And like the snub of a few weeks ago never happened, T.C. put out his hand to shake mine. "Name is Simmons," he said, "T.C. Simmons."

CHAPTER 4

LUKE

After T.C.'s triumph over Demerest, rumors started to spread of another of T.C.'s extraordinary abilities. He let it slip to me that he had a "shooting secret" which made him the very best with a bow and arrow. I spread the rumor, in an effort to enhance T.C.'s reputation. All of us played with bows and arrows, but I let it be known that T.C. had perfected a special way of shooting an arrow that was certain to hit a bull's-eye every time from up to fifty yards away. As I said, we all had experience with bows and arrows—some of us even hunted rabbits and other rodents with them—but none of us could shoot an arrow fifty yards, much less hit a bull's-eye at that range.

It was Wiggens, Jack Demerest's sidekick, who decided to unmask T.C.

"Ain't no way that lump can hit a bull's-eye at fifty yards," was Wiggens' pronouncement, and he set out to prove it. Demerest and the Kinsmen may not have been able to "whup" T.C., but he, Wiggens, could "show him up for the lyin' bastard he is."

And so one day Wiggens lay in wait, watching T.C. go off to the edge of the swamp where it was rumored he did his target practice. T.C. was armed with what appeared to be a sack of arrows. As soon as he disappeared from view, Wiggens ran after him, running hard until T.C. came into view, but staying far back enough so that he could hit the ground or jump into some underbrush if T.C. turned around to look. But T.C. didn't turn around. In fact, he seemingly unintentionally made it easier for Wiggens to follow him by stopping every so often to tie his shoe or adjust his coveralls. When he reached the swamp area, it became more difficult to keep him in sight, but he made a great deal of noise as he thrust his huge frame through the undergrowth. He was easy to follow. He moved with no stealth or thought of being tailed by anyone. Once Wiggens crossed the thick foliage of the swamp, it became even easier to follow T.C. as his huge body trampled down the bushes and swept aside overhanging vines in front of him. It was like tracking an elephant.

Wiggens suddenly became fearful. Not of discovery by T.C., but of quicksand. He had heard that there were quicksand pools in this part of the swamp and remembered being told that if you got caught in quicksand "the more you struggle the more it sucks you in. Then the sand gets up your nose and you breathe it right into your heart and you die."

His worry about the quicksand and fleeting thoughts of poisonous snakes were about to discourage Wiggens from his quest when he heard a loud "thwack" come from behind a clump of trees. It was clearly the sound of an arrow smacking into some solid target. He was apparently at the edge of T.C.'s target range. There was a pause and then another "thwack!" There were five sounds of impact in all until the ether fell silent again.

Wiggens was frozen in silence and fear. After a few more minutes, he heard T.C. exiting his target range. He remained immobilized until he was certain T.C. had left and then went to see what he had risked life and limb to discover. After proceeding only a few yards, he came into an opening. At his feet lay a bow and some arrows scattered on the ground around it. He assumed that was the place from which T.C. shot his arrows. Across fifty or so yards of damp, muddy but open ground he saw a huge piece of plywood about ten feet high and four feet wide. It was propped into a vertical position by being wedged firmly against two trees. As he walked towards the plywood, he could count ten red circles going from the top to the bottom of the plywood. In five of those circles an arrow was stuck almost mid-center in what was a circle of no more than six inches across. There were no arrows outside of any of the circles and no visible marks in the plywood from arrows since removed. It appeared to be a new target.

As he came within a few feet of the target, he could see that the arrows had burrowed with some force into the wood, eliminating the possibility that they could have been placed there by somehow hammering them into the board by hand. The loud "thwack" sounds he'd heard were also testament to the fact that the arrows had been shot into the circumference of those red circles with some force. He turned and looked back at the place where the bow and arrows lay on the ground. It was astounding to him that T.C., or anyone, could hit one bull's-eye, much less five, from that distance.

When he reached the huge piece of plywood, he was even more astonished at T.C.'s shooting prowess. He noticed that the red circles were purposely placed in an ad hoc alignment so that the shooter would not even have the advantage of aiming at circles that were aligned with one another. Wiggens just stood and stared in wonderment at the plywood with those arrows firmly stuck dead center of the circles.

When Wiggens returned from his adventure and told Demerest and the kinsmen what he had seen, disbelief turned to a grudging admiration. Not the kind of admiration that leads to fondness, but rather the kind that leads to resentment. They disliked T.C. even more, and now they had a reason. T.C. had improbably proven himself more skilled than any of them, not because he was born big, but because he had acquired a skill that they could never hope to master. T.C.'s "shooting secret" had confounded them.

Months later, after T.C. had become my best friend, I continually tried to pry out of him his secret shooting style that enabled him to shoot with such accuracy over such a long range. I pleaded, pestered and even threatened him with the loss of our friendship, but he would never betray his secret. I had just about given up ever finding out the secret behind his bow and arrow talent when what was a terrible tragedy to me turned into the key that unlocked the secret from T.C.

For two years I had been one of the few, if not the only, boys at school who owned my own camera. It was a cheap Brownie box camera, but I loved it. I couldn't afford to buy much film to take many pictures with it, but I cherished it like I cherished no other possession. Then one day, it stopped working. No one knew why. Not me, not my dad, not the person in town at the Fix-It shop who could fix anything ever made... except my camera. I was devastated, certain I would never get to own another camera. When I did receive a new camera from my father, the first one I told of my great good fortune was my new best friend, T.C.

As I showed T.C. the new gadgets on my new camera, he just kept staring at my old broken Brownie, which was lying on the floor near my dresser drawers. He allowed me to prattle on about my new camera. When I finally stopped talking, he nodded towards my old camera, and asked,

"Can I have your old camera?"

"But it doesn't work. It's broken."

T.C. just shrugged. "That's okay, I want it anyway."

I was about to lean over to pick it up to hand it to him when I suddenly realized that the palpable hunger in his heart for that camera could unlock the door to the secret that I had been lusting after for more than a year.

"You can have it, T.C. ... if you show me how you can shoot an arrow so far and so straight all the time..."

T.C. furrowed his brow in thought, grimaced, looked longingly at the camera, and then raised his head, a look of resignation on his face. "Okay, if you swear on the life of your mother that you will not tell a soul about how I do it... It means a lot to me that some people think of me as special because of my 'shooting secret.'"

I knew how important that secret was to him, and at first I couldn't understand why he would resist giving it up throughout a year of my constant entreaties and promises of all types of bribes, only to let it go for some broken-down old camera. I later found out how important that broken-down old camera was to a boy like T.C., who never had any possessions to display to his supercilious classmates. When I owned the camera, it never left my house unless I was using it because I was so scared of losing or breaking it.

But I noticed that T.C. often carried the camera in the bag he brought to school. He never took it out of the bag, but he left it in a prominent position where all his classmates could see his possession—one that few of them owned. He thought that it would be harder for them to look down on him for being the flea to their flea now that they could see that he owned his very own camera. T.C. couldn't have afforded film and developing costs even if the camera was in working order. But he didn't want to own the camera to take pictures. He wanted the camera so he could gain some self-respect.

T.C. told me to meet him the next day behind the outhouse in the field behind the row of tin-roofed hovels where he lived. He told me to come at night, because he did not want anyone to see us. I was bursting with excitement and curiosity when I arrived at the designated wood outhouse. The night was neither bright nor totally dark. There were no clouds in the sky, and the quarter moon and flickering stars cast a glancing light onto the ground.

T.C. was leaning against the outhouse when I arrived, a bow and arrow clutched in one hand by his side. I had worn my heaviest shirt, assuming that we would be walking through some very rough terrain to get to some secret location. I waved to T.C.

"Where do we go?"

T.C. waved back, "We don't go nowhere... we stay right here...."

I was confused. Why weren't we going to his secret location? Maybe he was so certain that no one would see us here, at night, that he felt it wasn't necessary for him to reveal his secret in a more private location. T.C. motioned for me to sit on a tree stump about ten feet from the outhouse. As I sat down, T.C. strung the arrow in the bow, walked about ten yards from the outhouse, stared at the wooden side of the outhouse for a moment, then pulled back the string of the bow and let the arrow fly. "Thwack!" it burrowed into the wood side of the outhouse. He just stood still.

Now I was totally confused. He shot the arrow just like I shot an arrow. And he shot it at ten yards into the side of an outhouse, not fifty yards into a tiny red circle. What was he doing?

As these thoughts swirled through my mind, T.C. put the bow and arrow down and walked toward the outhouse wall where the arrow had affixed itself. Just before he reached the wall, he reached into the pocket of his coveralls and pulled out a big crayon-like red marker, the kind we used in art class—in fact, the kind T.C. and I always *stole* from art class. T.C. put the marker firmly in his right hand and proceeded to draw a six-inch circle around the arrow. He then turned to me with a big smile on his face and said,

"I always figured it was easier to learn to draw a good circle than to learn to shoot an arrow into a circle."

When what he had done finally dawned on me, I burst out laughing. He had set us all up a year ago. No wonder, as Wiggens told us, the targets on that plywood board weren't aligned. T.C. just shot those five arrows anywhere on the board and then circled them with that giant crayon marker. And he didn't shoot those arrows from any fifty yards away either. I jumped off the stump, still laughing, and patted T.C. on the back, "But how did you know Wiggens was coming that day?"

T.C. shrugged. "I didn't know. I had that board out there for weeks. I knew when I told you about my 'shooting secret' you would brag on me, and it was just a matter of time until Demerest or one his boys would follow me out there... One day I saw Wiggens comin' after me, and I knew I had him."

I was still laughing,

"Wow, so you got us to make you a big star, like a big hero, 'cause we thought no one could shoot like you. You know we made you the Robin Hood of north Georgia. Wiggens even told how he saw you shoot at that target—he even said that you hit one of the targets with a blindfold on!"

All of a sudden the smile left T.C.'s face. He hung his head. His voice was almost imperceptible.

"No, no, Luke, I didn't do it 'cause I wanted to prate on myself. I did it to show myself that those kids who think I'm so stupid, well, maybe they're stupider than I am."

CHAPTER 5

LUKE

The outside world rarely pierced the hard shell of rural Georgia. Television, in its adolescence elsewhere, was still in swaddling clothes in Augusta. There was no radio news to speak of, and the headlines in the local newspaper rarely dealt with issues beyond the confines of local concern. World War II was winding down, and I have a recollection of the excitement, even cheers, of the older people reacting to the exploits of our soldiers recounted in the *March of Time* newsreel that preceded the motion picture at one of the local movie houses. But as soon as the war ended, even the adults seemed to lose interest in the outside world.

My parents had neither the means nor the desire to find out what was going on beyond the few miles that circumscribed our lives. We never took a vacation that required travel beyond Atlanta to the West, or Savannah to the south and east. We never even thought of traveling north. That is why I was pleasantly surprised when, shortly after my bar mitzvah, my father told me that we were going to Brooklyn to attend the wedding of my cousin Jackie.

My parents didn't talk much about their roots, which had originally been firmly planted in Brooklyn, New York. Nor did they discuss family members, most of whom still lived there. Except, of course, for my war hero Uncle Mike. It wasn't that they were hiding anything. It was just that it wasn't important to their lives or mine. My father did mention, with some regularity and obvious loathing, his older cousin Abe Lapinsky. Abe owned an important clothing company in New York City, and most of my cousins' fathers worked for him. In fact, my father was just about the only member of his family who didn't work for Abe.

Growing up, my only feeling about Abe and my relatives was

one of relief that I came from the Lipton branch of the family rather than the Lapinsky branch. I was sure that having the name of Lapinsky in Georgia would have made my life even more difficult. People with "un-American" names didn't do well in Georgia in the 1940s and 50s, and "Lapinsky" was just about as un-American a name as you could get.

What I didn't know then was that we were actually from the same branch of the family as the Brooklyn Lapinskys. Herman Lapinsky, my great-grandfather and the grandfather of my father and Abe, had fled Czarist Russia at the turn of the century. Herman came to America expecting to partake of its fairy tale bounties as soon as he stepped off the boat. The only bounty he found was a six-day-a-week, 12-hour-a-day job working as a stitcher in a garment factory. Only the coming of the Garment Workers' Union saved him and his family from abject poverty. He never made much money. He had fifty dollars to his name when he arrived in New York and sixty dollars to his name when he died fifty years later.

But if Herman had not found the streets of America paved with gold, at least they weren't paved with Jews. He bathed daily in America's greatest bounty, its freedom. He might have been forced to hide from creditors from time to time, but never again did he have to hide from the Cossacks as they hunted down any Jew they could find. Late in his life Herman never had to worry about poverty, because his grandson Abe had become a great success and a provider. Herman was proud of his grandson Abe, and proud that Abe, unlike many other ethnics trying to assimilate, had not changed his name. His pride in Abe, bolstered by Abe's largesse, allowed him to overlook the fact that Abe did his best to destroy the Garment Workers' Union which—before Abe came to his rescue—had been Herman's salvation.

I didn't know at the time that my father had changed his name from Lapinsky to Lipton when he and my mother moved to Georgia in 1937, three years before my birth. Dad wasn't trying to

shed his Jewishness so much as he was trying to shed Abe
Lapinsky. He left Brooklyn swearing that he would be the one relative to escape Abe's clutches.

Abe Lapinsky was a very wealthy man, known to those outside the family as an exceedingly generous and kind man who
hired all of his relatives—indeed, made them all managers in his
business and sprinkled beneficent contributions to Jewish and
Christian charities alike. But to those who knew him best—his
relatives—he was known as a man of suffocating control who
found his greatest joy in belittling and berating those closest to
him.

He did make sure that all of the relatives on his payroll were
in "management." As with all of his gestures, there was a reason
behind his kindness. He did not want any of his relatives in the
union anymore than he wanted the union. He deplored the
"Commie" unionists and was outraged and ashamed that their
ranks were riddled with Jews. But one could not escape unions in
New York. The union protected most of the workers from the
wrath of the likes of Abe, a protection that those in "management" did not have. Abe tortured and humiliated his relatives on
the payroll on a daily basis and made sure they understood that
the same rules applied when they were off duty as well as when
they were on the job. He carefully calibrated their pay, making
sure that he always paid them what they needed to live decent
lives, but not a penny more. In return for his "generosity" he
demanded total obeisance.

When my father graduated from high school, he was able to
avoid Abe's clutches by taking low-paying jobs that were just
enough to support a young single man. But after my parents were
married, my mother persuaded my father to swallow his pride
and go to work for Abe so they could afford to have a child. As
bad as it was for the relatives who had worked for Abe for some
time, the renowned Lapinsky hazing of a newcomer was unbear-
able. My father lasted two months. He decided he would rather

rely on the kindness of strangers than have his soul pounded to dust by Abe every day. He and my mother packed up, and with their newly-changed name and a few hundred dollars borrowed from two envious but less courageous uncles, took off to Georgia. They picked a town with few Jews because my dad figured there would be less competition and a greater need for a retail clothing store which he opened in 1938. The last thing a stunned and bitter Abe Lapinsky told him was "You'll come crawling back. They all do."

I did not have any contact with Abe Lapinsky until the celebration of my bar mitzvah. It was a simple affair held in a small hall in Augusta's Richmond Hotel. The ceremony and celebration reflected more of a desire to hang on to tradition than to take part in a religious ceremony. I invited none of my friends. If they knew I was a bar mitzvah, they probably would have figured out I was Jewish.

The best part of my bar mitzvah was the twenty dollar bill my father gave me. I had never had such a large sum of money. I debated whether to splurge on a new fishing pole or a new basket for my bike. My deliberations were interrupted when my mother handed me a letter sent to me by Abe Lapinsky. At first I just held it in my hand, not knowing what to do with a letter from an apparent family antagonist. My mother winked at me and said, "Better open it up before your father gets home. You know he doesn't like cousin Abe."

I ripped open the letter and pulled out a card with a commercially printed Happy Bar Mitzvah message stapled to Abe Lapinsky's gold embossed business card. He hadn't even signed it. But what fell from the envelope containing the card stunned me. As I pulled out the card, two crisp new one-hundred-dollar bills fluttered to the floor. Both my mother and I stood frozen, staring at the bills but afraid to pick them up. It was as if they were somehow contaminated. I looked up and my eyes met my mother's. She stared at me, then broke into a smile and said, "Pick it up. Are you such a rich man that you can afford to let two hundred dollars lie there on the floor?"

I scooped up the money just as my father came in the door. I could not control my enthusiasm. I waived the two bills at him: "Look what cousin Abe sent me for my bar mitzvah! I'm a rich man!"

My father stood frozen, and with narrowed eyes he grabbed the bills out of my hand.

"This is going right back to him as soon as I can get to the post office!"

"But dad…"

"No further discussion. The money is going back!"

I was furious, but if there was one thing I had learned about my father was that "no further discussion" did not mean that I could try to reason with him or even revisit the issue later. No further discussion meant case closed. I never forgave my father for that day… at least not until I found out the whole story about Abe Lapinsky and my father many years later. From that day until more than a year later there were four words that could never be uttered in my house, "nigger," "kike," "Abe" and "Lapinsky."

So it had obviously taken a great deal of courage and fortitude for my mother to persuade my father to go to my second cousin Jackie's marriage in Brooklyn about two years later.

I was so excited when mom told me we were going to New York City that I ran to the Augusta Central library and took out several books about that magical place. I spent the next day making a list of all of the places I wanted to visit: the Statue of Liberty, the Museum of Natural History, Central Park, and, best of all, the Empire State Building. The book said that you could go up to the very top of the building—the tallest building in the world! I wondered whether I would be able to see Georgia from the top of that incredible edifice.

We did go to New York, but I never saw anything beyond my uncle's apartment where we stayed and the synagogue where the wedding was held. My father said he couldn't take any more time off from work. I pleaded and even cried before we left, but he would not change his mind.

Actually, my disappointment in the trip began even before we arrived. The entire trip north along Route #1 in our Studebaker was taken in silence. It was as if we were going to a funeral rather than a wedding. My father was too upset about being forced to make the trip to take part in any conversation. My mother obviously felt that the icy silence was better than the furious screaming matches that would replace it. Maybe if my father had given me a reason—if he had explained to me that he didn't want me to see New York City because he was afraid I might fall in love with the place he most loathed, I would have understood. Or if he'd told me why he hated Abe Lapinsky. But with neither an explanation nor the joy of expectation, the trip was endless and colorless.

I did enjoy the one night the three of us slept in a Motor Cabin in Virginia—it was like camping out. And I also got a kick out of the many Burma Shave signs which were spaced along the highway. I read them aloud to break up the monotony and in an attempt to make my mother and father smile: The first sign was always the same: "Here Comes Burma Shave!" and then another sign, in poetic series, every 25 yards. One string read: "Cheer up face/the war is over/from now on/you'll be in clover/Use Burma Shave." Another one: "Romeo/Romeo/Romeo/if you have a beard/go homeo/Use Burma Shave." Or my favorite: "Heaven's latest neophyte/signaled left/then turned right/Use Burma Shave." I read them all aloud, but got not so much as a smile from the front seat.

My stay in Brooklyn lasted one day. My father wouldn't even let my cousins take me to Coney Island. The wedding was predictably loud and filled with forced good will. What I most remember is the bride walking down the aisle with her beaming father clutching her left arm—and cousin Abe clutching her right arm.

Someone on the outside would probably have thought that was some Jewish tradition. Those on the inside knew it was only an Abe Lapinsky tradition. After all, Abe had paid for and planned the entire wedding. The man deserved his recognition. Being cared for by Abe Lapinsky was a cradle-to-grave debt that had to be paid.

I saw Abe up close twice during the wedding. Once he came over so he could be included in the table picture taken of our family. He made sure he was there for every table picture. When he came to our table he hugged my father and said, "You'll be up here soon. We'll have your boy's wedding right here!"

He then bent down and kissed my mother and flattered her on her attractive good looks. How remarkable it was that she could look so good even in that dress "which he could never sell out of his company." My mother and father just smiled the forced smile of bad character actors. I could see that my father's right hand was balled up in a tight fist.

As we were leaving, Abe pulled me aside, whispering in my ear that he knew I hadn't been the one who wanted to send my bar mitzvah money back. He then shoved two one hundred bills into my suit pocket. I didn't even think of giving them back. I reached up and hugged him hard while he gave me a big wet kiss on my cheek. My effusive expression of gratitude was sincere. I was delighted to have the money and even more delighted that Abe had helped me get back at my father. I had never had any real feelings about Abe one way or other. He was my father's problem. But now I really liked him... a lot.

I was much more animated on our trip back to Georgia. I bubbled over with enthusiasm about our trip to Brooklyn and told my father it was really not a big deal that I didn't get to go up to the top of the Empire State Building. I told him it probably would have only made me dizzy. I kept chatting away, reading the Burma Shave signs, secure in the knowledge that I had gotten back at my father. Such were the thoughts which crossed my mind as I fingered the two crisp bills in my suit pocket. Of course I was glad we had come. Otherwise I would never have met cousin Abe and gotten back my two hundred dollars.

As we headed back towards Georgia, my father driving stiffly and silently, I never would have believed that before long we would all be back in the Studebaker, headed once again for Brooklyn. The old car would be packed full of the family possessions that mom did not want to trust to the shipping company. That time, we would be moving to Brooklyn to live.

CHAPTER 6

LUKE

Neither Georgia nor South Carolina are known for their natural lakes—in fact, not counting the Georgia swamps, I don't think either state has any large lakes. To make up for this, rivers are dammed up to form large bodies of water for fishing and boating.

Both states share the Clarks Hill Dam, which was made by damming up the Savannah River. It isn't far from Augusta, but it sure seems far when you've got to ride your bike there in the sweltering Georgia heat. That's where T.C. and I used to go on those days when T.C. wasn't helping some farmer with his afternoon chores. And that's where we were one hot day in the early spring when he first told me about the Klan. It came to me as a quite a revelation. Here was this loner who seemed interested in very little, but who had this powerful attachment to—of all things—the Ku Klux Klan.

Nobody in Georgia loved the Jews or Negroes—but I was of the opinion that nobody hated them either. At least that's what I thought until T.C. told me about the Klan. For a fellow who wasn't too smart in school, he sure knew a lot about that organization.

There were two reasons he knew so much. First, one of his ancestors, a preacher named Colonel William Simmons, had started the Georgia Klan 40 years ago, back in 1915; and second, having just turned 16, T.C. was looking forward to being inducted into what he called the "Invisible Empire." He told me of the organization and its history with great respect and the precision of someone who had committed it to memory.

I was surprised at T.C.'s vast knowledge of Klan history. Just the day before in class, when the teacher asked him to name the second President of the United States, T.C. had stared blankly back at her as if she had just asked him to give a full explanation of Einstein's Theory of Relativity. And now here he was talking about the Klan and sounding like a Ph.D. in history. I supposed it was because the history of the Klan was far more relevant to his life than American History.

He told me how the Klan had its beginnings after the War Between the States during the period called Reconstruction, when slaves in the South became free and were given political power. Some even became government officials. As T.C. explained it, the supremacy of the white race was being threatened. But worse, he said, and you could tell that he believed every bit of it, white women were being violated by former slaves who found it easy to revert to "untamed savagery." It seemed peculiar to hear T.C. use such words as "untamed savagery"—I wondered if he even knew what they meant.

He spoke in detail of the film *The Birth of a Nation*, which had been shown at an abandoned theater by a group of Klansmen. The movie was taken from a book written by Thomas Dixon, Jr. called *The Clansman*. T.C. was familiar with the book because, although his home had no other reading material, there was a single copy of the red-jacketed, dog-eared copy of *The Clansman, An Historical History of the Ku Klux Klan*.

He'd been just 10 years old when he'd seen the film. He and some other kids had been hanging out in town when they were invited in to see this movie, which showed how the drunken Union soldiers, carpetbaggers, and freed slaves were destroying the South. The film showed how the Klan had come to the rescue.

T.C. explained to me that at first the Klan had just tried to scare the former slaves from voting or holding office. They did this by burning crosses on hillsides or close to the homes of those they wanted to frighten. When this didn't work, they beat up, mutilated, and hanged them.

In 1867 some veterans who had fought for the South held the first Klan convention in Tennessee, and that's when the Invisible Empire, as the Klan then called itself, was formed. T.C. solemnly recited the titles of the official hierarchy: The leader was the Grand Wizard of the Empire. He was assisted by ten Genii. Then there was the Grand Dragon of the Realm, assisted by eight Hydras; the Grand Titan of the Dominion, assisted by six Furies; and the Grand Cyclops of the Den, assisted by two Nighthawks.

I almost started to laugh and couldn't help but smile when T.C. reeled off these names. To me they sounded like something from a horror movie. I couldn't imagine grown men giving themselves titles like that. But I stopped smiling immediately when I looked at T.C. He was deadly serious when he named these offices—in fact, his tone bordered on reverence.

T.C. explained to me that when the Federal troops went back north, the Klan began to take over and actually started to fill the seats of government. Through its chapters, known as Klaverns, it became stronger and even tougher on the blacks, who were quickly put down and restored to their diminished pre-war status. They weren't slaves anymore—but compared to what they had become, slavery might have been preferable.

When Grant became President, he began a crusade against the old Klan, arresting many of its members and disarming the Klaverns. But, as T.C. was quick to remind me, the mission of the Klan had been fulfilled. The whites had held on to their supremacy and the southern woman was spared the rape and defilement that surely would have ensued.

Then, just when the Klan was about to become lost in the arcanum of history, T.C.'s ancestor Colonel Simmons came along and began a new Klan—officially called The Invisible Empire, Knights of the Ku Klux Klan. Membership was restricted to native-born, white, Protestant males, 16 years of age or older. Blacks and Jews along with Roman Catholics were specifically excluded. Roman Catholics were particularly detested because they advocated practices which were "designed to destroy the American way of life." T.C. told me this without telling me exactly how the Catholics were going to bring about this destruction, or what activities they favored.

T.C., who everyone thought had very little to say, didn't stop talking until the hot sun started to slip behind the tall pines and the parents began gathering up their little kids and packing up their cars and station wagons. It was time to head back to town.

"You oughta join up," T.C. told me.

The thought of becoming a part of the Klan was the furthest thing from my mind as it would be from T.C.'s if he knew I was a Jew. What was on my mind was that my mother had told me that my father's business was having some difficulties. She was afraid that soon we might have to leave Augusta and my new-found friend for a place which the Klan would find a fertile field for their hatred—where Negroes, Jews, and even Catholics pretty much ran things.

CHAPTER 7

T.C.

"In the darkest hour of the life of the South, when her wounded people lay helpless amid rags and ashes under the beak and talon of the Vulture, suddenly from the mists of the mountains appeared a white cloud the size of a man's hand. It grew until its mantle of mystery enfolded the stricken earth and sky. An Invisible Empire had arisen from the field of Death and challenged the Visible to mortal combat."

—FROM *THE CLANSMAN* BY THOMAS DIXON, JR.

When he came home, T.C. smelled his father before he saw him. The smell was a familiar one. A mixture of sweat, unwashed clothing covering an unwashed body, and cheap whiskey. More of a stink than a smell.

"Where ya' been?" Duncan "Dink" Simmons asked the question out of habit, not concern.

T.C. didn't bother answering. He knew his father wasn't really interested in where he had been or what he had been doing. For that matter, he knew that his father was interested in very few things since his mother had taken off with a soldier from Camp Gordon a few years back.

Even before that his father's interest in his mother seemed limited to her ability to come up with enough of her earnings as a waitress to put food on the table and a bottle of bourbon in his hand. It was the same kind of interest the old man had in T.C.—as long as he kept his after school jobs working on the neighboring farms and brought home enough of his earnings, his father feigned an interest in him.

Dink Simmons had lived a trying life. When T.C. was born Dink was living his hardscrabble life with his family on Tobacco Road, that unpaved byway off Route 1 which Erskine Caldwell

39

had made symbolic of the Depression era south. The house where T.C. was born smelled of mildew and rot and resembled the run down two-room shack with a sagging roof that housed Caldwell's Jeeter Lester. And like the fictional Jeeter, Dink had despaired of growing tobacco or even cotton in the once rich, now leeched-out soil.

After his wife left him, he moved with T.C. closer to town so that he could find work enough to feed himself and buy the bourbon which allowed him to forget. And he had a lot to forget. Being black and poor was understandable and expected—being white and poor, as dirt poor as Dink, was to be "white trash," and that was about as low and undesirable as a person could be

When the school year ended in that June of 1955, all of the other kids rejoiced. All except T.C. To him school meant getting out of the hovel which he shared with his father—it also meant spending some time with me, his first real friend. Being in school had always been important to him. True, he was a loner and alienated from the others, but he did not feel alone when surrounded by his classmates. On the last day of class, unlike the others who ran from the schoolyard with shouts of joy, T.C. sadly plodded his way home—alone once again.

It was my father who, at my request, was able to get T.C. a job at a filling station. T.C. started work the day after school let out for the summer at an Amoco station on the Federal highway not a mile from his home.

On this particular day he was doing what he did on every other day. His job was to pump gas, empty and refill the crankcases of the too old cars, and change tires on the halfback trucks using retreads to replace the original tires which were worn down to the core. He spoke to no one and no one spoke to him which was all right with him. No one, that is, except old Mr. Knotts who owned the filling station and assigned him his chores. When he finished one assignment, he was given his next.

The only time he acted on his own was when a car pulled up

for gas. Then he dropped whatever he was doing to pump the amount of gas the customer requested. Usually it was two or three dollars worth. Sometimes a customer would ask for a fill up, but that was rare.

The rest of the time he did whatever he was told to do—but no one told him what to think. And he never stopped thinking. He thought about how little he had and how little he had to look forward to. If it hadn't been for me, he never would have known what it was to have a friend, and if it hadn't been for my father, he wouldn't even have had this job. He would have been shoveling shit out of barnyards and chopping weeds—the only kind of work he'd ever been able to get.

His father was a drunk, and he hardly remembered his mother. If it hadn't been for the kindness of Mrs. Jarman, he would probably never have known the tenderness of a woman. He also wouldn't have learned that for him good and beautiful things in life didn't seem to last—as soon as they were introduced to him, they were taken away from him. Even love—or at least what he thought was love.

Mrs. Jarman was T.C.'s eighth grade homeroom teacher. Her husband was an army officer previously stationed at Camp Gordon but just recently shipped over to Germany. To T.C. she was beautiful—as beautiful as any movie actress he had ever seen. Everything about her was perfect—her white skin and shiny black hair which she pulled straight back and tied with a bow. It seemed that every day she wore a different bow in a different color. And the way she smelled—such a clean, sweet smell, which seem to blow off her like a cool breeze. Without anyone telling him—no one had to—T.C. knew that he was in love. He also knew that no matter what he did or how good or smart he was, a woman like Mrs. Jarman would never know that he was alive— except as a teacher would acknowledge the existence of a pupil.

One day while sitting at his desk-chair combination, bending over his schoolwork, Mrs. Jarman stood over him. He smelled her—actually felt the cool breeze coming from her.

"'Catch' is spelled with a 't,'" she said to him in a voice so soft he was certain that no one else could hear her.

"Yes Ma'am," he said, "Someone with my name shouldn't be forgettin' T's."

She laughed. Such a beautiful laugh. Like bells, he thought.

"What are you doing after school?" she asked and continued without waiting for an answer: "I have some chores at my house and I could sure use your help."

"Nothing Ma'am—I mean I got nothing to do, nothing that I have to do." T.C. managed to get out.

"Good," she said. "I sure would appreciate it if you could give me a hand with some chores around my house. I live up on Juniper Drive in Sand Hills, you know where that is?" She was referring to a small subdivision between town and Camp Gordon, where many of the Camp Gordon officers lived with their families.

"Yes ma'am," he said.

"House number is 244 - 244 Juniper Drive. I'll be expecting you about 4:00," and having delivered that message and invitation, Mrs. Jarman moved down the aisle of desks—leaving her scent and an ecstatic T.C. behind her.

After school, T.C. rode his bike home to change. Even though the chores at Mrs. Jarman's would get him dirty again, there was no way he was going to visit her unless he was wearing his one clean set of overalls.

He pedaled his bike out of town and down Route 1 to Sand Hills which was just a mile or so north of Tobacco Road—the place where he was born. He couldn't help think of how lucky the people who lived in this development were. The neat row of single family houses, each with their own front and back yards, spoke, if not of opulence, at least of comfort. To Lester Jeeter, who tried to grow cotton on Tobacco Road not a stone's throw

away, they would have been mansions. To T.C. they were magnificent homes. In truth, they really were no more than modest two
bedroom, one shower, one bathroom ranch houses, built on a
concrete slab.

Some of the houses had TV antennas mounted on their
roofs and, as a sign of the greatest comfort which could be
brought to this sweltering land south of the Piedmont, bulging
out of some of the bedroom windows were air conditioning units.

He rode his bike down the serpentine treeless streets until
he came to Juniper Drive. A strange name for an area which had
never seen a Juniper tree, or any other tree for that matter. He
looked at the small children playing in the front yards. Front
yards that made a valiant effort to grow grass on their sandy
slopes. The sight of the children at play might have pleased some
visitors—even caused them to smile—but it made T.C. sad.
Something inside of him told him that he would never be able to
live in such a house. If he had children they would be condemned,
as he was condemned, to live as he lived.

244 Juniper Drive. Mrs. Jarman's house. As soon as he saw
the address on the mailbox he felt a pounding in his chest and a
most peculiar sensation in the pit of his stomach. Should he go to
the back door? Of course, he was here to do chores—he had no
business going to the front door.

The only way to get to the back door was to go down the
driveway, through the carport and around to where one step led
to the screen door, which in turn led to the kitchen. The inside
door was open to allow whatever breeze there was to do whatever cooling off it could.

T.C. parked his bike in the carport and walked to the back
screen door.

"Hi," he called instead of knocking.

"T.C.?" she called from another room, "Is that you?"

"Yes Ma'am," he responded with a voice which sounded
strange even to him. His usual gruff, too deep for his age voice

came out several octaves higher than usual. He sounded tentative and frightened. He was.

She came to the door dressed in very short white shorts and a white blouse with its tails pulled tightly around her waist and tied in front. She was wearing sandals. An hour ago she had been dressed as a school teacher was expected to dress—and now she was dressed...well, she was dressed like a young woman. Like a girl.

"Hi T.C.—you're right on time—come on in."

"That's all right, Ma'am." he said, "Just tell me what needs doin' and I'll get right to it." He still couldn't recognize his own voice. What was happening to him?

"First I want you to come in—now come on." She smiled and held the door open, but T.C. stood frozen, motionless. He knew it wasn't fear that arrested him—but he didn't know exactly what it was.

"Okay, T.C., if you don't want to come in for now, you can stay out there, but you must call me Maggie. We're not in school now, you know. And I should be calling you by your real name."

He remained motionless. "T.C. is my real name Ma'am."

Maggie continued to talk to him through the open door. "No it isn't, Thomas," she said, "T.C. is what they call you, but your Christian name is Thomas Caleb. Two good names: one from the New Testament and one from the Old. You should be proud of both." Of course she knew his real name. As his teacher she probably knew everything about him. Funny thing is, he had almost forgotten what his real name was. He wondered what else she knew about him.

"Yes Ma'am, ... er, Maggie, ma'am."

"No, just plain Maggie. Okay, if you won't come in just take the shovel in the shed and dig a bed around the house so I can plant some flowers." She wanted to make her house as attractive as possible. Her husband had been shipped out to Germany, and she thought she might have to sell her house soon in order to join him.

T.C. took the shovel and started digging into the hard-packed ground. It seemed the soil in this area was either sand or clay. Mrs. Jarman's house was built on a layer of clay. It wasn't long before he started to sweat like a hog. He looked up and saw Maggie leaning against the house staring at him with a look that wasn't the same as her earlier smile. It was a look he had never seen her wear before, certainly not in school.

"Is everything okay...Mrs...Maggie?"

"Oh yes, Thomas, but you know you're getting that shirt all sweated up and then you'll have a chill goin' home. Hand me your shirt, and I'll wash it out for you. It'll be nice and clean when you're ready to leave."

T.C. started to undo the straps on his overalls to take off his shirt, then hesitated.

"Come, on Thomas, take your shirt off."

He pulled off his large ill-fitting shirt, revealing his sweat-soaked muscular chest and arms strengthened by his years of toil chopping weeds and lifting sacks of seeds, fertilizer, tires, and tools.

"Here it is, Maggie, thanks...." She took the shirt, started towards the door, and then turned around and stared at the now bared upper torso of the laboring T.C.

"You just keep digging, Thomas."

She disappeared into the house as T.C. picked up the pace of his work. He had just about completed digging the trench on one side of the house when he looked up and saw Maggie peering at him from the window. She motioned for him to go to the back door where she met him. He stood, shovel in hand, bathed in sweat.

"Now Thomas, I am afraid you are working too hard. You need to take a rest. I insist you come into the house and sit a while."

"No, Maggie," he enjoyed the license which allowed him to repeat her name, "No, I'm okay...."

"T.C., you come in here now!" she snapped, reverting back to her schoolhouse manner, but with a smile.

T.C. leaned the shovel against the outside wall and walked inside the house. Maggie was holding a towel in her right hand.

"Now, Thomas, go sit in that big easy chair over there, and I'm going to dry you off a bit."

He sat in the chair. It was the most comfortable chair he had ever sat in—come to think of it, not counting the wooden chairs in school, this was one of the only real chairs he had ever sat in. He had sat on a lot of benches and stools and the worn seats in the motion picture theatre—and the one-holer in his backyard—but this was the first real chair he had ever sat in.

Maggie started to rub the towel slowly and gently over T.C.'s steaming body. T.C. just sat still, staring straight ahead, trying not to notice Maggie's sweet scent and warm breath as she leaned ever closer to him, almost caressing his body with the towel. Suddenly, she stopped and straightened up.

"No, Thomas, this just won't do...Do you have a shower at your house?"

"No Ma'am, I mean, no Maggie, I've seen one at the gym, but we use a tub at home."

She motioned with her hand to a door off of the room in which T.C. was sitting.

"Well, I have a shower in there. I want you to go in and clean yourself off a bit. It will cool you down."

T.C. looked toward the door and then glanced down at his overalls.

"Don't worry Thomas, you can take your clothes off in the shower room. Just shut the door... Now, go ahead."

T.C. didn't know what to think. He just knew he didn't want to take his clothes off in Mrs. Jarman's house. Reluctantly, he got up and without looking back, ambled slowly over to the door to the shower room. He was careful to close the door behind him. He started to take off his clothes, but then stopped to look back over his shoulder to make certain the door was closed.

He finally undressed completely and walked toward an enclosure with a huge showerhead as its centerpiece. It was slung over a pipe coming out of the ceiling and had what appeared to T.C. to be a drainhole in the floor right underneath. He looked around the room and could see nothing else—just the jerry-rigged shower with soap in a soap dish and two towels hung over a bar attached to a wall just outside of the shower enclosure.

T.C. stared at the showerhead, his back to the door. He wanted to make sure he did this thing right. He didn't want to break Mrs. Jarman's shower, or worse, show that he didn't know how to work it. He was about to reach up to pull the cord when he felt Maggie's hand on his back. Startled, he turned around, and found himself facing her, standing there completely naked. She smiled and, after a few moments, she wrapped her left arm around his waste to steady herself, her body against his, so she could reach up and grab the shower cord with her right hand.

"Relax, Thomas, I thought you might need some help."

She leaned against him even harder, pressing her breasts against him while at the same time pulling the cord and releasing a torrent of cool water.

"There, I think that should do it...."

She stepped back, allowing the water to cascade over her nakedness, and then diverted her eyes downward, looking directly at T.C.'s state of full arousal. T.C. flushed and tried to cover his erection with his hands.

"No, don't do that Thomas, you have nothing to be ashamed of."

T.C. could barely get his words out, "But Mrs...."

"Oh, Thomas, don't be embarrassed. You're not the first man I've seen, maybe the biggest, but not the first."

She reached over and brushed his hands away, putting her full hand around his throbbing hardness, gently squeezing, releasing the pressure, and squeezing again.

T.C. braced his hands against the shower wall to steady himself against the jolts of pleasure which coursed through his body. He felt his breath becoming labored as she lathered her hand with soap and gently stroked his erection back and forth. Every time her hand moved his knees weakened. T.C. had never been with a woman before, but he had been with himself, and he knew what was about to happen. He tried to warn her....

"Mag....."

Before he could get the words out, he exploded..

"Oh my gosh, I'm sorry...."

"Don't be apologizing Thomas. If it didn't happen, well, then you would have had something to be sorry about," Maggie said as she rose to her toes and gently kissed him on the mouth.

As T.C. attempted to steady himself, Maggie reached out and touched his penis with just the tip of her right finger.

"Oh my, Thomas, back again so soon?"

T.C. started to reach out compulsively to touch her breasts, but Maggie pushed his hand aside and dropped to her knees, taking him gently into her mouth. He caught his breath and felt his knees buckle. Then he felt her tongue darting back and forth, sending explosions up through his body. He again tried to brace himself against the wall, but his palms felt numb.

Abruptly, she pulled her mouth away. T.C. instinctively put his hand on the top of her head to force her back down.

"No, don't stop...please..." he said.

She ducked her head out from under his hand, and stood up on her toes so that her lips were next to his ear, "No, no Thomas, I want you to save this one for me.... It's time for you to start pleasing me. Follow me." T.C. followed her into the bedroom. The sight of her soft nakedness walking in front of him deepened his state of arousal.

The bedroom shades had been drawn against the day's sun, and the doors had been closed to retain the coolness generated by the droning air conditioner held tentatively in place by rusted metal brackets to one of the bedroom's window sills, the bedroom being the only room in the house with an air-conditioner.

Once inside the darkened room Maggie lay down on the bed, arms outstretched, beckoning him to come to her. "Come on, Thomas, get on top of me." Her voice was insistent as her breathing became more labored.

T.C. walked over to the foot of the bed and stared down at her.

"Thomas, what's wrong...come on...."

Thomas just shook his head in bewilderment, "No, no, if I lay on top of you, I'll hurt you...."

Suddenly she caught herself, she had forgotten to give him a condom. She bounced up from the bed and grabbed one from the top of the dresser drawer. She handed it to T.C., but he just held it in his hand, embarrassed to do nothing but even more afraid to do the wrong thing. He stammered,

"I don't know....I'm not sure...."

T.C. blushed as Maggie took the condom from his hands and placed it on his still erect penis. When she lay down again, T.C. said in a soft, almost whispering voice:

"Are you sure I won't hurt you if I get on top of you...."

"No, Thomas, not if you catch your weight on....but I have a better idea. You lie down and let me get on top of you." She gently pushed him down on his back, and, sitting on top of him, guided him into her. T.C. just lay back, bothered only by the fact that his heavy breathing seemed to be disturbing the silence.

She pushed herself onto T.C. And then began a steady bouncing rhythm. Soon the rhythm became erratic as Maggie threw back her head and, with eyes closed, slowly gyrated her hips in a circular motion, moaning softly as she moved from side to side and then forward and back, each movement sending pulses of ecstasy through T.C.'s body.

Just as T.C. was about to explode once again, Maggie put her breast next to his, the movement of her hips becoming a frantic pounding as T.C.'s body rose to meet hers. Their frenzy ended with both of them crying out and moaning between gasps for air.

For what seemed like an eternity both of them lay there silently, she on top of him, both completely spent. He put his arms about her to give her warmth against the coolness of the air conditioner, which now troubled their soaking wet bodies. They lay there for what T.C. wished could be an eternity.

T.C. had not uttered a word during the entire encounter, but now he felt compelled to speak.

"Maggie," he said, and after a long silence, "I love you."

As soon as he spoke the words, she pulled away from him. He heard her walk across the room and then the sounds of her getting dressed.

"T.C.," she said, "What we did had nothing to do with love and you're to forget that we ever did it. Promise me that." But before he could utter the promise, she continued, "Please get dressed and leave as soon as you can." Her change of mood was so abrupt, it left him stunned. He didn't remember much about what happened next. He remembered getting out of bed and getting dressed—Mrs. Jarman just seemed to disappear. He called after her, but she didn't answer.

As he was leaving the house he saw his shirt, still soiled, lying next to the back door. He called for her one more time and then picked up his shirt and left through the back screen door, slowly walked to his bike and pedaled away.

The next time he saw her was the next day in class. She hardly seemed to notice him—she acted like nothing happened. He should have known that something so good would end about as soon as it began. It just confirmed his belief that good things and people just didn't stay with him. He just wasn't able to hold on to anything or anyone.

CHAPTER 8

T.C.

A s he tightened one of the lug nuts on the wheel of a jalopy that had no business being on the road, T.C. was jolted out of his reverie about that afternoon.

"Stop your wool gatherin' and tend to the pumps." It was old man Knotts summoning T.C. out of his daydream and self-pity. It was getting late, and he guessed that this would be the last customer before he headed home. His two customers were talking too loudly—they didn't seem to care who heard what they were saying. They were talking about the Klan and a meeting that was going to be held that evening out near Phinizy Ditch.

One of the men, in shirt sleeves bathed in sweat, spoke while tugging at his tie which already hung loosely from around his bull-sized neck, "That's what I was told, Shelby himself's gonna be there." His reference was to Imperial Wizard Jackson Shelby, the National leader of the United Klans of America who lived over the border in South Carolina

"Sombitch." said the other, a too-thin, hipless apparition whose pants would have been around his ankles if it weren't for a pair of wide suspenders which also served a hooking place for his thumbs. "Shelby coming to Augusta! Hot damn, this is gonna be a night."

T.C. kept pumping gas while listening to their conversation about the Klan rally: how it was going to be open to the families of the Klansmen and how they were going to get there early with their kin so that they could get "a good place to where they could see and hear everything." T.C. could hardly contain his enthusiasm. He was determined to go to Phinizy Ditch that very night to witness the rally. His father's anger at his coming home late would be a fair exchange for doing what he had wanted to do all his life: Get close to the Klan.

As soon as the gas station closed, T.C. left for the rally. He was now 16 and, according to the Klan rules, eligible for membership. But he knew that there was no way the Klan would take him now. Some day, maybe—when he was worthy.

The dirt road approach was long and deeply rutted. Even worse was the route on which T.C. traveled to avoid being seen. It was almost impossible for his bicycle to navigate, but the glow of the lights, the sound of the country music, and the anticipation of being in the bosom of the Klan encouraged him to pedal hard enough to make it.

He stopped when he reached the edge of a small embankment that formed a rim around where the meeting was to be held. After concealing his bike, he snaked up the incline so that he could see and hear all that was about to transpire.

The first thing that caught his eye was groups of men wearing the same white robes that he had always identified with the Klan. The same robes which were worn by the hard-riding horsemen he had seen in the movie *The Birth of a Nation*. There were men wearing robes that were even more dramatic in design and color—rich reds and purples. There were also women present in all shapes and sizes, and although they wore no distinctive clothing, they clearly seemed to belong in this gathering of people who seemed to genuinely enjoy each other's company. There must have been at least 500 people altogether—mostly older, none as young as he.

The music came from a small roped-off area where a fellow was singing while playing a 12-string guitar. He was backed up by a fiddler and a very young-looking guitarist. T.C. would have expected the music to be more of the religious kind—it wasn't— it was good old country. Songs he had heard Roy Acuff and Hank Williams sing. The soloist was now singing a Lefty Frizell piece about how he "would walk miles, cry and smiles for his Mommy and Daddy," because he "loved them so."

Then the music stopped and with it the chatter and laughter from the gathering.

While everyone stood in silence, a large man in an ill-fitting suit walked to the area where the musicians had been playing. He was the Kludd, or Chaplain of the Augusta Klavern, and, taking the microphone in his hand, he asked for the assemblage to bow their heads for an opening prayer:

"Heavenly father," he began to a hushed audience, "We ask your blessings on this meeting, convened in your name to do Thy will. We are not unmindful of the word of Holy Scripture which tells us that vengeance is Thine—nor of the obligation we all share to do the Lord's work. We pray that You give us the strength to do Your work in righting the wrongs which others have been inflicting on You and on us and, in Your name, to smite down Thine enemies who are also enemies unto us."

He paused just long enough for those gathered to mumble a barely audible "Amen," and then continued:

"Members and friends of the Augusta Klavern of the Invisible Empire of the Knights of the United Klans of America—it is my great privilege to introduce The Exalted Cyclops of our Klavern. Let me present our friend and neighbor, John M. Peterson."

Peterson, wearing a scarlet robe walked to the front of the gathering to applause and hearty pats on the back:

"Brother Klansmen, sisters and friends. I thank God for this beautiful evening and for this wonderful turnout—both are a testimony to the blessings which have endowed our noble cause.

"But blessings alone are not enough. The good Lord blessed us with many things—good things—and we have seen them threatened and taken away from us by those who are anti-Christ, anti-white, and anti-American. As members of the Klan we are sworn to protect the greatness that is America from those who threaten this great land from within and without. If any of us—if any of you—fail to fulfill this sacred duty, then you lie when you call this your country." And after a dramatic pause: "And I know there are no liars here."

The crowd shouted its agreement and approval.

"And now, brothers and sisters, I am honored to introduce

you to our noble leader who has instructed us by word and deed that the Klan's work is God's work: our Imperial Wizard—Jackson Shelby."

T.C. was surprised at how slight a man this national head of the United Klans of America seemed to be. His bright green robes covered what must have been, judging from the portion of him which was visible, a very thin, almost frail man, but when he spoke his resonant voice was filled with conviction. He began softly, on a somber note:

"Today is May 17th. Remember this date—it is one which will live in shame. It was one year ago today—May 17th, 1954, that the niggers won a mighty battle in their war to dominate the white race.

"They didn't do it alone—they did it with the help of the Jew-Communist conspiracy. Their victory was handed to them by the United States Supreme Court which said, on this day of national disgrace: 'Segregation of white and colored children in public schools has a detrimental effect.' Listen now to the words: 'has a detrimental effect on *colored children*. It generates a feeling of inferiority.' Did you hear that? What they were saying is that it makes the *niggers* feel inferior?

"Heaven forbid we tolerate a school system which makes niggers feel inferior. They would prefer that white Christians feel inferior—that they be inferior. That black savages seduce and rape our white daughters and women—that they turn the white race to a bastardized dilution. They would prefer that the South, which has so far been able to retain its dignity and nobility, be finally brought to its knees to grovel at the feet of niggers, Jews, Catholics, Communists and every foreign-born, blood-sucking creature that was ever spawned in the bowels of Hell.

"Since the purgatory of Reconstruction, the Klan has prevented this from happening. We fought against the carpetbaggers, the scalawags, the Jews and the tools of the Pope—we have kept the niggers out of our schoolrooms and our bedrooms. But the times are changing. All we have fought for and died for, our 100 years of sacrifice are being threatened as never before.

"I pity the white Christian teenager." T.C., who had been listening in rapt attention, felt the hair rise on the back of his neck. The Imperial Wizard was talking about him—in fact, he would swear that he was looking right at him as he continued:

"What future does a young white Christian have in today's South? None. The Federal government and the northern industrialists have set themselves to the task of seeing to it that the niggers get the best jobs and take over the best businesses. And you know why no one knows what's going on? Because the Jews control the media and they see to it that you all are kept in the dark. But when you wake up—and one day you will—you'll find that you will be working for the niggers and the Jews and you won't have or be anything.

"I tell you that your only salvation—the only way you will be able to raise yourself up out of poverty. The only way you will be able to own anything and live in dignity and raise a family—the only way we can feel that our daughters, our wives and our sisters will be able to walk the streets in safety—will be to restore the South to its days of glory. That will be done by the Klan. That is our mission in this life, and we swear it to our death."

When he had finished speaking, there was no applause— only the hushed silence of understanding and resolve. Off to the side of the gathering a large wooden cross, which had been wrapped with kerosene soaked rags, was lit, casting an eerie and flickering light over the large gathering.

T.C. knew that he had just heard the truth from this man who seemed to grow in physical stature as he spoke. He knew now that his fear of failure, of never being more than a low-level wage earner and laborer, was predestined. The forces arrayed against him were too formidable for him to manage alone. He always felt that the Klan was in need of his support—now he knew that the opposite was true: it was he who needed the Klan.

CHAPTER 9

T.C.

A week had passed since T.C. had attended his first Klan rally—
a week spent by T.C. digesting what the Imperial Wizard had
said and noticing things that confirmed the truth of his message.
It seemed to him that the coloreds in town started to walk with
an offensive arrogance. They no longer looked away when he
tried to stare them down—instead they seemed to look at him
with a sort of defiance. It was the same sort of defiance they
showed when they came to the filling station where he worked.

And they seemed to have all sorts of money. The whites
would come in and buy gas by the dollar or the gallon—not the
coloreds. They invariably asked to have "fill-ups"—and they
asked for it with a sneer like they were showing off that they were
the ones who had the money. And their cars bore testimony to
the fact that, as the Imperial Wizard had said, "the niggers" sure
enough had "the best jobs and the best businesses."

But knowing the truth did not provide the reasons. How did
the niggers take over so quickly and so completely? He decided
that it was the fault of his father, and others like him, who didn't
give a damn. They had allowed the niggers, with the help of the
Jews and Catholics, to come in and snatch it all away. All that the
southern whites had created, built and fought for—all that the
brave Confederate troops had died for—had been sapped from
them. Sapped from *him* along with his future.

These were the thoughts that occupied his mind as he tended to the work assignments parsed out by Mr. Knotts.

"I saw you at the rally, son."

The words pierced his reverie. He looked up, but the sun
blazing through the garage window blinded him. The voice continued.

"Yup, I watched you lyin' there listening to every word. I

started to invite you down with the rest of us but I figured you had a reason to hide yourself."

T.C. got to his feet to see the stranger in a better light. "It's not that I was hiding myself," he said, "it's just that I didn't know what was right—me not being a member and all."

"Hell," the stranger said, "It was an open meeting. You would have been more than welcome. What did you think of it?"

"Great—I mean it was great," T.C. said fervently, feeling very much at ease with this man who he assumed was a member of the Klan.

"My name is Cantrell," the stranger said, extending his hand, "Lucius Cantrell, I'm a member of the Klavern which held the rally. Matter of fact, I'm what we call the Kleagle. which is..."

"The recruiter..." T.C. finished the sentence, anxious to demonstrate his knowledge of the workings and hierarchal structure of the Klan.

"Good for you," said the Kleagle, "I see you know something about our brotherhood."

"I know enough," said T.C. "Enough to have always wanted to be a part of it."

Cantrell was standing along side of his pickup truck. His wife, whom he introduced as Callie, was sitting in the passenger seat staring directly ahead as if she and Lucius were still driving down the highway.

Cantrell had heard what he had come to hear. From what he knew about this young fellow, he was an ideal recruit for the Klan. A strong, young, white Protestant southerner who had felt the pain of poverty and societal rejection.

As for T.C., he could hardly believe his good fortune. To be visited by the Klan recruiter was the equivalent of an invitation to become a part of the Invisible Empire.

"If you want ter join up, you best fill out this application."

"I do, and I will," said T.C., trying his best to conceal his elation. Somehow he felt that a demonstration of this sort of emotion would diminish him in the eyes of this man who had paid him the honor of this personal visit. "Where do I send it when it's finished?"

"Would be best if you do it while I wait," said Cantrell. "And if you have trouble readin' the questions or writing down the answers, I can help you."

"No, thank you sir, I can read n' write O.K."

The application was mimeographed on one side of what appeared to be inexpensive pulp paper. The questions were predictable and reflected the accepted truths of Klan dogma: "Were you born in the United States of America?" "Are you a Christian who fears the wrath of God?" "Are you of the White race?" "Do you believe in the supremacy of the White race?" "Are you willing to lay down your life to protect Christian ideals, American values, and the supremacy of the white race?" "Are you prepared to accept whatever duties, obligations, or other assignments as may be delegated to you from time to time by duly elected or appointed officers of the Invisible Empire?"

Neither the misspelled words nor the totality of the commitment dissuaded him. At that moment T.C. would have promised or signed anything Lucius Cantrell put in front of him.

He signed the application and handed it back to the recruiter who glanced at it briefly, put it in his pocket, and went back into his pickup where his wife Callie sat, still staring straight ahead without giving T.C. so much as a sideways glance.

One week later Lucius Cantrell returned to the filling station. This time he was not accompanied by his wife. He smiled on seeing T.C., who was just finishing up his day's chores. "Ready for your big night, boy?" he asked.

"Yes sir, Mr. Cantrell," he answered, "But no one told me—I'm not dressed proper."

"You're dressed good enough son—soon no one will know what your wearin'—hop in boy."

The Kleagle and his new recruit drove for no more that a

mile further out of town, past the guard post gates marking the entrance way to Camp Gordon, to a small dirt road leading off the Federal Highway. Cantrell took a sharp right hand turn onto the road, which T.C. had never noticed before, and, after driving another quarter of a mile they come upon a small brick building. There were no signs marking the location or naming the building or its purpose. And why should there be, thought T.C., this is the "Invisible Empire," after all..

Once inside the building, T.C. was blindfolded and told to wait for his "escorts." He was left alone to wonder what was in store for him. Of all the literature he had read concerning the Klan, including his father's tattered copy of *The Clansman* which he had read so many times, he knew nothing about the ritual of induction. He was about to learn.

After a few moments the blindfold was removed. He found himself in a small dark room with just enough light to allow him to see his two escorts. Both were dressed in the familiar white robes and peaked hoods of the Klansman. He knew that these two were "the Nighthawks" on either side of him. Each took T.C. by the elbow and led him through a door into a brightly lit room, so bright that it caused him to turn away from the glare.

When he was again able to focus his gaze, he saw that he was standing in a large room festooned with Confederate flags and filled to overflowing with hooded Klansmen. One of the Klansman walked up to T.C., a ghostly giant in white, and examined T.C. closely, his masked face only inches away.

One of his two escorts spoke: "We have a white Christian American who seeks admission to our brotherhood."

After a moment of silence the Klansman confronting him spoke in measured tones.

T.C., expecting a command, received a question instead: "Do you come in peace but prepared to do battle?"

He reflexively answered: "Yes."

After a dramatic pause: "And are you prepared to do that

battle to protect the Christian faith of your fathers, the supremacy of your race, and the United States of America?"

"I do," said T.C. with a determination and certainty that
echoed through the chamber.

"Then you may pass to the next station," said his questioner who stepped aside, allowing T.C., still led by his two escorts, to
move toward the center of room.

In that center was a neon cross which glowed with the red-
ness of fire above an altar. On the altar, seated on a chair which
resembled a throne, was the Grand Cyclops of the Den, the pre-
siding officer of the Klavern, his rank marked by two yellow circles with interlapping red crosses on his robe. Around him were
several Klansman whose hooded uniforms were complemented
by sashes of different colors, as well as others who had scarlet
stripes on the spikes of their caps. T.C. recognized the emblem of
the Grand Cyclops. He also recognized the Cyclops's voice as one
he had heard, it seemed so long ago, at Phinizy Ditch when he
first witnessed a Klan gathering.

The Cyclops spoke: "Thomas Caleb Simmons."

The last time T.C. had heard his full first name was when it
was spoken by Maggie. Oh, if only Maggie could see him now, in
this hall, with all of these men gathered on his behalf.

The Cyclops continued, but T.C.'s emotion was such as to
numb his hearing. He barely heard the exhortations which called
upon him to keep his blood pure and to right the wrongs inflicted
upon him and his race—wrongs perpetrated by foreigners,
blacks, Jews and those who swore allegiance to the Pope. He
avowed several oaths by saying "I do," and he trembled with the
realization that these were indeed sacred obligations. He silently
prayed he would be strong enough to fulfill them.

When he had finished his discourse the Grand Cyclops put
both of his hands on T.C.'s shoulders and, in a voice filled with
affection, he said: "You are now one of us. You have undertaken
the obligations of the Invisible Empire and have sworn to keeping

your heart and your blood pure. I welcome you to our family and, by the authority vested in me by the Imperial Wizard, I proclaim you a citizen of the United Klans of America and a member of the Ku Klux Klan. In the presence of this company and our almighty God I vest you with the most noble title which can be conferred upon a man: You are from this day forward a Klansman."

The hall filled with applause and T.C. found himself surrounded by his fellow Klansmen—all congratulating, embracing, and slapping him on the back. For the first time in his life he felt himself an accepted member of a community. The members of this community may have shared with him the shame of poverty and failure, but in this moment of comradery he felt a bond and kinship which elevated his spirit beyond the reach of suffering. To others these farm hands, factory workers, and garage menials may have been rednecks and white trash—but T.C. at that moment, felt as one with the noblest of men.

CHAPTER 10

L U K E

It's hard to explain my feeling of closeness to T.C. When we first met, he was considered the school oddity. I, on the other hand, was a popular leader who had developed a following among a large group of friends. That popularity was diminished by my spending more and more time with T.C., an affiliation that my friends found more than strange. My popularity was diminished even more by the growing discomfort that came from constantly hiding the fact that I was a Jew. And it was becoming more and more certain that my family would have to leave town, because my father's business was continuing to fail. I felt that I wasn't long for Augusta, which gave me a certain feeling of detachment from my old friends. When I was with T.C., I felt less like an alien in a strange land.

I knew it was curious for me to have such a strong connection to a person who shared none of my interests or values. A person who was from a cultural background completely different from mine, with a Klan mentality of aversion toward all minorities. But our connection was cemented with a powerful glue. It was based on the fact that we were both outcasts, a state of mind and condition that overrode all of those other differences. Outcasts remain bonded long after the cheerleaders and high school jocks have stopped seeing each other.

I'm certain it was my imagination, but when I met T.C. the day after the Klan ritual, he seemed like a different person. Of course, at that time I did not know he had become a Klansman. The hangdog look, which had been gradually disappearing, was now completely gone. Although he still bore a trace of his old reticence and the bearing of someone lacking complete confidence, he seemed to be much more sure of himself.

The day after his induction, I met him in town, still ambling, but with a more determined gait.

"How's 'bout goin' over to Clarks Hill Dam, Lipton? I got lots to tell ya."

"Sure," I said.

"This time, we're drivin'," he said.

In Georgia's rural communities you could be licensed to drive at 14, and T.C. had been driving since that age. But it wasn't until this year that Mr. Knotts had allowed him to drive one of the old cars he had at his garage. We walked together past the Dairy Queen and Andrew's Pharmacy to the car which was without fenders and seemed wired together.

"Old man Knotts been using this Lizzie for spare parts," he said, as he opened the door which was hanging by one hinge. I got into the passenger seat, which had a rusty spring protruding from its center, and after several grinding attempts the Lizzie started and we were on our way.

"How does it feel to be ridin' with a Klansman?" he asked with a broad smile.

I knew his induction was imminent but had no idea it had already occurred. "When did it happen? How come you didn't tell me until now?" I asked.

He then proceeded to tell me about Lucius Cantrell's unexpected visit and he described his swearing in as "the most awesome experience anyone could ever have."

And that was it. That was his total description.

"Tell me about it?" I asked, more curious than interested.

"You're my friend, Lipton, but I'd sooner die than tell the secrets of the Klan. In fact, if I did tell you, I *would* die." This was not said lightly and I knew better than to ask any more questions.

The rest of the trip we rode in relative silence.

When we arrived at the Dam, we went to our favorite shade tree. It was here that T.C. had first told me of his love of the Klan and here we were, just a year later, and he was a member—a full-fledged Knight of the Invisible Empire of the Ku Klux Klan.

T.C. lay on his back, with his arm playing the role of a pillow tucked under his head.

"Remember, Lipton, the first time we came here together, you were my first friend?" and then he spoke with an emotion which I thought him incapable of. "For as long as we live you'll be my first friend. And you're my best friend. Not a Klan brother, but a best friend. I know you're leaving soon, but I want you to stay being my best friend."

"You are my best friend, T.C., and I can't imagine having a better one." I answered, feeling an enormous affection for this overlarge poorly educated and impoverished boy who would undoubtedly grow up to be an overlarge, poorly educated and impoverished man.

He told me he had just seen this movie where best friends could become blood brothers by following a ceremony and pledging undying loyalty. Given his obvious attraction to ritual, and to make our friendship more binding, he suggested that we do the same.

"Okay." I said, "but how do you become blood brothers?"

T.C. took out the folding knife he always kept with him and put it on the ground between us.

"First we have to cut our fingers and mix our blood together. Then we have to prove our trust by telling each other a story about himself that he would never ever tell to anyone else, not even to his preacher."

I didn't mind the part about telling a secret, but I was a little worried about that finger cutting part. T.C. was real good with his fists, but he was real bad with his knife. I remembered the time he went to cut off the foot of a rabbit he had shot so he could have a lucky rabbit's foot. By the time T.C. was finished cutting and hacking, there was practically nothing left of that poor old rabbit, and T.C. had to wrap both his hand and wrist in a towel to stop the bleeding.

"Okay, I'll do it," I said," but I gotta cut myself."

"That shows you don't trust me."

"That's what you told the rabbit," I said.

I smiled, and T.C. smiled back. It occurred to me then that smiling was something he didn't do often. I took the knife and wiped the dirt off the blade on my shirt. I cut my finger deeper than I had intended and handed the knife to T.C. who gave himself a vicious hacking swipe with the blade. When we mixed our blood, T.C. sure contributed a whole lot more than I did.

As we put the wounds of our bleeding fingers together, we swore an oath to always be best friends, and to support and protect each other no matter what. We knew that I would be leaving Augusta soon so we promised that, although we might not be in the same place, nothing could ever separate us.

I told T.C. that seeing as how it was his idea to become blood brothers, he would have to tell me his secret first. He paused for awhile and appeared to be struggling with the unfastening of a secret that he was anxious to share but afraid to let go of. For a moment I thought that he was prepared to give up the secret sharing part of the ritual—and then he opened up.

And oh boy, did he ever have a secret. Seems he had all kinds of sex with Mrs. Jarman, our teacher. He told me that they did it at her house, of how he took a shower with her and how beautiful her breasts were. He kept on telling me of all the things they did, and how she even put it in her mouth. Once he got started he just went on and I wasn't about to stop him. I never thought I could get aroused listening to T.C., but I did. He ended his narrative by telling me how much he loved Mrs. Jarman and he intended one day to marry her.

"Now Lipton, promise again you won't tell anyone."

"Hey, we're blood brothers. I would never betray you," I said, then added, "but do you think that before you get married you could arrange for me to see her naked." I said this with a smile, but my blood brother saw no humor in it. In fact he seemed almost somber, no doubt feeling as though he had betrayed his lover by revealing their shared and intimate secret.

"Okay, what's your secret, Lipton?"

"Well, it's no big deal like your secret, but it is a secret that I have kept for awhile—one that could probably cause me a lot of trouble with a lot of people if it gets out."

T.C. looked at me with great anticipation. I think he expected me to tell him that I had done something physical to one of our mutual enemies, like stomping Demerest or maiming one of his kinsmen. The more he indicated his anticipation, the more insignificant I thought my revelation to be. It was like he had just described an eruption of Mount Vesuvius and I was going to tell him about a trained dog act.

"It's not really much." I said. And then after a long pause and a hesitancy which surprised even me, I spoke my secret out loud—I said just loud enough for him to hear: "I'm ...(ahem) I am Jewish."

I thought T.C. would be annoyed because my secret was not as exciting, interesting, and surprising as his. Instead, he sat up and stared at me with a rage that I could almost feel. His silence lasted just long enough to allow him to grab me by the collar and pull my face to within inches of his.

"Why didn't you tell me?"

"Let me go. It's no big deal. I just didn't want anyone to know."

Now he was standing over me, still holding me by my collar. With a shout of rage he lifted me clean off of my feet and threw me hard to the ground. He was pulling his leg back preparing to kick me when I scrambled to my feet and started to run.

I was grateful for his size and lumbering gait. That, along with my speed enabled me to put some distance between us. But he kept coming, swearing and shouting about how I tricked him. "Jew trick, Jew trick!" he kept shouting.

I realized then what I should have realized sooner. The most important thing in T.C.'s life was the Klan. I should have known that sooner or later, his friendship with a Jew would compromise his status within the Klan. I had a while to think about all of this as I tried to hitch a ride home. Clarks Hill was a long way from Augusta, but there was no way I was going to go back to the car and my crazed blood brother.

And that was another thing I should have realized. That blood brother oath thing was just putting him more in harm's way. It occurred to me that if the inhabitants of the Invisible Empire ever got wind of the fact that their most recent acolyte had taken a blood oath with a Jew, his days in the Klan—maybe his days on earth—would be numbered. It wasn't until many years later that I learned that T.C., in order to purge himself of his guilt, went to his Klan mentor, Lucius Cantrell, and confessed the pollution of his blood.

From that day until the day I left for Brooklyn, T.C. and I never spoke again. When I attempted to talk to him at school, he walked past me as if I didn't exist. He treated me the same way he treated his other classmates: with complete impassivity. The only difference was that he and I knew each other's greatest secrets and we had taken a blood oath. No matter what, there was that bond between us. A couple of weeks after that fateful day at the Clarks Hill Dam, he dropped out of school.

CHAPTER 11

LUKE

My father's business had always been an up and down operation. Part of the down times was caused by fluctuations in the wholesale clothing market. A mere ripple in the national market could swamp a small store owner like my father. But the major part of his problems came from his extending credit to people whom he did not have the heart to press for payment. And, I suppose, most of the problem stemmed from the fact that my father did not have Abe Lapinsky's talent for business.

Parents seldom seem to share their problems with their children—my mother and father were no different. When times are bad, children suffer financially and emotionally but often do not know why. I noticed that my mother and father were arguing more. Dad seemed to be turning grayer by the day, not only his hair but the color of his skin. Even though my mother had made reference in the past to the fact that my father's business was in trouble, and that because of this we might have to leave Augusta, I had no way of knowing how imminent all of this was.

Rumors started to spread that my father's store would be closing. Kids in my class, who'd overheard conversation from their parents, whispered that the bank would shutter his store and claim all of the merchandise as partial payment for loan payments far too overdue.

Although my classmates knew, it was never mentioned by them to me. It was strange that young people who may have harassed each other because of a different religion, a physical imperfection or countless other real or imagined shortcomings, never tormented another youth about a parent's financial problems. I imagine it was because, unlike other maladies that seem to uniquely target others, poverty is a malady which is perceived to threaten everyone—a threat that most young people fear.

When my father learned that my mother had called Abe to see if he had any "management" positions open in his company, he flew into a rage which seemed uncontrollable. In later years I came to believe that he was somehow grateful that my mother made that call—a call his pride would never have permitted him to make. I was wrong. It was more than my father's pride which kept him from making that call. He realized, as neither my mother nor I did, that any compact with Abe Lapinsky would be Faustian—that Dad's soul would be forfeit.

Cousin Abe could not have been nicer. There was always a place for dad at the company. After all, what was family all about except to help each other. He was delighted to have my father back in Brooklyn—where he belonged—where he ought to be. There was no need for Abe to taunt my father now. He had him caught in his web and could pounce on his prey at his leisure.

So we left Augusta for what I thought would be the last time. I was reluctant to go—to leave the world which brought me so much comfort with its familiarity. I would not miss my former schoolmates. I had been growing apart from them for some time—and now even T.C., my best friend, my blood brother, was completely alienated from me. But I knew I would miss Georgia. The summer heat and verdant lushness which smelled so sweet, the black sky pierced by thousands of pinpoint stars, the vast farms covered with a quilt of cotton balls popped open and just waiting to be picked, my house which, no matter what happened to me during the day, seemed to embrace me at night.

I wondered if my parents had any of the same feelings. There was no way of telling, because they kept their silence. On our way out of town neither of my parents gave even a sideways glance to our house, our neighborhood, or the tree-lined streets so familiar to us as we headed, once again, to Route 1 North.

I was as nervous as any 15-year-old would be who was heading into a new world and leaving his familiar hometown behind. But as soon as we crossed the Georgia/South Carolina line, my

mother started to speak putting on a non-stop display of optimism, telling me how great it would be to have so many cousins
my own age around, what great fun it would be to live in an apartment in Brooklyn, and how she had dreamed of this her whole
life. My father remained silent. I had no way of knowing then that
what crushed the life out him would make my wonderful life possible.

There was an early October chill in the air as the
Studebaker, dispelling all doubts of its indestructibility, entered
the borough of Brooklyn. Mom, huddled over the marked
Hagstrom's Street Map that Cousin Abe had sent her, guided my
father towards the apartment house which was to become our
new home. Every once in a while she looked up from the map and
commented on how empty the streets seemed. There were some
people, but not nearly the number one would expect in a borough
that had more people than the entire State of Georgia.

No sooner had my mother announced that our apartment
house was "right there on the corner" when all hell seemed to
break loose. Car horns started trumpeting, police sirens wailed,
and people who seemed deliriously happy came pouring out of
buildings and hanging out of apartment house windows.
Everyone was shouting.

Dad brought the car to stop in the middle of the street. The
cacophony of noise was so loud that mom's screaming to him
could not be heard from the passenger seat. People swarmed the
car, pounding on the hood and windows. My father stuck his head
out of the car window to ask someone what was happening when
a dowdy old woman planted a big kiss on his lips and let out an
ear-shattering whoop of joy.

I initially froze, startled at this upheaval which surrounded
us. Then I started to wave back at the people in the street who
were waving wildly at me, kissing each other and throwing kisses
at me. In Georgia I had always heard that New Yorkers were cold,
distant people. But there was nothing cold or distant about the

reception they were giving us. I wondered if cousin Abe had arranged all of this. I was busy watching a young woman twirling her terrified cat over her head in wild celebratory circles when I noticed my father again putting his head out of the window and shouting at a young man next to the car,

"Hey, kid, what's going on? This looks like the Times Square celebration after the Nazis surrendered."

The young man look incredulously at my father, then looked down at the Georgia license plates and smiled. He cupped his hands to his mouth so he could be heard and yelled back.

"No, sir, this is much, much bigger than V-E Day. The Dodgers, the Brooklyn 'Bums,' just won the World Series! We won the World Series!"

My father smiled one of his rare smiles and said to me and my mother, "Welcome to Brooklyn! Let's join the celebration."

I didn't have the slightest clue about the Brooklyn Dodgers. Nor did I have any idea why this entire borough was more proud of its Brooklyn "Bums" than it would ever be of the twenty-two Nobel Laureates who grew up there. We left the car right in the middle of the street, and it only took me a few moments to meld into the mayhem. At one point, I spotted a pretty young girl and screamed, not fully understanding what I was yelling: "I love those Bums!" then planted a big sloppy kiss right on her mouth. That probably would have gotten me lynched in the South. Here, the girl just shot her arm in the air and yelled, "Yahoo!" It was the first "Yahoo" response I had ever gotten from a girl.

When things calmed down a bit, we drove to the corner and our new apartment. My father told some of our new neighbors who were in the apartment house lobby that we were a new family moving into the building. In five minutes we had close to fifty people helping us unload the car of those possessions which my mother would not trust to a shipping company. They brought everything up to our apartment. The four rooms which were to be our new home were completely empty—we were going to stay at my Uncle Ben's apartment until the furniture Abe had person-ally selected for us arrived. If the rooms had not been empty, they never could not have held the crowd of still-celebrating people who followed us up to our new apartment. We were officially wel-comed into Brooklyn by a uniformed police officer, who held up an overflowing mug of beer and shouted:

"A toast to our new neighbors from the South. Some of us may resent that you didn't have to suffer all of those years like the rest of us when those damn Yankees beat us every year...(loud chorus of boos)...But what I have to believe is that God sent you to us as our good luck charm..."

My father seemed happy for the first time since we had left Georgia. He smiled at the cop and shouted: "Officer, you have met a Southern family who hates the Yankees even more than you do."

Whatever he said after that was drowned out by the cheer-ing. And so we celebrated well into the night, being handed over from apartment to apartment, none of whose denizens would hear of our not having some "homemade" food to eat. It was almost midnight by the time my uncle Ben could fight his way through the traffic and mayhem to pick us up and take us, ever so slowly, to his place for the night. Those personal possessions which mom found so dear that she kept them in the car rather than shipping them, remained unguarded and untouched in our new apartment. This whole magical event lifted my parents and me onto a cloud we hadn't ridden in years. When I saw my par-ents in a swirl of bellowing people actually hug each other, I only regretted that Georgia didn't have a Brooklyn Dodger team.

Unfortunately, the Brooklyn Dodgers never won another World Series in Brooklyn, and even more unfortunately, my father never had another happy day like that in his life. The next week he took up his new "management" position with Abe Lapinsky's clothing company.

Abe called a company-wide meeting—ostensibly to intro-duce my father to the employees of the company, but really to display his newest victim. The union employees eyed dad with resentment because he had been put into management his first day on the job while many of them had labored for years without any advancement. The non-relatives in management eyed dad nervously, knowing his filial relationship could vault him over them or even replace them in due time. And the other relatives in management eyed dad with pity, knowing he had just sold his soul to the highest bidder...actually, the only bidder.

Abe threw his arm around dad in front of the assembled employees and told them how lucky he was to have my father working for him now. He started joshing about how my father was the one relative who persisted in his refusal to work for him. He told the assemblage that no matter how much money he offered my father, my father refused to work for him. Then he tapped my dad patronizingly on the head and said with an obviously forced smile:

"I told you, you would come back, didn't I?"

My father just lowered his head and nodded affirmatively, wishing he had died rather than just failed.

"Well, let's hear a big company hand for my dear cousin who finally had the sense to come back to his cousin Abe..."

The thunderous applause for the cruel, thinly concealed taunting of my father rose in crescendo. As Abe strode off the platform one of the union men whispered to another,

"We all look like the fucking Politburo when Stalin used to give a speech...whoever stops clapping first, dies."

As the weeks went by, Abe stepped up the humiliation of my father, belittling him even more than the other members of management because on occasion my father had the audacity to defy him, albeit only briefly.

Of course, I never knew at the time that any of this was happening. To me Abe Lapinsky was the man whose two hundred dollar gift represented my victory over my father's summary "no further discussion." A victory that then seemed important to me.

I became even more enamored of Abe, who now insisted I call him "Uncle Abe" even though he was not my uncle and even though my father blanched every time I used the "Uncle" handle. Perversely, my father's obvious resentment of Abe only made me more resentful of my father.

*   *   *

I started to feel that I was a combination of my father, the perpetual outsider, and "Uncle" Abe, the outsider trying to claw his way to the inside. When I was growing up in the South I was viewed as an alien Jew among Southerners. When I moved up to a predominantly Jewish area of Brooklyn, I was viewed as an alien Southerner among Jews. The Southerners' outrageous stereotypes about Jews were matched only by the Brooklyn Jews' outrageous stereotypes of Southerners. I cannot count the number of times my classmates in Brooklyn asked me if I had joined the Klan when I lived in the South. I wondered if it was the God-given lot of the Jew to always be the outsider, reviled as the quintessential capitalist in Communist countries and equally reviled as the quintessential Communist in capitalist countries.

My first year in Brooklyn was very difficult. I joined classmates who had spent a lifetime together and who considered me a stranger, all the more because of my Southern accent. Abe even went so far as to pay for a special teacher to leach that accent from my speech. It never occurred to me that people speaking Brooklynese should be the last people on earth to make fun of anyone's accent.

I tried to fend off the shame of my outlander status by resorting to humor. I wrote a column for the school newspaper entitled "Oi vey, Y'all." But I never felt I was ever completely accepted by my peers. Had I not gotten credit for bringing the Dodgers their first World Series win, I don't know if I could have survived that first year emotionally intact.

When I felt the loneliest, I decided to write a letter to the only person with whom I really felt a close kinship, my blood brother, T.C. I still had frayed feelings from the way he carried on when he discovered that I was Jewish, but he was the only person who might understand the feelings I was having of not fitting in, of being the outsider. I didn't know if he would write back to me, but just writing the letter made me feel better. I was disappointed but not surprised when I received no response. I wrote him again a year later but still received no reply.

CHAPTER 12

T. C.

T.C. tried to sit up, but the pain and the heel of the man's boot pinioning him to the ground rendered him helpless. The other man shoved the muzzle of a twelve-gauge shotgun to within an inch of his face.

"Is what you told Lucius about your Jew buddy and that blood shit true or not!"

Sweat covered T.C.'s face as he tried to pull his arm free from the boot. The pain in his upper arm was so severe that he hadn't even noticed the loss of all feeling in his hand.

"You'd better talk soon, boy, or you'll end up dead."

This time the tormentor with the shotgun shoved the barrel hard into T.C.'s cheek, opening a gash in his face. The physical punishment T.C. had received at the hand of his father had instructed him on the futility and embarrassment of tears. Through clenched teeth he muttered his only defense:

"He tricked me. He tricked me!"

"What do you mean he tricked you, boy?"

The man standing on T.C.'s arm reached down and hauled him up to a sitting position. The blood had made ugly rivulets through his dirt-caked face. He wiped some of the blood from around his eyes, and looked over the top of the shotgun. His voice was more pleading than frightened.

"I never knew he was a Jew. He didn't tell me he was a Jew until after we became blood brothers. I didn't know. He tricked me!"

The other man spoke up for the first time.

"Ain't that just like a Jew, Carl?"

Carl Talbot took one hand off the shotgun and waved it in a way to signify rejection of the excuse.

"It don't matter how it happened. What matters is here's a

Klan member who took an oath to keep his blood pure—a member of our Brotherhood who's got Jew blood mixed with him now. Bad enough he violated his oath. He done become one of the enemy."

T.C. held up the finger he had cut in the blood mixing ritual.

"Here, you can cut my finger off. This is the finger. Go ahead cut it off."

Carl swatted the extended finger aside with the barrel of the gun.

"No, that won't do it."

He pressed the stock of the shotgun against his shoulder and pointed the barrel straight down toward T.C.'s gaping eyes. T.C. started to plead, but then an almost surreal calm enveloped him. He stopped trembling, and the blood no longer pounded inside his head. He put his left hand on the ground to steady himself, tried to get to his feet, but fell. He tried again, and this time managed to stumble to his feet. He wiped his hand across his blood-streaked face:

"Go ahead and do it. Only I'm gonna die like a man...on my feet..."

Carl's finger curled around the trigger and he raised the barrel of the shotgun, aiming it directly at T.C.'s face, which was only six inches above his own. Everything in the world seemed to stop for T.C. He saw nothing. He heard nothing, not even his own breathing. It seemed to him as though he had entered some other world, a world of total silence and tranquility.

"Did you hear what I said, boy?"

The barrel of the shotgun thumped against the side of T.C.'s head, shocking him out of his reverie. T.C. was no longer cowered. Now he was angry.

"Shoot me. Go ahead and shoot me!"

For the first time Carl lowered the barrel of the shotgun.

"I can't shoot you. It wouldn't do no good. You would still die a Klansman who was blood brother to a Jew."

T.C. just stared in disbelief. He thought it would be over by now. He wished it had been over, that he had been shot. He just stared at Carl in silence. He had a sense that he was about to be offered an alternative punishment, one that would allow him to expiate his sin. He was prepared to do anything asked of him except quit the Klan. After what seemed like an eternity of silence, Carl spoke:

"You gotta purge that tainted blood with blood. The devil sent that Jew to corrupt you into defiling your body and making a mockery of all we stand for. The only way you can undo the evil and re purify your blood is to spill his."

T.C. blanched. Still tasting blood in his mouth, he spat as if to rid himself of a curse. He looked down at his blood puddled on the ground. He kept his eyes on the blood in the dirt as he spoke haltingly.

"Kill...Lipton...I have to kill Lipton?"

Carl bent over and put a comforting hand on T.C.'s shoulder.

"You see, you already thinking wrong. He ain't Lipton. He's a Jew, the Antichrist in the form of a human. He's a messenger sent here from Satan. You'd be ridding us of a demon bent on corrupting, not only you, but others—our children, our women, our world. Killing him would be doing God's work."

No one spoke a word for seconds that seemed like hours. T.C. just kept staring at the ground, except he wasn't looking at the ground. He was looking at Lipton's face. He shook his head.

"Why can't I kill a different Jew? If they're all the same, what difference does it make?

"No, you gotta purge the blood from the one that tricked you...there's no way around it."

T.C. put both of his hands to his face covering his eyes, trying to blot out Lipton's face. He was not aware that Lipton had left town the week before.

"No, I can't, I ain't gonna do it. I ain't. You can kill me. I ain't gonna do it!"

Carl stared hard at T.C. He could tell that T.C. was not going to be moved because he was unafraid. He had no more fear. From his long service to the Klan, Carl knew that once the fear was gone, he had no more control. If T.C. had been black, he would have just shot him right there, just another dead nigger. But this was a fellow Klansman. If Carl shot him, there would be repercussions, and, worse, questions as to how a boy whose best friend was a Jew got into the Klan in the first place. His friend Lucius would suffer for that one.

Carl thought hard for a few moments, and then he pulled the other man, Will Morgan, over and engaged in a heated discussion with him out of hearing range. T.C. glanced over to the road, the thought of fleeing suddenly upon him. But he made only a tentative step in the direction of escape and then stopped. He knew he could get away...this time. But there was no getting away from the Klan in these parts. No police to go to...the Klan were the police. No money to flee elsewhere, and what would he do when he got there? There was nothing to do but await his fate.

"Okay, boy, me and Will talked this over, and decided that there is something you can do for repurification."

"You know that Jew Temple over on Greene Street?"

T.C. caught his breath. Were they going to ask him to kill the Jews in the Temple? His mind started spinning.

"You want me to kill the Jews, right in the Temple?"

Carl shook his head from side to side. "No, no, they sure as hell deserved to be killed. But if you kill a lot of Jews, they'll be hell to pay. It's not like you was killin' a lot of niggers—no, just burn the Jew devil's worship house down...completely down. All you gotta do is start a good fire, we'll make sure the firemen don't get there too fast."

T.C. felt relieved. "That's all I gotta do? Just burn down the Temple? Not kill nobody?"

Carl glanced over at Will who smirked back at Carl.

"Oh no, boy, you gotta kill someone too. In fact, you gotta do it right after you set fire to the Jew Temple, you gotta do both tomorrow."

Carl saw T.C.'s face go tight again.

"Don't worry boy, uh...T.C., it's only a nigger—a butt ugly black nigger."

"What did he do?"

Will laughed, "He didn't have to do nothing, he was born a nigger, ain't that enough?"

Carl just drew in his breath, "That would have been enough, but this nigger has got to pay for a bigger crime. He 'most raped a white women. Luckily the postman saw him through the window—buck naked he was and he had got her clothes off, too."

Carl's hands started to shake as he spoke, "We caught the bastard and got him penned up in a pump house. The nigger claims this white woman asked him to do some yard work and then asked him in to the house. The lyin' sonofabitch says she got him into the shower and took her own clothes off and then started to trot him off to her bedroom."

T.C. looked at Carl and then stared up to the sky, his eyes narrowing with anger.

"Lucky damn thing the postman came in when he did. Damn nigger grabbed his pants, putting them on while he hightailed it out the back door. There ain't a jury in this whole county that wouldn't string that nigger up...but hangin's too good for him."

T.C. became angrier as Carl talked. This was why he joined the Klan. This was just the kind of thing that he first heard about at the Klan rally, and the warning sounded that night was almost a prophesy which was now being realized. Niggers raping white women—a fear that has haunted the southern male for a hundred years.

Carl continued, "We gotta make an example of him. The postman knowed who the nigger was and some of the boys grabbed him as he was goin' into his shack out at Miller's Pond. Got him locked up in the pump house near the river. We're gonna take the black bastard down to the swamp and torch the sono-fabitch."

"Who was the woman?" Will asked.

Carl shrugged, "I don't know her name. She's a school teacher, lives over in Sand Hills up to Juniper Drive."

"Married?"

"Yeah, seems her husband shipped out of Camp Gordon for Germany."

T.C.'s mind went blank and then filled with a blind fury. He knew that Mrs. Jarman, Maggie, would never willingly have sex with a nigger. That nigger was trying to make her into a dirtbag whore —that nigger had violated Mrs. Jarman, and T.C. felt violated too. Carl and Will heard what they thought was a growl as T.C. started pacing back and forth like a caged animal. They were startled to hear the young man who seemed cowed just a few minutes ago, snarl through clenched teeth:

"Oh yes, I wanna get that nigger!"

*　　　*　　　*

The plan sounded so easy to T.C. The next day was Sunday. After he burned down the Temple, he was to meet Carl and Will at the corner of Tobacco Road and the Federal Highway. That was the part he was looking forward to. Not so much the Temple part, but the part when he would be getting the lyin' nigger. He couldn't sleep that night. He kept thinking about what he was going to be doing the next day. He also kept thinking about Maggie.

It had been years since his father had been to church—his drinking caused him to sleep late, and because he drank more on Saturday nights he usually slept later on Sundays. This Sunday was no exception.

T.C. left the shack he shared with his father and sat behind the wheel of Mr. Knotts' Lizzie. It crossed his mind that he still didn't own anything, except maybe for the clothes on his back.

He didn't even own the ability to think about that one secret he shared with Maggie—a secret no more since he told Lipton about it. It wasn't even a secret worth keeping since he heard about that story which that lyin' nigger told. Oh he was goin' to enjoy burning that sonofabitch—but first he had to take care of the Jew Temple.

He drove past the Temple and went around the block to be sure no one was looking. He didn't want to be caught and not be able to join Carl and Will when the fun began at the "Nigger BarBQue." He smiled at the thought as he pulled the Lizzie across the street from a tool shed attached to the rear of the Temple.

He had been told that the Klan would see to it that the fire trucks would be late in getting there. He figured that by the time they did get there, there'd be nothing but a pile of ashes, and he would be well on his way to the pump house near the swamp— on his way to set another kind of fire. He walked across the street with a book of matches in one hand and a kerosene-soaked rag in another. After looking both ways to be sure he was unseen, he slipped the rag under a piece of wooden siding which hung from the tool shed and touched it with a lit match. The fire started with a *whoosh*, and T.C. took off. He took off as fast as the Lizzie would travel, fast enough to attract attention, but not fast enough to prevent his vehicle and license plate from being seen by a half a dozen people who were walking their dogs and tending their lawns on an otherwise quiet Sunday afternoon.

Those same witnesses to T.C.'s retreat quickly summoned the fire department and ran to the Temple to do what they could to stop the fire.

*   *   *

Just as they had promised, Carl and Will were waiting by the side of the road. They told T.C. to park his car and get into the half-back driven by Carl. The three traveled down Tobacco Road

CHAPTER 13

LUKE

When it came time for me to go to college, it was assumed that I would go to the City College of New York—CCNY. At the time it was a great school, known as the Harvard of the poor. Even better, it was free. Mom was very excited that she was going to have a son going to such a prestigious school. And even though my father didn't say anything to me, I overheard him bragging to a friend that my grades and tests were so good that my teachers thought I would be placed into advanced classes at CCNY. In our Brooklyn neighborhood, going to CCNY was quite an accomplishment. That was where Felix Frankfurter had gone, and he became a Supreme Court Justice and top adviser to a President of the United States. And now Lukash Lipton would be following in Frankfurter's shoes and the shoes of all of those great scientists who went to CCNY.

I was all set to go to CCNY when Abe called me into his private office. He first slipped me some "spending money" that dad could not afford to give me. Then he put his hand on my shoulder.

"So I hear you want to go CCNY?"

I fairly glowed, "If I get in."

"Oh, with your grades and test scores you'll get in. In fact, your academic record is so good that I'll bet you could get into Princeton..."

Did he say Princeton? The Ivy League? The Big Three of the Ivy League? I had never even considered it. CCNY was the cynosure of a Brooklyn Jewish boy's universe. The Ivy League was in another galaxy.

"Uncle, Abe, I don't know if I could get in. I mean they only take a few Jews—and it's very expensive."

Abe just shook his head from side to side, "Lukash, Lukash,

Lukash. You should know by now there's nothing your Uncle Abe can't do. I already have a nice contribution check written out to Princeton, and I spoke to the Cardinal...you know when Catholic Charities made me Man of the Year—Well, he'll write you a recommendation. Believe me, if Uncle Abe says he can do it, he can do it."

I let all of this sink in for a moment. Yes, I thought, Uncle Abe could do anything, never thinking that my test scores, prize winning writings, and being second in my class might have had something to do with my chances at Princeton. The Lapinsky legerdemain was remarkable. Even when your own hand was in the hat, it still seemed as though it was Uncle Abe who was pulling the rabbit out of it.

"But my father could never pay the tuition...or maybe I could get a scholarship..."

"Scholarship? No nephew of Abe Lapinsky needs a scholarship. I will pay for your tuition and whatever else you need. It's not every day that a Lapinsky could go to Princeton..."

I did not even think to correct him by saying that a Lipton— not a Lapinsky—would be going to Princeton. Nor did I even think about how accepting Abe's largesse would further humiliate my father. I only thought the unthinkable. I might be able to go to Princeton. James Madison, F. Scott Fitzgerald, Woodrow Wilson... and now Lukash Lipton. Screw Felix Frankfurter. He was the Jewish dream. I was dreaming the American dream.

I accepted Uncle Abe's offer and Princeton accepted me. I also accepted Abe's explanation that the letter the Cardinal sent on my behalf, procured by Abe, was the reason I was accepted at Princeton. Uncle Abe had a copy of that letter framed for me. It read:

"To Whom it may concern, A good friend of mine informs me that his nephew Lukash Lipton would make a strong addition to your school. I am passing this information on to you to use as you may wish. Sincerely, Cardinal Spellman."

Across the cold light of several decades, that letter does not appear to be a real door opener, but at the time I thought it was my key to the Ivy League—put in my hand by all-powerful Uncle Abe.

When I was accepted into Princeton, I again had the overwhelming urge to write to T.C., but this time I didn't follow through because of a sense of guilt. How could I write him about going to Princeton when the only shot he would ever have at Princeton would be as a janitor there. I was afraid I would be rubbing his nose in the dirt if I told him of my good fortune. So I just tore up the letter and decided that if he gave a damn about our relationship, he would have answered one of my other letters.

My mother was very fearful that I would have a hard time at Princeton, the quintessential WASP school. But I really wasn't too worried. I was used to being the outsider. Indeed, I expected to be treated that way at Princeton. Besides, being accepted to Princeton gave me a great boost in prestige in my community. At Princeton, I might be viewed as that Brooklyn Jew, but in Jewish Brooklyn, I was praised, particularly by my friends' parents, as Mr. Ivy League.

The Princeton of my college years really did measure up to its reputation, both warts and beauty marks. Educationally, it was the best place in the world. There were small classes, outstanding professors, and a curriculum that could have kept even a Philistine fascinated for years. Socially, Princeton was also the Princeton of legend. It had the usual jock/geek split. But there was also an overlay of social and class stratification. There were the rich Waspy kids and then there were those who wished they could be rich Waspy kids. There was no such thing as ethnic pride in my college days. The only ethnic group we had pride in was the "All American white Protestant." No one back then could have ever accepted a black, an Italian, or a Jew as an "All American" boy—not even a black, an Italian or a Jew.

I thought at first that maybe I could blend in with the Southerners at Princeton. Princeton was probably the most southern of all northern schools. A good part of our student body came from the South. But I soon found that we shared little but geography. My South was Augusta, Georgia, the poor man's South. My friends in Augusta fantasized *Gone With The Wind*; the Southern boys at Princeton lived it.

The Jewish boys at Princeton tended to cling together, but for about the half of us who were trying to slither out from under our own skin, we tried to keep our "Jew Fests" below the campus radar. It never occurred to us that no matter how many skins we shed, to some in the Christian world we would still be the same old snakes.

What all of the Jews did have in common was the great pride we had in Albert Einstein who had lived in Princeton and had died just three years before I arrived on campus. When we were with Christian friends, we would casually point out where Einstein lived, taking great pride in the awe- filled reaction that the mere mention of his name would induce in our companions. It was, I suppose, our way of showing that Jews can be good for America, albeit all of us Jews wish he had done something with that goofy hair of his.

Princeton in the late 1950s was like a Shangri-La on Route 1, midway between Philadelphia and New York City, but it was light years away from both. The problems of the world rarely penetrated the bucolic Ivy skin of Princeton University. Unconcerned about racism, world conflict, and poverty, we could focus our concerns on the football team, what courses we were taking, how many dates we could get, and most importantly, what eating club we got into.

The Southern boys had a concern, however, that was not shared by the rest of the campus. Almost without exception, every Southern boy had an obsession with the Civil War, or, as they demanded it be called, the War Between the States. It was not an abiding historical interest to them. It was a real live concern that affected their lives every day. Whereas to them, the present Cold War was just a burning ember smoldering somewhere over the distant horizon, the Civil War was a raging inferno always lapping at their heels. To the Northern boys, the Civil

War was a course that you could take to fill your history require-
ments. To the Southern boys it was still alive and very much part
of their lives. I soon found to my detriment that you could more
easily curse God out to a Southern boy than make an even indi-
rect slander against Robert E. Lee.

I grew up in the South, but in the poor areas where I was
from, the people were not obsessed with the Civil War the same
way as these rich Southerners who went to Princeton. Unlike the
men at Princeton, they didn't go on endlessly about every battle,
every Southern general, every despicable carpetbagger, and
every slight, real or perceived, done to the South.

What effected my community in the South was not the
details of the Civil War and the Reconstruction but the detritus of
the Southern aristocracy's obsession with them. The flotsam of
the "Noble Cause" that my community grabbed onto was the hate
filled residue of the "Noble Cause." T.C. never talked of the battle
of Shiloh, or Reconstruction, or even the Thirteenth Amendment.
The words out of his mouth were "nigger, kike, commie Federals,"
and the like. The aristocratic South, by somehow convincing the
poor South that the loss of Tara in *Gone With The Wind* had been
their loss too, was able to avoid dirtying their own white gloves
by using people like T.C. as the bellows of bigotry. They worked
those lower-class bellows masterfully to fan the flame of hatred
throughout the South.

My Princeton classmates from the South were bright,
charming, friendly and utterly convinced that slavery was a good
thing for the blacks, the South had been concerned only with
states' rights in the Civil War, and that the white southerner, not
the blacks, not the Irish, not the Jews, and not anyone else, had
been the greatest victim in the history of the United States. I
found that, with few exceptions, I had nothing in common with
them other than a shared loyalty to all things Princeton.

My four years at Princeton were the best of times and the
worst of times. They were the best of times because I loved the

education it gave me and loved rooting for all of its athletic teams. It was also the worst of times because I so desperately wanted to fit in better. I once asked my Jewish classmate Charles Diamond Stone, the only blonde Jew on campus, how he could seem so happy and well adjusted at Princeton. He told me his secret for happiness at Princeton came from the advice his father gave him after he graduated from high school. His father pulled him close and said,

"Son, I have just one piece of advice to give you. Whatever you do in life, remember one thing...always, always, always, be yourself... and if that doesn't work, try being someone else..."

When Charlie finished imparting to me his father's advice, he took me into his room and pulled from under his mattress a bottle of blonde hair dye. The blonde hair may not have fooled everyone, but it fooled the only person who could make Charlie happy... himself.

Uncle Abe threw a big party for me when I made the Princeton Dean's List my freshman year. My father feigned sickness to avoid having to be there. Rather than showing a modicum of understanding, I was bitter at his not showing up. If his sickness wasn't bad enough to cause him to see a doctor, I couldn't understand why he couldn't at least make an appearance at the party.

I was also upset that my father never showed me the company newsletter where Uncle Abe mentioned my name. Every one of my achievements at Princeton, no matter how insignificant, was written up in the company newsletter under the heading, "The Lapinsky Scholarship." Uncle Abe told me he used that heading in an effort to be humorous, and I believed him. Of course, it was really Abe's way of showing that my father may have been responsible for my birth, but Abe Lapinsky was responsible for my being at Princeton. The employees were always congratulating Uncle Abe for my good works. No one ever congratulated my father.

Uncle Abe was proud, very proud, of the latest ornament on

his bracelet. He took me to the many big charity events he attended introducing me as his Princeton protege to the movers and shakers of New York City. Uncle Abe and I reveled in the glow. My father was never invited.

The more Uncle Abe showered me with his affection, the greater the torment visited on my father. In retrospect, it seemed as though Abe thought of new humiliations to heap on my father every day. He particularly loved to tell about my father's "crawl back" at all Lapinsky sponsored family weddings, funerals or bar mitzvahs. Then he would laugh and say to my father, "Everybody thinks I'm a nice guy...(laughing) It's really that I have a bad memory." Uncle Abe had a memory like an elephant. He would never forgive my father for ignoring or, worse yet, turning his back on his "generosity." Uncle Abe secured his revenge the Lapinsky way, by stripping my father of his dignity layer by layer...and then stripping him of his son.

I didn't find out the true story about Uncle Abe until he died shortly after I graduated from Princeton. That was two years after my own father had died of a heart attack that I am certain was brought on by years of having to swallow his anger and rage. Of course, Uncle Abe paid for my father's funeral and gave the oration over my father's gravestone, which he also paid for. He delivered a very moving speech about how my father had gone wrong early in his life but that we should thank the Lord that he finally saw the light and came home and died in the bosom of his extended family. At the time, I did not realize that my father had died because he had returned to the bosom of his extended family.

I was almost relieved when my father died. The more Uncle Abe praised me and showed interest in everything I did, the more I resented my father's silence and what I took to be his disinterest in my life. If my father didn't care about me, why should I care about him?

I was devastated when Uncle Abe died. Apparently, I wasn't alone in my grief or admiration. The daily newspapers carried articles about the death of the philanthropic business genius. The articles quoted the praise heaped on Uncle Abe by the head of every major New York philanthropy. Many of the articles also told of how his workers worshiped him, apparently mistaking groveling for genuine affection.

I was in the apartment getting dressed to go to Uncle Abe's funeral when my mother walked into the room. She saw me wiping tears from my face. She stared blankly at me for a moment and then she exploded, "How dare you cry for that bastard Abe Lapinsky when you didn't shed one tear for your own father!"

I spun around in shock. I had never heard my mother scream at me like that, and I had never heard her say a bad word about Uncle Abe. I shot back at her, "Because I loved Uncle Abe and I didn't love dad...and dad didn't love me."

My mother burst into tears and between choking sobs, poured out her grief. All my life I had enjoyed my mother's doting and affection and her calming influence. It occurred to me at that moment that I had never seen her in such an emotional state.

"Your father loved you more than life itself... which is why he's not here. It's about time you learned the truth about your father...and your so-called 'Uncle' Abe. I've wanted to tell you for years but your father wouldn't let me. He told me Abe could do more for you than he could, so he just kept his peace while Abe paraded you around and bragged on you. And you never for a moment allowed your father to share some of that pride in you. I was here when Abe called your father to tell him that the Abe Lapinsky scholarship boy had made Dean's List. Your dad heard it from Abe because Abe heard it first from you. Every day at work Abe humiliated your father, degraded him, ripped up by the roots any piece of self worth that your father displayed...."

She sat the foot of my bed, her head in her hands, still sobbing and laboring to fill her lungs with air so that she could continue her reproach:

"Your father went to Georgia, a hostile environment, to

escape Abe Lapinsky. He did it so that you and I could have a good life independent of this man whose sole goal was to subjugate your father and break his spirit. Your father was the only member of the family who dared to defy him and as a result Abe made him a target. Your father knew this, but I was too foolish to see it. I was the one who convinced your father to come up for Jackie's wedding—and when your father's business failed, I was the one who called Abe and pleaded with your father to come back to Brooklyn. Your father knew it would be his destruction—but he came. He came for us Luke, for you and me."

I sat on the bed next to my weeping mother and put her face, wet with tears, on my shoulder. She continued her account of my father's last years and my indifference.

"Every day he worked for that man was a day in hell. You think your 'Uncle Abe' did what he did for you out of love? He did it for two reasons: To have you earn him a kind of distinction and glory that he could never achieve himself, even with all his money, but more importantly, he did it to magnify himself in your eyes and life. By doing that he could further diminish your father's role in your life."

By this time, I too was weeping. My mother, more calmly now, told me more of the pain and torment suffered by my father. She told me that when my father's business in Georgia began to falter, she had called Abe without my father's knowing it to see if he would consider giving us a small loan to keep the banks at bay. Not only did he refuse, but, my mother was to discover years later, he took it upon himself to notify the bank that my father had an outstanding loan due Abe Lapinsky. My father's business failure in Georgia broke him and then Abe broke him again. And it wasn't just my father—Abe sucked the air out of everyone. There wasn't a penny that left his hand that didn't have a string attached to it.

The more my mother talked the more everything she said made sense. It was all so obvious now, I could not comprehend how I couldn't have seen it all along.

"Mom, why didn't anyone expose him?"

"Different reasons, I guess. Some needed him. Some were afraid of him. Your Uncle Ben could have done it. He had his own business and he was tough. One day your father said he was going to rip the veil off that charlatan, and Ben talked him out of it. Ben said, 'What difference does it make what Abe is really like...people think he's a great public benefactor and that makes him give more money to good causes and so what does it matter if it's all a myth?' Ben said bringing Abe down will make us all feel better, but it won't be better for the poor kids who get money from the Catholic Charities or the Jewish Federation, and it may make his employees feel better, but it won't feed them..."

"But why didn't dad just quit? We could have made do somehow..."

"It would have been worse for your father if you had to pass up Princeton and God knows what that will open up for you, just because he couldn't swallow his pride and stay working for Abe. And besides, your father couldn't leave Abe, nobody could. He breaks your legs so thoroughly, so completely, that no one can walk away. Your dad died many years before we put him in his grave..."

The tears that leaked from my eyes were not for Abe, and I was not crying for my father. I was crying for my own shame. I thought about what I would give to have realized years ago what I realized now. I wanted to be able to make it up to my father. I wanted another chance. I was feeling the terrible anguish of a person who has acquired wisdom far too late.

I remembered my reaction when mom called me at college to tell me my father had died. When I picked up the phone, I heard my mother sobbing. She had barely been able to gasp out the words, "Lukash, he's dead, he's dead. Oh my gosh he's dead..." Her anguished words slammed me back against the chair. The first, the only, thought that was flashing through my mind was that Uncle Abe had died. I didn't know what I would do now. I would have to drop out of Princeton because I couldn't afford the tuition. And I wouldn't be able to meet all of those power brokers Uncle Abe was always helping me to meet. What would happen to me now... and who would I have to mentor me? My mother had regained some of her composure by that time.

"Luke, I can't hear you. Are you okay?"

I still couldn't believe that Uncle Abe was dead.

"Mom... when is the funeral...?"

"Uncle Abe is taking care of it. He'll call you about it, I'm sure. In fact, please don't tell him I called you...He'll be mad that he didn't get to be the one to break it to you...since, well you two are so close..."

I blinked my eyes, "Uncle Abe... will call me?"

"Yes, he's taking care of your father's funeral. Are you okay? I really didn't expect you to take it this hard, but I'm glad..."

I didn't hear or remember the rest of the conversation because I was so relieved that Uncle Abe hadn't died. When I hung up the phone, I exhaled mightily, looked upward and thanked God that Uncle Abe was still alive.

As the thoughts of my reaction to my father's death mauled my brain, I started crying uncontrollably. Mom reached over and put her arm around me.

"Mom, I feel so damn guilty...what I did to dad..."

"Don't feel guilty...dad kept silent because he knew he was doing what was best for you even if you didn't know it. He knew that Abe, whatever his perverse reasons, could do more for you than he could."

"No damn it. I should have exposed him... someone should have exposed him."

"What good would it have done, Luke?"

"The truth, that's the good it would have done. It would have exposed the truth. How can people just sit there, people who know better and let people like that get away with...with destroying people...get away with perpetuating myths?"

My mother pried open my hand and placed the car keys in it. "Come on, Luke, we have to get to Abe's funeral. You have to give one of the eulogies... you know you were his favorite."

"No, Princeton was his favorite. I wouldn't be giving his eulogy if I had gone to CCNY."

She brushed her hand through my hair. "Whatever—come on, we have to go."

I stood up and gripped the car keys so hard that the metal pressed its impression deep in my hand, "Fuck it mom, I'm not going to Abe's funeral. They don't need me there. The Cardinal can take my place. Hundreds of people can take my place and give the eulogy, but, damn it, I'm not going. I have to do the right thing even if it's a meaningless gesture."

My mother stood still for a moment, shaking her head slowly up and down, weighing and measuring the thoughts flooding her mind. "Okay, you don't have to go, and I won't go either."

"Good, good, mom."

"But what will we tell them? Why didn't we go?"

"We'll pull an Abe Lapinsky on them. We'll tell them that we were too distraught to come. That Abe meant too much to us for us even to share our grief with anyone."

Mom stopped crying and started laughing, "You know, Luke, Abe taught you better than you know."

"Hey, mom, let's go take in a movie."

Mom put her arm around me, "I've got a better idea."

"What?"

"Let's go visit your father's grave."

And so while an overflow crowd of people from all walks of life were packed into the Jeffers Brothers funeral home singing the praises of Abe Lapinsky and wearing pasted-on mourning faces, mom and I were on our knees next to the tombstone of my father: mom crying over his death for the one-hundredth time, and I crying over his death for the first time.

CHAPTER 14

LUKE

Harvard Law School. The fact that I was accepted and Abe Lapinsky could take no credit made the acceptance even more rewarding. The fact that I was awarded a full scholarship and therefore had no need of Abe Lapinsky's "largesse" made the acceptance even more meaningful. Abe did leave me an income-producing trust, most of the proceeds of which I sent to my mother. Of course, I did not identify the source even though she had to know where it came from.

I was very nervous the first day at Harvard when they gathered the entire group of entering students in a large classroom. We had heard that the first thing they tell the incoming class was to look at the person to the right of you and the one to the left of you, because one of three of you would have flunked out before the second year started. Perhaps that is why so many students made an effort to sit next to the dumbest-looking student they could find.

We weren't put through that drill, but we were told that at Harvard Law School the exams would reflect a concern with our ability to think through a problem. They were not concerned with canned memorization. The assistant dean told us that there were no right answers to any questions. I mused that that if the assembled students had written that down as an answer on our Law Boards, not one of us would be here today.

When the assistant dean asked for questions, he was exposed to what was on the minds of the law students of the day—my day being several years before the cultural revolt of the late sixties and early seventies. Most of the questions related to grades, the chances for making Law Review, and the best way to get a good job with a top-flight law firm. Only toward the end of the session did one of the very few women in my class raise her hand, "Do we have any clinical courses here? You know, working in the community on housing problems, discrimination, things like that?"

The Assistant Dean looked stunned. He leaned over the podium, glared at the young woman and said with sarcasm: "If you want to work in a clinic, you should have gone to medical school."

The fact that Harvard Law School rewarded the ability to reason cogently rather than memorize effectively helped me immeasurably. The classes were all taught by professors skillfully questioning students, testing their ability to think fast and deeply, rather than by the lecture method. This method of teaching was called the Socratic method. There were many in my class who felt that the only thing the Socratic method proved was that Athens waited far too long before deciding to poison Socrates. I was not one of those, because I thrived on the system.

The only one I knew in law school who was not fixated on getting a job at a Wall Street firm was my friend Billy Metzger. Billy's dream in life was to one day drive the Zamboni, the machine that smoothed out the ice at Boston Bruins hockey games. During our third year he actually got up a resume and sent it to Boston Garden applying for the job of Zamboni driver. He was devastated when he was rejected. I assumed that the people at the Boston Garden thought that his application was some kind of Harvard Law School student joke. Billy was convinced otherwise. He sat on his bed, rejection letter in hand and sighed, "I guess they only take Law Review students."

Once I made Law Review, I had just one more goal left in my law school career, to get an offer to work at the law firm of Morton and Philips. Morton and Philips was the whitest of the white shoe Wall Street law firms. It had always attracted the best and brightest from the old Wasp ascendency, but, unlike almost every other Wall Street firm in the first half of the twentieth century, it did not completely exclude the best and the brightest of the lumpen proletariat, unless, of course, you happened to be a woman or black or both. In fact, even before World War II Morton and Philips had been just about the only Wall Street firm with a Jewish partner.

Due to my excellent grades, I was able to obtain a summer job working at Morton and Philips after my second year of law school. At the close of the summer, I was informed that if I applied after I graduated, the job was all but mine.

I was ecstatic that I was going to be working for Morton and Philips. I couldn't think of any greater vindication against those in the south whom, if they knew I was Jewish, would see me as a Jew spawn of the devil, and also against those Jews in Brooklyn who viewed me as some hick southern hillbilly. This would really show them all. Me, Lukash Lipton, working at *the* Morton and Philips. A displaced Lapinsky from Augusta, Georgia who used to cross the parched Savannah River with bandages on his toes working at the same place where the famous Doig brothers worked. Not since the first Rothschild made it to the House of Lords was a more unlikely combination of person and position ever effectuated.

The world seemed perfect to me. That should have immediately thrown up a red flag, because this world is never perfect. After I finished what I thought were merely perfunctory job interviews with various associates and partners at Morton and Philips, the managing partner called me into his office. I walked in thinking he would hand me a celebratory cigar; instead, he offered me an apology without so much as a gracious preface:

"You know, Lukash, that Morton and Philips was the first Wall Street firm to take Jewish partners, and we did so even though it did cost us some business—but the problem here is that we have already made job offers to three Jewish law students...and, well, there's a difference between accepting Jews as associates and even partners and becoming a magnet for Jewish lawyers. If we start becoming known as a Jewish firm or even a partly Jewish firm, that could really hurt us with clients...that's a hit we couldn't afford to take."

I sat staring at him, absolutely stunned. These were the brightest attorneys in town with supposedly the greatest integrity, and now they were going to dump me after they virtually promised me a job because some bigoted clients did not want too many Jews in their law firm? It wasn't right. It wasn't fair. I was furious.

The anger I felt at that time apparently had worked its way out of my memory fifteen years later when, as the Deputy head of the Litigation Department at Morton and Philips, I agreed with the senior partners that any women we accepted for jobs should be steered to the Trusts and Estate section, far from the disapproving eyes of our important clients. Those were large companies run solely by white males. I knew it was wrong to exclude women from my litigation section, but I had to deal with the reality that the men who controlled our big corporate clients did not trust women to handle their litigation or to be accepted as equals by judges and even juries. I knew if we became big heroes and put women in the litigation department, our clients would just take their business elsewhere and that would hurt everyone at the firm, including the women. Somehow my rationalization for keeping women in departments with little or no client contact sounded much more convincing to me when I said it than when I heard the same argument from the managing partner that disappointing morning.

I was so angered when I was told that there was no room for me that I was on the verge of telling the managing partner what he could do with his job and his whole bigoted law firm. But in the split second that it took me to take a more conciliatory approach, I saved my entire professional life. I just lowered my head and said,

"So, what you're saying is that you can't offer me a job."

The managing partner shook his head, "No, no, of course not. I assumed one reason you want to work here is because we are not only the best lawyers in the country, but we also have the most integrity of any law firm in the country. We told you last summer that we were almost certainly going to offer you a job...and we still want to offer you a job...only not now, not with this class. Next year, you will be the first one offered a job."

I knew that when he said I would be the first one offered a job next year, the "one" was a euphemism for Jew. I was going to be the first Jew in line for a job next year. Well, I thought, that shows that Morton and Philips really doesn't care that I am Jewish...they only care that their clients might care if I'm Jewish... and, well, the firm is not a civil rights group... it's there to service clients...I wanted to work there so badly that a slight delay on a career path that I hoped would be a lifetime at M&P seemed a small price to play. I looked up at the partner and smiled for the first time.

"I accept your offer...I am very excited about working here...but what do I do for a year? I haven't applied anywhere else, and no one will take me for just one year."

"Ah, Luke, if you don't know now, you will soon know that Morton and Philips always takes care of its own. I have a friend who runs a little boutique law firm; it does mostly criminal trial work and small commercial litigation. Now, I personally find doing criminal defense work to be rather unpleasant, but if you work there for even a year, you will get a lot of trial experience. In fact, you will probably do more hands-on trial work there in one year, than you will get in ten years in our litigation department. It's all set up for you, you just have to call and ask for Mr. Dingle."

That is how I got to work for one year at the firm of Dingle, Dingle, and Dingle, Esqs. The next day when I called the firm, the secretary answered, "Dingle, Dingle, and Dingle. Whom do you want to talk to?"

I suddenly realized that I hadn't a clue as to which of the three distinguished Dingles I was supposed to contact. But I was desperate to start work somewhere so I figured "any Dingle in a storm."

"I'll speak to any Dingle that will speak to me."

The Dingle I spoke to was Freddy Dingle. He welcomed me

to the firm on Monday, and on Tuesday I was helping him to track down an alleged alibi witness in a criminal case the firm was defending.

During my year at Dingle, Dingle, and Dingle, despite my inexperience as an attorney, I spent all of my time litigating criminal cases. It was not the size of the crime but rather the size of the retainer that determined which client I would handle. I was assigned the clients who could pay the least on the theory, I suppose, that one should get what one pays for.

In retrospect, I don't think my clients got shortchanged. I lacked experience, but as a new attorney, I had a real fire in the belly. I was stoked up twenty-four hours a day, and each client was zealously and ferociously represented. In my later years, I would describe the early years of a young trial attorney as being like the young baseball player when he first comes up to the major leagues. He doesn't have a lot of experience, but he can get by because he has a blazing fast ball. As the years pass, the pitcher loses a few miles per hour off the fastball, but he can make up for the lost velocity by using his experience to hit the corners of the plate. My last ten years as a litigation partner at Morton and Philips, I had completely lost the zip off my fastball, but, ooh, how I could paint those corners with my slow junk balls.

The fire in the belly smolders on a diagonal line downwards as your trial career continues. The experience you gain is a diagonal line headed in the opposite direction. To get a trial attorney at the absolute top of his game, you should hire him at that point where the two diagonal lines intersect... which usually happens in a trial attorney's forties. While at Dingle, Dingle, and Dingle, I was all fire in the belly and no experience, so what my clients bought was unbridled enthusiasm and an almost certain prison sentence. Judges rarely deducted time from a prisoner's sentence merely because his lawyer at trial tried really hard.

My lack of experience showed from my first day on the job. Fred Dingle allowed me to take the lead in interviewing the client, a middle-aged man of modest means and, thanks to Dingle, Dingle, and Dingle, soon to be of even more modest means. The man had been arrested for allegedly embezzling from his boss. I was not certain which questions I should ask. Only the first question seemed obvious to me,

"Well, Mr. Long, let's start at the heart of the matter. Did you do what you're accused of doing?"

The question was no sooner out of my mouth than Fred Dingle's eyes seemed to pop out of his head. It was as if I had just belched at an audience with the Pope. He rushed forward before Mr. Long could answer,

"No, no, no...don't tell us...You are presumed innocent, and we presume you are innocent."

I had learned my first lesson. Never, never ask a criminal defendant whether or not he actually did what he was accused of doing. If he admits to you that he committed the crime then, ethically, you cannot allow him to take the stand and deny committing the crime. It could also inhibit an attorney from forcefully arguing his client's innocence to the jury and getting into high dudgeon during a press conference about the government's persecution of the client.

Unlike today, at the time that I dipped my toe into the waters of the criminal defense attorney, criminal law was the black sheep of the legal profession. Firms like Morton and Philips would rarely handle a criminal matter. They even farmed out white collar criminal cases to specialized attorneys trusted by the firm. For the sake of the parent company, they wanted to keep some control of the criminal case, but did not want the embarrassment of being associated with it. None of the top students in my class would have thought of practicing criminal law at that time.

The very first client I defended was a schoolteacher accused of raping a 14-year-old female student. While the jury was out deliberating, Fred Dingle strode into the hallway of the courthouse where I was pacing up and down and sweating like a pig. Fred walked up to me, "Luke, you look like you're about to die."

I just rubbed my hands nervously together, "Fred, the jury has been out for over three hours. If I can get a hung jury, I can get a good plea deal...I'm so damned nervous."

Fred leaned over and put his arm around me, "Luke, who do you think you're defending, Sir Thomas Moore? The guy raped some little girl after he had her stay after school. He ought to be shot."

"But he's my client..."

He pulled me closer and whispered in my ear, "Luke, let me give you some advice. If you are a criminal defense attorney, your clients are your enemies. Some may turn out okay, but most will turn on you in a minute...these are people who think they can get away with anything. An acquittal is because they are innocent, and a conviction is because their lawyer screwed up. I often say that doing a great job for a criminal defendant client is like throwing an orgy for accountants...no matter how good it is, it ain't gonna be appreciated."

"So what do I do, just walk away from them?"

"No, you do what I do in these cases. Prepare like your own life depended on it, hammer away at the jury about the total lack of evidence against your client, and then sit back and pray for a gross miscarriage of justice."

I shook my head as I thought of what I was in for during this year, "But Fred, what about innocent clients, ones that really are wrongfully charged?"

"That's the worst client to have. At least when you know, or pretty much know, your client is guilty, you still hate losing, but at least it doesn't rip your insides out. The greatest burden a lawyer could have is knowing that his skill is the only thing that stands between an innocent human being and prison."

Fred raised up his head, grinned and continued, "Lucky for me Luke, that's a burden I have never had to bear."

After the conversation with Fred, I felt down. I did not think

I could get pleasure from representing people I couldn't trust and from either losing a case or getting a man off who deserved to be convicted. I couldn't wait until I could stop helping individual people break the law and could join Morton and Philips and spend my life in the far more rewarding and ethical task of helping big corporations avoid the law.

As it turned out, I didn't have to worry about getting guilty men off. During my year at Dingle, Dingle, and Dingle, I helped negotiate some good pleas for clients, but at trial I lost all five of my verdicts.

I never did fully adjust to doing criminal defense work, but my year at Dingle, Dingle, and Dingle turned out to be a blessing in disguise. It gave me a leg up on my incoming class colleagues at Morton and Philips. And it proved very helpful to me when I took on a criminal case later on in my life that I never could have imagined pursuing while I was passing my career at Morton and Philips.

There were 14 new associates with me in the litigation section of Morton and Philips when I started work there. One would think that the ties that bind would unite us as brothers (there were no sisters). After all, we all had the same insecurities and were facing the same challenge. But I soon realized that the ties bound us into an almost sick sadomasochistic relationship.

Theoretically, we should all have been best of friends. Indeed, anyone looking at us from the outside would think we were best friends, as we worked together, had after work drinks together, and even pretended to be best friends. But what kept a permanent wedge between us was the knowledge that partnership at any Wall Street firm is a zero-sum game. Each class in litigation would yield forth anywhere from zero to three partners after a ten year trip down the partnership track. Every step forward for your fellow associate was a step backward for you.

The relationship among the associates was best summed up by the aphorism that the failure of your friends can make your success complete. And since one never knew who would emerge as the new Caesar of the firm, another aphorism that applied was "Just remember that the toe you stepped on today may be connected to the ass you have to kiss tomorrow."

The unstated ferocious competition among associates led to some truly offensive activity. Everyone knew the story of the eighth year associate who dropped the Mickey Finn in his principal competitor's drink so that the poor fellow slept right through his crucial courtroom appearance with a rainmaking partner the next day. The day after that he was informed he was no longer on the partnership track. The poor guy never saw the train that knocked him off that track.

Tales of what one associate did to another in order to gain a slight advantage on the brutal competition were all well known and never discussed among associates. The paranoia became so great that when one of my fellow associates read a draft of a brief I had written for a partner and told me it was brilliant, I immediately ripped it up and started all over again. At certain times I felt less propelled by a need to succeed than by a desire not to fail.

We were all aware that anyone smart enough and ambitious enough to be hired by Morton and Philips was qualified to be a partner at any law firm, including Morton and Philips. The decision as to who made partner and who didn't would be dictated more by internal firm politics and luck than by skill and ability.

The most brilliant associate among us was sidetracked for five years defending a government anti-trust case against a client. He basically spent seven days a week, 51 weeks a year reading through stacks of dry reports, far under the radar of an approving partner's eye. My associate Jim Benson was a certainty for partner, because he had the good fortune to be assigned to the new emerging force within the firm, Roger Peters. For seven years as Roger Peters solidified his hold on the upper reaches of the firm's management, he pulled Jim Benson right along with him. And then one rainy night in Westchester Roger Peters lost control of his Bentley and crashed into a tree, killing himself and fatally wounding Jim Benson's legal career. Peters' adversaries took control of the firm's management, and Jim Benson was given his walking papers as soon as his executioners could dry their eyes from their weeping at Roger Peters' funeral.

I decided early on to take the advice of my mentor at the firm, Michael Trainor. He said always keep your nose to the grindstone and your lips to the buttocks. So for nine years, I traveled everywhere with a good pen and a tube of chapstick. By my ninth year of work at Morton and Phillps, the selection year, I was pretty certain I was going to make partner.

By that ninth year our incoming class in litigation had been whittled down to five. Several people left early because they couldn't take the 18-hour-a-day, six-day weeks, or just because they for some reason found spending all of their time looking for regulatory loopholes unfulfilling. By the fifth year, those with no shot at making partner were politely told that they should be looking for a job within a year. Their "dismissal" was supposed to be confidential, but everyone knew about it. Those people immediately became the other associates' best friends and closest confidants. After all, they were no longer competing with us for the partnership, so they could be trusted.

Those who did not make partner were, of course, upset, angry, and even humiliated. But they were free. No more long days, long nights, weekends, sucking up to partners, constant pressure, doing tedious, often boring, work working for companies you often detested, and, most importantly, no more being chained so tightly to a post that you never had the chance to really let loose and enjoy life. On the other hand, those who made partner had just been made an offer they couldn't refuse. A lifetime of highly compensated work at a high prestige job. There was no way out.

I had enjoyed myself during my time as an associate at Morton and Philips because it gave me what I wanted: prestige, intellectual rigor, and a social cachet my birth had denied me. I did not need "freedom." I had that as a youth down South. I didn't go from boarding school, to prep school, to college and then to Morton and Philips. I had already stretched my legs. What I had lacked was a sense of security and belonging. And now I was pretty sure I would have that.

Partners had dropped hints to me that I was going to be a partner, but one could never be certain. Our class received a big break when, due to a slight downtown in the economy, the class ahead of us suffered an undeserved complete downturn in partnerships, with no one making partner in litigation. As is the way of the Wall Street firms, one man's carcass is another man's meal. And my class figured it would feast on the carcasses of the class above us to the tune of three partnerships for litigation, a very high amount for a class.

The way the firm informs you officially if you are to be coronated or executed is that they call you in one at a time to face the managing partner and two senior partners. They tell you either the good news or the bad news, and it is never completely clear which is the good news and which is the bad news.

For the associate involved, being summoned to see the managing partner is very much as I imagined it would be to a Mafia button man being summoned to see the godfather. You know that either you are going to become a made man or you're going to be whacked. Either way, your life will never be the same.

When it was my turn to enter the inner sanctum of the managing partner, I was pretty certain I would be made a partner, but not completely certain. I had reached my conclusion by the hints dropped and by a process of elimination.

We received confirmation from a very good source that they had made three partners in the litigation section, a record for the litigation people. There were five associates left in the litigation section. One of them was brilliant, and a powerful orator, but he was small, swarthy and looked unkempt even in a Brooks

Brothers suit. It escaped no one's attention that he was never called to sit in on meetings with clients. As my mentor Michael Trainor put it, "Iconoclastic geniuses belong in science, not law. Law is all about conforming your actions to a community code of conduct. If you can't go through the entire day with your shirt tucked into your pants, you don't deserve to be a partner at Morton and Philips."

The other predicted "loser" was a smart lawyer and an even smarter operator. He didn't scratch his nose without a purpose behind it. He was the master networker at the firm. Unfortunately, for him he had recently networked himself with the Yorkist faction of the law firm, and this past year, the Yorkists had lost out in a palace coup to the Lancasters.

So, with two down, I figured the other three of us had it made. But I wasn't so certain that when I was summoned into the managing partner's office I didn't feel that same churning in my stomach that I felt every time I was notified that my jury had returned with a verdict.

I entered the office of managing partner Tim Kauper. He was flanked on his left by senior partner Josh White and on his right by senior partner Sam Alexander. I entered the room and stood in front of Tim Kauper's mammoth desk. Not one of the partners spoke. Instead they exchanged hard knowing glances with each other, obviously their way of purposely heightening the tension so they could play with me like a mouse pawing at its prey. Finally, the silence became too overwhelming for me. I spoke up. "Good afternoon, Mr. Kauper, sir."

I realized that "Good afternoon, Mr. Kauper, sir," was not exactly a speech that the National Archives would insist that I send to them for immediate preservation. But I thought it would get things moving. I then realized that I was so focused on Tim Kauper that I hadn't addressed the other two partners sitting there. I was about to remedy the situation when the managing partner spoke up.

"Luke, you ought to know after working here for nine years that partners here don't call each other 'sir.' So please call me Tim."

I did not respond. I was too stunned. I also wanted to make sure my mind was correctly processing what he said before I responded. Tim took my confused look for disappointment.

"I know Luke, you are probably thinking what my wife was thinking the first time I dropped my pants…"

Again I was stunned. For nine years, Tim Kauper had talked with me in the most formal of terms. Now, he's talking to me like a fraternity brother. I smiled and answered him, "What is that?"

Tim slapped the desk in glee in anticipation of his response, "She said, 'Is that all there is?'"

I waited for the laughter of the three senior partners to die down before I answered, "Well, no sir…I mean Tim… I was not surprised.…"

Josh White leaned over from his chair, "Well, Luke, it is a kind of an abrupt way to make someone a partner. Do you have any ideas for a more elaborate ceremony? I suppose Tim could knight you with his cane."

I pretended to join in the laughter, "Well, Mr., I mean, Josh, you know when I was a kid I once became blood brothers with my best friend by pricking our fingers and mixing our blood together."

Much to my surprise, rather than laughing, Tim waived off my jocular suggestion with his hand and leaned in toward me. He spoke very solemnly. "No, no Luke. None of that nonsense. What has just happened to you is very serious and very real. I know all of the tension, and bullshit you had to put up with for nine years—we all had to go through it. You had no opportunity to make real friends here, and we hadn't yet invited you into the family. But now you are in the Morton and Philips family, and you will see that our bond is deeper than the bond of blood brothers."

Sam Alexander spoke up for the first time, "Luke, did you ever read the St. Crispin's Day Speech in Shakespeare's *Henry V*?"

Yes, Mr. Alexander…"

He corrected me, "Sam."

"Yes, Sam, I had to memorize it in high school."

"Well, Luke, that's what we are here, a band of brothers. We are like those soldiers on the eve of Agincourt. When we do battle for our clients here, we form a bond like none other...not like with your wife, not like with your children, not like with anyone else. I'm not saying our bond is more important than a family bond, only that it is a unique bond like none other in the professional world." At that point, the room lapsed into an uneasy silence. Josh turned to me, "Well, Luke, you're from the South as I recall. Your blood brother must be some genuine trailer trash..."

I joined in the fun in an attempt to lighten up the atmosphere, "No, Josh, my blood brother was poorer than that. The trailer park is where my blood brother's rich relatives lived..."

"What is your blood brother's name?"

"T.C., T.C. Simmons."

Sam laughed, "They probably named him T.C. so there would be some chance he might some day learn how to spell his name. No sense giving him those killer three letter names like Bob."

A smile spread across Tim's face. "Hey, Luke, do you know what T.C.'s first girlfriend said when he first screwed her?"

"Nope, got me, Tim."

Tim leaned towards me, cupped his hands and either side of his mouth and said, "B-A-A-AH."

Everybody in the room laughed, and I joined in with them, although, for the first time, I felt a pang of guilt for making fun of T.C. The affection I felt for him during those days in the schoolyard and at Clarks Hill was still with me."

"Well, Luke, any questions?"

"Just one, how come if we are all brothers, these other three brothers have a chair, and I've been standing all of this time?"

We all shared a laugh and on that note, on a sunny Monday, April 7, I achieved my ultimate professional goal. I was made a partner at one of the best law firms in the country.

On my way home, I found my thoughts wandering from the joy of the news of my partnership, to the self-disappointment I felt because of my failure to raise even a modest defense of T.C. when he was being portrayed as a subject of ridicule by the partners. T.C. may have been big and clumsy—his upbringing may have invited the "trailer trash" epithet, but he was far from a fool.

In that moment of reflection I remembered the arrow incident from our youth. The one that happened after T.C. had proven himself capable of demolishing Demerest and intimidating his Kinsmen. It had proved to me that T.C. was capable not only of significant human thought, but also of human guile. Everyone, myself included for awhile, had taken T.C. for the fool, and so, he easily fooled us.

T.C. had gone through that elaborate ruse with his bow and arrow to get back at his tormentors. T.C. knew that they would never know how he proved himself smarter than they were—I guess it was enough for him that he knew. No, T.C. was no fool—and I should not have been a silent witness when my new law partners mocked him.

CHAPTER 15

T. C.

Prison visits are booked in advance by the prospective visitors to take place on either a Saturday or Sunday. The inmate is told that he will be receiving a "visit" and waits in his cell to be summoned, dressed in khakis previously worn and discarded by the military. After the visitor has been cursorily patted down and temporarily deprived of his parcels and handbags, he or she is ushered into a waiting room. The inmate's name is called over the prison loudspeaker and told he has a "visit."

For the prisoner, the "visit" is a welcome respite from the chaos that is prison life. A very temporary retreat from the sound of the keys that clang from the belts of the guards, the continual banging open of the cell doors and the smells of socks, sweat, and disinfectant.

When the inmate arrives at the area reserved for visits, he is escorted into an anteroom for a "strip search"—an exercise that is administered often and routinely to prisoners. Strip searches are designed more to humiliate the prisoner than to insure the security of the prison facility.

The designated guard has the prisoner strip and perform a virtual pirouette of bending and cheek-spreading, followed by the assumption of a position which reminded T.C. of the way in which a horse is positioned when being shoed. This allows for the inspection of the soles of the prisoner's feet. The finale is the digital inspection of the inmate's mouth by the guard's rubber gloved hand. After the completion of the exercise, the inmate gets dressed and is permitted to go into the "visit room."

Carl was anxious to see T.C., more to discern his commitment to silence than to give him comfort. The fact that his was the only white face in the visitor's room was not lost on him. When he came into the room set aside for the visits, it was easy

113

for him to spot T.C., who was also surrounded by a sea of black inmates and their families.

Carl walked through the room filled with embracing couples and children waving crudely crayoned drawings—gifts for their fathers. T.C. had found a table in the corner and motioned Carl to a chair placed opposite his. Carl, who a little over four years ago had pressed a 12-gauge shotgun against T.C.'s cheek, now hugged him as a father would a son. When Carl began disengaging from the embrace, he noticed how T.C. seemed to hold on to it—a gesture which indicated a great fondness and desperate desire to cling on to something. Carl was pleased at this display of affection and trust.

"Don't worry, boy, you're goin' to be all right." Carl said as he sat at the small table, "They figured when you tried to burn down that Jew Temple three years ago, it was part of a kid thing. You'll be outta here in a month's time."

"Hell, I ain't worried," T.C. answered, "Was my own fault— first with my hooking up with that Jew Lipton, and then with high-tailing it after the fire—I shoulda known better on both accounts."

"Well," replied Carl, "You proved yourself as a goddamned first rate Klansman. I'm only sorry that we couldn't spare you from all this. God knows we tried. Had the thing beat too, until they started changin' judges and ordering new trials. If it had been a nigger church I coulda kept you out."

"I was only afraid when they come after me the last time that they was comin' after me because of the nigger."

Carl put his finger to his mouth: "Shhh... Let's not be talkin' about that... That was a long time ago and that was Klan work.... We don't do jail time for Klan work, but we don't talk about it either."

"No, I know my brothers will take care of me..."

"You got that right," Carl smiled with the assurance, "and when you get out Will has a job waitin' for you at City Hall."

T.C. looked puzzled.

"Will Morgan? What's he got to do with City Hall?"

"He's gonna be Augusta's next mayor, that's all." Carl said with a smile.

"You ain't shittin' me are you Carl?"

"Nope, it's all set. Now you just keep your mouth shut and you're gonna end up with your ass in a tub of butter. Oh yes, Will Morgan is going to be our next mayor—it's all set."

T.C.'s eyes brightened. "That's good... that's real good..."

Carl looked at the vending machines lining the walls of the visiting room and reached into his pocket to retrieve a fistful of quarters. "What can I buy you, son?

"I'd love a bear claw," T.C. answered, referring to a large, very sweet raisin-filled cinnamon-covered cake.

Carl walked over to the cake dispensing vending machine and fed it four quarters. The machine began to grind, and its visible midsection exhibited a corkscrew like device that cradled a "bear claw," consigning it to a large open tray for customer retrieval.

While he was removing the bear claw from the tray, a large group of black children gathered around Carl to witness the machine's operation. He looked at a small group of little girls, their hair done up in small braids tied with white pieces of cotton, and gave each of them a quarter.

As he came back to the table he looked at T.C., nodded toward the little girls and said: "Pickaninnies gotta eat too."

T.C. thought about that as he endured another strip search after he left the visit room and returned to his cell. He guessed it was possible to hate some people as a group, but not hate every one of them individually. Maybe that explains why he felt such hatred for the Jews, and yet, despite all the misery Lipton had caused him, and nearly four years since he had seen him, he could still not move himself to hating his one-time best friend. He regretted, once again, not answering his letters.

Lipton had written him two letters. When he received the

first he threw it away without reading it. He read the second out of curiosity—to see where Lipton had ended up. Lipton wrote of his new home in Brooklyn. T.C. guessed that Brooklyn was a place where most Jews ended up.

*   *   *

It was on a Sunday morning. T.C. was just returning from religious services that were held at the prison chapel. Being a Christian was still an important part in his life, and this morning's services were very special. A group called "The Philadelphians" had come by bus all the way from Knoxville, Tennessee. They brought their own musical instruments and sang the most beautiful Christian music he had ever heard. Hearing their music made him feel close to Jesus. The music and words to: "Give God the Glory/Are You Washed in The Blood/Mighty is Our God" uplifted him in a way he could not describe.

It happened before he knew it was happening. Walking toward his cell, still humming "Give God the Glory," someone grabbed him from behind and immobilized his arms by holding his wrists behind his back while a second person, his ebony face glistening with hatred, thrust a homemade shiv against T.C's throat.

"You fuckin' redneck piece of shit, I'm never goin' to get out of prison, but I'll enjoy my stay knowing that I took one Klan cracker down."

The sudden attack froze T.C., who found himself staring at the pointed twisted end of a spoon. He stared wide-eyed and helpless, bracing himself for the blow as the man facing him lifted up his arm to plunge the shiv into his throat. Just as the lethal blow was about to strike, a large intercepting hand came from nowhere and knocked the shiv rattling to the ground.

"What the hell are you doin'?" the surprised assailant said to the unexpected intervener.

T.C.'s savior was a huge black prisoner called "Buck" by the other white inmates and guards. The term "Buck" probably derived from the word "buckwheat" which was a low grade animal food, and was considered pejorative and one notch above "nigger." It was usually used to describe blacks of considerable size. In this case "Buck" was aptly named. He was considered a gentle giant who spent most of his time sitting in his cell playing a harmonica. He played with such a sweet sadness it could make you cry, but when he was on his feet the size of him was frightening. T.C. had seen him in the shower once, and the man's mammoth arms and legs convinced T.C. that Buck was not human...he was some kind of beast... But it was this beast who had saved him.

The man who had the shiv reached to the ground to retrieve it, but Buck kicked it off to the side before the man could reach it.

"Hey, man, you know who you savin?' Guard sergeant tol' me he was Klan. That the sonofabitch been lynchin' niggers when he on the street an' been lyin' on us since he been inside."

Buck spoke: "If he such a piece a shit, why you put yourself in harm's way by cuttin' him? Don' you know they'll fry your ass you cut a white man?"

"Not this white man," came the response, "The sergeant say he see that nothin' gonna happen to us we ice this cracker."

T.C. took advantage of the opening and tried to run past the three black prisoners in front of him. But the man who had just saved him stuck out an arm, wrapping up T.C. like a rag doll and lifting him off the floor.

At this point, the other prisoner had retrieved his shiv and was rushing at T.C. with the weapon extended in his thrusting arm. Buck dropped T.C. to the ground and flicked the aggressor away with the back of his hand, sending him skidding to the other end of the room.

"Now you two, get the hell out of here."

He turned back to T.C., "And we'll forget this ever happened. Just watch your back from now on. An' watch out for that guard who appears to have a hard-on for you."

T.C. quickly nodded his head in the affirmative as he watched the other two black prisoners disappear from his sight. Buck turned back to T.C.

"You Klan don't understand that people that's got nothin' got nothin' to lose. One day they's gonna explode, and your kind'll be the first to go."

T.C. was still nervous...and confused....

"If you believed those things—that I was Klan and did those things—why'd you save me?"

The big man gathered himself up so that he was virtually leaning over the top of T.C.

"I'll tell you why. First off, when a white guard tries to have a nigger off another white, I gotta ask questions about somethin' else goin' on. An' more important, 'cause our enemy ain't in here. He's out there... only he wants us to keep killin' each other so's we don't wake up one day and kill him...So you see, we're really brothers, you and I, only your kind is too stupid to know it."

Rather than gratitude, T.C. felt a surge of resentment. He knew he was no brother to a nigger. He glared at this huge black man, angry that he, a white man, was powerless to control him...and angry that a black man had to save his life. He was more determined than ever to make certain that the world outside the prison didn't become like the world inside the prison.

"You don' believe what I'm sayin', do you?"

T.C. backed up as the huge black form loomed over him. "I ain't sayin' either way."

The man looked at T.C. and smiled. "Well whether yo' know it or yo' wan' to believe it or not, we be brothers." And saying that he put a big wet kiss on T.C.'s face and, with a deep guttural laugh, walked away saying over his shoulder: "Watch yo' back."

*　　*　　*

The Georgia prison system prides itself on the fact that every inmate is given a job. Carl had promised T.C. that he would see to it that during his sentence he would be given the job that all of the prisoners wanted: "Garden Tender." That was about as close to farming as you could get, only a whole lot easier.

Every now and again a guard—or "hack" as they were called—would walk up to an inmate, clipboard in hand, and tell him what his job assignment was. Jobs ranged from the best, which was working in the vegetable garden as a Garden Tender, to the bad, which was ladling grease off the top of the grease pit, to the worst—which was working in the cotton shop. Now you would think that working the stinking grease pit in 110 degree heat would be the nastiest—but it wasn't. The cotton shop had them all beat.

The cotton shop was where raw cotton was spun, twined, and woven into cloth. The air was so filled with lint that you went from coughing to spitting blood within a week. You knew that if you were kept there too long you could be buying a death sentence, which is why most of the inmates sent to the cotton shop were the prisoners whom the guards wished dead. They were usually blacks who were convicted of messing with white women, or men of whatever color who were convicted of messing with children. T.C. had spent three years in the relative ease of Garden Tending.

When T.C., headed for the Garden area as usual, was stopped by a clipboard-toting hack and told that he was to report to the cotton shop, his reaction went from surprise to rage. His response was unequivocal: "Fuck you!"

"You best wise up, Simmons," the guard said, "The Sergeant says if you give me a hard time you'll go to the cotton shop by way of the hole."

"Fuck you," T.C. repeated, whereupon the guard blew his whistle and two other guards appeared—ready to cuff and drag T.C. off to solitary confinement.

But T.C. needed no escort nor did he offer resistance. He indicated that he would go voluntarily to solitary or anywhere else, but that he would not go to the cotton shop. The guards led him, handcuffed, to one of the solitary confinement cells located in the lowest level of the prison.

T.C. had lived his life in poverty. He had felt the discomfort and squalor which often comes with deprivation, but he had never suffered from the abject misery which comes with being penned like an animal. In solitary confinement—which he thought was properly called the "hole"—he learned what it was like to be physically uncomfortable and spiritually hobbled.

Solitary—the hole, seclusion, SHU (secure housing unit), whatever you wanted to call it—was a row of ten-by-twelve foot cells, each with its own steel sink and toilet. Against one wall there was metal rack covered by a thin, oil-covered pad. That was the bed. The door was a slab of solid steel with a small vertical slot that allowed the hack to peer in. A small knee-high horizontal slot was used to deliver and return food trays. That same slot was used for the prisoner to stick his handcuffed hands through so that his cuffs could be removed from outside the cell once he was safely ensconced inside the cell.

The walls were of concrete block. There were no windows, and the sole source of light was a large fluorescent tube that burned day and night.

Once he was inside his solitary cell, T.C. was told to strip and pass his clothes through the food slot to the waiting guard. He was told that this was done so he wouldn't use his clothing twisted into a rope to harm himself or others. He was convinced that there as another reason—he was stripped to further dehumanize him—as if that was possible.

He had only been in the hole for two days, but he found the confinement, the heat, and the deprivation of natural light to be beyond oppressive. If he wasn't pacing back and forth he found himself sitting on the floor pressing his back against the comparative coolness of the cell wall. Only two days, but it felt like an eternity.

"Hey T.C." A disembodied voice came from the other side of his cell door. "Carl says to sit tight—he's goin' to square this thing for you."

T.C., sitting naked in a corner of the cell, smiled. He knew it. He didn't doubt for a minute that Carl and his brothers would come through for him. "Tell him to hurry!"

The next morning T.C. was awakened by the sound of clothes being shoved through the door slot. "Suit up Simmons, the sergeant needs to see you."

So finally he was going to see this sergeant who seemed determined to either have him stabbed, choked on cotton lint, or suffocated in this hole. He guessed that Carl had arranged for the sergeant to get off T.C.' s back—but why, as Buck had said, did the sergeant have such a hard-on for him in the first place?

With a guard on each side of him, T.C. walked handcuffed through the barred entrance of the seclusion unit and across the recreation yard. Although the sight of a handcuffed inmate being escorted across the yard was not novel, the other prisoners seemed to always stop what they were doing to stare as one of their fellow prisoners was being led like a chained dog from one unit to another. T.C. hated being stared at by these niggers and lowlives while he was being led along like a chained animal. The walk across the yard was no longer than 50 yards, though it seemed like a mile.

They entered the unit housing the sergeant's office, and T.C.'s handcuffs were removed. The sergeant was standing behind his desk. T.C. recognized him instantly. It was his old nemesis from school days, Jack Demerest. Too young to be a sergeant, T.C. thought—and too stupid, too.

Demerest fingered through some papers without taking his eyes off the desk. "Well lookee here," he said, "We got a big fellow who likes to fight but refuses work assignment. You was up for parole too—too bad, looks like your ass is going to be mine for quite a spell." He now looked T.C. in the eye and smiled broadly, "and I'm goin' to see to it that you're going to be down to that cotton shop 'till your blowin' lint outta' your ass. You read me, big fella?'"

T.C. stared right back, "You the same little prick you always was."

Demerest stopped smiling. "And for someone who didn't speak 'till he was grow'd up you sure gotta' lotta shit to say." With that he signaled for the guards to remove T.C. with the order: "Take this turd back to the hole for the night and tomorrow take him to the cotton shop. Chain him to the fuckin' loom if you have to."

T.C. tried to control his rage. He kept his eyes closed as he was being escorted back to seclusion. That night he pounded on the walls of his cage until his hands bled. Where was Carl? Where was God?

The next morning came, but no one came for him. It wasn't until late in the afternoon that a guard opened his cell door and smiling said: "C'mon, T.C., you're going back to the general population."

T.C. put out his hands expecting to be cuffed.

"Naw," said the guard, "You're outta seclusion—in fact you gonna be outta here and back on the street by week's end."

"What the hell happened?" said T.C.

"Seems the Warden took your file and cancelled the standing order that kept you in the hole so long, along with the sergeant's turn down and reactivated your parole date."

"And the sergeant didn't complain?"

"Hard to complain when you got no mouth to complain with."

"What are you saying?" T.C. asked the question hoping he knew the answer.

"Oh, I guess you don't get much news down here. Last night on his way home Demerest got his head blown off with a 12 gauge shotgun."

CHAPTER 16

LUKE

One year ran into another. I was lost in work—corporate work, done with diligence and integrity. But not everything we did at the law firm dealt with the law. We all accepted as part of the job what we called "CS," or client stroking. There were some clients whose company I genuinely enjoyed, but there were others with whom we spent no time at all unless contact with them brought significant business to the firm. Even time spent with unpleasant clients was easily tolerated, because we could discern a straight line between the boring golf game and our huge bonuses at the end of the year. But it was hanging out with and supporting crooked or just obnoxious politicians that I found most unpleasant. Because the line from our support of a politician to our year end bonuses was more oblique, the forced fraternization was even more odious. The politicians rarely helped our firm directly, but if they helped our clients or if our clients perceived that our relationship with a politician helped them, then it helped us.

Dealing with politicians was a task for which law school had not prepared me. In retrospect I wished that instead of teaching such courses as Advanced Business Law at Harvard, they had offered more important courses such as: "Sucking Up To Politicians 101." I eventually became adept at cultivating these denizens of the deep—my biggest problem being that it took me almost ten years to master the art of laughing heartily at lousy jokes. Of course there were well-motivated, intelligent and gracious people in politics and government—I don't mean to paint with too broad a brush. These other, more civilized, politicians were a delight to spend time with, but somehow the ones we were assigned to suck up to were not in that category.

The most detestable of all the politicians I met was also the closest to our law firm. My partner Lou Howard had served as his campaign treasurer for his last two elections. I speak of Senator Allan Kirk, who had lived the professional politician's dream. He rose from being a Deputy City Clerk to the United States Senate pausing along the way only for the purpose of raising enormous sums to fill his and the party political coffers and to destroy those whom he perceived as a threat to his vaulting ambition.

Allan Kirk rose in the County ranks strictly on the merits of his skills as a bookkeeper. He kept meticulous records of every unlawful payoff from and to party members. He captured the Republican nomination for Senator mainly because of his ability to shake down almost anyone by promising them almost anything. His early promises of zoning changes and exclusion from jury duty matured into promises of sought after government contracts and sweetheart land grants as well as the empowerment which governmental and administrative licensing can bestow when properly, or improperly, influenced.

It was this aggressive talent as a fundraiser on behalf of a Presidential candidate which brought him to the attention of the national chairman of the Republican Party. The local and county Republican leadership knew Kirk for the disreputable person he was, but when the national chairman pushes for a candidate's nomination, the local organization does not object. Besides, Kirk would be running against a popular Democratic incumbent whom few thought anyone, no less Kirk, could unseat.

One of Kirk's great strengths was that people underestimated him. They mistook sleaze for ineptitude. Even before he became a United States Senator, he had demonstrated his shameless cruelty by eliminating anyone within his county organization whom he thought of as a threat to his advancement or even his starring role. But the callousness he evinced before his Senate nomination was eclipsed by the tactics he employed during his first campaign and after he assumed the role of Senator.

His opponent, an elderly, avuncular, slightly overweight political moderate known for his honesty, integrity, and hard work was characterized as "a liberal who would rather feed than lead." Kirk had raised millions for the campaign and spent most of it on television ads which had as a tag line: "Allan Kirk: A Man Full of Life" this was followed on the screen by a black and white picture of his opponent slouched in a chair looking somnolent, obese and very old.

Television campaigning had not yet taken on the negativism that is now an accepted part of political life. Kirk's campaign was one of the first to use this form of media as a destructive weapon. Because of his enormous time buys and the entry into the race of fringe parties which sapped votes away from his opponent, he won. He garnered only 42% of the vote in the three-way race, and no one was ever sure what he stood for or against—but he defied all odds and won that first election.

Senator Kirk had a particular loathing for Italian politicians, blaming them for what he called the "Italian Cabal." It was this cabal that he blamed for holding back his early political career. He once told his chief of staff that the only things the Italians brought to this county were the Mafia and pizza, and they really had nothing to do with pizza. Of course, none of that stopped him from telling the Loyal Order of the Sons of Italy when they chose him as their "Man of the Year" that his one regret in life was that he wasn't born Italian. The line brought thunderous applause, his big smile masking the fact that he had nothing but contempt for every individual in that audience.

He was now poised to run for his fourth term and his incredible malignity and cruelty toward others—even those who considered him a friend—had become legend. He was said to have been the first person in history to have broken the Ten Commandments in perfect order from One to Ten. Once, at a party, his chief of staff Corker Reed was listening to Senator Kirk gleefully recount to all of those in attendance how he had ruined yet another person whom he felt was in his way or had crossed him. Midway through the Senator's diatribe, Corker leaned over to me and whispered: "The only thing more dangerous than being Allan's enemy is being his friend."

Nobody knew that better than Corker. For three Senate terms he had been the Senator's chief of staff, watching the Senator degrade and figuratively spit on anyone who couldn't spit back. And, not counting restaurant waiters, who for some reason were the Senator's most hapless targets, nobody got spit on more than Corker Reed. He suffered daily humiliations at the whim of the Senator, even while Corker was spending his every waking hour covering up for the Senator's misdeeds, some big and some small.

Corker never blew the whistle on the Senator for the same reason many other people kept their peace. Everyone close to the Senator had a stake in his continued success. Many also had their fingerprints on the same cookie jar in which the Senator almost always had his greedy hand. There was nothing to gain, and a pretty damn good life to lose, by blowing the whistle on Senator Kirk.

Those who had knowledge of his misdeeds but not a great stake in Senator Kirk's career, remained passive because they feared that if they shot and missed, they would never live to see another day. The political highway was littered with real and imagined enemies of Allan Kirk. His capacity for vindictiveness was as large as his ego.

The Senator was a survivor, making it alive through public maelstroms that would have killed almost any other human being. One does not take on a survivor lightly. There was a reason Senator Kirk was called Rasputin behind his back. Rasputin, the Russian mystic and favorite of the Czarina, who had been shot at close range, beaten, and poisoned, still survived. It seemed that nothing could bring the man down. Rasputin was eventually killed because after the shooting and poisoning failed, the aristocrats who wanted his death were able to drag him to the river in broad daylight and drown him. Senator Kirk's enemies knew there was no aristocratic immunity in the United States. They were afraid that if Senator Kirk survived the shots to the head and the rat poison, they would never get the opportunity to drag him down to the river.

The highlight of the Senator's career came when he won his second election by viciously attacking his opponent's ethics. Kirk attacking his opponent's ethics would be like Hitler running a campaign during which he attacked his adversary for being an anti-Semite. But Kirk pulled it off, and even his enemies marveled at his effrontery.

Most people concerned with good government were hoping that the Senator would be taken down, sooner rather than later. They also knew that Corker Reed, who knew all there was to know about the Senator's nefarious ways, would have to be the one to do it.

Unfortunately, just two weeks before Kirk was expected to run for a fourth term, Corker Reed suddenly resigned as chief of staff. He left to take a job in the private sector as a vice president of an export-import company whose president was a very close friend of Kirk's. The rumors that there had been a break between Reed and Kirk were quieted when Kirk gave Reed an impressive going-away party and announced that he had arranged to get Corker the private sector job because "it was about time that Corker earned some decent money after all of his years of public service." Corker Reed could not have been more effusive in his praise for the Senator in his letter of resignation. The "Some day we'll get the sonofabitch" investigative reporters all over town broke their pencils in anger.

Lou Howard was later to tell me what really had happened. It seems that the staff threw a birthday party for Senator Kirk in the back hall of Bleemer's Restaurant in Manhattan. By the time most of the guests had arrived, the Senator was already four sheets to the wind. When the Senator had too much to drink, which was often, he lost touch with reality —so much so that he actually thought the attractive women he dated went out with him because of his charm. Whenever the Senator showed up at any of our parties, he always had a beautiful woman on his arm— this for a man who had to pay his best friend's sister to go with him to his senior prom in high school.

Senator Kirk was as arrogant and thoughtless with his dates as he was with everyone else in his life. He had the reputation among the women he dated for always arriving late and coming early.

By the time Corker arrived, Senator Kirk had already managed to insult most of the females at the party. Corker came with his wife Betsy, and his 16-year-old daughter Maxine who was thrilled at the prospect of meeting Senator Kirk in person. Corker had always kept his family as far away from his work and Senator Kirk as possible.

Corker, clutching the hand of his daughter Maxine, made his way over to the Senator.

"Senator, I want you to meet my daughter Maxine. She's your biggest fan. She has no picture of me in her room, but she does have that picture you autographed for her right on her night table."

Senator Kirk blinked once or twice and then steadied himself. His eyes went like lasers from Maxine's rather plain face to her cleavage.

"Hey, Corker, you didn't tell me your daughter had such big tits... Hold old are you, honey?"

Maxine was startled. She could barely get the one word out: "Sixteen."

Kirk slapped his hand against his forehead. "Sixteen! Corker, you trying to get me arrested?"

The Senator laughed and then put his hand on Corker's shoulder, "Hey, Corker, I'm sure any daughter of yours at 16 is a virgin, but when she decides to do it, you make sure she remembers that Old Uncle Allan has first dibs."

Senator Kirk burst out in laughter. No one joined him until he picked up his head and looked to the right, then the people to his right joined his laughter. As the Senator rotated his head, laughter followed his gaze.

Finally the Senator turned back to face Maxine only to find that her mother, Betsy Corker, had stepped in between them, saying nothing, but glaring at Kirk. Corker caught Betsy's eye and shook his head surreptitiously from side to side, signaling her not to do or say anything rash.

The Senator seemed a bit taken aback by seeing Maxine's mother in front of him. At first the room fell into a tense silence as the Senator glared at her. But then his eyes went down to her breasts and a smile broke out on his face, "Oh, now I see where your daughter got her big tits, Corker...I always liked older women anyway."

With that remark, the Senator leaned over and gently pinched each of Betsy's breasts saying,

"Boop! Boop!"

Before anyone could react, Tim Johnson, one of the Senator's bodyguards, swooped in and gently pushed the Senator away, moving him to another table. It did not matter. Corker wouldn't have done anything anyway. He knew that anyone who rebuked the Senator in public did so at his peril. He had learned how to handle these occasions: keep your mouth shut and make believe nothing happened. But this time was different. This was his wife and daughter. This time he quit. But he didn't just quit—he had learned well from the master.

Corker Reed had made certain to obtain copies of the documents he had been sneaking out of the office for more than ten years—hard proof of the Senator's misdeeds. He kept one stack of these papers in his desk at home and the other in a rented safety deposit box along with a copy of his detailed explanation of the bag jobs he had run for the Senator, as well as a note telling whomever opened that box to destroy its contents if he had died a natural or unsuspicious death.

For the entire week after he quit, Corker shuttled between his office and the safe deposit box. He was torn between his rage over what the Senator had done to his wife and daughter and the more "reasonable" emotion which calmly took stock of the money he could earn at the job arranged for him by Kirk. Into this decision-making equation he also calculated the blowback he would face if he exposed Kirk.

Lou Howard had told me at that time that there were rumblings that Corker Reed might be blowing the whistle on the Senator. I immediately called a very select meeting of the firm's five management partners. We'd had such a meeting five years earlier, when there were strong rumors that the Senator was about to be indicted. At that time we decided to do nothing. Everyone knew that if Senator Kirk was actually brought down, the truth-tellers would come pouring out of the woodwork. But until that time, until everyone was certain that Rasputin was actually dead, everyone would hold his fire.

We were as hypocritical as everyone else. Whatever his personal failings, Senator Kirk had been good to us and good to our clients. He had delivered, and all we had to do in return was to stoke his war chest with legal bribes known as campaign donations. We also could rationalize that no matter how despicable a human being Kirk was and how dishonest he had been, at least he was a Senator who "brought home the bacon." In the long run, that was one of the things for which we constituents were paying him. As Lou told me, after I complained about having to put the arm on some clients to contribute to the Senator's re-election campaign, "You can't eat integrity." Still, I was disturbed about our support for so loathsome a human being. I was even more disturbed after my meeting with my old college friend, Jon Weinberg.

Jon Weinberg had become a well-known, top-flight investigative reporter. He had exposed and brought down countless miscreants, but he could never quite catch up to Senator Kirk. Jon was always taunting me, urging me to come forward and help nail the Senator. He knew how close our firm was to him—at least professionally.

One day Jon invited me to meet with him at an out of the way restaurant. He told me in the strictest confidence that he had a mole close to Kirk. This person had given him some explosive information, but Jon's editor said he had to have everything confirmed by at least two independent sources. He wanted me to be one of those sources or, better yet, to have the information confirmed by Lou Howard without letting Lou know that I would be passing the information on to Jon. Jon pushed four pieces of paper towards me. They summarized the allegations made by the alleged mole. Some I had heard in general, some Lou had confirmed to me as true, and some were totally unknown to me.

As I read his notes, I was tempted to help Jon. I wasn't worried about exposure. I knew Jon would spend the rest of his life in prison rather than give up a source. But I was worried about being part of the collateral damage if Kirk was taken down. Our firm would not only lose a valuable contact, but we would look bad for having been so close to him. Indeed, when the indictment scare arose five years before, we discussed how to carefully calibrate our reaction to it. We decided that as long as it looked as though he might beat the rap, we should stay with him, but the minute he went down we had to stay ahead of the curve. It is no surprise that every time an important person is in difficulty, the summer soldiers immediately head for the high grass. That attitude is not good for friendships, but it's perfect for business.

I knew my law firm could head for the high grass fast. After all, we had never participated in any activity concerning the Senator that even came close to the legal or ethical divide. It was precisely because our firm had the deserved reputation for having honest attorneys of paramount integrity that we could safely express our shock, our absolute shock, about any verified revelations about the Senator. But I saw no need to help bring down the Senator so I passed the papers back to Jon.

"Jon, I don't really know first hand about anything. Some of these things are vaguely familiar. Hell, I probably heard some of these rumors from you. I really can't help you."

Of course, Jon knew that if Corker Reed would open up to him, he could virtually put a Pulitzer on the mantel. Jon said that he had hoped that Corker Reed would talk when he left the Senator's employment, but that it appeared the separation was amicable. I just nodded and said, "That's my information too."

As it turned out, it wasn't necessary for anyone to prod Corker. Corker was being heated up by his own fuse. The Monday after the Senator had abused Corker's wife and humiliated his daughter, he had stormed into the Senator's private office, not to resign, but to demand an apology. The Senator snapped at him, "Hey, I don't even remember much of that night, but everyone around here says I was funny as hell with your wife and daughter. Not one person told me there was anything wrong in what I did— why the hell do you bring your daughter to a party where you know we always drink and crap around?"

Corker interrupted him, almost yelling, "You pinched my wife's goddamned tits right in front of everyone, and I was such a chickenshit wimp I just stood there."

"Take it easy, Corker, it was probably the best foreplay she's ever had. It's too bad you left so early, I also could've given her the first good lay she's had in years."

Corker stammered. He never could stand up to the Senator. Even with this humiliation, he seemed tongue-tied. His only demand was for a personal apology to his wife and daughter. The Senator refused and finally ordered Corker out of his office. That is when Corker quit and gave the Senator an earful of spite that had been lingering in his innards 12 years.

Rather than talk him out of quitting, the Senator immediately agreed that Corker needed a respite from his job. The stress of working for a Senator had obviously overtaken him. Kirk never wanted anyone of questionable loyalty being close to the every day workings of his office. When the Senator caught so much as a whiff of waffling in an employee, he acted quickly to isolate the contagion lest it infect the entire office and possibly even effect the health of the Senator himself. But, of course, he always made sure that a friendly set of eyes was looking over the isolated contagion. Countless numbers of people who had been trampled by the Senator now worked for companies whose owners were steadfastly loyal to him. Corker would be no exception. Corker's anger was overcome by the $400,000 a year job—courtesy of Senator Kirk.

It was only when Corker's daughter broke down and, sobbing, wanted to know how he could just stand there silently while the Senator humiliated them that Corker decided to take at least a half step. Corker had a bruising verbal spat with his daughter during which he called her an ingrate for not appreciating that everything they had was due to the Senator. In tears, Maxine told him she would rather have nothing than to trade their dignity for money and position.

The more Corker thought about his daughter, the angrier he became. It was not so much what she said that so unnerved him. It was that look on her face, the shame she felt for her father's cowardice. He knew that he had to do something. It was then that he met privately with Lou Howard and told him that if the Senator ran for another term, he would take him down. He had the documents to do it, and he had an extra copy of everything safely hidden away.

The threat was duly relayed to the Senator. He just laughed. It wasn't that he didn't believe that Corker had the ammunition to blow him away. He just didn't believe that he had the guts to do it. The Senator had been threatened like this before. Now, he just leaned back in his chair and said,

"Don't worry about old Corker. When he calms down a bit,

he'll see that swapping a great job for a prison sentence and poverty is not a very good trade. If I had thought he was the kind of guy with balls like that, I wouldn't have had him as my chief of staff in the first place."

The very next day the Senator announced that he was running for a fourth term. Corker swore to himself that he would act within the week. Whether he would or would not have acted will never be known, because within the week, Senator Allan Kirk was dead.

The day after Senator Kirk announced he was running for a fourth term, he went over to New Jersey to film a campaign commercial. The ad agency had festooned a trained circus elephant with a large GOP FOR KIRK cloth saddle. The Senator was to be hoisted onto the elephant's back while a flood of off-camera security people monitored the elephant's movements.

While the Senator was waiting for the filming to begin, he walked behind the elephant and, puckering up his lips, he leaned in towards the elephant's butt. Laughingly, he called out to one of the cameraman, "Hey, take this one. The caption will say: 'Senator Kirk has to kiss the GOP's ass so why don't you? Give money now.'"

A security man tried to rush in to pull the Senator away from the elephant, but the laughter from the sycophants standing around the beast inspired its tail to stand straight up. Apparently, having Senator Kirk so close to his rear end was an inspiration of a different sort.

Before the security man could reach the Senator, one huge pellet after another started flying from the elephant's rear end. The Senator was so startled that he fell backwards and slipped on one of the larger pieces of excrement. The laughter from the sidelines, now spiked with some shrieks of fear, apparently spooked the elephant because it suddenly rose on its hind legs, and, as its handlers tugged on the ropes, the elephant pulled back and in the process trampled Senator Kirk. By the time the handlers managed to pull his crushed, fecal-spattered body from under the elephant's hind legs, it was clear that nothing could be done to save him.

On hearing the details of his death, the public was in shock. They were stunned by the news that someone so prominent should die such a gruesome and unexpected death. The Senator's constituents were very proud of the way the Senator chose to exit this world. Even Jon Weinberg, the investigative journalist who had always been after the Senator, was taken in by the contrived story of the Senator's demise. He conceded in his column that the courage the Senator showed in giving his life in an attempt to rescue one of the elephant's handlers, who had been caught up in the ropes while the elephant was rearing, was exemplary.

Perhaps it showed that the Senator's critics, himself included, had really misjudged the man after all. Nobody seemed to notice the very fortuitous and heightened job placement some of the eyewitnesses to the Senator's death secured after that terrible day. There was no need to entice the handlers and ad people to go along with the mythic heroic death story. The Senator's "heroic death" saved all of them from a public's wrath for allowing the Senator to get so close to an elephant they were unable to control. The good story allowed the emphasis to be placed where it belonged—not on their negligence but on the Senator's heroism.

The heroic death cover story only confirmed what some people believed about the goodness of Senator Kirk. The populace's clamor for public recognition for this heroic man resulted in the new FBI building in Manhattan being named the "Allan J. Kirk Federal Building." Lou joked with me that they named the FBI building after Senator Kirk just to torment the Bureau. Senator Kirk had died with a clean criminal record. Every day the agents came to work they would have to see the name that represented their greatest failure. I told Lou that if they wanted to be true to the memory of the Senator, the building would have a cashier in the lobby selling everything from liquor licenses to pardons for felons.

136

Lou, of course, told me the real story of how the Senator died. When I read the Senator's obituaries and heard people from all walks of life rending their garments for television, I thought to myself that I hadn't seen such fawning over a miscreant since I read Abe Lapinsky's obituaries. But with Abe, I had not known about his true nature until after he was dead. When I did discover the truth, I could have vented my anger at those who knew the truth, but remained silent or actively suppressed it. But with the Senator it was different. I had known the truth all along about him, but I had acted just like those whose lives depended on being within Abe Lapinsky's orbit. I swore to myself that I would never turn my back on the truth again. And I somewhat salved my sore conscience by convincing myself that no one had ever been able to bring down the Senator, and I would doubtlessly have failed where better and stronger men than I had failed. No human being I knew could have brought down Senator Kirk. I took comfort in the advice my old Uncle Ben gave me, "Never send a man to do the job of an elephant."

The night of Senator Kirk's death, his present and former employees spontaneously drifted into their favorite watering hole near his local Senate office to mourn together. Early in the evening they cried together and hugged each other for comfort, but as the evening and drinks wore on, the sobbing turned to the recounting of numerous tales of degradation and humiliation that Senator Kirk had heaped on everyone in the room at one time or another. The room became noisier and noisier, until at about three o'clock in the morning, Corker Reed climbed atop a table and signaled for silence. Recognizing the former chief of staff, the crowd quieted down and Corker spoke, his eyes still red from earlier crying and his legs a bit unsteady from later drinking,

"I am happy that we could all be here tonight to share our feelings and our grief. And I know that this is a very, very tough night for all of us. And no matter what each of you thought about Senator Kirk, he deeply affected all of our lives. Although some of you might disagree with me, I think we should recognize how our lives were all effected by our nationally revered Senator, a man who is being mourned well beyond the borders of our state and even beyond the borders of our country. I think I can capture our feelings in a three word toast."

The crowd was deadly silent but soon shouts of "Here! Here!" and "Say it!" ripped around the room. Corker bowed his head as if to hold back his tears, raised his drink in his right arm towards the ceiling and cried out:

"To the elephant!"

The crowd burst into laughter and ear shattering unceasing applause as years of pent up anger were turned into a purging laugh-fest. Corker got down from the table and exited the tavern with the crowds' answering shrieks of "To the elephant" ringing in his ears.

A decade after the Senator died, Lou said he bumped into Corker Reed at a fund raising event for the senator who replaced Kirk. Corker said he did not finally make his peace with Senator Kirk until one night at 3 A.M. when, in a moment of impulsive inspiration, he drove his car to the "Allan J. Kirk" FBI building and paid condign homage to the Senator by relieving himself on the honorary plaque affixed to the cornerstone of the building. Corker told Lou that he knew that a few seconds of pissing on Kirk did not make up for ten years of Kirk crapping on him, but it made him feel better nonetheless.

I would have admired Corker more if he had the courage to show his manhood by peeing on Senator Kirk while the bastard was still alive. After-the-fact courage was a cowardly trait that I felt shame about possessing myself. I never forgave myself for allowing Abe Lapinksi to die happy and unexposed. My father died an unknown hero, unheralded and unmissed by all but me and my mother. Abe Lapinsky and Senator Kirk, two of the most abhorrent human beings ever, died revered and missed by the multitude. I swore that if it was ever in my power, I would do my

CHAPTER 17

LUKE

Some people burn out sooner and some later. But they all burn out some time. My burn out had come on gradually, but I didn't realize the need to do something about my life and living it until many years later when I received a late day call from my doctor. Whenever the doctor himself calls you a few days after a routine examination, you know that he isn't calling to tell you that you are perfectly healthy.

"Luke, the radiologist found something on your chest x-ray." (Well, tell him not to spill his coffee on my x-rays next time.) "It is a nodule, and we have to send you for a CAT scan to see what it is. Of course, it could be bad, but I'm sure it's nothing. I wouldn't worry about it." (I wouldn't worry about it either if it were on your lung.)

I was told that what was found on my X-ray was called by the medical community an "anomaly." Every profession has its euphemisms. What the medical profession calls an anomaly, lay people often call a death sentence.

Emotionally, I was extremely agitated after receiving the call. I had always thought a great deal about dying, going back to my childhood in Augusta when I was convinced I would be deprived of going to heaven because of my failure to "accept" Jesus. I have always been terrified and bewildered when I contemplate the prospect of dying and its connection to God and religion.

The greatest scientific mind could never produce a salve to heal the wounds inflicted by life so well as does the balm of faith. God does make life tolerable and comprehensible in its incomprehensibility, and He does so even if He does not exist. It is the *belief* in God that is so comforting. But you can't will yourself to faith—I've tried. I have prayed to a God I don't think exists when I have felt powerless to control events that were threatening the life or happiness of myself or a loved one.

I knew that whether my anomaly would be benign or fatal would not be determined by the measure of my life. One characteristic that makes God God is His infinite capacity for total ingratitude. You can lead the mostly saintly of lives and end up dying at an early age being run over by a car driven by your drunken, wife-beating, bastard of a neighbor who lives happily until the age of 90. The Calvinists knew that this lack of disparity between the lives of the good and the evil escapes rationalization by even the greatest theological minds. So they cut the string that tied good works to good lives and even heaven by proclaiming "predestination." Whatever happens to you is predetermined the day you're born. Unfortunately, predestination proved a very poor control mechanism for human activity, so Calvinism really never caught on.

Sitting there in my plush Wall Street office it struck me that if there is anything more inexplicable than the mystery of death, it is life. What is the point of life if everyone is really born with a death sentence hanging over his head, a final, eaten by the worms, no soul to heaven death? The randomness of tragedy and death always provided the greatest challenge to believers in any kind of deity. Why does one baby get cancer and another not? Why did Stalin live into his seventies while Martin Luther King never saw forty? Someone once said that God can either be omnipotent or compassionate; He cannot be both.

All of these thoughts of life and death, of the concept or reality of God, flooded my mind as I waited for my doctor's call. The truth is that his initial call was far more meaningful than the call I finally received telling me that my "anomaly" was not going to kill me. I did not die, but I did peer into the abyss for the first time. Intellectually, I had always known that I was going to die someday, but then, for the first time, I truly knew it. It turned out only to be a dress rehearsal. But I knew there was going to be a full performance in the not too distant future. I really did have a near death experience. The fact that I was not near death did not negate my near death experience. Near death is objective. A near death experience is subjective.

I realized that although my death might not be imminent, my burnout was well on my doorstep. I also realized I had to do something with my life before either of them happened—before I died or, more imminently, burned out. I first realized that I was hitting that singed wall when I found myself looking forward to the monthly partners' meeting where the discussion centered on what *pro bono* work the firm would undertake for the month. Somehow, following the trajectory of a death row appeal was becoming not only more meaningful but also more exciting to me than the work I was doing. So it was with a not unpleasant antici- pation that I entered the partners' board room for that month's *pro bono* meeting.

For the past thirty years it had become *de rigueur* for the major New York law firms to undertake significant *pro bono* work, that is, free work for some person or entity that otherwise could not have afforded even ten minutes of Morton and Philips repre- sentation. The partners' motives for undertaking this *pro bono* work were varied. Some did it for the purest of motives. Some partners felt it was a necessary evil to fend off social critics— doing *pro bono* work for minorities in order to avoid having to actually hire minorities was the lesser of two evils. For others, doing *pro bono* work was part of a sense of *noblesse oblige* which only confirmed the firm's exalted caste status. For other partners, the *pro bono* program was a vestigial remain from the unbridled '60s and early '70s when even the brightest students would demand to see how much *pro bono* work a firm was doing before agreeing to work there. Of course that was no longer a justifica- tion for a firm's having a *pro bono* program, since law students today asked only what their bottom line pay was going to be and what their chances were of making partner.

Although I always participated in the process, I had never suggested any particular client for *pro bono* status. But now, as I filed into the meeting room with the other partners, I knew I was going to break that precedent, and I knew I was in for a real struggle.

*　　　*　　　*

I had heard news stories about a Klansman who had been arrested in Augusta, Georgia for the brutal murder of a black man. Because the crime had been committed so many years ago, I only half-listened to the television and radio reports. It wasn't until several days after the story broke that I heard the name of the alleged murderer—it was T.C. Simmons.

It had been more than 40 years since that day at Clarks Hill Dam—more than 40 years since I had seen my "blood brother," who was now being held in an Augusta jail for trial on the charge of murder. The newspapers seemed convinced that T.C., as a member of the Klan, had murdered the black man by torching him while he was still alive. The body of the victim was recently discovered and accompanying physical evidence, DNA and a mystery witness had implicated T.C.

The crime allegedly took place around the time T.C. and I had last been together. I did not know what T.C. had been doing these last 40 years, but I was certain that my boyhood friend, my blood brother, could not have committed such a crime.

My partners knew of my unusual interest in the case, which, as I said, had been a topic of national discussion. I took my seat at the *pro bono* round table and rocked back and forth in my chair. Silence hung heavy in the room for a few very elongated seconds. Then I stood up and faced my friends.

"You should know that when I lived in Georgia, I knew and was a close friend of T.C. Simmons." A questioning silence filled the room. A palpable disbelief that one of "theirs" could have known—much less been a "close friend" of—a murdering Klansman.

"I have decided that I am going to go down there and offer my services, and I will pay for whatever it costs to learn exactly what happened. I am convinced of this man's innocence and I intend to prove it."

Fran King, one of the senior partners, who was once quick to tell me that becoming a partner at Morton and Philips was much tougher for a woman than it ever was for a Jew, argued for the uncomfortable assemblage.

"What makes you so sure he's innocent? He sounds like a redneck bigot to me—one that has gotten away with a murder for far too long. Besides, what do you prove if you get him off—that we have a particular affinity for the Klan? That we don't have enough potential *pro bono* clients up here who have lived decent lives and have earned the right to due process of law?"

"I'll tell you what it proves," I shot back, "It proves that in this country we have the presumption of innocence, a presumption which applies to those accused of crimes whatever their color or background—even if they are poor whites in Georgia."

"Even if they're Klansmen who have a criminal record which includes the torching of a synagogue? Give me a break, Lipton." The speaker was another partner, Tim Costello, a large beefy-faced specialist in the newly developing field of "intellectual property."

I stared at Costello, wondering how this fatuous oaf could be a specialist in matters which had something to do with anything "intellectual." I also wondered how a person with so little hair could manage to arrange it in such a turban like sweep so as to convince himself that he was not bald.

"What do you know about the burning of that synagogue?" I asked.

"Only what I read in the paper," answered the hirsute wannabe Costello. "Seems he did it about the same time he murdered that poor black man. He did it on a Sunday morning. Damn fool thought that Jews had their services on Sundays and wanted to incinerate the whole congregation."

"Wrong " I almost shouted the defense. "I'm certain he knew the synagogue would be empty on Sunday, and the whole fire consisted of burning a small corner of the storage space behind the building. The fire was nowhere near the Sanctuary."

Those sitting at the table stared at me. Fran was again the first to speak.

"How the hell do you know so much about that incident? He set that fire forty years ago."

"Research, Fran, research, but that's not important. What is important is that this firm authorize my *pro bono* representation of T.C. Simmons whom, I am convinced, is being falsely accused of a murder committed more than 40 years ago—a murder he did not commit."

"And what if we recommend that we have more important things to attend to?" asked Costello.

"Then I'll take a temporary leave from the firm."

"What if the firm disapproves?" Costello replied, and then, adding with a slight smile, "Representing a Georgia Klan member who torched a synagogue and a living black man is not the kind of representation we could be proud of. Kind of makes a mockery of the spirit of *pro bono*."

"Then I'll take a *permanent* leave from the firm."

The room fell silent. Finally, Fran leaned over toward me and, putting her face close to mine, almost whispered:

"Luke, think about this. Think about this first."

"Fran, I've been *thinking* all my life. It's time I started doing. I'm going to Georgia."

*   *   *

After I informed the members of the firm that I was going to Georgia to defend T.C., several partners made it a point to talk to me—each separately and all earnestly. They felt that my decision to surrender the jewel of the legal profession, a partnership at a prestigious law firm, in order to defend a redneck bigot in what they considered a backwater state defied both logic and reason.

What my partners did not understand was that I had spent my entire professional life yoked to logic and reason. I had dreamed for years of breaking free, but I had a family to support and a job that most lawyers would kill to have as their support system. Every time I was tempted to go where my heart rather than my mind led me, I would be brought back to reality by opening the top draw of my desk to look at a copy of my latest tax return. It did indeed defy logic and reason to walk out on a guaranteed yearly salary in the middle seven figures. And the profession I had chosen taught that one must never defy logic and reason. Unlike actors, lawyers do not wait on tables while dreaming about that one-in-a-million break.

A person who has grasped the logic of law well enough to be made a partner at one of the Wall Street law firms of New York City knows all too well that, absent independent wealth, one cannot afford to walk out on a partner's salary.

Oh, I had thought about it. Once I thought of joining the Peace Corps as a friend of mine had done only ten years before. I even thought of starting up my own solo practice... just me, all alone sitting in my office, coming and going when I wanted, returning or not returning clients' always "urgent" calls. I would not have to worry about how I yelled at women associates (always keep it gender neutral, call her an idiot but never a bitch), whether a client was incensed that I did not call him back on a Sunday, or even whether I was properly attired during my work hours. I could even download a pornography site or two from my computer during a break. The worst that could come of that would be that my feminine side could sue my masculine side for creating a hostile work environment. I remember smiling as I wondered if any solo practitioner ever sued himself for sexual harassment.

Yes, I really wanted to go down to help T.C. But I also wanted to break away and do something wild and unfettered. The prospect of acting irrationally in the sense of not making rational decisions was a great attraction to me. I guess in some ways I was going to have my Age of Aquarius later in life. My decision to leave to go down South to defend T.C. was an agonizing and grinding one for me to make, but as soon as I pulled the trigger, I felt completely liberated. I felt almost giddy, knowing that this could all turn out to be a personal disaster, a blunder of monumental proportions. But that was part of the excitement of it all.

I felt a rush of fresh air pouring into my life for the first time in years. I had enjoyed my work, loved my firm, and felt a degree of satisfaction from the legal work I had done. But I could not remember the last time I felt the exhilaration I now felt. And if things did not work out, big deal. It was not as if I could ruin my career. I had already lived my career. Now, I was going to chase excitement and a few dreams.

BOOK TWO

CHAPTER 18

Back when I had lived in Augusta there had been a seafood restaurant in town called the "Ship Ahoy." You knew they didn't catch fish in that part of the Savannah River, so that whatever fish they did serve had to come from a long way off. Given the fact that there was no airport in Augusta, and that there were more stifling hot days than cool ones, it was hard for me to believe that a seafood restaurant could stay in business. Apparently it didn't —because the Ship Ahoy Restaurant went the way of the Dutch Inn, the Kalico Kitchen, Mike's Candy and Soda Emporium, and the old grand dame Hotel Belle Air—all gone. Swallowed up by history in the development of a new Augusta.

They even had a main street named for a native son, a *black* native son, the popular singer James Brown. Camp Gordon had become Fort Gordon, and almost all of the landmarks of my teens were gone. I'd been certain those landmarks would be as enduring as my youth. I was wrong on both counts.

T.C. had stayed in Augusta all these years—kind of a living landmark. According to the news accounts, he had apparently lived a decent life after his release from a short prison stay. Besides, everyone believed he pleaded guilty to torching the synagogue for someone higher up in the Klan.

T.C. had served only a relatively short prison term for the arson, but now he stood charged with a far more serious crime. Murder.

Again according to the press, at or about the time of the synagogue torching, T.C. and two other Klansmen had dragged a black man, one Aaron Boddie, into a swamp south of Augusta and set him afire while he was still alive. The crime in all its horror would never had been discovered except for a diversion of the river downstream that drained that portion of the swamp, leaving

Aaron's remains coated with silt and baking in the hot Georgia sun for forty years.

The grisly discovery of the encapsulated charred bones was made by a construction crew preparing the area for yet another housing development in yet another Augusta suburb. Uncovered close by, also concealed by baked silt, was a faded, torn, and partially decomposed piece of cloth that bore a dark stain. The cloth was from a shirt and the stain was determined to be blood. The DNA from the blood was very degraded, but on the fourth test the pressured laboratory chief made a match to the blood taken by court order from T.C. Simmons.

T. C. had been ordered by the court to provide a blood sample because a bone from some small animal was found near the scene. There was a hole drilled through its metal casing. This apparent talisman was engraved with the name "T.C. Simmons." Prosecution might not have been possible given the degraded DNA sample and the fact that the defense could claim that T.C. had given his bone talisman to someone else, or even lost it; however, as a result of the news story about the horrific discovery in the swamp, the District Attorney received a telephone call. It was a preemptive call from a witness who said he could and would skewer T.C. for the heinous crime.

Prosecuting a member of the Klan in a state court had never been a popular pursuit in Georgia. It wasn't that prosecutors admired or feared the Klan, it was just that getting a jury conviction was next to impossible. In addition, a prosecutor who went after a member of the Klan usually had to pay for it come election day.

All that had changed as much as Augusta had changed. The Klan was now a remnant, devoid of political clout and an embarrassment to the new generation of Georgians and the great majority of southerners. There was also a new generation of prosecutors who delighted at the promise of convicting those guilty of the kind of atrocious bigotry which marred the reputation of the

New South. A prosecution that was once a political handicap was now an attribute. And if that targeted abominable bigot happened to also be a member of the Klan, or a former member of the Klan, the attribute became a blessed political virtue.

CHAPTER 19

I demanded to see the Warden. They had promised me that I would have a private room for the visit. I was not about to see and speak to T.C. after more than forty years through a heavy wire mesh screen. The local Georgia attorney I had hired, Payton Simkins, entered the room with the Warden in tow. The Warden, a tall black man with close-cropped hair and a ramrod posture, stuck out his hand, "I'm Warden Johnson, Hector Johnson."

I was to learn that there was a more significant change in Augusta than the Ship Ahoy's disappearance. It was Augusta's new breed of black citizen. I could remember when most southern black men seemed to affect a kind of disengaged presence, a detachment that could easily be mistaken for ignorance. You never knew whether they were concealing an intelligence, but you did know that if it was there, you were never intended to see it.

I didn't know quite how to approach the Warden. I could appreciate the fact that if he was a product of the South, he had good reason not to want to do any favor for a present or former member of the Klan or his attorney. On the other hand, I also knew that this was a big-publicity case, and he wouldn't want the media to portray him as anything less than an enlightened administrator who served as a sentinel at the gates of justice.

"Glad to meet you Warden Johnson. Look, I really don't want to make any trouble but...."

"Save your breath, I'm having your client brought to the private visitor's room. But you will only have it for half an hour."

"Thank you, Warden," I said respectfully, not only because of his accommodation, but because I was genuinely impressed by his demeanor and directness.

"Think nothing of it," he said with a slight smile, "I think Klansmen who have murdered innocent black people deserve every break they can get, don't you? I mean, that's what you're here for, right? That's your noble mission, isn't it?"

I found myself fumbling for a reply. "Well, I came here for..."

"You came all the way here from New York because you thought this was another Scottsboro case, right? You're like that other fellow from New York, who came down South at risk to his life to defend those innocent black boys back about 80 years ago. Only difference is, you're coming down here to defend some poor innocent Klansman 'cause white folk can't get no justice down here."

He caught me completely off guard. It was as if he'd been waiting for the chance to ambush me. I fumbled on: "No, I don't know. I mean I came down...."

"You mean you couldn't find one case in New York more important than this, than defending a bigot scumbag who burned some poor black man forty years ago while he was still alive and probably pleading for mercy. You know what kind of pain that poor man must have been in?"

I was embarrassed, but I felt the need to explain—to tell him that I wasn't here just to defend some racist Klansman.

"It's really nothing like that, Warden. You see, T.C. Simmons was a good friend of mine. I grew up in Augusta and, well—in fact, we were blood brothers." I put that at the end with a smile, hoping to lighten up our conversation.

"Oh really—were you blood brothers before or after he torched that synagogue?"

It seemed the Warden was determined to either embarrass or belittle me. My dismay became apparent.

He finally smiled, "Oh don't take it so to heart, Mr. Lipton. We in the South, white and black, are used to northern hypocrisy. We had over 4,000 lynchings of blacks in the South and still couldn't get anyone from the North—not even President Franklin D. Roosevelt—to say a word of condemnation. But we welcome you anyway." Saying this, he looked beyond me to acknowledge a wave from a distant prison guard.

"Okay Mr. Lipton, and Mr. Simkins, your room is ready and your Mr. Dreyfus is ready to see you."

Dreyfus? How did he know of the Dreyfus case—the case of a Jewish captain in the French army who was humiliated and persecuted not because of what he did, but because of what he was—a Jew. "How do you come to know about the Dreyfus case?"

"You shouldn't be surprised. Black people have an affinity for innocent people who are railroaded by a bigoted society. Even innocent Jewish people. But believe me, Mr. Lipton, Simmons is not a Dreyfus."

A guard walked Payton and me to the prisoner conference room, but T.C. had not yet arrived.

"Remember," the guard cautioned, "I'll be standing here. No touching the prisoner. No handshakes."

Payton smiled. He obviously had no intention of shaking T.C.'s hand. I had been greatly impressed by this young Payton Simkins, but I had to wonder why he was willing to work on the case of a former Klansman accused of murdering an innocent black man. I knew it couldn't be easy for a young black attorney to do that. And given the fact that his offices were here in Augusta, it couldn't be very good for his career. I hadn't mentioned this to him because he never brought up the subject. But now my curiosity got the best of me.

"Payton, weren't you a little surprised that the Warden, being black and all, didn't ask you why you were working on this case?"

"No, not at all. Don't you think he gets shit for being a warden of a prison filled with young black men? He knows where I'm coming from."

"Well, maybe he knows more than I do then, because truth is, *I don't* know where you're coming from. I called up the senior partner in your firm and asked him to get me the best young criminal attorney in his office—one with a fire in his belly—and he came up with you."

Payton's eyes suddenly went cold.

"Bullshit. First of all you didn't ask for the best young criminal attorney in his firm. You asked for a young *black* attorney to work on the case. I don't even think you asked for a *good* black attorney. All you wanted was a black attorney."

I was taken aback more by Payton's knowledge of my request than by his obvious anger. I *had* asked for a young black attorney. But I never thought that the senior partner would tell Payton that I had specifically asked for a black attorney. Those things happen all the time in litigation, but some things are better left unsaid.

Yes, I wanted a black attorney for all of the obvious reasons. I knew in the "new" South we were going to get black jurors, and I knew they probably wouldn't relate to me, and they certainly wouldn't relate to T.C. I also knew that even a white juror would have to think twice before convicting a man whom a black attorney thought was innocent. No one would believe that a black person would defend a white person who really had so gruesomely murdered a black man.

Of course I knew T.C. would have a much better chance of being acquitted if he had a black attorney at the table. What was I supposed to do, be virtuous and colorblind at the cost of T.C. spending the rest of his life in prison? Besides, Payton Simkins turned out to be a fabulous attorney, even if that attribute was only an added starter compared to his major attribute—his color.

"Payton, if you knew I was asking for a black attorney just because he was black, why did you take the job?"

"I thought it was a milestone for affirmative action. For the first time, black attorneys could also take part in getting white racists off for lynching black folks. That's a great step forward for my race, don't you think?"

"Seriously, the truth, why did you do it?"

Payton slumped against the wall and exhaled a long deep

breath.

"Actually, I didn't agree to do it until I was able to interview T.C. twice, and until I was able to investigate the case. There are two reasons I decided to stay with it. First, he never denied being there, seeing it all happen. I think this country still needs reminding of what was going on here, the horror of those days still infects this country and everyone should be told the story so no one ever forgets. T.C. told me he would be willing to describe the horror of that lynching."

"And the second reason?"

Payton's eyes narrowed into angry slits as he glared at the empty wall.

"The second reason was that I believe him. I believed him when he told me that the real person behind this was Will Morgan. That Will Morgan was there—that he was the sonofabitch who did it. You know what that means? That it was Will Morgan who did it? That Will Morgan torched that poor soul?"

"Who is Will Morgan?" I asked

"He's Mr. Big around here. He's our Mayor. He was Klan 40 years ago, then he graduated to the White Citizen's Council. You have no idea how big Will Morgan was and still is around here. He's been mayor for forty years, kind of a 'Mayor for Life.' The only mayor to serve a major city for a longer period was Erastus Corning of Albany, New York. But Morgan is more than Mayor. He runs everything and everyone in this town. He's everyone's hero. Even my nephew works for his lumber business and loves him— just loves him..."

"So you want this trial to expose Morgan?"

"Oh yes, oh yes, big time. He represents something to me— something I despise and have always despised." He took on the look of a crusader. "It's always burned my ass that the George Wallaces and the Strom Thurmonds just walked away from the damage they caused...forgiven by everyone, white and black and their past forgotten by everyone. Even my son said George

Wallace was only fighting for 'state's rights.' Well, when the son of a bitch was sworn in as governor of Alabama, he yelled: 'Segregation Now, Segregation Forever.' He never said a damn thing about states' rights."

"Yeah, but Morgan is no George Wallace or Strom Thurmond."

"He's no different. You know the DeBeckwiths and guys like T.C., they were just the disposable white trash. They're scum all right, but they just carried out the orders. You know, people today just don't understand that the White Citizen's Councils, all respectable white business people, did more harm to blacks than all of the Klansmen combined."

"Payton, I know and understand how you feel, but you know your job is to defend T.C. If that means getting Morgan, okay...."

Payton whirled around and faced me, his anger obvious as he raised his voice for the first time.

"Hey, I don't give a shit about T.C. He's scum. But he's only a pawn. We've been settling for the pawns for too long. I want the king this time. And I'm going to get him."

"What if T.C. decides to take the plea they offered him. Then no one is going to find out about Morgan. What will you do then?"

Payton's voice was now a shout and he slammed his fist against the wall.

"Damn it, T.C. promised me he wouldn't take a plea. He says he's innocent. He promised me he was going to fight, and he damn well better follow through."

I didn't say anything to Payton, but I knew what he was doing was wrong. No lawyer has the right to sacrifice his client on the altar of some moral crusade that the client has not agreed to join. But I also knew I had no choice. I needed Payton. He was already deep into the case. He was smart. He was a good attorney. He was fired up for the case...and he was black. I decided to change the subject.

"When are they going to get T.C. here? You know I haven't seen him in over forty years. I wonder what it will be like to see him again after all these years."

In fact, I hadn't spoken to T.C. since we had become blood brothers, and he had flown into a rage when he found out I was Jewish. Payton had told me that T.C. was divorced with two grown children and two grandchildren. He had been working at times during the last forty years for Will Morgan at City Hall, a detail which did not escape Payton's notice. The fact that T.C. had been breeding—well, I found that a little frightening. With my blood in them too!

I was startled out of my reverie by the abrupt opening of the door. I turned toward the clanging noise of chains as a prison guard led T.C. into the room. He was wearing an orange jump suit and had a chain around his waist. Other chains were secured to his ankles and wrists, all attached to the chain around his waist. As he shuffled into the room, I stared at him in silence. He was just as big as I remembered him, but it seemed that all of his strength had been sapped from his large body. He avoided my stare. Could it be that he still resented me for "tricking" him? I felt I ought to say something fast to break the tension. "Damn, T.C., you old bastard, look at you, you still have all your hair."

T.C.'s face lit up.

"Yeah, and where's your hair?"

"Oh, I still have all of my hair too. It's in a shoe box in my top dresser drawer."

T.C. laughed and turned to Payton.

"Hello Mr. Simkins."

I waved my hand at T.C.

"Hey, T.C., we're a team here. You call me Lipton like you always did and you call him Payton."

Payton interjected curtly, "No, I don't care what he calls you, but he'll call me Mr. Simkins."

I caught my breath, stared somewhat surprised at Payton, but then turned to face the guard trying to change the subject and defuse an awkward situation.

"Hey, can't you take this shit off of him while he's in here with us? We don't need him in shackles here."

The guard just shook his head.

"No sir, the last thing we need in here is to have some lawyer taken hostage."

"Well, at least leave us alone with him," I requested.

"O.K.," the guard said, "but I'll be standing right outside and remember—no contact. You got thirty minutes."

As soon as the guard left, I motioned T.C. to sit down. I wanted to talk to him, to renew contact with him, talk about old times. But I knew every minute I had with him was precious so we had to talk about new times or at least recent times. Before I could say something clever to break the ice, he began:

"Mr. Lipton..."

"What is this Mr. Lipton shit," I interrupted, "I told you—you call me Lipton or Luke."

"Luke, " he began again, calling me by my first name for the first time I can remember. It seemed unnatural, but then this whole scene seemed unnatural. "Luke," he repeated, and then with a steady stare of sincerity: "I never killed that Negro."

"Look, T.C. if I believed that you had, I wouldn't be here."

Payton stepped in, correctly sensing that this was not moving as fast as it needed to.

"Look, we don't have a lot of time. Let's get down to business. T.C., why don't you tell Mr. Lipton what you told me, how the whole thing happened."

CHAPTER 20

T.C. lowered himself into a chair in the small room and tried to stretch his cramped legs, but the shackles prevented him from fully extending his limbs. He paused for a few uncomfortable minutes and then began in a low almost mumbling monotone.

"Well, you know I was young and I had been in the Klan for just about a year, and a couple of the Klan leaders told me that I had to prove myself as worthy. They told me that I had to prove myself by killing this ni...Negro who had raped a white woman whose husband was in the army."

"Did you believe that the guy had raped the woman?" I asked.

T.C. looked at me seemingly confused by the question.

"Well, we didn't think much about whether they done it or not in those days. We felt...we had a notion that we had to protect white women...and...well, I guess I never really thought about it...they said he done it, so I thought he done it."

T.C. put his hand to his chin in what appeared to be an effort to recapture his train of thought. I had been away from the 1950's South too long to realize that "did he do it?" was a totally irrelevant question when applied to black people.

"Anyway, me and Carl Talbot and Will Morgan got in a car and drove to where they had got this black boy locked up."

"Now listen to me," Payton interrupted with an edge in his tone, "We're not talking about a 'boy' here. When you refer to him from now on you call him a 'man' or refer to him by name. His name was Aaron Boddie. Do you understand what I'm telling you. Aaron Boddie. He was a person—he was a man!"

"Yes sir," T.C. said with genuine contrition. He started again: "This man, Aaron Boddie, he was locked up in this pump house way back down river."

"How was he locked up?" I asked.

"Chained," T.C. answered, holding up his own chained wrists as if to illustrate, "chained to the pipes in the pump house."

He then described in detail how he, Carl, and Will dragged the manacled pleading and weeping black man into the flat bottom skiff.

"Was anybody saying anything?" I asked.

"Well, the black man kept saying that he didn't do anything, that the white woman was playing with him." When T.C. said this, I thought I saw a spark of anger—gone as fast as it came. T.C. continued: "...when he said that, about the woman having played with him, Carl lost it—he stood up and kicked the ni..—black man up side his head. Carl kept kickin' him, sayin 'you're a lying bastard.' and the black man's face started bleeding and swelling up."

My stomach knotted up—the picture of a handcuffed man being kicked in the head while being rowed to his death was sickening.

"Did you do anything to stop them?" I asked.

'Not then," T.C. answered.

"Okay, go on."

T.C. continued with the story, talking while staring at a blank wall, seeing images that were playing across his mind as he recounted that horrible day. He told how they traveled about two hundred yards downriver, maneuvering the skiff into a tangle of mangrove trees where they dragged Aaron Boddie, his body soaked in sweat and blood, into the brackish water of the swamp. Carl kept kicking the man as they dragged his semiconscious body free of the skiff and on to some land. Blood was pouring from his nose, ears, and the shattered teeth of his opened and gaping mouth.

The beatings did not stop until Carl went to relieve himself in the bushes. T.C. described how he watched with growing terror as Will Morgan went back to the skiff and returned with a can of gasoline which he proceeded to pour over the helpless Aaron

Boddie.

"It was when the gas was being splashed on him and I knowed they was going to set him on fire that I decided I couldn't just watch this happen. That's when I went for Carl's shotgun, which he had stacked against a tree. I put it to Carl's head and told him that if he didn't give it up, I was going to blow his head off."

Remembering the guard's admonition, I did not physically touch T.C., but seeing how visibly shaken he was, I wanted to reach out and hold him. Here it was 40 years later, but revisiting the horrors of that day had obviously taken an emotional toll. I felt a revival of the affection I felt for the boy T.C. once was. This made it even more difficult for me to ask a very important clinical question.

"T.C. this is very important. At the point when you tried to stop it, was the man alive? Did it look like, if nothing else was done to him, he would live?"

"Oh yes, yes, fact is, he looked up at me to thank me. To thank me for saving his life."

"He said that?"

"No, he didn't say nothing. But I could see his eyes, big red eyes, bobbing his head at me. He knowed I was saving his life."

T.C. continued with his narrative. He told us how he stood with the shotgun to Carl's head ordering Will Morgan to untie Boddie. After Boddie was untied, T.C. told how he bent down to try to help the mutilated black man get to his feet when Morgan slammed a knife into his shoulder blade knocking him hard to the ground. When T.C. fell, Carl grabbed the shotgun and pointed it at T.C., who was writhing in pain. Will yelled: "Shoot the nigger lover," but Carl, who had developed an affection for this young man, just glared at T.C. He glared, but did not pull the trigger.

"I have a question that's bothering me. You must have known when you took Boddie out of that pump house that you and the others were going to kill him. Why did you suddenly change your mind? Why did you decide that you didn't want him to die?"

"Well, I really didn't know they were going to kill him. I just thought he was goin' to get a good beating. And I sure didn't know they was goin' to burn him alive. I didn't even see the can of gas in the boat. I didn't feel anybody should die that way." After a pause, T.C. continued, "And there was something else. When I saw Carl beatin' up on that black man, I suddenly felt an overwhelming pity for him. I felt like even though he was black and I was white—that somehow we were brothers. There was another time I had that feeling about a black man, a time when one of them saved *my* life."

"What are you talking about?"

"When I was in prison, I was blindsided by a couple a' inmates who were out to cut my throat when this big buck," T.C. looked quickly at Payton, "That was his name, Mr. Simkins, 'Buck' was his name, that was his name, I swear. Anyway this Buck fellow he beat off two people had a shiv to my throat. He saved my life. And after he did, he reminded me that all men—black and white—are brothers. That was the same feeling I had that day in the swamp. That all men, black and white, are brothers."

When a lawyer listens to a person telling a story lived in the real world he has to translate it in his head to determine how it will sound in the court world. Jurors have expectations about how people will act even in stressful situations. They will hold it against a person who does not react "properly" to the death of a loved one, or who suddenly acts in a manner not consistent with their notion of how a person should react under certain circumstances. I was relieved that now I had a handle to explain T.C.'s almost inexplicable conversion in the middle of a murder upon which he willingly embarked and a reason for that epiphany— that conversion to tolerance inspired by *compassion*. Plain old fashioned Christian compassion. A compassion which T.C. was able to identify with an unrelated incident when he was in prison. An incident which saw a black man save his life. An incident that demonstrated to him that if a black man can save his life, he can save the life of a black man. I believed that the portrait could be painted in real life colors for a jury.

"And when I seen Will lighting a bunch of matches, I tried my damndest to get to him. The ground was boggy and I couldn't use my hurt arm to prop me up fast enough. God knows I tried, but I kept slippin' and before I could get to him he dropped the matches onto the black man. That poor boy—er, man—just seemed he blowed up, turned all fire—and all the time screaming and throwing his arms around. I kept trying to get to him, but Carl and Will held me back. And them just laughing while that poor soul burned."

At that point, T.C. just fell silent. He didn't weep. He didn't tremble. His body slumped in his chair, but he sat perfectly still, staring straight ahead... at nothing and nobody. I turned to look at Payton for the first time since T.C. had begun talking. Payton had his head in his hands, and I could see tears running through his fingers. I cursed myself for making any black person work on this case. T.C. remained still—and silent. I had to move things along, our time was too valuable to waste on human emotion.

"What happened next?"

"Like I told you, there was this whoosh of flames. I was hoping he was so near being dead when it happened that he wouldn't feel nothing—but when he blowed up he gave the most horriblest shriek I ever heard. It was beyond horrible, Luke." And with this T.C. finally showed a sensitivity of which I never believed him capable and for which, as a trial lawyer, I was grateful. This man whom I always considered incapable of compassionate emotion, broke down and cried, his body shaking violently as he tried to speak through an agony of tears.

"It was beyond horrible. I couldn't stop seeing that poor soul burning ... If only I had been able to stop it... I prayed to the Lord to get that picture of that poor man out of my mind...of that poor man burning and shrieking like that. I went to drinking but that didn't help—God just wouldn't take that picture out of my head.

"I got married and had kids, but my drinking and the night-mares which kept me screaming at night—just like that poor man was screaming, like he possessed me—drove my wife and children out of my house. God punished me by having everything I loved disappear from my sight—everything 'ceptin the picture of that black man burning."

"And do you still have those nightmares?" I asked.

"They stopped five years ago when I found Jesus. He forgave me... He gave me forgiveness."

"How did you know of His forgiveness?" My question was not asked to discover the mystery of T.C.'s faith—I was shamelessly trying to envision my direct examination at trial.

"My preacher told me."

"Your preacher?"

"My preacher at the church I go to. He told me that if I gave my life to Jesus—if I sought salvation in Him—there was hope. That Jesus had died for the sins of others and that belief in him could bring redemption to me. I told my preacher of my pain. I told him of my criminal intent and my realization, too late, that a "brother" of mine, a black brother, was about to die—I told him of my inability to save a man's life. I confessed my sin. I gave myself to Jesus."

I never thought I would hear such eloquence from T.C. This was no redneck Klansman, this was a man who truly believed.

A trained attorney can cut through human emotion like a scythe through grain. He can also sift that grain to separate the chaff from the golden wheat. All I heard in the story about the minister was the evidentiary rule known as "prior consistent statement." If he told this minister his story *before* he had any idea he would arrested, it could be used as evidence to prove the truth of his story that he withdrew from the murder plot. It would be powerful evidence. I looked up at Payton.

"Do you know this minister? Did you check this out?"

"Yeah, the minister considered it a confidence until I got word to him from T.C. that it was all right for him to talk to me about it. He let me know he believes T.C.'s story. And, by the way, T.C. forgot to tell you that the rev is black. T.C. goes to this Episcopal Church that is the only mixed denominational church around here. Black and white pray together in that church."

I couldn't believe our good fortune. A black minister. Oh thank you Lord. And what made me feel even better was that this was legit. No lawyer told T.C. five years ago to go to a mixed race church with a black minister. And T.C. didn't even mention that the minister was black. Whatever T.C.'s failings, he was a person without guile. I was convinced that his going to a church with a black minister was proof that he was a changed man. The problem was getting a cynical society and a cynical jury to believe it.

As T.C. had been talking, I had been writing down clinical questions on a yellow pad. I now ran through them with T.C. Most important was that shirt with his DNA on it.

It seems that after the burning, Will and Carl buried the remains of Aaron Boddie in a shallow mud grave. T.C. watched the burial in a numbed silence. Carl instructed T.C. to take off his bloody shirt—or what was left of it—which he tossed on the ground next to the burned body. They rowed the skiff back to the car that was parked near the pump house. They then drove in silence back to the Federal highway where Will Morgan got back into his car with the parting warning that if T.C. ever spoke of that day to anyone, he would end up like Boddie.

Carl drove T.C. to a "friendly" doctor who admitted him to the emergency room of the Augusta General Hospital where he stitched up his stab wound.

Looking for confirmation of T.C.'s story, I was anxious to see his stab wound. I started to ask T.C. to pull his shirt off when Payton, anticipating me, said, "I already checked. There's a mean, ugly keloid scar there, and I got the hospital record, and it all checks out. Except, and I expected this, the hospital record says he got stabbed in a drunken brawl. It was just luck that the hospital had stored its old records."

I scanned my notes for questions that I could envision coming up during cross-examination.

"Weren't you worried about leaving your shirt at the scene?"

"Carl said there was no need to clean up—that the swamp would clean itself up. And Will Morgan said it didn't make no difference anyway 'cause no one was gonna care or weep over this nigger's death,' and, looking quickly at Payton, 'It was him used that word...'"

I looked at my notes: "Where is this Carl Talbot now?" I asked.

"Dead a long time. Truck ran him off the road. Carl didn't drink, but the truck driver was real drunk. He lived, Carl died."

I smiled. "Every lawyer's dream, a dead person to take the blame for everything."

Payton was not amused. "I'm not for pinning it on the dead guy, I want the live guy...Morgan..."

The interview was over and, as if on cue, there was a hard rapping at the door. The guard stuck his head in. "Time to go. I already gave you extra time."

As he shuffled out of the room, T.C. turned to me: "I'm sorry about that synagogue, Luke, and I'm sorry I acted like such a damn fool when we were together last. You're still my best friend." And then, with a catch in his voice, "You're still my blood brother."

CHAPTER 21

I was almost relieved when the guard took T.C. out of the room. If he had stayed any longer or said any more, I may have wept. I don't know exactly why—pity for poor Aaron Boddie? Sympathy for T.C., whom I felt was in many ways a pathetic victim? Or regret for my own lost youth, which I would never recapture? I turned to Payton.

"So what do you think?"

"I told you I believed him, or I wouldn't be here."

"So you think we got a shot?"

"No, I think they're going to convict him."

My look must have been more than quizzical. "Why?"

"Why? Because it's good for everybody. These guys always get convicted years later. It makes blacks feel good because they get a sense that there's some payback. The whites love it because it washes away their sin and they can now say that this proves that America is no longer racist so black people should stop their bellyaching. And neither the whites nor the blacks care what happens to the likes of T.C. No one has any interest in seeing some poor piece of white trash get off."

From my own sense of personal morality, I didn't know what punishment, if any, T.C. would have deserved. He was a member of the Klan and, even giving him the benefit of the doubt, he did mean to harm a defenseless man. On the other hand, he put his life on the line to save that poor fellow. Given the time this happened, you could fit all of the white people in the South who would have reacted that same way into the navel of a flea and still had room left for all of the white people who would have been upset at the lynching.

"You know, Payton, that story about the black guy in prison saving his life could be an interesting piece of this case. It is almost allegorical. Here he tells how a black man saves his life in prison, which gives him the impulse to reflect on his righteous behavior in attempting to save a black man's life. It would almost serve as a reaffirmation of his affinity for Boddie—a mystical payback. Do you believe a black man really saved his life in prison?"

"Absolutely," said Payton.

"Good, so if the prosecutors check it out, verifying the name and the incident you think it will all check out?"

"I'd bet my life on it," Payton said.

"Great—it's a sound explanation as to why T.C. was now reflective and suddenly wanted to help a black man—because one saved his life. So we can go with it."

"No we can't."

"Why not?"

Payton smiled. "Like I said, the story was true—the problem is it happened three years *after* the lynching, when T.C. was doing time for the synagogue torching."

So the incident with "Buck" in prison had nothing to do with an epiphany or a "payback" or anything else for that matter. I asked Payton: "If you knew he was lying about this being one of his reasons for saving Boddie, what makes you still think he's innocent?"

"Because I don't think that it was an intentional lie—I just think that he got the time sequence mixed up. Besides, like I said, I believe his story about his antipathy to the lynching and I believe that some part of his conscience took refuge in the fact that he had a bond with blacks because of the prison incident."

"But then why *did* he suddenly decide he wanted to save Boddie?"

"I think it was because he was a coward. You know it takes some kind of guts to burn an innocent man to death or even to put a bullet through his head. T.C. was the kind of racist who would vote to acquit any Klansman accused of a crime. The kind of bigot who would attend Klan rallies and congratulate the murderers on their good work—but he wouldn't have the guts to be the one setting the fire or pulling the trigger."

"But it took some kind of courage for him to try to stop the thing from happening, didn't it?"

"That was instinctive—it was a civilized reaction, and that's why I feel he deserves to be defended, but I wouldn't call it courage. A courageous man doesn't join two other men with a shotgun to brutalize a man who is chained and frightened half to death."

"So you're willing to defend him because he exhibited a 'civilized reaction?'"

"Yes, and because I think he's genuinely changed and changed before all of this shit came down on his head... and because by getting him off I'll be able to get Morgan. And I want Morgan."

I shook my head in silence. I wondered whether Payton really believed T.C.'s story or whether he was so anxious to get Morgan that he really didn't care whether T.C. had the civilized conscience of a saint or the murderous heart of a villain.

We left the prison and walked towards Payton's office. He told me that he had spoken to many of the parishioners in T.C.'s church. White and black alike had been extremely fond of the man, so that the charges of this 40-year-old crime had come as a shock to them. Although they wanted him to remain a member of the congregation, they also went out of their way to avoid him. The media had reported only the prosecution side of the case, so T.C. was believed to be the prime culprit—the one who actually set fire to Boddie. The other participants in the crime were referred to only vaguely. Morgan was not even mentioned.

The District Attorney knew that we were aware of Morgan's involvement. He was not only a good friend of Morgan's, he had been hand-picked by Morgan for his position. The D.A. could not obscure the facts of the case while the klieg lights of the national media were in such sharp focus, but he could still try to protect his good friend Morgan. Morgan knew and controlled too much to be tampered with.

CHAPTER 22

One of the first meetings Payton had arranged for me on my arrival to Augusta was with the District Attorney, Eddie Rabison. I had done my research on this prosecutor, who represented all I detested in this species. The man, who first gained notoriety when disparaging the insanity defense of a diagnosed schizophrenic, said: "Nobody hears voices I don't hear."

T.C. kept telling me that the truth would come out at the trial, and the prosecutor would drop the charges. I didn't have the heart to tell him that this prosecutor wasn't searching for the truth; he was searching for a way to punch his ticket to fame and fortune. There was no way he was going to let this once-in-a-term opportunity slip through his fingers. Having the opportunity to prosecute a case involving a high-profile defendant or high-profile crime was like having manna from heaven dropped in a prosecutor of his sort's lap.

The high profile case was the Holy Grail of prosecutors on the make. A prosecutor who had a superb record of both obtaining convictions and clearing the innocent in 99% of his caseload would remain forever anonymous. But the prosecutor who brought down a Mafia don, a congressperson, a big business tycoon or the subject of a high profile crime would be set for life. It was like winning a Pulitzer Prize where the recipient, no matter how badly he wrote in the future, would be forever lauded as a person who won a "Pulitzer." The prosecutor who could forever be known as the man who brought down some famous or infamous person would have the only notch on his belt that truly counted. It would not matter if the prosecutor uncovered the "crime" through brilliant investigative work or merely had the "crime" drop in his lap all gift-wrapped and ready for the press. It was the outcome that mattered.

What infuriated me even more was that the prosecutor in this case had all of the attributes of the very worst aspects of out-of-control prosecutors. He was a bully of the first order who, like many prosecutors, had never been in the position of having to defend himself or a client against the might of the State, and confused the power of the office with his own power.

I will never forget the perceptive observation of President Harry Truman, who stated that he was always very careful not to confuse the President with the Presidency. Truman knew that the power resided in his office not in himself. This prosecutor, Eddie Rabison, was known to throw his weight around with such reckless abandon that he was known as Nutty Eddie—an appropriate sobriquet given his frequent tirades. A starving homeless man who was caught sleeping on a park bench would pop Rabison's veins.

"Nutty" Eddie first gained fame around here by separating himself from the prosecutors whom he felt were not sufficiently adamant in pursuing the death penalty. He would have made disagreeing with him a capital offense if he had the power.

I felt there was a conflict of interest in his rabid pursuit of the death penalty since he himself looked like a cadaver. Tall and thin with a pasty complexion, he resembled an artist's rendering of Washington Irving's Ichabod Crane.

Rabison was a big favorite of the local press because he always made for good copy. A former aide of his had told me that he had to fight his way through a horde of reporters every time he tried to get into Rabison's office to discuss a matter. Reporters always managed to somehow obtain knowledge about secret Grand Jury proceedings. But should there ever be a favorable article about a defendant or an unfavorable article about a "victim" or government witness, Rabison would be on the phone with the defense counsel threatening the defendant with dire consequences if any further such "improper" publicity appeared.

The Code of Ethics for Prosecutors states that they are to merely announce the indictment and not engage in any public discussions that might jeopardize a defendant's right to a fair trial. It should have taken Rabison about five minutes to read T.C.'s indictment. As it turned out, it took him four hours to get through his philippic when announcing the charges against T.C.

I watched the tape of the indictment announcement. Rabison had all types of law enforcement people lined up behind him, one carefully selected from each ethnic group. No one but Rabison was permitted to speak, but he complimented them all for "breaking this case which proves that racist murders can run and hide for years, but they will never, never be beyond the reach of the law." Rabison thundered on about the vile nature of T.C.'s act. I just watched the cadaver come to life, ranting on while I thought to myself, "I wonder when he's going to get to the part about the presumption of innocence."

I knew that as T.C.'s counsel, if I ever acted like Rabison, I would be up before a disciplinary committee before the day was out. Any defense counsel knows of the double standard. A prosecutor can secure a witness' testimony by offering him money, immunity from the most horrid crimes and even a new job. But if a defense counsel offers to send a witness a thank-you card in exchange for his testimony, he will be facing a Grand Jury investigation.

I had not yet arrived in Augusta at the time of T.C.'s first court appearance. Payton had represented him. The first order of business had been Rabison requesting and obtaining a "gag" order from the judge. No talking to the media because it might interfere with a "fair trial." Of course Rabison really was bothered by the fact that if the defendant could fight back in the media, it might interfere with the propaganda he had already unleashed into the public consciousness. He shoots his missiles into my house and then demands that the judge impose a peace treaty on the parties.

I soon found out that the gag order seemed to choke only me. Almost every day there were items in the newspapers splashing more mud on T.C. I complained to the judge, but as the judge pointed out, I had no "proof" that the leaks were coming from the prosecutor's office. If I had his Grand Jury, I knew I could prove it in a finger-snap.

I thought seriously about unleashing people to the media who were not covered by the gag order, but I knew it was hopeless. Besides, I knew I just wasn't any good at the extra-judicial counter-punching that is such a necessary part of a defendant's arsenal in a high profile case. For the first time, I had some sympathy for the Johnny Cochrans and Bill Kunstlers, whose antics had so appalled me in the past.

I knew that T.C. would really have been better off with a Bill Kunstler than he was with me, a white shoe lawyer who had spent his life filing two-hundred-page motions where the harshest language I used was "I respectfully disagree with learned counsel." Rabison knew this was his one shot at eternal fame. God Himself could have told him that T.C. was innocent, and Rabison would not have slacked off his assault one iota. It is not self-flattery for me to say that T.C. had a student of the law, a legal scholar, as his lead defense counsel. What he really needed was a street fighter.

I came down to this trial as a man who had an almost religious zeal for the preservation of law and order, and I knew I would leave with the same conviction. But, damn it, there ought to be a requirement that nobody can be a prosecutor who hasn't first been on the receiving end of a government investigation. Many prosecutors become defense counsel; unfortunately, they do so after they have left the prosecutor's office. It should really be the other way around. Being a defense counsel should be a training ground for being a prosecutor, not vice versa. It is both good and necessary that prosecutors have certain power, but they should have some concept of what it is like to be the recipient of that power before they are allowed to wield it.

Every day that I received news of another witness being bullied and threatened by Rabison, I became more incensed. I didn't know what would adversely affect me more, watching T.C. unfairly convicted or watching Rabison become a national hero by securing that conviction.

Rabison had nothing to do with "busting" this case. It had fallen right in his lap. A national magazine referred to him "as a courageous warrior who will not rest until justice is done." As if this were a tough prosecution. The man was going after an admitted former Klan member, who was viewed even by the right wing as embarrassing white trash, for the lynching of a completely innocent victim in a stomach-turning way. This was a courageous pursuit?

He declared that he was certain he "could put this vile creature where he belongs and keep him there until he rots." That was his public pronouncement, but he knew that when cases are old, memories tend to fade and evidence becomes more questionable. For that reason, and because he feared that a loss of this case would damage his career, he made us an "off the record" offer of ten years in prison if T.C. agreed to plead guilty within the month. The District Attorney thought it best "to get all of the unpleasantness of this dastardly crime behind this town and this state."

Payton and I both knew that what the District Attorney really wanted was to get this crime behind "him," before some newspaper reporter started uncovering some skeletons that were liable to come tumbling out of the closet. Whatever his motives, it was a good offer, and I tried to convince T.C. to take it. T.C. kept telling me that he didn't do what they said he did, and he wouldn't admit to something he didn't do. I told him that in our system of justice the truth is less important than what can be proved in court. Our courts are concerned with evidence, not truth. God is concerned with truth.

I also tried to explain to T.C. that with his prior felony conviction for the synagogue arson and his Klan background, we might not even be able to put him on the stand. The DNA on the shirt would place him at the scene, and it was apparent to me that if they had to call Morgan as a witness, they would. Morgan, the only living witness to the crime other than T.C., was obviously the "mystery witness" giving the story to the D.A. about how T.C. burned Boddie to death—and it was probably the D.A. who was leaking that story to the press. Morgan would be a hard witness to discredit, and he could get just about anyone to corroborate anything he wanted. Sometimes it makes good sense for even innocent people to plead guilty.

I will never forget T.C.'s answer to me as I implored him to consider pleading guilty as being only an accessory to the murder. I told him that he could then give his version of what happened to the media, even though I knew no one would believe an admitted felon and Klansman over an upstanding public servant like Morgan. T.C. became adamant—he would not take a plea.

"I will not plead guilty to this murder even if I would get no time in prison. I will spend the rest of my life in prison if that is what I deserve for what I did. But my story is true. They told Mr. Simkins that I was lying. I know what I said isn't a lie. I have already destroyed my life. I will not destroy my soul."

Fred Dingle had told me when I was a very young lawyer that no greater burden can be placed on the shoulders of a criminal defense attorney than defending an innocent man. The presumption of innocence is an essential element in our justice system, but it bears little relationship to actual guilt or innocence. My problem was that I felt certain that T.C.'s story was true—I was also certain that if we stuck with his story, he would probably end up serving the rest of his life in prison. I explained to him that the District Attorney would accept what is known in the law as an Alford plea, much like the one Spiro Agnew took—he would accept the conviction without admitting to guilt. But T.C. would not budge. I admired him for this strength, but I also feared the consequence.

I could not begin to imagine what T.C. must have been going through. Here was an insignificant man with an insignificant life who had suddenly become the cynosure of a nation's wrath. For varying motives, everyone wanted him to take the fall for a long-ago sin. Everyone had deserted him, even the few friends who cared about him but cared more for their own well-being and reputation.

Payton told me that T.C. had reestablished a relationship with his two children about five years ago when he was "born again;" however, his recent arrest had caused a rupture in those relationships. T.C. wrote to his son every week from prison, and, like clockwork, the letters came back unopened and unclaimed.

When I heard how his arrest and the relentless and vicious publicity had shattered T.C.'s reconstructed life, I could understand why he wanted to see this thing through to the end. He had nothing to lose. If he pled guilty, he would not win back his Church, his family, and everything else that mattered in his life. You would have a hard time convincing T.C. that America believes in the apothegm that everyone should be considered innocent until proven guilty.

I wished that every person who howls for law and order at all costs could spend just one week on the target end of a government accusation. Putting the full weight of the government on an individual is like striking a piece of glass with a hammer. Even if it turns out that the hammer blow was unwarranted, the shards of glass can never be glued back together. This is as true of a person charged with a blue collar crime as one charged with a so-called white collar crime. Once charged by the government you are injured beyond repair, regardless of the outcome of the case. That fact occurred to me as I turned to Payton one last time before leaving his office.

"Payton, you know what really bothers me about all of this? We know that T.C. is no longer a Klansman—hasn't been for 40 years. They're going to punish a man who is not the same man who committed the crime...whatever crime it is that T.C. might have committed. They are looking to send a God-fearing, God-loving man to prison for a crime that was committed by a Klansman two generations ago. Only they won't be sending a Klansman to prison for the crime."

"So you think that we should just live and let live at this point."

"Well, I guess that would be one way of putting it. It was over 40 years ago, and T.C. is the just the meaningless detritus of a long ago horrible explosion."

"Did you feel that way when they tried to prosecute the 85-year-old Nazi concentration camp guard 60 years after he was just a 'meaningless' cog in a much bigger machine?"

"I hadn't thought of that... but that was genocide..."

"Well this was certainly genocide for Aaron Boddie. It didn't matter a damn to him whether six million others died with him or not."

"But what's the purpose of going after T.C.? What's to be gained?"

"You know, every group has its grudges, some going on for centuries. People can understand why the Jews don't forgive the Holocaust, how the Serbs still burn with resentment over their defeat by the Ottomans over six hundred years ago, and the Iraqis and Iranians slaughtered each other in 1988 over wounds that had been festering since Cyrus conquered Babylon more than 2,500 years ago. It seems it's only with blacks that people demand that old injustices be forgotten. We should get on with our lives. We should forget about slavery. We should forget about Jim Crow. We should forget about some nobody like Aaron Boddie being burned alive because of some fantasy in some white woman's mind. Well, I'll get over slavery, Luke, when you get over the Holocaust."

"I'm not asking you to get over anything or to forget any of that, Payton. You should never forget it. What I'm asking you is what is gained by ruining the life of someone like T.C.?"

"I'll tell you what... something an awful lot of people take for granted, but black people are still hungering for... justice."

"So why are you defending him?"

"I already told you why. I do believe him, but that's not why I intend to work 'til 2 A.M. every day on his case. He was still in the Klan and God only knows what else he did, but I told you the main reason I wanted this case. Let me put it in terms a New Yorker like you will understand. He may be no more than a Sammy "the Bull" Gravano and maybe he's just as guilty, but I want John Gotti."

"Look, Payton, I hope you get everything you want out of this case. But I've go to remind you again: don't forget, you are here to defend a client, not to right any social wrongs."

I walked out of Payton's office, uncertain about Payton, uncertain about T.C. and uncertain about myself.

CHAPTER 23

We were not surprised that Will Morgan was the People's principal witness. On his direct examination, he had claimed that he had been with Carl Talbot and T.C. Simmons when someone told them that a black man who had raped a white woman was chained up at an old abandoned pump house down by the river. He testified that Carl and T.C. were going to question the black man to be certain that he was the one who did it. Morgan said he tagged along after them to see to it that if the suspect appeared to be guilty, he would be turned over to the police.

He said that when they got to the pump house, Carl and T.C. insisted on putting the black man in a small boat. Morgan testified that he pleaded with them to let the man go, but they pressed on with their mission which, as he said T.C. put it, was to teach "niggers what happens when they fuck around with a white woman." He told how he jumped into the skiff to continue his attempt to have the black man freed but was restrained by T.C. while Carl began kicking the handcuffed black victim.

At that point, Morgan testified, T.C. moved to the back of the skiff, apparently to fetch a can of gasoline. Because he then knew the intended fate of the black prisoner, Morgan said he pulled out his hunting knife and stabbed T.C. He then turned on Carl, but before he could reach him, Carl struck him with a mighty blow to the head with the butt of his shotgun. When Morgan regained consciousness, he found himself lying in the marsh next to the charred remains of the black man. T.C. and Carl were gone. Morgan testified that next to him was a note that read: "If you talk, you will end up dead like the nigger lying next to you." He said that after the event, he talked to only three close friends about the incidents leading up to the murder. I knew we would be seeing those people later in the trial.

I had to concede that Morgan's demeanor was superb during direct testimony. He cried what looked to be real tears. He talked about how hard he has worked over the years as a respected public official to heal the sort of wounds caused by people like Carl Talbot and T.C. Simmons. He said he left the Klan forever after that fateful night. The "amens" coming from the blacks in the audience elicited a grin from Rabison and were not stopped soon enough by the judge as far as I was concerned.

CHAPTER 24

Payton and I stayed up until almost 5 A.M. the night before the cross-examination of Will Morgan. It was not until after midnight that I agreed to let Payton conduct the cross-examination of Augusta's Mayor.

My reluctance had nothing to do with my confidence in Payton as a lawyer. I was impressed by his reputation and brilliance and was certain that he could do the job. In addition, he had a real fire in his belly. My concern was that in this case, the fire was fueled by his need to shatter the myth that the Klan was an illiterate mob of white trash bigots, while the upstanding citizens of the South, like Mayor Morgan, did no more that drift about their periphery for a couple of years of youthful indiscretion.

I was not troubled by the prospect of Payton ripping the hood off Morgan in his testimony. Any good defense attorney wants the trial to be about the crimes of a key government witness, or even about the alleged misconduct of the law enforcement officers who pursued this case—anything but a trial of the defendant. But we had to keep in mind that our sole obligation was to defend T.C. Simmons, not to educate the public on what truly went on back in 1957 in the deep South. The prize Payton had his eye on was the destruction of people like Mayor Morgan who had been the pillars of the white supremacist movement in the mid-20th century. People who had now slid effortlessly into leadership roles in the "New South" without having paid any penalty for the human misery they had left behind.

I had been honest with Payton about my concerns, and he had assured me that he knew his obligations as T.C.'s lawyer. He felt I was wrong in thinking his goal of exposing "the White Citizen Council" types and the goal of getting T.C. off might be in conflict. Besides, he pointed out that one goal of any good cross-examiner is to suck a key witness into a heated, nasty battle with the cross-examiner. Right now, the jury had only seen the kind, humble, apologetic man who had testified on direct, led through a litany of good deeds by Rabison. Payton had objected time and again to the unimpeded flow of good deed testimony that the prosecutor elicited, but, unfortunately for us, this very Protestant judge had a very Catholic view about how far afield a prosecutor could wander in pumping up the character of his witness. Payton insisted that if we wanted to crack Morgan's phony veneer of sweetness and light on cross-examination, the best way was to have an uppity "nigger" in his face, demanding that he answer the questions.

Payton smiled at me and said, "He'll just shrug off kike questions. But nigger questions will burn him to his soul."

The tipping point in my decision to let Payton conduct the cross-examination came at the end of the day when Morgan had finished his direct testimony. The prosecutor had earlier filed what is called an *in limine* motion. That is a motion filed to prevent the other side from doing something or presenting certain evidence at trial. Rather than wait for the allegedly inadmissible evidence to reach the jurors' ears, a party may ask the judge for a prospective ruling regarding the evidence in question. Judges, of course, can reserve their ruling until the precise nature of the evidence becomes clear, but that usually occurs in front of the jury, and even a favorable ruling from the judge at that point rarely erases the toxic effect of the jury having heard the inadmissible and prejudicial evidence.

Rabison had filed a thirty-page brief requesting that the defense be constrained from delving too far afield in Morgan's past life. As the prosecution pointed out, Simmons, not Morgan, was on trial. The prosecution wanted to focus like a laser on the murder of Aaron Boddie and claimed that wandering off into areas not directly related to that murder would serve only to distract the jury from the principal issue in this case.

Our opposition brief had stressed the fact that Morgan's beliefs and actions of forty years ago were central to this case. The jury had to decide if Morgan was the type of man who could have orchestrated this murder and prevented T.C. from stopping it, as we alleged. In order to make that crucial credibility determination, the jury had to size up the Morgan of forty or even thirty years ago.

In his reply papers, the prosecutor argued that the evidence of Morgan's bad choices as a young man would be far more prejudicial than probative. The danger was that the jury would reject what Morgan had to say just to punish him for the person he had been forty years ago, not because he was lying about what he said had happened. The prosecutor pointed out that, as a general rule, that is precisely why courts do not allow a jury to hear about all of the past crimes of a defendant—the jury is supposed to decide if the defendant committed the charged crime, not if he is a bad person.

In sum, it was the age-old battle between prosecutor and defendant. The prosecutor has to prove a case beyond a reasonable doubt and so does not want the jury distracted from the principal issue in the case—whether the defendant committed the crime charged. The defense only has to create a reasonable doubt, so it wants to throw up as much garbage in the air as possible in the hopes that something sticks to the jury. However, in this case it was not just tactics involved. The prosecutor genuinely felt that the kind of person Morgan was forty years ago was not relevant to T.C.'s guilt beyond how they interacted to commit the crime. We genuinely felt that the kind of person Morgan was had everything to do with whether T.C. or Morgan engineered and committed the crime.

Initially, the judge ruled that he would not rule on whether to limit us in our cross-examination until he heard the questions we were asking the witness. He said he would rule on each piece of evidence or testimony that the defense intended to elicit. I was upset we had not won a more definite victory, but I was relieved that the judge had rejected the prosecutor's demand that we make an offer of proof. That is, the prosecutor said that we should have to disclose precisely what evidence we intended to elicit. What he really wanted, of course, was a preview of what he could expect and to prepare his witness accordingly. He knew that. I knew that. Fortunately, the judge also knew that.

We caught an unexpected lucky break just as we were leaving the courtroom for the day after Morgan had finished his direct testimony. The judge suddenly called all of the attorneys into his chambers with the court reporter. While glaring at Rabison he said, "I have decided to amend my ruling on your *in limine* motion, Mr. Rabison. In view of the fact that you spent so much time on your direct testimony downplaying and minimizing Mr. Morgan's role in the Klan. I think you have opened the door to a more wide ranging cross-examination on his activities and beliefs back in those days. As a substantive issue, it may be somewhat remote, but you have now turned it into a credibility issue that might indeed effect how the jury views his testimony about the murder. Before you explode, Mr. Rabison, I am taking no further arguments on this issue, you have your exception...."

Nutty Eddie spat out his reply, "Yeah, I have my exception, now if only Your Honor can get me a right to appeal."

CHAPTER 25

Rabison knew that if there was an acquittal, the government had no right to appeal, no matter how many errors the judge had made. He knew that as soon as the judge declined to rule on his motion before the trial began, he lost any right to appeal a judge's decision. Even as a defense counsel, I admired judges who ruled for the prosecution on some close questions, knowing that they might be inviting an appellate court reversal on their record while if they ruled for the defense, they were, by legal definition, always correct, or at least not reversible.

But this time, I thought the judge had done the right thing. And now Rabison knew that he had been hoisted by his own petard. He had taken advantage of the judge's failure to rein in his endless elicitation of "good character" evidence and had subsequently marched himself right into a trap. He told the jury Morgan was a good young man, badly misled. Now the defense can show he was a bad young man, doing the misleading.

Just as we were leaving the chambers, the judge called out to me,

"Mr. Lipton. Don't take this as a license to drive all over the country. I will still entertain objections as to relevance regarding any particular evidence you elicit. You saw what happened to Mr. Rabison when he pressed his advantage too far... don't make the same mistake."

"I understand, your Honor."

This last remark did give me cause for concern. One of the key pieces of evidence we had related to 1968, almost 11 years after the Boddie killing. Two weeks before the trial started, we had received a phone call from an unidentified person who told us that he had some interesting evidence for us to see. He had insisted that we meet him in some rural tavern 25 miles outside of Augusta. Receiving such calls was not unusual. Ninety percent of the time such tips turn out to be a total waste of time, the evidence is irrelevant or inadmissible. Nine percent of the time, the evidence proves to be helpful. It was the other one percent that concerned me. Those are the times that the attorney never returns from that out-of-the way meeting place.

Payton was as leery of the rendezvous as I was, so he arranged for his investigator Jim Cory to precede us undercover into that tavern and to keep an eye on us while we met with the informant. The subsequent meeting was neither as perilous to our safety as I had feared nor as helpful as I had hoped.

The tipster turned out to be a gnarled, old, very frightened man who had worked for the principal newspaper in Augusta, the *Augusta Gazette,* for forty years, before retiring back in 1985. He told us that he remembered that back when George Wallace first ran for President back in 1968, Will Morgan, in his capacity as mayor, had caused quite a controversy in town by writing a letter to the editor viciously attacking George Wallace—attacking him because he was a phony white supremacist. The letter raged that Wallace supported the rights of white people and white culture only because he was an opportunist, not because he really believed in what he said. The informant then went on to tell us what he recalled was in the letter as to the specific indictment of Wallace. The old man said many of the City's citizens had wanted Morgan removed from office, some for his attack on Wallace, some because the vicious racist views he openly espoused could dissuade businesses from locating in the Augusta area, particularly businesses with a national reach. There had actually been a vote in the City Council to mandate a recall. It was narrowly defeated.

As the story came tumbling out, I began thinking about how we could get hold of the edition of the newspaper containing that letter. I also started thinking of arguments to make to the judge to convince him that this 1968 event was relevant to the 1957 murder. I was trying to figure out how to approach this whole matter when the old man pulled a yellowed old newspaper from under his jacket and handed it to me. I was pleasantly surprised, and let the informant know it,

"Hey, you just saved us a huge investigator's bill. Is that the letter to the editor?"

The man shook his head from side to side. "No, no. I always hang around the newspaper. It's what I do with my time these days. I am kind of their mascot I reckon. Anyway, I went to the newspaper morgue to get the newspapers. I didn't know exactly when it was in, but I knew it had to have been within about a few months of the election primaries. Only problem was all of the newspapers containing that letter and the subsequent dirt it kicked up were missing... six days in a row of newspapers missing. It can't have been just a coincidence. I checked all of the newspapers for that year and no other newspapers were missing. Unfortunately, the newspaper could never afford to put any of their back issues on microfilm."

I held up the newspaper he had handed me.

"So what's this?"

"Oh, that's from the seventh day. Whoever cleaned out the files missed that little article on page 9 just talking briefly about how the newspaper found out that there was a secret ballot in the City Council to try to get a recall. That was the only piece left on the incident."

Lawyers are a cynical sort. When an unsolicited tip like this one comes in over the transom, you almost feel relieved if the person is looking for some kind of money or other reward. If not, you are left to wondering if this is not some type of set-up. Prosecutors are forever laying traps all over the terrain in the hopes that a defense lawyer or defendant will try to swipe the bait and end up getting himself snared in the trap. This old man had asked for nothing, and given us no reason for taking what he clearly saw as a risk to tip us off to this newspaper letter to the editor. He certainly didn't look like a champion of civil rights, and he certainly expressed no desire to expose Morgan as a bigot. Yet, I couldn't conceive how this could be a trap. Payton wasn't so sure. After the informant left, Payton read the little article on page 9.

"You know, Luke, this article just talks about the City Council vote on the recall. It doesn't talk about what precipitated the vote. We can challenge Morgan about whether he wrote such a letter with or without the letter—even if he denies it, the jury will assume it really happened—but if the judge determines we had no basis for this question, it could poison him against us for the whole trial. This evidence is not important enough to risk alienating a judge."

"Well, we should be able to show our good faith basis for the questions if we tell the judge we received the information from an informant who did not want to be identified, but we have to hold the line there. Even if we tell the judge it was someone who worked for the newspaper, it might expose him, but the information, that letter, could really rattle Morgan. He played himself off as just a camp follower, someone with only a desire to belong to a group with no real racist bones in his young body—this puts the lie to that."

"*If* it's true."

"What do you mean, Payton, *if* it's true?"

"We don't know if there ever really was such an article or such a controversy based on a letter to the editor. This could be a set-up. I could ask the question. Morgan could adamantly deny it, the judge could demand to see the letter to the editor, which we don't have and we don't have a witness who will say he read the letter. And the chances of finding anyone who remembers that letter from way back forty years ago is about nil. The jury could think we're just bastards trying to smear this poor guy."

"You know, now that you mention it, we could also get screwed by the collateral issue rule. You know, if the judge determines that this issue is collateral, he will not allow us to have a mini-trial on this issue, so we will be bound by Morgan's answer even if it's a complete lie. We couldn't disprove it even if we had the witnesses to disprove it."

We batted around the pros and cons of using the newspaper and decided Payton would just play it by ear. Our hopes were that if what the informant had told us was true, Morgan might feel compelled to admit he wrote such a letter if he saw we had an old copy of the *Augusta Gazette*. He might just think that this was a copy of the issue with his letter in it. Neither of us had any clue as to whether the judge would let us get into a 1968 incident at all.

The morning of the cross-examination, Payton and I were just about to leave the hotel room when I pulled a cheap little click pen from my pocket and threw it to Payton.

"Hey, I forgot to give you this."

Payton looked down at the 50-cent pen and said, "What is this piece of shit, an old bar mitzvah present?"

"Nope, that's my special clicker weapon. Whenever a witness is lying or exaggerating, there are always times when you can show there were other people present or other material that could document their assertion. Of course, you would have no time to check out their answers in the course of a trial, but they don't know that, and they're afraid of perjury. So I just click that old pen right in their face and demand to know the names of the people there, and then I press them for the addresses, and then I ask them for more names."

"It's amazing how witnesses 'forget' even the last names of their dearest friends when pressed. It really unhinges them and makes the jury realize what liars they are. Even professional experts can't beat the click—just last year, a plaintiff's expert had said on his direct testimony that he often testified for defendants in order to show how objective he was. I knew it was bullshit, so I clicked my pen and asked him to name for me the last five cases in the past two years in which he testified for a defendant. He couldn't name one. He finally he came up with one name; it was a four-year-old case that didn't even go to trial. I knew if I had asked him to name one, I could have gotten screwed, but I knew there was no way he could name five. That click unnerves them every time."

"What if they give you names, all the names you ask for?"

"No problem, I just write down the names and continue on. But it never happens. You only click them when you know they're lying, and they never have the balls to give you the phony names."

CHAPTER 26

Morgan walked up to the stand, sat down, turned and warmly greeted the judge, and then nodded toward the jury and said, "Good morning," a greeting they returned in unison. He then leaned back in the chair and smiled at Payton, who had just reached the podium and placed a stack of papers and documents beneath the top of the podium. The judge turned to Payton.

"You may begin, Mr. Simkins."

Now this was the point at which an attorney usually graciously introduces himself to the witness and explains to the witness if he does not understand a question to just ask to have it repeated and blah, blah, blah. But not Payton, He sprang from behind the podium, placed himself in front of the podium, glared angrily at Morgan and then reached back and grabbed my click pen from atop the podium. I felt a chill go down my spine as I thought,

"Oh, my gosh, Payton is going to click him right off the bat."

Payton's voice came out strong, nasty and insistent, but not loud. I could see the jurors suddenly whip forward in their chairs, surprised and delighted by the sudden attack right out of the box. To jurors, cross-examination is a blood sport, and unless they really like a witness, the bloodier the better.

Payton snapped off his first question,

"Mr. Morgan, give me the names of everyone you told about the Boddie murder within a year after it happened!"

I could see Morgan recoil in surprise at the unexpected sudden attack, and a question that had been wrenched totally out of any chronological order. Now he leaned forward in the witness chair clutching the underside of the front rail with his fingers. He voice was practically stuttering,

"Well, I guess, I wish I had told some law enforcement people, but I was too scared...."

Payton didn't let him finish, and his voice became angrier, louder and filled with more disdain, "Mr. Morgan, I didn't ask you for the names of the people you didn't tell!"

Payton paused, reached back and pulled out a little pad. He walked towards the witness chair and clicked the pen right in Morgan's face. Rabison leaped to his feet.

"You honor, could you instruct Mr. Simkins to back off the witness."

Payton turned to the judge. "I just wanted to make sure that I received all of the names exactly right when he gave them to me, but I'll back up."

Payton backed up but kept facing Morgan, who looked absolutely stricken. The jurors were sitting on the edge of their chairs, mouths agape. This sure wasn't like the sweet, plodding love-fest of Morgan's direct examination. They were seeing a different man: the drama that Payton had created by itself seemed to contradict the picture that Rabison had painted of Morgan.

"Okay, Mr. Morgan, I am ready to write, give the names of the people you told about this."

"Well, it was so long ago...."

"Oh please, Mr. Morgan, I take it witnessing a murder did not take place every day for you."

"Of course not..."

"You are not trying to tell this jury that you confided in no one?"

"Well, I told Billy Johnson..."

(click) "Give me his address, where he lives now...."

"He died of a heart attack five years ago."

"Who was your best friend back in those days?"

The questions were being fired at Morgan so fast that he barely could catch his breath between answers, and he certainly didn't have time to figure out where all of this was going.

"Ah, ah, Tom Billings...."

"Good, give me his address and phone number."

"I didn't tell him about the murder. You see..."

"Who was Billy Johnson?"

"Just someone I knew from work."

"A good friend?"

"No, more of an acquaintance."

"So, you confided in an acquaintance but not in your best friend?"

"Well, I didn't want to involve Bill...."

"The other Klan members must have demanded to know what happened. Did they?"

I could see that Morgan was desperately trying to outthink Payton on the fly. He was trying to give answers that were credible without backing himself into a trap. I could see things were sliding out of his control... He knew now he had to avoid giving an answer that would require him to give names.

"I don't think so."

Payton stopped and glared at Morgan like he wanted to step up and rip his heart out. Payton then turned to the jury and pointed to them. Now he spoke slowly and deliberately, but sternly,

"Now, Mr. Morgan, are you telling this jury that you take part, at least as a witness, in a Klan-ordered killing, and they don't even ask you what happened..."

"I'm not saying they didn't. I just don't remember."

"Well how about you? Who did you confront about this?"

"Who did I confront? I don't understand."

"On your direct examination, when Mr. Rabison was asking you the questions, you testified you didn't know that Mr. Boddie would be killed and that you didn't want Mr. Boddie to be killed. Do you remember saying that?

"Yes."

"What I'm asking you now is: Did you demand to know from the Klan people if they ordered the murder?"

"I don't think they ordered it. I think T.C. did it on his own."

Payton rocked back in faked disbelief.

"T.C. did it on his own? Well, I am sure that you reported his reprehensible conduct to the Klan."

Morgan's eyes were almost glazed over now at the pace and ferocity of the questioning, "Yeah, yeah, of course I told them what he had done...."

Now Payton's voice became sarcastic, "Oh, and Mr. Morgan, were they shocked that a white human being would do such a despicable thing to a black fellow human being?"

"I don't remember what their reactions were. I was too scared."

Payton took a step towards Morgan and gave him another facial with the click, "Okay, give me the names of the Klansmen you told about what T.C. had done."

Morgan looked up to the ceiling as if trying to recall, "Well, there was John Simons and Tim Bellows."

"And their addresses and phone numbers are?"

"They've both passed away."

Payton turned purposely to the jury and smiled at them, letting them know what he thought of the answer. "Now, Mr. Morgan, all of these people you told your story to, all seem to have died. Do you think your secret put some kind of a curse on them?"

Rabison sprang to his feet but not before the jury's laughter enveloped the courtroom,

"Objection, and will you instruct Mr. Simkins to slow down with his questions?"

Payton snarled back, "If you're having trouble keeping up, just tap me on the shoulder, Mr. Rabison."

The judge's voice boomed out, "Alright, calm down both of you. Mr. Simkins, you may proceed at whatever speed you like, and Mr, Morgan, if you need for him to slow up, just say so."

Payton paced back and forth in front of the podium for a few seconds, and then he spun to face Morgan, "Mr. Morgan, from the time of the murder until today are there any people you told about what you testified to on your direct testimony, who are still living today?"

"I just don't... you have my mind so jumbled up. You know it's not something I am proud of."

"Why not? You said you put your life on the line to save the life of a poor black man way back in those sorry racist days. Why aren't you proud?"

"I mean I'm not proud about being in the Klan."

Payton spit out his words hard, "I didn't ask you if you told anyone about being in the Klan. I am asking you if you told anyone about your heroic effort to save the life of Aaron Boddie?"

"I don't know who I told what at this point."

One key to cross-examination is to break chronology of all the time so that the witness cannot get a linear thought process going. The jury may lose track of where everything is going but you can pull it together for them in the summation. What the jury will see is a witness and a story unraveling. Payton switched gears without so much as catching his breath.

"Now, Mr. Morgan, do you remember testifying on direct that you joined the Klan not out of ideology, but because it was the thing to do for a young person in Georgia back in 1957?"

"Well, yes, I said that because it was true. I don't want anyone to take it the wrong way, but you have to understand back then, in those times, for a young man joining the Klan was like you would join the Boy Scouts today."

I could see Payton flinch at this surprising answer. I knew he would pounce at this unexpected opportunity. "Like the Boy Scouts?!"

"Well, I knew you would try to twist what I said."

"No, no, I won't twist anything. Was it like the Boy Scouts in the sense that both organizations taught you how to tie knots in ropes?"

"Objection!"

The judge's voice was more annoyed than angry, "Why

don't you move on to another topic, Mr. Simkins."

"Okay, your Honor, I had planned to ask him if he received a merit badge for murdering Mr. Boddie, but I'll move on."

"Objection and move to strike."

The judge turned to the jurors,

"Disregard that last statement from Mr. Simkins. I know he won't engage in such improper conduct in the future. Now continue."

"Would it be fair to characterize your relationship with the Klan in 1957 as 'go along to get along?'"

"Well, I think you finally said something we could agree on."

"Mr. Morgan, could you tell the jury what a Kleagle was back in 1957?"

"A silly name."

"Well, tell us what that silly name meant in the Klan."

"Well, the Kleagle, he was sort of the recruiter in the Klan."

"It was a pretty exalted position wasn't it? Yes or no?"

"It was a stupid name for a stupid position. The whole thing was stupid."

"Did you tell your fellow Klan members you thought it was a silly position when they made you Kleagle back in 1957?"

"Objection, argumentative!"

"I'll allow it. Mr. Morgan, answer Mr. Simkins' question."

Morgan just put his face in his hands and shook his head in frustration, "I don't know what you want me to say. I was made Kleagle when Lucius Cantrell stepped aside. I am ashamed of what I did back in those days."

"What was that name? Lucius Cantrell? Is he dead too?"

"I don't know, I'm not even sure that was his name, I've already told you I was ashamed of what I did in those days."

"One minute, Mr. Morgan. Back in those days you would have been ashamed to have tried to save a black man's life like you claimed you did, isn't that true?"

Morgan became angry rather than scared for the first time,

"Well, I did try to save him, whether you believe me or not. Your client over there is the one who insisted on killing him."

Payton walked over to T.C. and put a gentle hand on his shoulder, "Was T.C. a Kleagle?"

"No."

"Was he the Grand Cyclops or the Grand Wizard or was he even a Nighthawk?"

There was a scattering of laughter in the courtroom at the roster of titles.

"No, he was just a member, that's all."

"Are you telling the jury that in a quasi-military organization like the Klan some poor little piece of white trash could order a Kleagle around?"

"Objection as to form."

"Sustained. Reword your question, Mr. Simkins, and leave out any reference to white trash or anything about the military nature of the Klan, there's been no testimony about that."

"Okay, Your Honor. Mr. Morgan, in the Klan or the Klavern you were in, could a regular member tell a Kleagle what to do?"

"To do about what?"

"About murdering someone."

"I told you T.C. insisted on it."

"And you tried to stop it?"

"Yes, and I wish I had succeeded."

"Did you report this insubordination of T.C. to the Klan?"

I saw that Payton glanced up at the clock. He knew that the judge always took a break at precisely 11:30 A.M. I knew Payton wanted to spring at least one more trap on Morgan before he could regroup at the first break.

"I'll withdraw that question. Now, Mr. Morgan, you stated on direct examination that you never would consider yourself a white supremacist at any time, that you had prejudices against blacks but you didn't like to mix in politics, is that right?"

"Well, I just didn't think about it all day. I didn't hate black people. I am ashamed to say I believed in segregation, for the good of both races I might add, but, no, I never was what you would consider a white supremacist like that was all I thought about day or night."

"But you knew the Klan was a white supremacist group?"

"Yes, and I told you that it was stupid of me to have joined the Klan, and I never really believed in their hate."

Payton and I had prayed that Morgan would attempt to minimize if not deny his role in the Klan. Had he straight up admitted his odious views of that time, we would have been in a tough situation. But it is part of human nature to minimize and rationalize past mistakes. Moreover, for Morgan, a man in his position, a pillar of community, it would have been social even more than political suicide to admit to such a horrific past. We knew once he tried to back away from the Klan, the facts and common sense would rise up to trip him every time.

"How about ten years after the murder, were you a white supremacist then?"

"No, I was in my second term as mayor then; I was more mature. I had long been out of the Klan by then."

"Yes, you had graduated to the White Citizens' Council by then, right?"

Morgan snapped back, "The Council was not the Klan!"

Payton bowed towards Morgan, "I apologize. The White Citizens' Council was made up of businessmen, pillars of the community, wasn't it?"

"It was good people. We just didn't like our states' rights being taken away from us."

"And the Klan was filled with just stupid, poor ignorant white trash folks, right?"

"Objection."

"Sustained!"

"Well, isn't it a fact, that contrary to myth, many pillars of the community were in the Klan, weren't they?"

"What do you mean, 'pillars of the community?'"

Payton reached inside the podium and pulled out a list he had.

"Well, let's see, in 1957 Sheriff Natt was in the Klan, right?"

Morgan looked agitated, his eyes searched the packed courtroom—he was looking for his longtime friend and assistant, Corine Pastore, not for answers but seemingly for comfort.

"Look, I don't want to drag these people through the mud for something they might have done forty years ago. I don't see the relevance of this."

"Well, Mr. Morgan, don't you think that who was in the Klan at the time of the Boddie murder is as relevant as the fact that in 1995 you established a scholarship at Georgia State for a black student each year from Augusta—as you felt the need to tell the jury during your direct testimony?"

The judge did not even wait for an objection, "Jurors, disregard that statement. Mr. Simkins, I don't want to warn you again, .you are starting to skate on thin ice."

"Your Honor, I have a right to ask him if he thought..."

"Mr. Simkins, you have a right to ask him what I say you can ask him. Now ask your next question."

"Yes, your Honor."

Payton reached into the podium and pulled out the yellowed newspaper that the informant had given us. He plopped it down on the table next to the podium in full sight of Morgan. Morgan leaned forward in his chair to try to determine what the yellowed document was, and what could possibly be coming next. I held my breath because I didn't know if Morgan would buy into the bluff and assume that we had a copy of his letter to the editor.

"Mr. Morgan, do you remember writing a letter to the editor of the *Augusta Gazette* in June of 1968 regarding the candidacy of George Wallace?"

Rabison shot up to his feet like a rocket, "Objection. This is totally irrelevant! 1968!"

"Your Honor, this relates to that open door we discussed in your chambers. I'm just walking through it!"

"I demand a side bar, your Honor, and an offer of proof!"

The judge became angry. "You will demand nothing, Mr. Rabison. You will request of me. But I will allow Mr. Simkins to proceed. But remember, Mr. Simkins, just because the door is open, it doesn't mean you can bring any irrelevant junk through it that you wish—now proceed."

Payton pointed to newspaper as he talked, "Mr. Morgan, you wrote a letter to the editor of the *Augusta Gazette* about George Wallace in 1968, didn't you?"

"Oh my Lord, how am I going to remember a letter I wrote back in 1968?"

Payton picked up the newspaper and scanned it as if reading it, "Well, Mr. Morgan this letter ended up causing quite a flap in the City Council, didn't it?"

Morgan turned to the judge, "Your Honor, this is ridiculous, that letter has nothing to do with this trial."

The judge leaned towards Morgan, "I will decide what is relevant for this trial, Mr. Morgan. Now I let you testify at length on your direct examination about how little you had to do with any racial politics back then, and I'm going to allow..."

"But, Judge, this was 1968, it had nothing to do with Aaron Boddie."

The judge flared with anger. "Mr. Morgan, don't you ever interrupt me again. Now, I'm going to let him proceed a bit longer with this line of questioning. I know you jurors understand that what Mr. Morgan did and felt in 1968 has a marginal relation to murder in question, but in view of what Mr. Morgan testified about on Tuesday, I am letting it in on the issue of credibility and, perhaps, bias. So continue, Mr. Simkins."

"I believe a question was on the table, your answer..."

The judge turned to Morgan, "Do you remember what that

letter was about?"

Morgan shook his head, obviously irritated. "Pretty much, it was a big to-do about nothing. It was about the George Wallace Presidential campaign."

Payton jumped in fast to retake control of questioning, "In fact, you were telling people not to vote for George Wallace, isn't that true!"

I looked over at the jurors, several of them turned to each other with quizzical looks. Why would Payton bring out the fact that Morgan opposed Wallace in 1968? That elicitation seemed to be swimming upstream against the current we were trying to ride.

"Yes, that's what I did."

Payton let a few very pregnant seconds pass to add to the drama and suspense.

"And was that because you disapproved of Wallace's racist policies?"

Morgan gestured to the newspaper, "You know darn well that wasn't why I wrote that stupid letter."

Payton picked up the newspaper in his hand. "Why don't you tell the jury why you wrote that letter?"

"Sure, I wrote the letter because I was uninformed and somewhat naive in those days."

"Well, you were not some young kid. You were the Mayor then as you are today, correct?"

"Yes."

"And on the White Citizens' Council, is that correct?"

"Yes."

I had to suppress a laugh because I could see juror number two mouth silently to juror number three in exasperation, "What did it say?" But Payton knew how to prep the area so that the bomb would do more damage when it fell.

"And that letter caused the City Council to consider a recall vote, isn't that correct?"

Rabison didn't know what was in that letter, but he knew he

didn't want the jury to find out. "Objection, this is going so far afield. May I have a side bar?"

The judge frowned: "No, sit down, Mr. Rabison. I'll give you a few more questions along this line, Mr. Simkins. It is getting awfully attenuated."

Now Payton moved in front of the podium again, signaling to the jury to be alert because he was about to lower the boom.

"Isn't it a fact, Mr. Morgan, that you didn't want people to vote for Wallace because you thought he was insufficiently racist?"

"Objection!"

"Overruled. Answer the question, Mr. Morgan."

Morgan was disappointed that the judge did not rescue him from the questions he knew would follow. He seemed to peruse the courtroom, looking for some sort of salvation, again resting his eyes on his chief of staff Corine Pastore. Finally, he just shook his head in exasperation, "I wouldn't characterize it like that. I just thought Wallace was a phony..."

"A phony racist, isn't that right?"

"No, that isn't right."

Payton strolled over to the newspaper, opened it up, ran his finger along it as if reading the letter, put it down and said, "Would it be fair to say that in this letter you pointed out that before he became Governor when Mr. Wallace was a county judge he was the only judge in Alabama who addressed black attorneys and black parties as "mister" rather than "boy" or by their first name?"

"Well, I..."

"Yes or no?"

Morgan turned to the judge, "Can I explain, your Honor?"

The judge shook his head, "You can explain when your lawyer asks you questions on redirect."

I knew there would be no redirect questions. Rabison was too good a lawyer to prolong the agony. Redirect would invite re-cross, and there was no guarantee that the blind, unplanned re-direct would bring forth the answers the prosecution wanted. Witnesses like Morgan were like loose cannons when they were without a script.

"Well, Mr. Morgan, did you not criticize Wallace for addressing black attorneys as 'mister?'"

"You're taking it out of context. I said he was an opportunist."

"And not a genuine racist!"

"I didn't think he really believed in anything."

"But this letter complains that he cannot be trusted to uphold the white race, didn't it?"

"Well, you've got it there. I don't remember exactly what it said, but if you say so..."

"Mr. Morgan, I am not asking you what I have in this newspaper. I am asking you if your letter stated, if not in exact words, that George Wallace could not be trusted to uphold white supremacy and now that he was running a national campaign, he would sell out the white race so he could get northern votes?"

"Well, I told you I don't remember those exact words."

"But that was gist of it, wasn't it?"

"Yes, sort of, yes, I guess it was, but now you tell me what that has got to do with this case."

"Don't you think, Mr. Morgan, that someone with those views might actually murder a person just because his skin is black and he was perceived to have offended the white race by having relations with a white woman?"

Morgan jumped to his feet for the first time, "I didn't kill him. Your damn client did, and he knows it!"

As the court marshal ran towards Morgan, the judge stood up,

"I think this would be a good time to take a break."

Payton strode forward a step. "Judge, can I ask one more question?"

"Mr. Simkins, I know the most unreliable words in the world are when a lawyer asks for just one more question. But I will hold you to it."

Payton fixed Morgan, who was still standing, with a laser stare and said, "As you stand there today, Mr. Morgan, in this courtroom, it bothers you, doesn't it, to hear the judge refer to me as 'Mister' Simkins?"

The judge waived his arms. "Don't even answer that! I knew I should have never let you have your question Mr. Simkins. Next time you pull something like that, I will hold you in contempt."

I was upset with Payton for letting his bile overwhelm his guile. Sometimes it makes sense to snap off a statement or question that will upset the judge just to get it before the jury or to rattle a witness. But this was unnecessary, and we certainly did not need to alienate a judge who could abruptly narrow the wide playing field he had allowed us to roam so far. This was precisely the type of thing I was concerned about with Payton.

We walked off the break together. I knew now was not the time for negative comments. Besides, I knew on the whole he had done a great job. Morgan was definitely badly shaken, and he certainly didn't look like a saintly human being on the verge of beatification as he had during his direct testimony.

Payton spent the entire afternoon and the next day cross-examining Morgan. He shredded him on every topic he explored. The only problem was that Payton did not spend what I considered sufficient time taking apart Morgan's day-of-the murder story. That story had so many holes in it, a fleet of trucks would have had no trouble in navigating it. Payton and I had reviewed at least fifty areas where that story would not hold up. Yet, Payton spent only about twenty minutes reviewing the murder story and about three hours showing that the White Citizens' Council did more to enforce white supremacy and harass and hunt down civil rights advocates than did the more reviled Klan.

Payton made good progress in tearing Morgan apart on this

Council issue because, unlike with the Klan, Morgan felt a current need to defend the myth of the White Citizens' Council as some states' rights organization. He had to defend the Council. Its members were still running much of the South. Many still were truly the pillars of the community. And when Morgan claimed no one could have stood up to racism in those days, Payton pulled out a list of courageous black and white Southerners who had stood up to racism and read them to Morgan to acknowledge.

As I said, my concern with Payton's cross-examination was that it did a better job of unmasking the myth of the "good cause" white south than of unmasking the falsity of Morgan's murder story. But, of course, I knew Payton had been out for much bigger game than merely springing T.C. He wanted to bring down Morgan and his ilk more than he wanted to free T.C. Simmons. I wondered if I had made a mistake in keeping Payton on the case after I realized that he had an agenda that might require the sacrifice of T.C. Simmons. But, yet, Payton was such a skillful slash and burn cross-examiner that destroying Morgan might have been enough without having to destroy his murder story directly. The cross examination drew to a close at the very end of the trial day.

CHAPTER 27

Payton and Morgan had just finished another one of their running battles. The judge's patience was wearing thin, Morgan looked like he was ready to pass out, and I was soaked with sweat. But Payton, fueled by the inexhaustible power of a righteous cause, looked fresh as a daisy. The judge pointed up to the clock,

"Bring it to a close, Mr. Simkins. I have given you more than enough time, and probably way too much latitude. So wrap it up."

Payton started to reach for some more papers on the desk, but then withdrew his hand. I could see the judge give a sigh of relief. He knew every time Payton grabbed a document, it meant he was going to approach the witness, and the judge knew once he got there, he would be shouting in Morgan's face again. The judge had thought of making Payton give the papers to the court officer to bring to the witness, but that was not how the judge had run his courtroom, and he probably didn't think it fair to single out one side for that special treatment. So he just backed Payton off as quickly as possible.

The judge seemed relieved because it was apparent that this protracted cross examination was about to conclude. Payton rocked back and forth on the heels, and then, talking uncharacteristically softly, said: "Mr. Morgan, when you testified on direct, you said, it was important that your actions be judged in the context of the times, is that correct?"

"Yes, that's correct."

Payton rocked again, paused and this time his voice was a little louder,

"And in those times, in places in the South, a lot of people would take great offense to a black person talking to a white person, particularly a white person of a high station, the way I have talked to you today, isn't that so?"

"Not all, but...yes, some would I imagine."

"Well, you would have back in 1957, wouldn't you?"

"Yes, I...many of us were foolish back then, yes. I really guess I would be more surprised than angry. It just wasn't done in those times."

"In fact, back in those times, to get things in context like you said we needed to do, a black person like me could have gotten himself lynched for talking to a white person like you the way I did today, isn't that true?"

Morgan thought for a moment and then replied, "Well, I don't know if you'd have been lynched."

"Well, black folks did get lynched for being what white folks thought was too uppity to them back then, isn't that true?"

"Well, I don't think it happened as often as people seem to think it did, but yes it did happen."

"It happened to Emmet Till, didn't it, you know, the teen-age boy from up north who was lynched for sassing a white woman in Mississippi when he was visiting his cousin?"

Rabison started to object, but thought an objection at this time would bring emphasis to a line of questioning which made him as well as the witness very uncomfortable.

"Yes, I remember something like that. Well, okay, I told you it happened some times, just not that often."

Payton closed the gap between himself and Morgan, stopping about ten feet away. The judge and Rabison both started to say something but I guess the late hour, an exhausting day, and the promise of finally having a finish to all of this, glued them to their seats. Neither said anything.

"Now, Mr. Morgan, several times here today, you became very angry at me, enraged by the way I treated you, isn't that true?"

"Well, yes, you were trying to smear me and..."

All of a sudden Payton exploded and screamed at Morgan,

"And isn't it a fact that you sat there thinking that you wished you could lynch that uppity nigger Simkins just like you lynched poor Aaron Boddie?"

Rabison, from a seated position, started to cry out, but the judge's stentorian bellow drowned him out, "Okay, that's enough! Strike that last question! In fact, I'd like to strike that last questioner. No more questions...Thank you, Mr. Simkins! Any re-direct, Mr. Rabison?!"

Rabison rose to his feet, "Your honor I would like to address that outrageous outburst by Mr. Simkins."

The judge became even more insistent, "Any re-direct Mr. Rabison?!"

"No, your honor."

The judge turned to Morgan and said, "You are excused Mr. Morgan."

Morgan looked up at the judge, "Do I have to come back tomorrow, judge?"

The judge blanched. "Great goodness, Mr. Morgan, you want to come back tomorrow? Perhaps I could arrange for Mr. Simkins to burn some lit cigarettes into your back."

The courtroom erupted into laughter.

The jurors filed out. The spectators and media filed out. And as the lawyers filed out of the almost empty courtroom, the judge called out, "Mr. Simkins, I have to give you this much. You are consistent. You rode out on the same horse you rode in on."

I felt totally spent, and I hadn't asked one question. I felt pretty good about things. Payton had destroyed Morgan, but I was afraid Payton had also caused some needless self-inflicted wounds on our own case by being too carried away by his personal vendetta. I was concerned that some jurors might have even felt a bit sorry for Morgan after a while. From a legal standpoint, I was convinced that Morgan's general credibility was destroyed, but I still wished that Payton had at least made a pass or two at the murder story. With some witnesses, you need not shred the principal story to destroy the effectiveness of a witness. Indeed, it is often better to leave the principal, and usually well-rehearsed, story alone and go after the witness' credibility on other issues, hoping that the lack of credibility on those issues would bleed over into the principal issues. But with Morgan, you couldn't avoid dealing with the murder story, and I didn't think Payton dealt with it enough. But he sure took care of Morgan and his ilk.

CHAPTER 28

I was furious that the media was so supportive of Morgan during his testimony and after he testified. It occurred to me that the reporters must have been at a different trial than the one I was attending. It seemed the reporters heard what they wanted to hear. To them Morgan was an embodiment of the New South, and they didn't want to hear anything that would dispel or disparage that image.

Payton took Morgan apart cut by cut—unfortunately, the media views a death by a thousand cuts as no death at all. If they don't see a decapitation, they think the witness has survived unscathed. Even the sophisticated *New York Times* was sucked in. Its article said something about the best of the New South ripping off the scab protecting the worst of the Old South. The author of the article wrote that one need only glance from the slouching, steely-eyed defendant to the emotionally trammeled, courageous Morgan on the witness stand to see the great progress that the South had made in race relations. It was sickening.

But the press would not determine the outcome of the trial—it was going to be up to the jury. That had to be our concern as the trial continued. It continued the next afternoon which was to be far less successful for our side than the euphoric experience of Morgan's cross-examination.

The court rules require opposing counsel to submit "witness" lists to one another. In this way neither side could claim surprise and seek additional time for preparation. The one name on the District Attorney's list that was a puzzlement and caused me some concern was that of Bummy Thornton. I asked Payton and T.C., "Who the hell is Bummy Thornton?"

Neither knew, so I assumed that he must be the "mystery witness" that the press kept talking about. The press had report-

215

ed that a secret witness was being kept in protective custody. *Protective custody*—as if T.C. were so connected that he could order a death from prison with the snap of a finger. They knew no witness, mystery or otherwise, was in any danger from anyone. Putting someone in protective custody and then leaking that fact to the press only underlined the danger and guilt of T.C.—which is precisely why Rabison put that mystery witness in protective custody.

I quizzed T.C. again and again about who this Bummy Thornton could be. He told me that as hard as he tried, that name just did not ring a bell. Payton again retained his favorite investigator, Jim Cory. Cory and I had met when he protected our backs in the meeting with the ancient former reporter from the *Augusta Gazette*. Now Cory set himself to the task of scouring records and interviewing half the citizens of Augusta to find out who Bummy Thornton was. He came up empty. Who could this Thornton be and what would he testify to?

Payton was certain Bummy Thornton would turn out to be someone who was in prison with T.C. either two decades ago or perhaps in some drunk tank more recently. Jailhouse snitches know they can work off some pretty serious time by ratting to the government on admissions that "important" defendants did—or, often, did not—make. T.C. need not even have met this guy. If he was in prison at the same time as T.C., Rabison would have the handle of a cudgel which could be used to beat our case senseless.

CHAPTER 29

"The People call Bummy Thornton to the witness stand."

I glanced at my watch. It was 3:00 P.M. on Friday. That was good in that we would have the weekend to do whatever investigation we needed before starting Monday's cross-examination. The downside of late Friday evidence was that if this testimony was devastating, it would simmer in the jurors' minds all weekend. By Monday, it might have come to such a boil that no amount of cross-examination would be able to cool it off in the minds of the jurors.

I was sitting next to Payton who was, in turn, sitting next to T.C. As the stooped old black man made his way to the witness stand, I whispered to Payton to ask T.C. if he recognized the man. T.C. said he never saw the man before in his life.

Rabison began in slow measured tones knowing that he was about to unleash a bombshell, "Now, Mr. Thornton, did you know an Aaron Boddie?"

"Yes, sir, he was my half brother, we had the same Momma."

"And were you with your brother late in the afternoon on Friday afternoon the 21st of June, 1957?"

"Yes, sir, I was, until he got killed by that man over there."

The finger he pointed at T.C. went right through my heart. I could tell from the look and demeanor of this witness that he was going to be hard to undermine, no matter what his testimony. And his testimony was devastating.

Bummy Thornton testified that he had heard that some white folks had picked up his brother Aaron Boddie claiming that he had "messed with a white woman." He was told that Aaron was tied up in the old pump house down by the river, so he went to see if he could set him free. He told of walking for miles until he saw the pump house and was about to run to the door when he heard a truck pull up. He quickly hid in the bushes. He saw T.C. and two other men, one of whom fit the description of Carl Talbot, get out of the pick-up truck. From his hiding place he watched as two of the men dragged Aaron out of the pump house and into a skiff.

He would have tried to do something, but there were three of them and besides one of them was toting a shotgun. He could not hear everything they said, but they were yelling something about Aaron raping some white woman.

Bummy testified that he followed the two men at a distance and tracked behind them in the swamp, "sometimes chest high in muck," as they guided the skiff into a stand of mangrove trees. He described how he saw T.C. kicking Aaron while Aaron lay chained and helpless in the boat. He saw T.C. pour gasoline onto Aaron and then he saw him burst into flames and heard the worst screams he ever heard in his life.

At that point, there had to a be a break in the case because Bummy couldn't go on. As he was being helped off the witness stand, he suddenly turned to T.C. and said, with almost eerie calm, "Why you do that to Aaron? He never hurt nobody." I was up on my feet objecting as soon as I could react, but I knew my objection was meaningless. The bell could not be unrung. The Judge told the Jury "to disregard the witness's statement made to the Defendant."

I knew that the Judge's admonition to disregard the testimony would be as effective as giving a five-year-old a pea and telling him not to put it in his ear. Whatever reluctance the child might have had to putting that pea in his ear would immediately vanish as would the pea. The surest way to arrest the drifting minds of jurors is to have the Judge tell them: "Jurors, disregard that last statement." You can be sure that will be the one statement that the jury will pay special attention to. That is precisely why some wily trial lawyers ask questions calculated to elicit answers they know will be disallowed and why witnesses seem so often to "spontaneously" blurt out testimony that the court will be bound to strike and instruct the jurors to disregard. Futile attempts to unring bells of this sort have brought down many a case.

When Bummy came back to the stand, he went on with his testimony, getting more emotional as he continued. His emotion was a controlled emotion, dramatic because of how calmly and without rancor it was delivered. He seemed more confused than angry. He could not understand why anyone would kick and beat and then burn another human being for no reason. 'Cause I knew Aaron Boddie was a good, God-fearing man who would never hurt anyone, no less a woman."

I glanced at the jurors. Several sobbed openly and others tried to remain detached but they betrayed a pain born of the compelling testimony they were hearing. It was the third day of the trial, and I already knew that the clammy hand of defeat was taking hold of my case.

"Now, Mr. Thornton, do you recognize that person sitting in the back row? The man over there in the green shirt?"

I was taken aback. I had not seen Will Morgan in the courtroom.

I rose quickly to me feet, "Objection, your Honor, he is a witness in this case and should not be in the courtroom."

"Counselor, he was a witness."

"But what if I choose to call him?"

"Overruled, I'll allow the question."

"You may answer the question," said the prosecutor, and Bummy Thornton studied Morgan's face for awhile.

"Can he come up to here closer?"

The judge nodded to Morgan and he approached the witness until he stood just three feet in front of Thornton.

"Oh yes, I sure do, 'cept he looked much younger and he didn't have gray hair back then." Bummy said this with his first smile of the day.

"Have you seen this man recently??

"No, sir, I ain't seen him since the day they killed my brother. I got out of town fast after that and swore I'd never come back 'cause I figured if they knowed what I seed they were sure gonna come after me. I didn't come back to Augusta until ten years passed."

"Well, when did you last see this man?"

"I seed him when he tried to save my brother's life—must be goin' on forty years."

The judge spoke, "Counselor please have the gentleman return to his seat..."

Bummy turned to the judge, "Judge before he go, can I get down from my chair and shake his hand. That man was sent by God—he tried to save my brother's life. He put his own self in harm's way tryin' to save my brother."

"No, no just continue with your testimony."

"But judge, I ain't never got the chance before to thank him."

Rabison suppressed a smile, grateful for this unexpected testimonial bonus. "I have no other questions, your honor; however, I reserve the right to recall this witness."

"Thank you Mr. Thornton, you may step down," the judge said. "But please remain available in the event you're needed. We're going to recess for the weekend."

I leaned over to Payton and told him to get the investigation going. As he turned to me, I noticed that his eyes were moist. I passed him a note that said, "I think T.C.'s fucked." He passed me back a note that said: "Yes, but he fucked us first."

Payton knew what I knew. Bummy Thornton's testimony had the ring of truth. Juries often cannot accurately discern what is dramatic true from what is dramatic false. Lawyers know the difference. That man's testimony was true. I knew it. Payton knew it. And we feared the jury would know it.

I felt like the world had crashed in on me. All of that work. I had put my guts in this case, and it was all for nothing. I had been taken in, big-time. I was going to be a national laughingstock. At that very moment the talking heads were probably practicing their attacks on the Morton and Philips dupe who had been sucked in by a rednecked Klansman.

As the court officers led T.C. to the holding cell off the courtroom, I had to fight my impulse to just turn around and leave the courtroom and get the next plane home. But, finally, reluctantly, I walked over to the cell.

T.C. was sitting in a chair as far as possible from the door where the court officer sat guard. "Well, T.C., you fuckin' lied to me from A to Z."

T.C. looked startled, "You didn't believe him did you?"

"Yes I did believe him. And so did Payton. And so did the Judge. And so did the jurors. And so did anyone who heard him who doesn't happen to be brain dead."

"He was lying... I swear..."

I wanted to pounce on T.C. and beat him senseless.

"I know a liar when I see and hear one. At least I thought I knew liars until I met you. I gotta hand it to you, you sonofabitch, you're good."

T.C. didn't even argue with me. He seemed resigned to the fact that he had finally been exposed. There were just too many details of Bummy's testimony that rang true, things about which he could not have known without being there. But more than that, his testimony was clearly unrehearsed which added to its believability.

I knew my obligation as a lawyer. When I worked as a criminal defense attorney before going to Morton and Philips, I often attempted to tear to pieces a witness whose testimony I knew to be true. The adversary system requires it; the right to counsel demands it. But I didn't see how I could hurt this witness on cross examination even if I wanted to—and I didn't want to.

That night Payton and I went out drinking for the first time. We sat in a local bar watching ourselves on the local news as reporters asked us what we could do to undo the harm caused by Mr. Thornton. Payton just glared at the microphone and snapped, "Just wait until Monday!" And now we were in some seedy out-of-the-way bar with Payton raising his glass and saying, "To Monday!" I raised my glass, "To Monday!"

I couldn't sleep that night. I had experienced failure and shame and even defeat in my life, but never betrayal. I had believed in T.C.—I believed in him so deeply and passionately. I didn't want to return to court on Monday.

CHAPTER 30

I didn't know whether it was sheer exhaustion or the disappointment of the day before, but I found it difficult to get out of bed that Saturday morning. If it weren't for the insistent ringing of the phone, I would probably have slept through the weekend.

"Hello," I answered through a sleepy haze.

"Good morning, my dear friend."

I recognized Payton's voice, more cheerful than it should have been.

"What have you got to be so cheery about?" I asked.

"I'm down here with Cory—and we got something big to drop on you. I'm coming up with donuts, coffee, and news that will blow your socks off."

I knew it was going to be good news, Payton's buoyancy tipped me off to that. But what the hell could it be? I started imagining all kinds of positive scenarios, but none could have matched the one which Payton delivered to my hotel room as he spread an assortment of donuts and three containers of coffee on the small table.

He and Cory sat down—both smiling.

"Well?" I said, finding the anticipation difficult to deal with.

They both started to speak at once, but Payton deferred to Cory, who began his narrative:

"You know, a lot of so-called investigators are no more than computer nerds. They take an assignment, go on the Internet, and get a lot of information that anyone could get if they had a computer, subscribed to America Online, and had a little patience. Then there are the other, old fashioned, gum shoe types like me."

I showed my impatience: "Get to the point, Cory."

Cory ignored me and continued, "Anyway, it's not only patience that's required of a good investigator, it's also intuition.

Now when I saw that fellow Thornton on the stand, I was struck by something very strange."

I couldn't imagine what he saw that escaped both me, an experienced trial lawyer, and Payton, a savvy and intuitive guy.

Cory continued, "Remember when he was asked if he remembered Will Morgan? He asked if he could get a closer look at him. And then he said he hadn't seen him since the day of the lynching. Now by his own testimony he moved back to Augusta ten years after the crime—that means he's been living here for the last thirty years."

How could I have missed that? Will Morgan was no ordinary citizen. He was the Mayor for God's sake. He was Augusta's leading citizen, admired by blacks as well as whites. How could Bummy not be familiar with his face? And that bullshit about asking the judge if he could shake Morgan's hand to thank him—he'd had thirty years and more than a half a dozen political campaigns to shake Morgan's hand. How could I have missed that?

Cory told us that after Bummy Thornton's direct testimony on Friday, he, Cory, was determined to prove that he was the phony he suspected him to be. He then told us what seemed to me at the time to be the unfolding of a miracle.

When court recessed for the weekend, Cory walked outside and noticed the crush of media and cameras surrounding Bummy. What also caught Cory's trained eye was Mayor Morgan standing off beyond the fringe of the crowd heatedly talking with Corine Pastore, his chief of staff who had been in the courtroom throughout the trial.

The Mayor was leaning close to Corine, whispering to her in a very excited manner. Corine just kept nodding her head to acknowledge she understood what he was saying. At one point, in response to something the Mayor said, she nodded her head and patted the purse that was strapped to her shoulder. After a few more minutes of animated conversation, Morgan strolled, smiling, toward the cameras while Corine walked briskly away from the crowd, clutching her purse tightly with her hand even though it was securely fixed over her shoulder by its strap.

"Now someone less experienced," Cory continued, "would have followed Bummy or even Morgan, but I knew that Corine Pastore is known as a virtual appendage of Morgan. In fact, I had picked up rumors around City Hall that for years she was not only an appendage of the Mayor but was the routine recipient of the Mayor's appendage, if you get my meaning."

Cory saw that his weak attempt at humor didn't draw so much as a smile—so he continued.

"You gotta understand that while the Mayor kept his personal relationship with Corine locked securely out of sight, he flaunted his professional relationship with her. Where he went, she went. It was a rare event when the Mayor would even have a conversation with anyone without Corine hanging over his shoulder. And that is what made me so suspicious. It was almost inconceivable that the Mayor would not be huddling with Corine to brainstorm strategy, legal and public relations strategy, or even sharing ideas after the trial had just recessed for the weekend. After all, Bummy had just given the Mayor the free pass he so desperately needed by hanging the entire lynching on T.C. and practically turning the Mayor into a near martyr for civil rights. But instead, they had separated at this most crucial moment. I figured that whatever was pulling them apart must be damned important."

So Cory trotted along after Corine, keeping a safe distance away but always keeping her in sight. After walking for some ten minutes, he saw her approach a red Mercury Sable. She stopped, looked around furtively, and got into the car. Cory ducked behind a tree, took out his cell phone, looked up at the street sign and called for his back-up aide to get his car over to him as quickly as possible.

The wait seemed endless, but Corine just sat in the car, bent over her purse, fiddling with something in it. She then took out a cell phone and had a rather lengthy conversation with someone, and seemed to be writing information on a pad that she had propped up on her lap. Before she finished, and none too soon, Cory's aide drove up, parking his car along the curb several cars in back of Corine's Sable.

Cory slid into the driver's seat of what was to be the vehicle in which he would follow and keep Corine under surveillance. He told the aide to walk back to the courthouse to follow Bummy or Morgan as best he could if either were still hanging around being interviewed.

Cory checked to make sure the miniaturized Cannon Elph camera was in the glove compartment. He then looked over to the back seat floorboard to make sure the "P" bottle was there. He didn't know if he would need the camera, and he didn't know if he would need the bottle, but he always made sure both were present and accounted for. The camera was there in case he needed to surreptitiously take pictures of anything or anyone. Sometimes, he just took pictures of the area where a subject had gone. The bottle was more essential. Some stakeouts lasted longer than a human bladder could endure. The camera was ready to go. But Cory noticed that his assistant had put an empty wine bottle in the back of the car. Cory interrupted his narrative long enough to tell us what he thought of his aide's preparation of the stakeout vehicle.

"That jerk. How I am going to piss in that? My aim is good, but I ain't no Annie Oakley. I must have told him a hundred times. Skippy Peanut Butter. Get me one of those Skippy Peanut Jars, the jumbo kind you get at Price Club. A drunken sailor full of beer couldn't miss one of those..."

Payton, who knew what was coming, sat back eating a donut and smiling. I was on the edge of my chair. Cory continued his story. He waited until Corine had pulled away from the curb, then eased his car into traffic staying several cars behind. Corine headed toward Route 1 and took the long bridge over the river into South Carolina. She drove a few miles and pulled into a mini mall, parking her car in the middle of the parking lot. Cory pulled his car just far enough away not to be noticed, and watched.

Corine read from a small piece of paper, and then stuck her head out of the car window and began scanning the stores until she spotted a store front with a neon sign which read: "Bella Cosa, Emporium of Delight. Adult Videos." She drove her car to a parking space in front of the Emporium and pulled out her cell phone, making a call while her eyes searched the area. She finished the conversation, put the cell phone down, and just sat in the car, continuing to look around. She then pulled out the cell phone again, and this time her conversation seemed to be a bit more animated. After concluding the call, she got out of the car and started walking toward the strip of stores.

Cory quickly exited his car and started walking in the same direction, but before he could reach Corine, she had vanished into a laundromat next to the Emporium. Cory walked up to a newsstand next to the laundromat, purchased a magazine at random, and sat down on a bench strategically located so that he could keep an eye on the laundromat while at the same time appearing to be reading the magazine. Cory could see Corine sitting in a chair in the laundromat, not talking to anyone or doing anything.

"Now get this," Cory said, "Here I am reading this magazine, sitting on a bench. Sounds innocent, right? But what do you think the magazine was that I just grabbed blindly from the newsstand? Get this—it was 'Bride and Groom.' I mean, talk about a rookie mistake! Here I am tailing this broad, trying to look inconspicuous, and I'm reading 'Bride and Groom.'" Seeing that we were no more amused by his magazine story than we were about his "P" bottle woes, he continued with his tale.

"Corine just sat. I just sat. I couldn't figure out why she would go into a laundromat to meet someone. She put a few quarters in a washing machine and let it run. She was sitting there all alone. At first I figured it didn't make sense—to be sitting there in an empty laundromat. Looking at an empty machine tumbling water around. But then I figured it out. About every ten minutes, she would walk outside, look around, talk on the cell phone and return to the laundromat. Apparently, she was waiting for someone. If she just sat in the car, she might draw attention. But no one would be suspicious of a woman sitting in a laundromat waiting for her clothes to be done."

Cory just sat, waited, watched and, for a buncombe read his 'Bride and Groom' magazine, learning how he could buy a wedding dress that would accent his bosom without having too much of a plunging neckline. He looked up at the newsstand and became even more upset when he saw that if he had randomly grabbed for a magazine only one magazine over, he could have at least grabbed a "bridesmaid" magazine which had as its lead story: "Lingerie can Make your Wedding Night Sheer Delight."

Cory wished he had looked before he had bought that magazine. Even more he wished he had used that bottle in his car— all the more as he watched that washer tumbling water in the laundromat. But he was afraid that if he walked back to the car, he might lose Corine just when her contact arrived. So he tried, oh how he tried, not to think about his bladder pain, with only limited success.

Cory was subtly trying to fan his pants with the magazine to dry up the small amount of moisture that he couldn't hold when he looked up and saw an old black man staring at Corine's car and shaking his head up and down. Cory stood up and started strolling slowly towards the man, holding the magazine in front of his damp groin area.

"And then I saw him," said Cory

"Saw who for God's sake?" I said, tired of hearing about Cory's incontinence and magazine preferences and eager to hear the end of the story which had apparently brought such pleasure to Payton.

"That's the trouble with you lawyers," Cory responded, "You're too damn impatient. What I'm trying to say is then I saw the man who Corine had come here to meet—it was Bummy Thornton."

He let that sink in for a moment, then continued: "Corine came bounding out of the laundromat and threw her arms around Bummy. They engaged in some conversation for a short while. Then she looked furtively around the mall as I purposely started walking diagonally away from the two of them so that I wouldn't catch their attention. The mall wasn't crowded, but there were enough people moving around to make the movements of one person seem to be unremarkable. I could see Corine out of the corner of my eye get into the driver's seat of her car and lower the window. She reached into her purse and handed Bummy a large brown paper lunch bag bulging with something. I pivoted towards the two of them, staying far enough back to avoid suspicion, took out my camera, held it just off to the side of the magazine and started the continuing shooting function of the camera. This little camera could shoot consecutive pictures for up to three minutes.

"Bummy was standing outside the car right next to the driver's window. Corine was seated in the driver's seat facing towards Bummy. He took the bag, and flashed Corine a smile as big as the whole outdoors. My mind was working furiously as the camera ripped off picture after picture. But how the hell could I find out what was in that bag?

"And then it happened—like a prayer being answered. Corine started to raise the window when Bummy tapped on it, motioning for her to lower the window again. She did, and Bummy reached into the brown bag and pulled out a small handful of paper money, not enough to make a dent in the bag, but more than enough of a sampling to prove what was in the bag. It was obviously full of money, and a whole lot of it. He started giving the handful of bills to Corine, but her eyes almost exploded out of her head. She pushed his hand away, refusing the offer. She looked all around her almost in a panic, yelled something at Bummy, raised the window, gunned her car and backed up so quickly out of the parking space that she almost ran Bummy over. Bummy watched after her, slowly got into his car, and drove off.

"Then I got into my car, checked the camera to make sure it had been working okay, and when I was sure everything was all right I called Payton with the good news. We met this morning and here we are."

Saying this, Cory cleared the donuts and coffee from the table and reached into a large manila folder. With a huge grin, he took out a deck of photographs which he spread across the table with the expert hand of a Las Vegas blackjack dealer.

The pictures were better than Cory's ten thousand words. They were far from perfect, and I was concerned about how effective some of them would be if introduced into evidence. But they told the whole story, from the moment Corine kissed Bummy, to Bummy's taking the greenbacks out of the envelope in an apparent attempt to reward Corine for her role as the middle person fixer.

I sat staring at the photographs for a very long time. I congratulated Cory and told him—at great length and with much genuine admiration—how incredible he was, how he brought virtue to his profession and how justice only triumphs when the Corys of the world free truth from the bondage of deceit. He seemed appreciative of the praise and, telling us how much he looked forward to Monday, took his leave.

As soon as Cory left, I hugged Payton and shouted, "We're back in the ball game!"

But Payton, who just a few moments before seemed as full of elation as he was of donuts, suddenly fell silent.

"Hey Payton, my man, where's the smile? We just got raised from the dead."

"Yeah," he said, " after we dumped all over our client."

I hadn't even reflected on that. He was right. We had been brutal and beyond cruel to our client. I guess it was kind of a game to me, the lawyer. We'd been down, and now we were up. But this was no game to T.C. We had stomped on him. We had disbelieved him when he needed desperately to have someone believe in him.

"Of course, you're right," I said. "Damn—this should teach us both a lesson. Our profession has turned us into such cynics that we look for reasons not to accept the truth—even when it's sitting right there in front of us. Which one of us gets to give T.C. the good news?"

"I have a better question—who gets to explain to him why we didn't believe him?"

"That'll come later. The best way to make it up to him is to pulverize that sonofalyinbitch Thornton when we get him back on the stand."

CHAPTER 31

Payton and I spent the rest of the day relaxing. I had ordered a couple of bottles of wine from room service and we sat sipping and philosophizing. The more we drank, the more profound became our philosophical discussion—at least it sounded more profound to us.

"You know," I said, "The reason we were so quick to disbelieve T.C. is because we know the truth about the bigotry which infected his younger years. And like I said, our profession made us so cynical that we refused to accept the truth when it was right there in front of us. Even Cory saw through Bummy—he saw the truth."

"Let's not be so hard on ourselves. Sometimes it's good not to see what some people call the 'truth.' Sometimes the truth can challenge your whole belief system, and then it can be dangerous."

I knew the wine was starting to dull my senses because as hard as I tried, I couldn't understand Payton's point. It sounded erudite, but how could realizing, understanding and accepting the truth be dangerous?

"So, Payton," I said, "if truth is so dangerous, perhaps we should undertake a massive attempt to rewrite and whitewash history."

"No need to. We already have done it. You know you make me think of this cartoon I used to have over my desk in my dorm in law school. It showed the young David, still holding his slingshot, standing over the prostrate body of Goliath. Goliath is lying on the ground shrieking in agony with his hands grabbing his groin. Next to the two of them is a scribe writing on his stone tablet and saying, 'History will record that he was hit in the forehead.'"

The wine made me laugh more than the word picture deserved. I imagined a Sunday school class filled with little boys and girls all dressed in their Sunday best. "Oh yeah, Payton, I can just envision the Sunday school teacher saying to his Bible studies class, 'And then David put a stone in his sling shot and hit Goliath right in his balls.'"

Payton, who had drunk as much wine as I, added to the humor, "Would that be the St. James version of the Bible or the original Vulgate?'"

"I think it's from the Hugh Hefner version of the Bible."

Payton then pointed up towards the ceiling, "And then when David goes to heaven, God says to him, 'David, I can easily overlook your persistent philandering and even having your good friend killed to steal his wife, but that thing you did to Goliath, man, that just wasn't right.'"

"And David answers: 'But, God, sir, I had to kill him.' 'Hey, David, I'm no Pollyanna. I know war ain't beanbag. I wouldn't have minded if you had gouged out his eyes. I probably also could even have lived with a hot poker in his nether regions, although I might have given you a couple of weekends in Purgatory for that...but hitting a fellow in the testicles, we don't do that up here...maybe that's acceptable behavior in Hell, but we don't approve of things like that up here. You know I am very compassionate and understanding. I accept deaths caused by a thrust through the heart without question, a blow to the mid-section is already beginning to push the envelope—but a rock to the genitals is definitely beyond the pale.'"

"You know, Payton, the more I think about it, the more I think that David would have been better off if the truth about Goliath had been known. He would have been given the keys to Sodom and Gomorrah. Better yet, ain't no one would take Israel on. You can imagine some hostile chieftain calling his elders together and saying, 'We can sack the cities of Assyria, we can rape the women of the Parthians, but whatever you do, don't piss that David guy off.'"

We did a lot of laughing that night. We didn't sleep much, but did manage to finish off the two bottles of wine before Payton went back to his room. It took all of Sunday to catch up on our sleep and regain our focus for the trial.

CHAPTER 32

On Monday morning Payton and I met in the counsel's room just behind the courtroom. The first decision we had to make was to decide which one of us would cross-examine Bummy Thornton. In Payton's favor was the fact that he had done a great job on Morgan's cross-examination. We also knew that the black jurors might be more forgiving if a black attorney beat up on a black witness than if a white lawyer ripped his gizzards out. But Payton's cross-examination style was more slash and burn, perfect for a cocky white collar type like Morgan, but Thornton would have to be dismantled in a much more controlled manner. We both felt that I was better suited for that job.

In addition, Payton doing Bummy's cross would be too obvious. It is precisely because the jurors would expect us to use a black attorney to cross-examine a black witness, that we might gain credibility with the jurors by *not* playing the race card. Besides, Payton was near total exhaustion since he not only had prepared for Morgan's cross examination, but had also been orchestrating the behind the scenes investigation of the case. We decided I would cross-examine Bummy.

I knew there was a great danger in cross examining a sympathetic witness like that sweet old black man Bummy Thornton who, as far as the jury knew, had endured watching his half brother burned to death by some white racists. There are some witnesses that a jury becomes almost proprietary about, and they resent any attacks on them. Yet I knew that even the most sympathetic jury will turn on a witness if they feel he has been lying to them. In other words, taking on a witness like Bummy Thornton was like trying to kill the king—if you decide to shoot him, you had damn well better not miss.

I had Cory's pictures ready to go. They weren't bad, but

they weren't that good either. They looked like they had been taken by someone who had just wet himself which, of course, was the case. There were about fifty pictures in perfect sequence. Corine and Bummy were readily identifiable. There is no doubt that she was passing the brown bag to him. But when Bummy took out the money to give Corine a "tip" for her effort, Cory probably was caught by surprise because the camera suddenly lost its focus and shot more of Bummy's arm than the money. You could tell it was money in context, but if you just showed the pictures cold to someone, he would never be able to tell it was money in Bummy's hand. Worse still, Corine wasn't in the picture at all when Bummy removed the money from the bag. You could just see a blur that I assumed was her hand pushing the money away.

I knew I could call Cory to testify about what happened. Indeed, to get the picture in evidence, I would have to call Cory to lay the foundation unless I could get Bummy to admit that the picture accurately reflected what went on that day. In one sense, I would have liked Bummy to deny that the bag and money exchanged hands so that I could undermine his credibility even more.

On the other hand, I didn't want anything to turn on the credibility of Cory or any other of my witnesses. Jurors are very cynical. They liked Bummy now. They wanted to believe he was honest, and they might think that Cory was just some sharpy detective pulling a fast one on some helpless old black man. I wanted to bluff or scare the truth out of Bummy himself. I didn't want to have to call Cory. A good prosecutor would just walk Cory through all of his stealth and plotting and invasions of peoples' privacy. Private detectives are in a dirty business, and many jurors don't like it, regardless of the evidence turned up. I wanted them concentrating on Bummy not Cory.

What we had going in our favor was that Bummy was no genius. I didn't think he could hold up well when surprised with the pictures on the stand. There is no way that Bummy Thornton would be able to come up with a spontaneous creative answer when confronted with such damning evidence. Bummy did very well on direct, but that was because Rabison, though a detestable human being, was a good lawyer. He had Bummy well rehearsed, probably even down to that flip little dagger he thrust into T.C.'s heart when Bummy "spontaneously" asked T.C. why he murdered poor Aaron Boddie as he stepped down from the stand. I doubted that Bummy had received any rehearsal for the payoff story. Both Payton and I agreed that Rabison almost certainly did not know of the payoff from Morgan to Bummy.

Prosecutors often slide a foot over that ethical line by telling witnesses, "I absolutely don't want to put words in your mouth, but it certainly would help us if you had seen that knife on the table." And lo and behold, the witness, especially one who wants a good deal from the prosecutor, suddenly remembers that knife on the table. Yet, neither I nor Payton, who was far more skeptical of prosecutors than I was, thought that a prosecutor, even Rabison, would be part of or even allow a witness to be "paid off." And if Rabison didn't know about the Morgan payoff to Bummy, then he didn't prepare Bummy how to deal with the payoff if we confronted him with it. Moreover, in Georgia, the defense had no obligation to warn the prosecutor ahead of time of this kind of looming ambush.

The prosecutor has a legal obligation to give the defendant any evidence that might help the defendant, but there is no corresponding duty on behalf of the defendant. It's not exactly fair, but it's about time the law let a defendant at least have a pea shooter to aim at the prosecution battleship. We gathered up our pictures and headed for the courtroom.

The judge peered down at Bummy on the witness stand and instructed him that he was still under oath from last Friday. The judge then nodded to me as a signal to begin my cross-examination.

I knew I had to strike hard and strike fast. I wanted to knock Bummy off balance immediately and then deluge him with lethal blows before he could regain his equilibrium. But unlike Payton's style in his cross examination of Morgan, I would talk in a reproachful, controlled voice, not yelling but letting my disdain ride with each query.

"Mr. Thornton, could you please tell this jury how much money Mr. Morgan paid you for your testimony last Friday?"

I could hear the air get sucked out of the room. Bummy just fell back in the witness chair, a shocked look on his face. Rabison was up on his feet like a rocket. "Objection! Objection! Objection!"

The judge just smiled at Rabison who continued in a stammer, "This is outrageous, and in bad faith. Uncalled for, your honor. I demand the question be stricken and the jury be instructed that a lawyer's questions are not evidence."

The judge turned to face me, "Mr. Lipton, I will uphold the objection as to form. There has been no testimony that this witness took any money from Mr. Morgan or anyone else. So, assuming you are acting in good faith, and you had better be—why don't you rephrase the question."

I stepped in front of the lawyer's podium and took a step towards Bummy,

"Quite right your Honor, I will lay a foundation. Now, Mr. Thornton, last Friday after you testified you met with Mayor Morgan's chief of staff, did you not?"

Bummy looked over to Rabison as if pleading for help. It seemed he stared forever at Rabison until he realized no help was at hand.

"Well, I don't know who this chief you talkin' about...."

"Well, how about Corine Pastore. Did you meet with a Corine Pastore over in a mall in South Carolina just the other side of the bridge?"

"Oh, I meets with so many people these days...I don't...."

"Mr. Thornton, I am talking about at a mall in South Carolina after you finished testifying here. Did you meet with a woman about five feet, seven inches tall, a white woman, rather thin, with short black hair?"

Bummy turned towards the judge, but the judge directed his attention back to me.

"Can you answer Mr. Lipton's question, Mr. Thornton?"

Bummy looked again towards Rabison. Every lawyer's nightmare, a witness who shows his distress by looking to you for help right in front of the jury. Rabison just looked away.

"Yeah, yeah, now that I think, I think I did meet that lady, but weren't nothing that happened."

"Move to strike everything after "Yeah, yeah.""

The judge thought for a moment and then granted the motion to strike. I did not care about what was stricken, but I wanted to keep a tight control on this witness. Forcing him to march to my cadence was the best way of doing that. Don't let the guy start to get creative.

"Now, Mr. Thornton, this woman—by the way, did you know her name?"

"No, I mean, it was you said, Corine, only I didn't know her last name. I was just there and I seen her."

"Move to strike."

Rabison was on his feet, trying to break my rhythm.

"Judge, please tell Mr. Lipton to let the witness complete his answers."

The judge turned to Bummy. "Mr. Thornton, on cross examination, an attorney can require you to answer yes, no, or I can't answer yes or no. You can make your explanations when your lawyer gets up on redirect examination. Okay, I understand you are not used to testifying, so just try to answer the question that is being asked of you and only that question."

I paused long enough before asking my next question so that I would let the jury know that whenever I made a pregnant pause between questions, I was about to drop another bomb on the witness.

"Well, Mr. Thornton, this Corine woman gave you something

in that mall, didn't she?"

Now Bummy looked totally confused and panicked.

"No. I mean, did she tell you that?"

The judge intervened before I could go on. "No, Mr. Thornton, the question is not what anyone else said at this point. We're only interested in your testimony. Did that woman give you something?"

Bummy looked up at the judge, thankful for his intervention—an intervention which I regretted.

"Oh, Mr. Judge, sir, I can't really remember what that woman gave me on Friday. I am thinking hard, but I just don't remember."

I saw the opportunity for some freelancing here. When an opportunity to land a punch unexpectedly arises during a cross-examination, it is not always wise to land that punch, especially if the diversion might deflect the force and cadence of the more powerful blows you have been landing on a more important issue. But I couldn't resist.

"Mr. Thornton, could you please tell this jury how on your direct examination, you could recall in the most extensive detail events that happened forty years ago, but you can't remember what a woman gave you last Friday?"

Up popped Rabison, "Objection. Argumentative!"

The judge shrugged his shoulders, "Well, probably so, but why don't you move on, Mr. Lipton?"

I figured that now was the time to strike the fatal blow. I reached in under the podium and pulled out the stack of pictures.

"Mr. Thornton, would it help refresh your recollection about what went on with Corine on Friday if I showed you some pictures?"

I could see Rabison come to the top of his chair, not quite springing up but ready to do so. Another lawyer's nightmare is that stiletto in the back. Bummy's eyes flashed open in terror, "Pictures—I didn't take no pictures."

The judge signaled me and the District Attorney over to the

side of the bench near the court clerk.

"Mr. Lipton, why don't you have your pictures marked for identification and then show them to the witness and see if that refreshes his recollection about what—if anything—that woman...."

"Corine, your honor..."

"Well, thank you, Mr. Lipton, but there is no evidence of the woman's name before this jury, so I will refer to her as 'that woman.'" And then with a smile, "Sounds Clintonesque—makes me feel Presidential." This caused the rest of us to smile—not because we thought it particularly humorous, but because it was said by the judge.

I went over and handed the pictures over to the court clerk who marked the fifty pictures for identification. Bummy was rising halfway out of the witness chair trying to take a peek at the pictures. Rabison was engaged in a hurried whispering conversation with his assistant, then he rose. "Judge, can we have a sidebar?"

"Okay, counselors, come to the sidebar, and Madame court reporter, please come up here to take down the discussion. Ladies and gentlemen of the jury, to save time we will have this discussion here out of your hearing rather than sending you out of the room. You're probably getting used to this by now."

Rabison and his assistant and Payton and I gathered tightly around the judge, all of us aware that our body gestures would be watched by the jurors for the minutest clue as to what was happening and who was winning the argument. Rabison raised his voice as loudly as he could without having it rise above a whisper:

"Judge, I have not seen these pictures. I don't know what they are all about, and it is patently unfair that this ambush is sprung on us. I don't even know if they are untouched, or played with or, these days you can even have objects and people inserted in pictures, and it would take an expert in a lab time to find that out."

"Well, Mr. Rabison, you can look at the pictures before they are shown to Mr. Thornton, but what do you suggest I do?"

The red was beginning to flow into the whiteness of Rabison's cadaverous face. I knew that whenever he colored up like this, he was upset, real upset. He shook his finger at me.

"I suggest that this was bad faith. I know if I suggest a mistrial, Mr. Lipton would refuse to join in the motion and then would come running in here later yelling double jeopardy. But what I would ask your honor is that we adjourn until tomorrow so I can rush these pictures to the State Police lab to have them looked..."

I exploded, "No way, your Honor."

I knew that Rabison had made a tough decision. On the one hand, he knew that by adjourning at this point on this issue, he was making the meeting with Corine a huge focus of the jury. By adjourning for another day, he would only emphasize more an issue he should want to get past as soon as possible. Jurors' memories have a short shelf life. Things that seem devastating when they happen in front of a jury find their rightful place in the full context of the trial by the time it is over, if they are not dwelled upon too long during the trial.

That being said, I knew that Rabison was making the right move. One of his key witnesses was on the ropes. Bummy was a good witness as long as he was swinging at the softballs that he was being fed on his direct testimony. But old Bummy couldn't think his way out of a paper bag when the pitches came unexpectedly. The prosecution needed time to regroup and get Bummy set up with some good answers to the questions that were heading his way.

Of course, Rabison knew that the judge would inform Bummy that during any adjournment he could not talk about his testimony with Rabison or his staff. When that order is given to a defendant it is problematical, since it might be viewed as depriving a party of his right to counsel. But Bummy was the witness, not the client of the prosecution. My concern was that Rabison, and any other sharpy lawyer, knew how to get around the boilerplate gag order. Just play telephone. Have someone not under the gag order talk to the witness. Better yet is the "inadvertently" overheard conversation. Rabison decides what he wants to tell Bummy, and then has a conversation with an assistant about what Bummy should testify about within obvious earshot of Bummy.

Perhaps, even more importantly, I knew Rabison wanted time to regalvanize his own staff. He wanted time to find out what this was all about and then find some way to minimize or even totally eliminate any damage from the grenade that had just been lobbed at his witness. I desperately wanted to hit Bummy while he was reeling. An adjournment for an entire day would be a disaster for us.

The judge scratched his chin and leaned back in his chair. He put his hands together in front of his face, lacing the fingers of each hand through those of the other. It was clear he was thinking. A dangerous sign.

"Well, you know, Mr. Lipton, maybe technically you did not have a legal obligation to turn these pictures over earlier, though if you read the reciprocal discovery rules that is in no way certain. And I don't really see the harm in giving Mr. Rabison a chance to...."

As the judge droned on I knew I faced the need to come up with something fast. The ability to think fast is more important for a litigator than the ability to think deep. Right now, my mind was racing. I had to head the judge off at the pass before he granted that adjournment.

"Judge, just a minute. I'm not even offering the pictures in evidence, yet. I'm just trying to refresh his recollection as to what changed hands—anything can be used to refresh someone's recollection."

I could tell from the smoke curling out of Rabison's ears that he knew I might just have hit on my key to victory on this point. The rule in every state is that a lawyer can use anything to refresh a witness's recollection. This rule always amazed me for its breadth and lack of limits. When I was facing a "forgetful" witness, I always wanted to walk up to him, kick him in the shins and say, "Does that refresh your recollection?" Many a chunk of prejudicial information has reached a jury's ears through the "anything to refresh" doctrine. Rabison wasn't buying what I was selling,

"Judge, you know that's not the real reason he wants to show the witness those pictures. My God, look at the jurors already trying to see what those pictures are all about—even if you denied putting them into evidence—after all, we haven't even heard foundation testimony from the person who took them as to where they were taken, when they were taken, under what circumstances they were taken, who developed them, whether there are any other pictures that might contradict these pictures..."

I jumped in before Rabison was finished, "Judge, as to putting them in evidence, all we need is for this witness to say that the pictures accurately reflect what happened, and if he doesn't I can call the person who took them later."

The judge waved his hand, "Enough, enough. Okay, here is what we will do. Mr. Lipton, you can try to refresh Mr. Thornton's memory with the pictures, but if you want them into evidence, I will give the prosecution some time to examine them first—but not until tomorrow—if you move the pictures into evidence, Mr. Lipton, we will adjourn until 3 P.M. And one last thing, Mr. Lipton, unless and until those pictures are in evidence I don't want you 'accidentally' to place those pictures so that the jurors can see them, understand?"

"No problem, judge, but can I make a request that goes the other way?"

"Yes, go ahead."

"Throughout this trial, I have been constantly objecting because Mr. Rabison always makes what he knows are frivolous objections just to tip off the witness as to how to answer. In this instance I would like you to instruct Mr. Rabison not to jump up and yell at the first hint of hesitation by Mr. Thornton; something like, "Objection, Mr. Thornton said it didn't refresh his recollection" so as to tip Mr. Thornton off that if he says those talismanic words, he can safely repeat his testimony that he doesn't remember what was exchanged. You know that without a tip-off he may suddenly remember something after seeing a picture."

The judge could see that Rabison was about to explode, but he signaled him to be silent.

"Mr. Lipton, Mr. Rabison has been a vigorous adversary, just like you have been. I will not warn him in advance about any conduct. He knows what is proper and what is not. Now, let's continue. Mr. Lipton show the pictures to Mr. Rabison and then show them to the witness."

Rabison and his assistant hovered over the pictures, whispering back and forth to each other. I just smiled because I knew what they really wanted was to be whispering to Bummy, but now that they did not have their adjournment, they could not do that. I knew if I were Rabison, and I had the chance, I would tell Bummy that the picture was fuzzy, and it was not clear at all what was in the bag or being taken out of it. Then we could all put our heads together and figure out what Bummy could say was in the bag, without, of course, putting words in his mouth.

I gathered up the pictures and showed about five of them to Bummy. Since he knew what was in the bag, he would think that he could clearly see in the picture that there was money being pulled out of the bag. Before, I could ask a question, Bummy looked up the from the pictures, "Yeah, that's the lady."

The judge interrupted, "Please, Mr. Thornton, wait until there is a question asked of you."

I walked towards Bummy for dramatic effect, "Do those pictures refresh your recollection that there was money in that bag that Corine gave you?"

I knew Rabison would jump up to object to something just to disrupt my attack and give Bummy some time to think. "Objection, your honor, there's been no testimony about any 'Corine.'"

"I'll allow it. Please answer the question, Mr. Thornton, but ignore the name. Do you know that woman's name, Mr. Thornton?"

"He said, your Honor, Corine, only I don't know her last name...."

I'd gotten an unexpected opening and I quickly jumped in. I could sense that I'd put Bummy into that magic position—a witness who is becoming too scared to lie since he fears he will be exposed. "Mr. Thornton, that Corine, she works for Mayor Morgan, correct?"

"Well, I don't know that for sure, but that is what she told me."

"Fine, now tell me, does that picture refresh...."

Rabison was out of his chair: "Objection, there's been no testimony that he needs to have his memory refreshed."

I quickly out-shouted Rabison before he could further tip Bummy off about what to say.

"He's doing it already, Your honor!"

The judge held up his hands, "Both of you keep silent. Mr. Thornton, do those pictures refresh your recollection about what was given to you, if anything, by Corine?"

Bummy just leaned back in his chair and almost sighed out his answer.

"Yessir, judge, those are pictures of Miss Corine handing me money, but that weren't bad money."

Rabison flew to his feet. "Objection and move to strike. The pictures are not in evidence. What is in the pictures is irrelevant!"

The judge turned to the jury, "I am granting the motion to strike the answer of Mr. Thornton. You are only allowed to see or hear about items that are in evidence. Those pictures are not in evidence."

The judge turned back to Bummy. "Now, Mr. Thornton, do those pictures refresh your recollection as to what was given to you by Corine?"

"I jest told you that she gave me the money, but it wasn't bad money."

The judge pulled him up short, "Okay, the pictures refreshed his recollection. She gave him money. Next question, Mr. Lipton."

"Okay, Mr. Thornton, why did she give you money?"

"I don't know why, why don't you ask her?"

"Let me get this straight, Mr. Thornton, you were in some mall in South Carolina the same day you testified in this court, and this woman, Corine, comes up to you and hands you a brown bag full of money?"

"That's what I told you because that is the truth."

"Mr. Thornton, you are one heck of a lucky fellow."

"Objection!"

"I'll withdraw that, Your Honor. Mr. Thornton, now Corine gave you this money last Friday after you testified, is that correct?"

"If you say so."

"It's not what I say. It's what you say. This happened last Friday, right?"

I picked up the picture just to remind Bummy that he better stay on the straight and narrow. He looked at the picture and said, "Yeah, I suppose that is when it was."

"Where is the money?"

"At home, I 'spect."

"That would be your home, I assume?"

"Yessir."

"How much money was in the bag?"

"How would I know, it ain't my money."

"Are you just holding it for Corine?"

"I suppose so, why don't you ask her, it's her money."

"Did you ever suggest to Corine that it might be more prudent to keep that money in a bank rather than at your house?"

"You should ask..."

The judge interjected, "Just answer yes or no, Mr. Thornton, like I told you before, Mr. Lipton can ask for a yes or no answer. Now did you ever tell this Corine it would be better to keep the money in a bank?"

"No."

Now that the judge had put Bummy back on the leash, I decided to take him for a walk.

"Mr. Thornton, answering yes or no, did Corine ever tell you what the money was for?"

"No."

"Did you ever ask what the money was for?"

"No."

"Did she tell you who the money was from?"

"No."

"Did you ask who the money was from?"

"No"

"Has anybody called you about this money since Friday?"

"No."

"Has anybody told you that someone was going to call you or see you about this money?"

"No."

"Before Corine came up to you in the shopping mall, were you expecting anyone to bring you money?"

"No."

"Did Corine say anything to you about the money when she handed it to you?"

Rabison knew he had to interrupt this slide into oblivion, "Objection, asked and answered."

The judge knew the purpose of that technically correct objection. "I'll allow it. Answer the question, Mr. Thornton."

"No."

"Did you ever tell anyone in the prosecutor's office about this money?"

"No."

"Did you ever tell anyone about this money before you testified here today?"

"No."

I then stopped and just rocked back and forth as if I was thinking of my next question. What I really wanted was for the jury to collect itself for my summing-up question. I knew I would ask it slowly and deliberately so that it would have its maximum impact on the jury.

"Now, Mr. Thornton, tell me if I have this right. After you testified Friday, you drove down to a mall just over the South Carolina border. Some woman who said her name was Corine and that she worked for Mayor Morgan walked up to you and handed you a bag filled with money and said nothing about who the bag was from or what you were to do with the money. You asked no questions of her and you took the money without counting it and have told no one about it, not even the prosecutor, until today?"

Rabison sprang up again, "Objection, it's a compound question and it's confusing..."

"I'll allow it. Answer the question Mr. Thornton."

"I already told him that's what happened Your Honor."

At that point, I had one of those split-second trial lawyers decisions to make. I had at least five hours of cross examination ready concerning Bummy's testimony about the murder. I knew the more detail I spun out from him, the more I could show the contradictions in what he had testified to on his direct testimony. I was pretty sure if I pressed hard on the edifice he had constructed on Friday, the rotten foundation would cause the entire house to cave in. But I also knew that, unlike his testimony today, Bummy had rehearsed and been rehearsed on the murder testimony and might have more plausible explanations ready than he gave when pressed to be creative on his own. Also, like it or not, T.C. was a Klansman, and he was at the scene of the murder. I was not sure it would be wise to give Bummy another chance to recount to the jury the terror of that awful night.

Besides, I knew you could undermine the credibility of a witness two ways. You could do it the slogging way—by chipping away at the details of the story the witness told; or you could do it the fast way—by showing the jury that witness was totally compromised either by bias or that he had been paid off in some way, or that he had lied to the jury on some collateral matter that was important enough to have the jury totally disregard the principal testimony without having to attack it directly. Moreover, there is some drama to having a short, hard-hitting cross-examination, particularly since I knew that the prosecutor could only redirect Bummy on the areas I had gone into that would not include the night of the murder. All of that flashed through my mind in an instant. I decided to wrap it up and declare victory.

"Now, Mr. Thornton, those pictures refreshed your recollection, correct?"

"That what the judge said."

"Well, that's what you said?"

"Okay, yes."

"Well, what I want to know is if that money you received in the bag refreshed your recollection about the testimony you gave on Friday?"

I got just the response I wanted.

"Objection!"

"I'll withdraw it. Nothing further your Honor."

The judge turned to Rabison, "Any redirect, Mr. Rabison?"

Rabison stood up, but before he could say anything, Bummy interrupted him with a whine, "I got to answer more questions?"

The courtroom erupted in laughter. I would have preferred that we had kept up the somber, dramatic mood, but I thought that Bummy's response showed that he was very uncomfortable with what had happened in court that day.

I knew Rabison would be reluctant to ask too many unrehearsed questions of Bummy. I could not imagine how he could, going blind on redirect testimony, weave a rehabilitating story out of testimony that stated someone came out of the ether to dump a bag full of money in Bummy's lap.

"Mr. Thornton, I have just one question. Was what you told us Friday about the murder true?"

"Yup, it sure was."

"Nothing further, your Honor."

"Mr. Lipton, any further re-cross?"

"Yes, your Honor, I also have only one question."

"Proceed."

"Mr. Thornton, was the testimony you gave on Friday as truthful as the testimony you gave today?"

"Objection!"

The judge shot back immediately, "You opened the door for it, Mr. Rabison—please answer the question, Mr. Thornton. Was the testimony you gave on Friday as truthful as the testimony you gave today?"

"Sure was, your Honor."

"Fine, you may step down, Mr. Thornton. Thank you for testifying. Call your next witness, Mr. Rabison."

While the testimony proceeded, Payton and I again reviewed our decision with respect to using Cory. If we put him on the stand we could get the pictures into evidence. But to what end? The jury already knew that Bummy had been given a bag full of money. Cory could further discredit Bummy's testimony by testifying to the furtive nature of the meeting and how Bummy tried to "tip" Corine. But with all of that we finally agreed not to call Cory. As Payton put it, why take the risk of calling a witness—and there is always a risk with that alternative. If the jury didn't disbelieve Bummy now, they would never disbelieve him.

What we did decide to do was to subpoena Corine Pastore, have her identify herself as chief of staff to Mayor Morgan, and then simply ask her if she gave the money to Bummy. She would know that we have the pictures and would be aware of Bummy's testimony, so she would have to admit passing the money to

Bummy. That's it, just those two questions. Rabison would be insane to try to run an innocent explanation by the jury on cross examination after we finished our direct. If they did, then we could really tee off and tear her up on redirect testimony.

As it turned out, we never did question Corine Pastore. Her lawyer informed the Judge at a closed meeting in his chambers that she would take the Fifth Amendment if called. I wanted her to do just that in front of the jury. But the judge denied my request—denied it, that is, if the prosecutor would agree to tell the jurors that all parties agree that Corine Pastore was chief of staff to Mayor Morgan and that on late Friday afternoon at the Green Mall in South Carolina, she passed a bag containing an indeterminate amount of American currency to Bummy Thornton. Rabison reluctantly accepted the offer he couldn't refuse.

CHAPTER 33

"Payton, do you have any idea why they want us over in the D.A.'s office?"

"Probably after the way you took apart Thornton, they might be offering us a sweeter deal."

"You know, I have no idea why they put him on without thoroughly checking him out. It's the most common mistake litigators make—thinking it's a good move when they have more witnesses. I always instruct new litigators to shave every case with Ocham's razor. The simpler the better. They had a pretty lockshut case without Thornton because they knew we couldn't put T.C. on the stand."

"Well, it's far from in the bag yet," Payton said. "It will take a very courageous jury to let T.C. go given the murder and given that we have to admit that all of the testimony about his Klan activity was truthful. It's like admitting that your client was a prison guard at a concentration camp but that he didn't kill the people you said he killed. Tough to ask of a jury. And don't forget the jurors know that no matter what the details of the evidence are, the sound bite heard 'round the world will be: 'Admitted Klansman Acquitted by Georgia Jury.'"

When Payton and I entered the D.A.'s office, the door was closed and locked behind us. There were two men whom we had never seen before seated in the corner of the room and a tape playing machine of some kind in the center of the room. No sooner had we entered than Rabison handed me a court order. Payton tried to peer over my shoulder.

"What does it say?"

"It says we can't reveal anything we hear in here unless we get permission of the court."

I had no idea what all of this was about, and I didn't fully find out until after the trial was over. We were instructed to return the next day to hear some tape recordings that would be of interest to us.

*   *   *

It seemed the FBI had been conducting a two-year-long investigation of corruption involving some state and county judges as well as some local politicians. Will Morgan had been a prime target of the probe, and for the past two years all of his conversations from his office in City Hall had been monitored.

The wiretaps had serendipitously picked up conversations between Will Morgan and T.C. just when the Boddie case broke and about a week before T.C. was arrested and jailed. The investigation was being orchestrated from the top levels of the FBI in Washington, but one of the local agents had made the mistake of sharing certain of the wiretap evidence with District Attorney Eddie Rabison.

After the World Trade Center disaster, the FBI had promised to cooperate more closely with local law enforcement officials. That may have been a helpful rule in general, but Fritz Maier, the FBI agent in charge of this corruption case, should not have shared the evidence he had gathered with District Attorney Rabison without first clearing it with Washington. He hadn't cleared it with Washington, and as a consequence his career as well as the corruption investigation were in jeopardy.

When it was discovered that the FBI had aided the local authorities in the Boddie murder probe, the FBI knew that there was no getting around the fact that this was what was known as "Brady" material. The rule governing "Brady" material, derived from a Supreme Court decision, required that evidence in the possession of the government which might assist the defendant in his defense was required by law to be turned over to the defendant. In fact, Rabison had already violated the rule by not turning over this material after Morgan testified in the Boddie trial, because it contained prior statements which Morgan had made, and which had been recorded during the FBI monitoring operation.

The top FBI brass was furious that they had to endanger their big corruption investigation by turning over evidence in connection with the Boddie case. They knew that the Boddie case was now hotter and of greater interest to the public, but it was really a one-year wonder. Whatever happened to T.C. would not affect anyone's life one whit. But taking down corrupt judges and politicians could have a real and lasting impact. However, after the Oklahoma bombing case, the last thing the FBI needed was to be exposed again as playing fast and loose with discovery rules. The material had to be turned over. Their only hope was that it would never surface in the Boddie trial. The last thing they wanted was to have some of the targets of the investigation tipped off.

The Bureau sent down a deputy director to put pressure on Rabison to give T.C. a plea deal he couldn't refuse. If T.C. would agree to plead guilty, the trial would end and the tapes would remain sealed until such time as they could be used in the more important corruption case.

Rabison adamantly refused to offer T.C. a deal, even the ten-year deal he had offered him before the trial. The Deputy Director accused Rabison of wanting the tapes played at the trial so that his friend, Mayor Will Morgan, would be tipped off to the corruption investigation. Rabison's face turned blood red, and he shrieked at the Deputy Director that he was not going to give a break to a former Klansman who had murdered a black person just to save the FBI investigation.

Rabison, giving a hint of his volatility, shoved his face into that of the Deputy Director and shouted, "This case will be compromised over my dead body. The South needs a conviction in this case. The country needs a conviction in this case. Justice *demands* a conviction in this case!"

The Deputy pushed Rabison back and said, in measured tones: "The only thing that demands a conviction in this case is your bloated ego!"

The two almost came to blows before the local FBI Agent Maier stepped in to keep them apart. Maier, who had shared the information from the case with Rabison in the first place without clearing it with the Bureau, saw a chance to redeem himself with the suits in Washington. He knew that the Deputy and Rabison had backed each other into a corner. Maier also thought he knew how to cut the Gordian knot. The Deputy approved of the Maier's plan, but didn't think Rabison would buy it. Maier, who knew Rabison better than the Deputy, felt his plan could be sold to the self-absorbed District Attorney.

That night Maier went to Rabison's house unaccompanied by the Deputy. Maier explained to Rabison that the Bureau had not done a sufficient job in explaining how important the corruption investigation was to the Bureau, and the nation. It was bound to get nationwide publicity when broken. Maier told Rabison that the Bureau thought it was very important that the local law enforcement official, the District Attorney, be part of this investigation. It would be good for the Bureau to show it was now cooperating with local law enforcement officials unlike the bad old days. And, for Rabison, it would save him the embarrassment of not being in on the corruption probe with the implication that he could not be trusted. Of course, what was left unsaid was that Rabison had been left out of the investigation up to this point precisely because the Bureau *thought* he could not be trusted, particularly since he was a Morgan protege.

Nor would the Bureau be in the position of having to trust him now if Maier hadn't met Rabison at a party and foolishly whispered what he felt was a very insignificant piece of information about Morgan to him. He hadn't even told Rabison his source, which was the wiretap. But what he had done was enough to implicate the *Brady* rule and require the Bureau to make the wiretaps relating to T.C. Simmons available to the defense.

Rabison leaned back in his chair as Maier explained the importance of the corruption investigation.

"*Now* I understand the importance of the corruption investigation," Rabison said after Maier explained it more thoroughly. Of course, Rabison had understood the importance of the investigation all along. He just didn't want the embarrassment of the story of the investigation being the subject of a press conference without his being a part of it. He could not imagine a worse scenario than having to watch the FBI announce the indictment of local officials without the participation of the local District Attorney. Even the few friends he had would be able to read between those lines. But now Rabison sensed the possibility of getting great press. Nothing was more important to Eddie Rabison than getting great press.

"Well, if I am going to get involved in this investigation, and particularly if it might take down Mayor Morgan, who was good to me, though mind you, if he is corrupt, I don't care if he was my father, I'd take him down in a minute, I want to make sure that I get equal credit for this."

Maier had been told by the Deputy that the Bureau would still try to keep Rabison as far away from the investigation as possible, but the Deputy said that he could promise Rabison a joint press conference when the indictments were announced. The Deputy wasn't sure Rabison would buy into that, but Maier assured him that he knew Rabison and that Rabison would like that just fine since it was the credit not the work that would entice him. Maier put his arm on Rabison's shoulder and smiled. "Well, what do you mean by equal credit, Eddie?"

"What I mean is that if I get Simmons to take a deal and these tapes never see the light of day, I want to be standing right next to whatever pooh-bah executive the Bureau sends down to hold the press conference. I don't want an acknowledgment from the studio audience. I want full-fledged equal time at the indictment press conference."

Maier stuck his hand out: "You drive a hard bargain, but you've got deal. Now go make the sale to Simmons. I hope you can persuade his lawyer to take the deal. You may be in over your head in trying to out negotiate a Jew lawyer from New York."

Rabison laughed. "I pick my teeth with New York Jew lawyers."

CHAPTER 34

The next day found Payton and I once again in Rabison's office. This time it was only the three of us and the FBI agent named Maier.

"Well, counselors," Rabison began, "Here is my offer. If you don't make me play these tapes for you, your guy gets off with five years, period." I shook my head. "He won't do it."

"How do you know he won't do it?"

"Because after Thornton came on the way he did in his direct testimony, I asked T.C. if he would take a lesser sentence if it was offered, and he said no, adamantly no. He is desperate to clear his name, and his conscience."

Nutty Eddie raised his voice: "I'm giving you the Goddamned courthouse."

"He won't take the courthouse."

Maier spoke: "Look, these tapes don't even help your man. We don't want them released for other reasons."

I smiled politely at the agent, "Sir, I didn't begin practicing law yesterday. If these tapes hurt my client, Rabison here wouldn't be sweetening the deal—I mean he's not that nutty." I couldn't resist the dig that caused Rabison to turn a bright red. "And if they didn't help my client, you wouldn't have to turn them over as *Brady* material."

"Well, I'm going to be up front with you," said the FBI agent, "It's *Brady* material because it contains statements from Morgan that could hurt his credibility—but believe me, these statements don't help your guy."

I walked over to the far side of the room with my arm around Payton, whispering in his ear. "Do you think he's bluffing?"

"We'll never find out unless we call him."

I turned around and looked at the FBI agent: "Play the tapes."

"Okay, you got it."

"Wait a minute, can we take notes?"

"Not now. After lunch you can come in here alone and take all the notes you want, but there will be a guard outside and you cannot remove the tapes from the room."

"We have a right to those tapes."

"Not until the judge orders it, you don't."

I expected to hear a scratchy, barely audible tape of a conversation between T.C. and Morgan, but, in fact, the tape was amazingly clear. There was no doubt that it was T.C.'s voice on that tape—

Morgan: "Look T.C., I can't let my career be ruined by what I did forty years ago. Remember, I'm the one who's seen to it that you've had a job all these years. I've always taken care of you. If you just take a plea, I'll see to it that you get taken care of, anything you want. I'll even see to it that some trust funds are set up for your kids."

T.C.: "Listen, I know it was you who fingered me. It was you who called the D.A. telling him it was me to cover up for yourself. You were the big boss, not me. This was all your idea, that murder, you're responsible for the murder, not me. You hurt me bad that night."

Morgan: "Look T.C., let's not rehash that day. It's over. Think about it, no one is going to believe you over me. I can get all the witnesses that I need. You press me, I'll press you—and you'll come out the loser."

T.C.: "I just can't do it. Why should I take the blame when I tried to do the right thing. I can't admit to guilt I don't feel. I didn't do anything to feel guilty about that night and you know it. You are the one who did it, not me. I was the victim of you. I didn't do nothing wrong. Nothin' that God hisself wouldn't of wanted me to do."

Morgan: "Look T.C., I admit it was my fault for setting things up that night, my responsibility not yours. But so what? What good will that do? They aren't going to let you go anyway. I can help you plenty, or by God I can hurt you plenty."

At that moment, another FBI agent burst into the room and shut off the machine. He turned to Maier, "Fritz, headquarters needs you immediately on a secure phone."

Maier turned to us: "Okay, counselors, I'll be right back. Don't touch the machine until I get back."

As the Agents left the room I turned to the District Attorney. I could not conceal my anger.

"You sonofabitch. You hear that tape? How in the hell could you prosecute Simmons with Morgan practically confessing. When does my client get his apology?"

"I'm not giving an apology to anyone."

One thing that burns every defense counsel is that the government never admits it was wrong. Someone is "acquitted," never " innocent." The French have still never officially admitted that Dreyfus was innocent.

"Do you guys have any idea what this has done to my client? You destroyed what was left of his life and you bastards knew all along that it was Morgan who was behind this, you knew that T.C.'s story was true."

"We knew nothing until the FBI called us yesterday with the tapes."

"Now you're just game-playing. Someone in government was sitting there knowing there was a lynching going on, only this time it was a white man getting lynched. It isn't politically correct to be concerned with a white man being lynched, is it?"

Payton had to grab me to keep me from hitting Rabison.

"Take it easy, Luke, just cool down."

I slammed my fist into the table. I was furious with the government, my government. And I was furious at myself for having doubted my client, for imploring him to plead guilty to a crime that he did not commit.

I wasn't only angry at the prosecutors. I was also angry with myself and all of my intellectual, high-minded friends. I knew damn well why T.C. felt he had to keep proving to me again and again that he was innocent, that he had done the right thing on that horrible night many years ago. T.C. knew he could never gain my full trust for one reason—he was a member of the only group in this country that unites blacks, middle class whites, Hispanics, conservatives and liberals in their disdain and contempt. T.C. was a poor white man who grew up in circumstances that we would call heroic if applied to poor blacks or poor immigrants. But when it is a poor white man who grows up in such wretched circumstances that indoor plumbing is as rare as a chance at a decent education, we just call them White Trash. And then we give them the same respect we give to our trash.

These thoughts plagued me as Maier re-entered the room. "Sorry guys, emergency business. Okay, let's let it roll again."

T.C.: "Why should I take the fall since it was your damn fault this whole thing happened?"

Morgan: (raising his voice) "I already said it was my fault. I admit that I'm the one that ordered him killed but you know, I changed my mind. I chased you down and tried to stop you."

T.C.: " You didn't just chase us down. You fucking tried to kill me. You stabbed me to save the life of a fucking nigger! And now you want me to cover your ass?"

Morgan: "I've come too damn far—and brought you and a lot of others along with me—to have my life ruined by something that happened a long time ago."

T.C.: " That's your problem. You tried to kill me to save a nigger. I'll never forgive you for that."

Morgan: "Boy, you got a damn short memory. Wasn't for me and Carl you'd still be in the Goddamned lock-up taking it in the ass for torching that synagogue."

T.C.: "Yeah, and you and Carl were the ones told me to torch that synagogue. And had me do it on a Sunday when the kikes weren't even in there. You musta laughed your asses off sending 'the stupid kid' on a fool's errand. What good did it do to burn a

Jew building—they got enough money to build a hundred build- ings. You just never had the guts to have the Jews burned out— just like you didn't have the guts to burn that nigger Boddie. It's 'cause of yellow bellies like you the Klan fell apart. You sold out."

Morgan: "T.C., you gotta realize that the Klan is over. It's dead. We've all got to live in a new world. We were wrong and God has led us on a new path."

T.C:: "We weren't wrong. God was with us that night and He would be with us now if people like you just had the guts it took to win."

Morgan: "Don't you see it was wrong what we did, T.C. It was wrong taking Boddie like we did, and it was wrong for you to kill Boddie—and, damn, the way you killed him! I knew it was wrong even then. That's why I tried to stop you."

T.C.: "You yellow belly scum. We shoulda burned you with that nigger. You say we were wrong? Shit, you know whenever I feel down, I just think how that nigger shrieked and smelled like a grilling piece of Bar-B-Que meat and it just picks me right up."

I didn't wait for the tape to end. I just scooped up my papers and stormed out of the room, telling Payton to come back after lunch and take notes on the tape. I felt like some great hand had reached out and squeezed all of the life out of my body.

CHAPTER 35

U nder the law governing wiretaps, the government must stop taping a conversation after a certain period of time unless the conversation being taped relates to the purpose of the wiretap order. Any material or conversations taped during a period when the recording should have been turned off cannot be used. The judge would have to suppress that portion of the tape that incriminated T.C. It could not be used to convict him.

I suppose I should have been happy when the judge did just that with respect to the taped conversation between Morgan and T.C. By the time T.C. and Morgan began talking about the murder, the FBI should have realized that T.C. had nothing to do with the purpose of the tap, namely the search for evidence of the corruption of judges and politicians. The government argued that, at least on the surface, Morgan was talking about a crime, bribing a witness and covering up a murder, but all of that came way after it was apparent that T.C. was not a relevant target of the tap and the FBI should have signed off. I thought that Rabison purposely tanked the suppression motion because the FBI did not want that tape to see the light of day, just in case they could still salvage their corruption investigation before the existence of the tape tipped off possible targets. That's why Rabison agreed to have the suppression motion taken in private in the Judge's chambers with the resultant transcript seated.

Payton and I decided not to tell T.C. about what was on the tape. There was nothing to say, and it would only have gotten me angrier and more confused than I already was. We had to tell him, our client, about the *existence* of the tape without revealing its content. When we did, T.C. was cool as a cucumber. He said he didn't need to hear the tape or see any transcript. He said he never talked to Morgan about this case, they must have mistaken someone else for his voice. I acted convinced. I would have been convinced if I had not heard the tape. T.C. was that good a liar. But I already knew that by now.

I didn't want to give the summation in the case. I had been so furious earlier in the case the first time I thought that T.C. had lied to us. And then I thought I found out he hadn't lied, and I felt terrible for not having believed him, and on and on. There had been so many reversals of emotions in this case for me, that I no longer felt angry or sad—I no longer felt anything at all. I just didn't have it in me to give the summation. This case really had to be sold to the jury, and I just didn't have the fire to be a decent salesman. Payton tried to talk me into giving the summation.

"What's wrong, Luke? Do you think you are the first defense counsel who was lied to by his client? Get over it."

"This isn't just any case. I gave up my job to come down here. I did it not only because of my remembrance and affection for T.C. I did it because I thought it was for something important. Something righteous, to help a person who needed help, who deserved help."

"Forgive me if I don't weep for you or your client—our client. Knowing what you know now I would think that you would be grateful to see the sonofabitch caught out. But that still doesn't relieve you of your obligation as his lawyer. You've got to give that summation."

Payton reached into his pocket and pulled out a plastic baggie with a tape inside. "And just so you won't go away empty-handed, I have a souvenir to take home with you when this thing is over."

"What is it?"

"It's a tape—the FBI tape we just heard."

I was stunned. "How the hell did you get it?"

Payton smiled. "I filched it."

I palmed the tape in my hand staring down at it as if it were radioactive—which in a sense it was. I couldn't believe that

Payton had risked a prison sentence and his license to practice law to smuggle out a copy of the tape. I understood that the danger of being caught or found out was diminished once he smuggled a copy of the tape out of the District Attorney's building. There were probably several copies of the wiretap tape being held by various agencies and people in government. Moreover, in the course of the lengthy corruption investigation, there were certainly a good number of people who had access to the tape and could have copied it.

Some of my reflexive concerns about the discovery of the theft—or of the identity of the thief—were allayed by my belief that the government would be less than enthusiastic in pursuing such a matter. There were just too many government people with a motive to leak that tape. There were even those in District Attorney Rabison's office who might want to leak the tape. Whether or not T.C. was convicted, Rabison's people would have a motive to show either that the verdict was correct or that it was wrong. Eddie Rabison would, at best, conduct a phony investigation to find out who leaked the tape lest the trail curl back to someone in his office or the suspicion fall even on him. The FBI would be no more eager to vigorously pursue an investigation for fear that the culprit might be one of its own, and the investigation might reveal some of the "sharp," if legal, practices it had engaged in during its sweeping corruption investigation. Payton and I would appear to have had the least opportunity and motive to steal the tape. After all, it showed our client to be guilty.

I looked up at Payton and shook my head in amazement. "How the hell did you pull this off?"

Payton smiled. "It wasn't easy. The deal Rabison and I worked out with the judge in chambers was that I would get one hour alone with the tape, but I could not remove it from the room or the tape recorder, though I could stop it and rewind it and play parts over."

"I'm surprised Rabison agreed to that."

"He didn't agree to that. It was a compromise. He wanted a person in the room with me while I listened to the tape and took whatever notes I needed. I demanded to have a copy of the tape to take to my office and then return it later. The judge compromised. He said I could not take the tape out of the building or the room. He said I should thank him for that ruling because it would keep me off the hot seat if the tape disappeared or an unauthorized copy of it was made. Anyway, the judge agreed with me that it was a violation of my work product privilege to have a government official in the room with me watching what parts of the tape I noted down and which parts of the tape I emphasized by replaying. "

I kept nodding my head as he spoke, fascinated with how he had managed to execute this *Mission Impossible*. "Okay, I understand that, but how did you get a copy of the tape?"

"Well, when I showed up at the designated time to listen to the tape, I showed the security screener my personal dictation tape recorder. The D.A. had told me that the wiretap tape of T.C. lasted 26 minutes. The tape in my dictaphone recorder lasts 60 minutes."

I was surprised, "He let you take your dictaphone machine into the room with you?"

"Well, not at first. He called down to Rabison. Rabison came up and told me he would not let me take my dictaphone recorder into the room with me. I could only take handwritten notes of the tape. I became indignant and told him that it was none of his damn business how I took notes. I don't like to take handwritten notes, which I often can't read later. I also told him that our agreement was that I had only one shot at this for one hour. If I had to take handwritten notes, I was going to ask the judge for as much additional time as it took me to write down everything I wanted to write down. I told him that if he made me take notes by hand, I might transcribe the entire tape even if it took me all day."

"And?"

"And, I guess he didn't want to have to go back to the judge.

He probably knew that the judge would probably side with me because he had already leaned too far in Rabison's favor by refusing to allow me to have unlimited time with the tape at a place of my own choosing. I also knew that Rabison didn't want to give me any more time than the one hour. We argued back and forth, and eventually I let him save some face by agreeing to only 50 minutes with the tape because I could save some time by using the dictaphone."

I still couldn't believe that Payton had gotten that tape. "Why didn't you tell me that you were going to do this?"

"Because even I didn't know I was going to do it until I got into that room. I really did want to use a dictaphone to take oral notes, both to save time and for better accuracy. Something just overcame me when I got in the room with the tape."

"But weren't you afraid that you were being observed?"

Payton raised his eyebrows and laughed. "Sure was. In fact, Rabison had posted an Assistant D.A. near a window in the door. I started the wiretap tape while I held the dictaphone in my right hand by my side where the Assistant D.A. couldn't see it. I clicked on the dictaphone when I started the tape. Every so often I would stop the tape and then pretend to click on the dictaphone, but I was really clicking it off. Then while the tape was stopped, I would lean over my dictaphone and whisper into it, whispering into a stopped tape. Then I would start the tape again and appear to click the dictaphone off, but, of course, I was really clicking it on.

"I didn't stop the tape too often the first time through, just two or three times. I wanted to be sure I got the whole tape on my machine, and I didn't want too many cuts on my copy—I was afraid it would look like it had been fiddled with—though I wasn't too concerned about that because the context made it clear that our copy was recording an uninterrupted conversation."

"The guy at the window didn't get suspicious?"

"No, why should he? I assume he was just watching to make sure I didn't try to remove their tape from their tape machine and to make sure I didn't do anything to their machine but start and stop it. Anyway, when I had gone through the tape the first time, I figured I still had at least half an hour left on my dictaphone tape. So, this time around, I started and stopped the tape more often, and really did dictate some "legal" thoughts and analysis of the tape into my dictaphone. At one point, I even stood up and paced with the dictaphone to my mouth near the door so that the Assistant D.A. could actually hear that I was talking into it."

"So that this tape has some of your meandering thoughts on it?"

"No, I already erased that part of the dictaphone tape. The only thing you have left on that tape is the full wiretap conversation between Morgan and T.C."

"Damn, Payton, I still can't believe you did this!"

"I did have one big scare. When I left the room, the Assistant D.A. who has been posted at the door demanded that I play my dictaphone tape back for him to hear. Inside of me I was dying, but I made damn sure to show only anger on the outside. My first thought was that if he tried to confiscate the tape when I refused to play it for him, I would just rip the tape up 'as a matter of principle.' But it never came to that. I just went ballistic, shouting that he had no right to hear what I said in the tape—that it was privileged information. I was howling that 'this was all a trap set by Rabison to get his hands on my work product and our privileged thoughts about our defense, and I was not going to take that crap from them!'"

"Did he buy it?"

"Almost. He knew I was right about that. So he pulled out his cell phone and called Rabison. From what I heard him say, Rabison was probably quizzing him to make sure he had watched me carefully the entire time I was in the room—the guy kept saying 'Positive, I'm positive. I didn't take my eyes off of him for one second.' He let me leave the room with it—and now it's yours."

"What do you expect me to do with it?"

Payton smiled, "You should save it and play it every now and again as a reminder whenever you're tempted to rush off to another 'do good' assignment. Next time you have that feeling come over you, sign up to work for the Red Cross."

"Here, take it back, I don't need it."

"No, keep it. I haven't given up on squashing Morgan yet. You wounded him when you beat up Thornton on cross about Morgan paying him off, but I want him dead."

"You think they'll go after Morgan for trying to bribe Thornton?"

"No, no the government witnesses never get banged for lying or bribery. Defense witnesses will get the chair for spitting on the street, but if you testify for the government, you get a free pass forever. If they can still get him on that corruption thing, they will, but I don't want him for corruption. I want him for being in the Klan, for being a White Supremacist who tried to put the black people back to the days of slavery—for using people like T.C. to do his dirty work for him."

"And how do you suppose I'm going to help you nail him?

"All you have to do is address a nice big envelope to the *Augusta Gazette* and drop that baggie with the tape in the envelope in the mail and both T.C. and Mr. Morgan will get their due. But don't leave your prints on anything. The newspapers would never turn in the envelope anyway. They would die to protect a source. But who needs to take chances?"

"Why don't you mail it?"

"Because wherever I go I'm recognizable. Most everybody in this town knows me by sight, particularly since the trial. It would be hard for me to mail it from a public box without someone seeing me do it—and, like I said, who needs to take chances? Besides, it's your call, not mine."

I looked at the encased tape. In some ways I was delighted that I now had the smoking gun. Not so much to please Payton by "getting" Morgan, but rather to place that smoking gun in T.C.'s hand where it belonged. Whether he was convicted or not, that tape would show T.C. for the murderer he was.

Yet with power comes danger and hard choices. I did not mind the danger. In fact, I thought what Payton had done to get a copy of the tape was exciting. I found it exhilarating to be in on the caper now. It had been so long since I had risked anything. What I was less thrilled about was having to make a very hard choice—whether to publicly disclose the contents of the tape. I did feel some relief that I did not have to make that very difficult choice at that moment.

CHAPTER 36

When I arrived at my hotel the night I heard those awful FBI tapes, I poured myself into the big overstuffed chair in the center of the hotel room. I threw my briefcase against the wall, causing all of its contents to spill on the floor. Those papers representing so much work, so much faith, were now evidence of my failure, lying on the carpet along with the assorted shapes of the dust balls that proved that the cleaning lady was as big a failure as I was.

I knew I had to make an immediate choice. Should I destroy myself or T.C.? I knew now there could be no happy ending. I couldn't decide what would be worse, having T.C. convicted or having T.C. acquitted. The lawyer in me, weaned on the adversarial system, still wanted a "victory." The moral ideologue in me wanted T.C. to get his just desserts.

Many years ago, just after my family left Augusta for New York, I met my great Uncle Jeremiah Lukash—one of the few of my mother's relatives. He was a man filled with wisdom who had a wise answer for everything. I tried to think about what Uncle Jeremiah would have said to me at a time like this. He used to say, "God always make certain to stitch at least a shard of silver lining into even the darkest clouds. For reasons we cannot possibly understand, God will often strip a human being of his possessions, of his dreams, and even of his loved ones. But," he used to say, "the one thing God will never strip entirely from a human being is hope. He will always leave a man or a woman a toehold in life, a little silver lining."

My father used to make fun of Uncle Jeremiah's eternal optimism. Dad said that optimists look at a half-filled glass and proclaim it half-full, a pessimist looks at a half-filled glass and finds it half-empty, while Jeremiah looked at a completely empty glass and marveled at how much room there was in the glass that would be available when we eventually found something to fill it with.

I was never one to let God off the hook with the defense that "God works in mysterious ways." Frankly, God's sense of humor often totally escaped me. I did not find what He did to Job funny, and I did not find what He had just done to me funny either.

When my father asked Uncle Jeremiah where the silver lining on the Holocaust was, old Uncle Jeremiah launched into the founding of the State of Israel; the refuge that many survivors found in the United States, the greatest country in the history of the world; the growing taboo against overt anti-Semitism for the first time in two thousand years, and on and on. In fact, Uncle Jeremiah made the Holocaust sound like just about the greatest thing that God ever did for the Jewish people, or at least those few who survived God's wondrous "gift."

I was locked into a trial I could not get out of which had only two possible outcomes, each one of which would be devastating to me. It was time to search for Uncle Jeremiah's silver lining.

It took some creative thinking, but I finally found it—sort of. The existence of those FBI tapes would allow me to slip the dilemma we had wrestled with about T.C. taking the stand in his own defense. It wasn't a big silver lining; it was actually closer to a gray lining. In fact, it was like having your legs amputated but then realizing how much you would save on shoes and socks. But at least it was something.

The decision on whether or not to put T.C. on the stand in his own defense had caused Payton and me more concern and anguish than any other tactical decision in the trial. The problem was that the decision involved ethics as well as legal tactics.

I asked Payton his opinion as to why criminal defense counsel were so reluctant to put their clients on the stand. I told him I knew the judge had to tell the jurors they could not hold the defendant's failure to take the stand against him, but I also knew that they always would. Payton told me that I was right up to a point. Jurors would certainly be suspicious that a defendant was not testifying because he was guilty, but suspicion or even surmise does not amount to proof beyond a reasonable doubt. On the other hand, listening to a defendant lying, contradicting himself, and looking and sounding like the criminal he is accused of being shoots that meter needle way beyond reasonable doubt. It's the old case of it being better to be silent and therefore being thought to be stupid rather than talking and therefore removing all doubt. Innocent or not, defendants are best left off the stand.

I had to twist Payton's arm even to fully debrief T.C. Payton told me it was tantamount to malpractice for a criminal defense attorney to ask his client if he actually committed the crime. As I had learned at Dingle, Dingle and Dingle, a criminal defense lawyer cannot knowingly put a defendant on the stand if the lawyer knows the defendant is lying. On the other hand, there is no problem with putting on the stand a guilty criminal defendant who is lying to you. Even if you know in your gut he is lying, you can put him right on the stand and let him rip. The major problem for a criminal defense counsel is if your client tells you the truth. It is a real problem if your client tells you that he is guilty and then proceeds to propose telling a false exculpatory story that is so brilliantly conceived and smoothly delivered that you know it would convince the most cynical jury.

That is why, Payton informed me, the first thing he told his clients was that if they told him they did it, he would not put them on the stand. It is not a hard signal to pick up. Payton agreed with me that the worst nightmare for a criminal defense attorney is having the burden of defending an innocent, honest person. Even worse, however, is having an honest guilty client. The dream, of course, is to have a dishonest guilty client.

I had insisted that we get the "truth" from T.C. no matter what the consequences. Every defendant, no matter how heinous his crime, is entitled to a vigorous competent counsel. But there was no law or ethical decree stating that I had to be that counsel.

I had not come to this as just another day at the office in the career of a criminal defense attorney. I had come to this case because I truly believed that an old friend of mine was innocent and would be railroaded into a lifetime sentence if I did not come down to help him. Had T.C. not convinced me of his innocence, I would have turned right around and headed right back to New York.

As I said, before the mind-numbing experience of listening to the FBI tapes, back when we thought T.C. was an innocent man, Payton and I had agonized over the decision as to whether we should put him on the stand. We stayed up all night on the first Saturday after the trial started, debating the pros and cons of allowing T.C. to testify. We knew there was some play in the joints depending on how the trial went, but basically, we had to make the decision at that time.

At that time Payton and I were very concerned about walking T.C. into a perjury trap. The Constitution prevents a defendant from being tried twice for the same crime, even if new incriminating evidence is found or if errors were made in the trial that prevented the government from getting a fair trial. But a trial for perjury would not be considered retrying the defendant for the same offense for which he had just been acquitted.

We were afraid that if we put T.C. on the stand, the prosecutors could try him again for perjury, even if he was acquitted and even if he was innocent. We did not want to give the prosecutors two bites at the apple by opening up a possible perjury prosecution if they were unsatisfied with the jury verdict or with the sentence T.C. received from the judge.

We had worked our way through twenty other considerations in deciding on whether or not to put T.C. on the stand. We decided to visit him in the prison the next day, a weekend day, and put him through a cross-examination run-through without telling him why we're doing so.

This was, of course, well before we had any idea of the existence of the FBI tapes. What we were trying to determine was how good or bad a witness T.C. would make. Innocence or guilt had nothing to do with it. At that time we were both certain of his innocence, but an innocent person who sounded guilty would be a disaster, while a guilty person who sounded innocent would be an excellent candidate for testifying. A good attorney must discard irrelevant concerns when making decisions involving what testimony to put on at trial—and guilt and innocence are two of those irrelevant concerns. Unfortunately, the truth is also an irrelevant consideration. Any lawyer who decides to put on a witness merely because the witness is telling the truth is greatly harming his client if that witness is not essential and would make a lousy witness. Some of the best witnesses are the biggest liars, and some of the most unbelievable witnesses wouldn't even lie about what they ate for lunch.

During our run-through T.C. turned out to be the worst god-awful witness I had ever heard. When he gave his name "to the jury" he looked to me like he was lying through his teeth. After Payton ran him down with a series of fast-paced questions, I just leaned in and shouted at him, "You killed O.J. Simpson's wife, didn't you?" T.C. glared at me like a frightened deer caught in the headlights. Had I not known better, I would have been certain I had just ended O.J. Simpson's never-ending search for his wife's killer.

T.C.'s story unraveled, came back on itself and then totally morphed into a different story as Payton sunk his teeth into T.C. without surcease. Trial attorneys would recognize T.C. immediately for what he was, a lousy witness who could be confused over his gender and made to look like he was lying about just about anything he was asked. The problem was that we knew that jurors would think they were watching a liar and a guilty defendant. And, at that time, we believed him to be innocent.

When Payton was finished we knew we had cemented the decision we had reached the night before. No way we could put T.C. on the stand, however convinced we were of his innocence. I laughed and put my hand on T.C.'s shoulder, "T.C., I must say that was the most abominable presentation I have ever heard. You, sir, will not be allowed within ten feet of the witness stand. In fact, if you even so much as lean towards the witness stand, I will personally throttle you."

T.C. did not laugh. He pushed my hand off of his shoulder and glared at me.

"I didn't do it. I'm testifying."

I was taken aback. Payton and I had taken the most minute considerations into account in reaching our decision about whether to put T.C. on the stand. The only thing we'd forgotten to take into consideration was T.C.'s opinion on the matter.

"T.C., I know you're innocent. I wouldn't be here if you weren't innocent. We're not talking innocent. We're not talking truth. We're talking getting you acquitted. The best chance of getting you acquitted is to keep you off the stand."

I tried to explain to T.C. that his testimony involved too many "stories." I told him a "story" was an explanation for why something did or did not happen in a manner one expected it to happen. For instance, if a person was claiming he was badly injured, he would have to give the jury a "story" as to why he did not seek immediate medical help. A "story" could be either true or false. But what was important was that a jury will accept one, and, at most two "stories." When they start hearing labored explanation after labored explanation, they start thinking they are just hearing a bunch of bullshit, even if every word is true.

T.C. stared at me blankly. I realized I was not making contact.

"Look, T.C., let me give you an example. If you take the stand, the prosecutor is going to ask you about all of the people to whom you admitted that you torched the synagogue, and you didn't tell one of them that you were the Klan fall guy. And they have evidence from your indictment that seems to show that you did it. Now, I know that you were the fall guy, but you still have to give the jury a "story" about why all that happened in a way that seems to defy logic."

"But it did happen the way I told you!"

"I'm not saying it didn't. I'm just saying it requires a 'story' to tell. Now, when you get to talking about the murder, they'll get into your blood on the shirt at the scene, your name on that little good-luck charm, your membership in the Klan, and a whole bunch of other evidence, not to mention Morgan's testimony. Now, I know your explanation for that, and I believe it, but it's another story. And I have three more stories written down here that you tell about other things. Eventually, the jury just says, 'Hey, this dude always has an explanation for everything, a story for everything. No one is that unlucky—with all that smoke he's blowin' at us, there has got to be a fire somewhere.'"

I looked at T.C.'s face. He was looking at me, but I didn't know if he was even hearing much less understanding what I was saying.

I stopped my pitch, because T.C. was just staring at me and shaking his head "no."

Payton pulled out of his bag the yellow legal pad on which we had listed the many reasons why T.C. should not take the stand. He held it out to T.C.

"Look T.C., there isn't *one* reason why you shouldn't testify—there are *twenty-three* good reasons why you shouldn't testify."

T.C. brushed the pad aside with the back of his hand. "I don't need no yellow pad to tell me nothing. I didn't do it. I'm gonna tell those jury people what really happened."

"But they won't believe you."

"God will believe me. That's all that matters."

As an attorney I was furious that this idiot was slitting his own throat. He knew nothing about trial work. He was going to destroy all of our work and his own life as well. Yet I couldn't help but admire him. We cared more about his escaping conviction than we cared about the truth. He cared more about his own personal convictions than his legal conviction. I felt almost guilty about virtually ordering him to forego his opportunity to tell his story to the jury, and the world. Maybe his passion would overcome his ineptness as a witness, after all.

Looking back on it, I had to admit that I was moved by T.C.'s genuineness and insistence on telling the jury "the truth" whatever the consequences. We knew now that the man was lying through his teeth to us, and both Payton and I bought it. Two trained litigators had been completely taken in by a semi-literate Neanderthal of a murdering bigot.

After I heard the FBI tape, I was too furious to think of anything but strangling T.C. Payton took it all in stride. On the way out of the courthouse, he put his arm around me:

"Hey Mr. Lipton, remember when we thought T.C. was innocent? Do you remember what clinched our decision not to put T.C. on the stand?"

"I can't remember my own name right now."

"We did that cross-examination run through with him and decided that, even though he was innocent, he was such a bad witness that nobody would believe anything he said. And then he tells us he has to testify because he is innocent and he has to tell his story to the jury, and we buy it, the whole package. This guy whom we, two experts, thought was the most unbelievable witness we ever heard sold us the Brooklyn Bridge *and* took back a mortgage on it."

Payton and I realized that the FBI tape took us out of the pan and into the fire. On one level, it pretty much eliminated any question about T.C.'s taking the stand to testify. Payton was almost certain that he could get the tapes suppressed since the government was obliged to have minimized the conversations and cut out as soon as they realized that there was no discussion relating to their corruption investigation. Moreover, the Feds were clearly going to punt on the suppression since they didn't want the tape revealed and their investigation totally wrecked.

But even when some evidence is suppressed, courts allow it to be used to cross-examine a defendant. The FBI wouldn't want the tapes used in open court, period. But I wasn't so sure about Rabison. The theory is that the courts don't want a suppression of probative evidence to be a green light for perjury by a defendant. So, it was all pretty easy: if T.C. gets on the stand, the tape comes in, and T.C. is fried.

"Payton, if T.C. still insists on testifying, I'm getting off this case."

Payton laughed.

"What's so funny about that?"

"There isn't a judge in the world who would let you withdraw from this case now. Too many problems, not to mention the extra year it would take for a new lawyer to get up to speed. The judge would have to declare a mistrial. Even the fact that you suddenly disappeared from the jury's sight would be so harmful to T.C.... and you know no judge is going to ever declare a mistrial if he doesn't have to—especially in a high-publicity case like this. Nope, buddy, we're in this for the long haul."

Payton decided, and I reluctantly agreed, that it would be best if he went to the prison to talk to T.C. without me there. I was so angry that there could only be big trouble if I faced off with T.C. at this point.

"Like it or not, Luke, we're still T.C.'s lawyers and we still have to do the best damn job possible for him."

"I know. I know, but it isn't easy. I thought I was defending Dreyfus, and it turns out I was defending Esterhazy."

"Who the hell was...."

"Never mind, it's just another screw-the-Jew thing."

Payton left on his mission. Given his history of stubbornness, I thought there was no way in the world that T.C. would agree not to testify. Payton was on a mission, a suicide mission, but a mission nonetheless.

Much to my surprise and delight, Payton succeeded in persuading T.C. not to testify at the trial. Payton told me that his success was due to his magical powers of persuasion, aided by a pair of pliers clamped down hard on T.C.'s testicles.

"Seriously," I asked Payton, "How did you do it?"

"I looked the sonofabitch in the eye and told him that I had heard the FBI wiretap tape of his conversation with Will Morgan. I said that if he insisted on testifying you and I were going to get out of the case and throw his redneck ass to the wolves. That got his attention."

"Well, now that we don't have to worry about training T.C. how to testify on the stand, we have to teach him how to testify *off* the stand."

For both offensive and defensive reasons, we knew it would be essential that T.C. learn how to testify without taking the stand and without the prosecution ever actually cross-examining him. The defensive need for such "testimony" arose from his failure to take the stand to testify.

Jurors want to feel they know a defendant, want to read him, size him up. If they cannot do that while he testifies, they watch him like a hawk in the courtroom for evidence of "guilt" or "innocence." Even in civil cases, I always told my clients not to ever joke or laugh until they were at least fifteen minutes away from the courthouse. Even a juror seeing a client laughing with someone in the courthouse corridor might signal to that juror that the client didn't really take all of this seriously. And if, God forbid, a criminal defendant should laugh while chatting with someone during some down time in the courtroom, it would signal that he has no remorse at all for what happened to the "victim." Laughing is definitely out.

Non-testimonial "testimony" is often the greatest tar pit for a defendant. Every individual and thus every juror has an expectation about how a person should act or react to any given situation, even stressful ones. Let the local news program show a tearless, almost automaton father talk about finding his wife dead in the house, and the viewers will deem him "guilty" because grief stricken people should be showing more emotion. Should that same father bawl like a baby while describing finding his wife's body, and the viewers will judge him guilty because his "performance" was just too over the top. No psychiatrist has ever nailed down exactly how a person is supposed to react to a stressful or sad situation, but every citizen, every juror has his own idea about how guilty or innocent people should react.

We knew if we told T.C. to keep a blank, expressionless look on his face at all times, many jurors would interpret that as the look of a cold-blooded bastard without feelings. The person who doesn't flash even an iota of anguish as someone on the stand testifies about finding the incinerated body of an innocent black man in the marsh is probably a person who could have been responsible for that cold-blooded murder. Yet if we told T.C. to react with emotion to testimony on the stand or events in the courtroom, jurors might think he was just programmed and play-acting.

"Payton, have you ever figured out exactly how an innocent man would react in the courtroom?"

"Apparently neither one of us has any idea how an innocent man would react, since we both thought T.C. was innocent. It's impossible to guess how a juror would expect an innocent person to act. But since the non-testimonial testimony also has a lot to do with getting the jury to like your client, I always go with nervous. I always tell my clients to look nervous and scared and confused, like you can't believe this is happening to you."

"So we're going with nervous, scared and confused. With T.C. we're set on the confused, but we have to beat the arrogant and bullying into scared and nervous..."

Payton was in charge of the non-testimonial testimony, teaching T.C. how to behave and look while in the courtroom and how to react to various happenings. He made sure that T.C. would be the first one to reach to refill our water glasses, and we even arranged for T.C. to help a seated old lady out of her chair in the courtroom visitors' section as the jury was leaving the court-room. And, of course, we went to T.C.'s church, urging them to send parishioners of all colors and from all walks of life who would, in a Christian way, hug and throw kisses his way during breaks in the testimony.

I was in charge of the offensive non-testimonial testimony. I told T.C. that when there was some damning testimony that was being given, I would step on his foot underneath the table. That was a signal for him to start to rise from his chair, eyes ablaze with indignation. I would put my hand on his shoulder and push him down in the seat before he could straighten up. I would save this "testimony" for one or two shots. But it would be clear to the jury that T.C. was testifying "he's a goddamned liar." That kind of reaction looks genuine, and, best of all, is not subject to cross-examination.

For example, earlier in the trial when Morgan had testified, we had still been debating whether T.C. would take the stand. So, to be on the safe side, I had utilized to perfection one of our non-testimonial testifying tricks. I had choreographed the entire dance several times with T.C., and I must say that he performed flawlessly. He and Payton executed the *pas de deux* with perfec-tion.

The second day of Morgan's cross-examination, Payton stood up with his papers under his arm. As he was walking over to the lectern to begin his cross-examination, Payton bent down to T.C. sitting in his chair. They then carried on what seemed to be an animated conversation in whispers, with T.C. gesticulating as if he had a gun in his hand. To the jurors, it was obvious he was giving Payton some of the details about how the murder actually happened. It looked very real.

Next, according to plan, Payton walked over the lectern, fixed Morgan with a killer stare and barked, "Mr. Morgan, isn't it a fact that you took your gun, aimed it at that innocent black man lying on the ground begging for his life and threatened to shoot him...."

At this point, right on schedule, Payton pivoted and looked over to T.C. T.C. pointed to his left eye. Payton pivoted back to face Morgan.

"...and pushed that gun right into his left eye? Yes or no?"

Of course we knew what the answer would be, but T.C.'s non-testimonial testimony as relayed to Payton really had the ring of truth to it, or so we hoped.

At two other points in the cross-examination, as planned, T.C. signaled Payton over to him after Morgan had given some damaging answer. Payton would then confer with T.C., return to the stand and rip into Morgan.

"Mr. Morgan, isn't it a fact that it did not happen that way? What really happened...."

And so it had gone. The non-testimonial testimony had worked so well that my vanity in remembering it almost made me forget the anguish that the better part of my nature felt over T.C.'s betrayal.

CHAPTER 37

It was three o'clock in the morning on the day of my summation in the case. I sat alone in my hotel room, knee-deep in papers, exhibits, transcripts from the trial and Payton's notes. Throughout the trial, I had been taking notes for my summation. But that was when I had assumed that I was going to give the summation of a "true believer." Now that I had to give the summation of a "true mercenary," I had changed my approach entirely. My summation would not be fueled by faith and passion but, I hoped, by cunning and oratory brilliance. This summation would be coming from the head, not the heart.

I had taped to the wall the names and descriptions of our jury. There were four blacks, six whites, one Pakistani or Indian—I wasn't sure which—and one person of undeterminable origin whose appearance made him look like he had been conceived at an orgy at the United Nations. He looked like he had black blood, Indian blood, Jewish blood, Italian blood, Native American blood, and Payton swore that he had the gait of a man from Ulan Bator.

The only firm decision Payton and I had reached before picking the jury was that we didn't want any Jews on the jury. At that point we were assuming that somehow that synagogue burning would come into play, and Jews were more likely to take that personally than, let us say, Christians.

The few times a Jew had come up for questioning, Payton and I took copious notes and asked copious questions until we came up with an impenetrable pretext for challenging that person. We needed a pretext because, by law, we could not challenge a person based solely on race or ethnic origin. Push hard enough, and any decent lawyer can find a "legitimate" reason for illegitimately dismissing a juror. Three Jews up, three Jews down, albeit we may have wasted a challenge on a Mr. Wolfe who was seen holding rosary beads as he gathered up his belongings to leave. Payton whispered to me, "As you can see, even the Jews are Christian down here."

It probably surprised the prosecutor that we made no effort to keep blacks off the jury. In fact, we wanted as many blacks as possible to serve. The horrendous murder of Aaron Boddie so many years ago had understandably become a *cause celebre* for the black community. That one brutal, unprovoked and unpunished lynching stood as a horrible metaphor for the old Jim Crow South. Because this lynching had gained such national notoriety and was so important, particularly to the black community, Payton and I felt that the Leo Frank syndrome would work to our advantage with black jurors.

It was the Leo Frank syndrome that made so many people refuse to accept that such an important person as President Kennedy could have been killed by such a nobody as Lee Harvey Oswald. People could not accept a world in which a JFK could be eliminated by a Lee Harvey Oswald acting alone. President Kennedy deserved better assassins, more important people, bigger catches. When the family of Martin Luther King Jr. insisted that the CIA, J. Edgar Hoover, and other "important" people were directly involved in the killing of their saintly father, they were also expressing an unwillingness to accept retribution from only some worthless piece of white trash. The Leo Frank syndrome infects us all at one time or another.

Leo Frank had been convicted of a crime he did not commit because he was a far more "worthy" murderer of the victim than the person who actually committed the crime. At the turn of the last century, many Northern industries had set up factories in the post-Civil War, economically devastated South. The South welcomed the businesses but detested the businessmen. The South considered this a second Northern invasion.

One of those Northern "invaders" was Leo Frank. He came down South to manage his uncle's pencil factory in Georgia in

1913. To add insult to Southern injury, Leo Frank was Jewish. Being a Jewish Northerner Scalawag, Leo Frank started out his turn at bat with three strikes against him.

One day in 1913 a young female white factory worker in the Frank plant was found sexually assaulted and murdered. The evidence strongly implicated a black janitor who worked at the factory. The problem was that for the enraged white community, a black janitor would not do. Hell, they could lynch a black janitor for committing even a minor crime or no crime at all back in those days. The gods of White Supremacy required a far more substantial sacrifice than a mere "nigger janitor."

A rich Jew from New York, now there was an apt sacrifice. Leo Frank was arrested for the murder and convicted based primarily on the evidence that he was a rich Jew from New York. The courageous John Slayton, governor of Georgia, commuted Frank's death sentence, thus causing the good and decent Slayton to flee not only his office but the state. The commutation only meant that the people rather than the state would carry out the death sentence. Leo Frank was lynched by an enraged mob of white people.

Payton and I figured that the blacks on the jury would demand a more important killer than just another piece of white trash like T.C. After all, we were not asking black jurors to leave the murder unsolved. A "not guilty" verdict would clearly implicate Morgan in the murder. The T.C.s of the South had been made to pay for the sins of the Old South that benefited primarily the Morgans of the area. We were betting that the black jurors would want to nail Leo Frank, not the janitor. Moreover, black jurors were less likely to be dazzled by Morgan's high standing in the community since blacks were rarely included in that community.

I knew I would be aiming at those black jurors. They would be most receptive to my arguments, and I hoped and assumed that the other jurors would give great deference to their views because the victim in this case was black and was killed because he was black.

The key to my summation, as I saw it, would be my ability to trump the prosecutor's race card with my class card. They'd be aiming at T.C. I'd be aiming at Morgan. I would, of course, review all of the other issues, but the sale I really had to close was the class issue: that T.C. was being made the scapegoat because he was dispensable white trash who was being sacrificed to protect the respectable Will Morgan.

I knew that one way to drive my class point home was to convince the jury that my argument on that issue was fueled by passion and belief. I had been careful to husband my emotional explosions so that when one did come, it would appear genuine and heartfelt. I had done my share of yelling and shrieking during cross-examinations in other cases, but in this case my cross-examination was firm, tough and controlled. My only loss of control would come during the summation when I flipped over the class card.

There are many lawyers who try the whole case in a state of high dudgeon. They are screaming, flailing their arms, and engaging in constant histrionics from day one to the last day of the trial. They are constantly in first gear. Such lawyers are a great show, often garner wonderful reputations, and invariably are asked to be talking heads on the television shows. But they are rarely effective.

I'd had a partner named Franklin Stanton whom we all called The Mad Lawyer. We called him that because in court he always acted like he was mad. Or funny. He was always cracking up the courtroom. I felt that if he spent as much time working on the case as he spent working on his one-liners, he would have been far more successful. As it was, Franklin always packed the courtroom and had jurors swarming about him after a trial. But he rarely was the beneficiary of significant verdicts. You see, the jurors thought Stanton was a hoot, a great show. A very impressive show, but a show nonetheless. I used to joke that a "Stanton" verdict was when the jury Foreman came in with the verdict and turned to Frank's client and said, "First the good news, your lawyer was extremely entertaining."

I wanted to be sure that when I faked outrage, it would be appear to be spontaneous, sincere and heartfelt. The more I practiced the summation, the further my mind retreated from the reality of the situation—I was defending an unrepentant bigot, anti-Semite and murderer. But the summation was what I did for a living. It was the jewel in the crown of the adversary system. The champion from each army, lined up *mano a mano* and then the judge says: "Ready, Set... Shovel!"

The adversary system is based on the assumption that the best way to get at the truth is to have each side tell the most outrageous version of what happened just this side of perjury. The unspun truth will be about the only things the jurors will not hear. They will be watching a well-orchestrated display of synchronized spinning. Myth versus myth.

Yet, the longer I practiced law, the more I appreciated our system, which, to paraphrase Churchill, was greatly flawed and better only than every other system in existence. The adversarial clash is invaluable in beating the wheat from the chaff. And the anchor of the system is the jury. Ask any litigation attorney, and he or she will tell you how much respect they have for juries. Jurors can be standing hip deep in crap and still be able to reach down and find the diamond of truth. Jurors have a remarkable ability to go through the shifting sands of legalisms and lawyers' shenanigans and still come to the bedrock of truth. At one time I considered that a great virtue. In this case it scared the hell out of me.

CHAPTER 38

And so it began. I had been standing about ten feet from the jury box and methodically analyzing the evidence. As a rule, I never crowd the jury box. It makes the jurors nervous, and they tend not to listen to what you are saying if you crowd their space either by leaning in or by fixing one of them with direct eye contact. But this time I started moving towards the jury rail, and the closer I got the lower I dropped my voice. I knew my back was to both Payton and Rabison, and the judge would only have an oblique view of me. All would have to strain to hear what I was saying. I knew what I was about to do was improper, but I was hoping that it was not so improper as to invoke wrath from the judge.

I walked up to the jury rail, swept my eyes over all of the jurors, walked dramatically from one end of the jury box to the other and then stopped. I stared into the box, appearing to stare at each juror but really looking at none. I knew that a pregnant pause lasting for only seconds during a trial makes for great drama. Now the jurors were watching me expectantly, knowing that this was going to be something different. I narrowed my eyes and whispered in a hard voice, "Do you really think I, a Jew, would come back all the way down from New York, and that Payton over there, a proud black lawyer from Georgia, would be here if we thought for one second—if there was even the slightest possibility—that we were defending an anti-Semitic and racist Klansman who lynched a black man many years ago? And, what's more...."

"Objection! Objection!"

The prosecutor's voice rent the air with its high pitched shrillness. I did not finish my whole statement, but I got much farther than I thought I would. Payton later told me that the prosecutor had been leaning over toward me with his hand to his ear as he strained to hear what I was saying. When he finally realized where I was going, his face became beet red, and he leaped to his feet.

I sucked in my breath as I waited for the judge's reaction. I could deal with thunder. What scared me was the possibility of lightning. I saw the judge swivel his chair towards the jurors. "Ladies and Gentleman of the Jury, you are to disregard what Mr. Lipton said about his or his colleague's personal feelings. What a lawyer feels about anyone's guilt or innocence is not relevant. They weren't witnesses in the trial. It is up to you to decide guilt or innocence based on the evidence, not based on what anyone else either inside the court or outside the court feels about whether this defendant is guilty or innocent. So just wipe that last statement out of your mind. Proceed, Mr. Lipton."

Thank goodness, not even a storm, more like a gentle rain. Of course, I knew a jury could be dead asleep, but when a judge suddenly says, "Strike that. Disregard that," they suddenly wake up. Moreover, as I expected, the fact that there was an objection and a court remedial charge would only serve to highlight what I had said.

One of the few significant advantages a defendant has in a criminal trial is that his attorney does not have to protect the record. In a normal civil case, I knew I had a stake in making sure a judge would not make an erroneous ruling, even if it was in my favor, because the verdict might be reversed by an appellate court. Then my client would have to incur the enormous costs and concomitant uncertainties of a new trial. In a criminal case, however, if a defendant is acquitted, he cannot be tried again—no matter how many errors the judge made in the defendant's favor or how outrageous the misconduct of the defendant or his attorney.

So a criminal defense lawyer does not have to protect the record. He can just rear back and try anything and everything that might work to the defendant's advantage, so long as it was within the murky confines of ethical behavior. I took full advantage of the nothing-to-lose aspect of defense lawyering in this trial. I knew if we did not receive a fair trial, the appellate court would give T.C. a new trial. If the prosecutor did not get a fair trial, there would be no appeal.

The only real gamble I was taking when I pushed the envelope was that the judge would sanction me or declare a mistrial. I knew I would never engage in the kind of misconduct that would result in my being personally sanctioned by the judge. And I knew that the chances of a judge declaring a mistrial were remote at best. Some judges are pro-plaintiff. Some judges are pro-defendant. Some judges are pro-government. But all judges have a top priority of clearing their calendars. I did not believe there was any way in this case that the judge was going to declare a mistrial—particularly for anything I did. If I asked for a mistrial and the judge failed to grant it, the appellate court could determine if the judge should have granted the mistrial. If I did something that prejudiced the government, or if some evidence wrongly came in on my side and the judge erroneously failed to grant a mistrial, the mistake would be buried beneath the double jeopardy clause of the Constitution. My client could not be tried again for the same crime.

What was strange was that I had planned very few of these court tricks or sharp practices when I passionately believed in T.C.'s innocence. It was only after I became solely a mercenary that I tossed off my restraints and reached deep into my bag of litigation gamesmanship tricks. Indeed, the trial had *become* a game for me now that I knew I was not defending an innocent man. Hell, that's the way it is supposed to be. The outcome of the trial should be based on what the evidence shows or what the lawyers convince a jury that the evidence shows. Only God can and does make decisions based solely on the truth.

The game probably had even higher stakes for the prosecutor. Win or lose, I was going back to New York. For the prosecutor, he would either end up as the reviled loser of a big case or the brilliant winner of the biggest conviction in his office's history. And, yes, I was going to fight to the death to defend a man who probably deserved death. But what of the prosecutor?

At least a defense counsel is supposed to seek an acquittal, period. A prosecutor is supposed to seek justice. Oh sure! If that bastard Rabison found out for certain today that T.C. was innocent but could still be convicted on the evidence, there was no way in the world he would call a press conference to announce that he was dropping the charges. That prosecutor, that old Ichabod Crane lookalike Eddie Rabison, wanted this conviction so badly that he could taste it. He would never let something as minor as a defendant's innocence get in the way of his one chance to launch his career into orbit.

I decided that now was the time to lower my voice and approach the jurors for a more intimate discussion about an issue that many defense counsel choose to avoid entirely for fear of bringing undue emphasis to it. I was going to confront head-on the fact that T.C. had not taken the stand in his own defense.

When the prosecution had rested its case, and it was our turn to put in a defense, our entire case consisted of showing the jury the videotaped statements that T.C. made to the FBI after his arrest. In that video T.C. admitted going to the swamp to administer what he thought would be a beating to some black man who had raped a white woman. On the tape, T.C. expressed his shock and repulsion at the murder and told of his "heroic" efforts to save the black man from his horrible fate. District Attorney Rabison chose not to show that videotape in his own presentation of evidence. Instead, he had the FBI agent who took T.C.'s post-arrest statements testify as to what T.C. had said in substance, though not verbatim.

I guessed that Rabison did not use the videotape in his case because he did not want to propound our defense for us. Quite to the contrary, throughout the trial he did everything he could to bait us into making T.C. take the stand so that Rabison could slice and dice him in front of the jury. After all, T.C.'s post arrest statements had been an almost free ride, void of any harsh cross-examination and interrupted only by gentle prodding by the questioner. Moreover, even though the FBI agent gave an accurate characterization of what T.C. had said, he did so with such a slight and undetectable spin to it that it sounded even worse than T.C.'s rather lame rendition of events.

I knew that Rabison had to know he was taking some risk that we would only call his bluff halfway. We would not call T.C. to the stand, but we would use the videotape of his post-arrest statements. I supposed Rabison felt that he was in a win-win situation. If we were compelled to use the videotape, then the jury would twice hear T.C.'s version of the events, which Rabison was confident the evidence and common sense disproved. In addition, when the jury first heard the FBI agent recount the events as told to him by T.C. and then heard T.C. himself on the videotape, they would have been reminded at two separate, crucial points in the trial that T.C. himself did not have the courage or belief in his own credibility to walk the few steps to the witness stand and testify on his own behalf.

T.C. did less than a stellar job in his post-arrest statements. He had not yet had time to polish his "story," and he was also obviously nervous. But it was all we had; so, we went with it. Now, in my summation, I had to deal with the fact that T.C. had not taken the stand.

*   *   *

I walked to within four feet of the jury box, close enough to signal the intimate nature of what I was about to say, yet not so close as to make the jurors uncomfortable by crowding their space.

"You know, ladies and gentleman of the jury—one of the great things that makes this wonderful legal system of ours unique is the constitutional guarantee that allows a defendant such as T.C. to sit silently throughout a trial and not have his silence held against him." (pause)

"I emphasize to you the word 'constitutional.' What we call the Fifth Amendment was not just some law passed by some congressmen. It was put right into the bedrock of our government, the United States Constitution, by our own Founding Fathers. It was that important." (pause) "Now, the judge will tell you later that you cannot hold it against T.C. that he chose to follow my advice and not testify in this case. Why? Because the *government*, here in the person of Mr. Rabison, has the burden of proving T.C.'s guilt beyond a reasonable doubt and they clearly did not do so."

I slowly swept my eyes from juror to juror, establishing an agreement among all of us.

"I am absolutely 100% certain that you will follow that very important instruction from the judge and not hold it against T.C. that he did not testify." (long pause) "But you know, I also live in the real world, and I know it is human nature to want to hear from a defendant—and there's nothing wrong with that. You wouldn't be human if you didn't have those feelings."

Now I began to back up a little, allowing my voice to rise ever so slightly,

"What I want you to realize is that you have heard from T.C. You heard from him first when the judge told you when this trial just began that T.C. pleaded innocent to all of the charges against him. When T.C. pleaded innocent, it was like he came into this courtroom and yelled at the top of his lungs that he did not do what Mr. Rabison accused him of doing."

I paused for a moment to signal the jury that I had an even better point to drive home.

"Better yet, you heard from T.C. in that videotape. And I would remind you that hearing from him in that videotape was even more significant than if you had heard him here in court. Why do I say that? Well, if you saw him testify here in court, you would have said, 'Well, he sounded convincing, but look how long he had to work on that story. Heck, he even had attorneys to help him calibrate every word according to the available evidence in the case.'"

I smiled, "Yes, I see it in your faces—you know I'm right. You *should* be skeptical about the testimony that comes to you after so many rehearsals. Heck, you saw how rehearsed Morgan looked in his testimony."

"Objection!"

The judge turned to the jurors, "It is up to you to determine if anyone's testimony looked rehearsed, and frankly, I didn't hear Mr. Lipton say anything different. Continue."

"Well, ladies and gentleman, one thing you know for sure. T.C. Simmons' statements after his arrest were not rehearsed. He had no time to rehearse them. He had no lawyer to help him. Yes, he had every right to have a lawyer with him. You all have heard about the Miranda warnings. Every defendant has the right to remain silent and have his lawyer with him. Yet, T.C. chose not to remain silent. He chose not to wait for his lawyer before he spoke. He chose to give a spontaneous, unrehearsed and *true* rendition of the events that happened. And this statement was made right after his arrest. I will leave it to you to determine if a guilty person would act that way—give a videotaped statement before he could think a story through—before he even knew what evidence the government might have that could contradict what he was going to say. But you see, T.C. did not have to worry about what evidence the government could have to contradict his statements, because he knew his statements were the truth. There could not be any evidence that truthfully contradicted what he had to say."

I backed up to the counsels' table because I was about to rise into high and pre-planned dudgeon. My fist came down on the table with a "thwack."

"And why did prosecutor Rabison hold back that videotape

from you?! Why did he have the FBI agent filter T.C.'s statements to you through government eyes when he could have shown you what T.C. said word for word and you could have seen T.C. making the statements and how credible he looked making them?"

I was now practically shouting, "Please, in your deliberations, don't overlook the government's conduct in this case! Do not forget, you can do whatever you want in this case. The verdict in this case is totally up to you. You are the final—and I stress "final"—arbiters if you choose, as you should, to acquit my client of all counts against him."

Rabison fairly flew to his feet, "Objection, Your Honor! The government is not on trial here. He's asking the jury to disregard the law."

Before the judge could answer, I shot back, "I am not! I'm merely pointing out to the jury that they should not be intimidated—that they have the final right to render whatever verdict they think of as being right."

Rabison shouted back, "Your Honor, he's asking for a nullification verdict."

A nullification verdict is a verdict where the jury purposely disregards the law, because they disagree with the law or because they want to send a broader message to the public or merely because they do not want to convict the defendant, even though the law demands it. In almost every jurisdiction in this country there are two rules about nullification verdicts. The first rule is that they are perfectly legal verdicts, in the sense that the jurors rendering them face no punishment and the defendants receiving them are as free as defendants acquitted in accordance with strict adherence to the law. A nullification verdict is a right of every jury. The second rule is that no attorney or judge is allowed to inform a jury that it has that right. Much to the contrary, the jury is instructed that it must follow the law.

The judge swiveled his chair towards the jury, "Members of the Jury, Mr. Rabison is quite correct that the government is not on trial here. You are here only to judge the guilt or innocence of T.C. Simmons. Nor are you to disregard the law. This courtroom is not the proper forum to send any messages to anyone or to express your displeasure with any law that I tell you applies in this case. All that being said, you should also understand that it is perfectly proper for you to take into consideration the government's actions or words where such actions or words are relevant to your job—your job being to find the facts in this case and to render a verdict. What do I mean by that? Well, let me give you illustrations that have nothing to do with this case. Let us say a defendant claims that the police planted some drugs on him. Well, that defendant has the right to ask a jury to examine that claim because it is important to the jury's task of determining the facts and guilt or innocence, and that is so even though, in a sense, it is putting the government on trial.

"The same thing goes for what the government may have told you. If the government told you something that you found not to be so, you may use that conclusion of yours in weighing the evidence in this case, even though that too could be characterized in a sense as putting the government on trial. I see from the nodding heads that you all understand what I said and agree with it. Am I right, do you understand what I just said? Again, the nods. Okay, Continue Mr. Lipton."

I listened intently to the judge deciding on whether or not I should take another stab at letting the jury know about its nullification powers.

"Thank you, Your Honor. Well, I repeat that you jurors have the ultimate say on this verdict. Do not feel intimidated by possible repercussions from your verdict, not from the District Attorney, not from your neighbors and, indeed, not from me. But please do look closely at what the government has done and said to you in this case. What do I mean?"

Out of the corner of my eye, I could see Rabison spring loaded and ready to go should I put even one toe over the line.

"Let me give you an example. Remember Mr. Rabison's opening statement? He railed and screamed and pounded his fist telling you how T.C. had lynched, by burning to death, poor Aaron Boddie. And how much of his case was an attempt to prove that T.C., and not Morgan actually did the dastardly deed? About 90%? Yes, that's about right. Well, when the District Attorney gets up to give his summation, I will bet dollars to doughnuts that he will remind you that on the felony murder and conspiracy to commit murder charge, the government doesn't even have to prove that T.C. was the one that killed poor Mr. Boddie. Well, if—rather, *when*—he does that you just ask yourselves, if it doesn't matter who killed Mr. Boddie, why did the D.A. bust a gut to prove it was T.C. that did it? Smart people like Mr. Rabison don't kill themselves to prove unimportant things."

I could see that the jury was totally taken with what I was saying. I assumed the jurors were surprised to hear that what they thought the trial was all about, *who killed Aaron Boddie,* might not even be important—at least according to the prosecution. I paused long enough for them to digest what I had said before I continued:

"I will tell you something. The judge will instruct you after the summations, when he delivers his charge to you, that on two of the four murder counts here, a defendant *can* be convicted even if he did not so-called 'pull the trigger'. I'll tell you something even further: the judge will tell you a defendant can be convicted even if he did not know that a murder was planned or, with felony murder, he can be convicted even if a murder was not planned by any of the participants."

Two of the jurors' jaws were hanging halfway to the floor.

I smiled. "So, is the jig up for us? I mean, T.C. admitted that he was there as a participant in a scheme to hurt Mr. Boddie. Does that mean it's all over for T.C.? Well, you know for sure that it means no such thing. You know there was a reason why the District Attorney knew it was essential that he convince you that

T.C. *killed* Aaron Boddie. You see, the judge will also tell you that T.C. can *not* be convicted on any count unless he killed Boddie or knew Boddie was going to be killed or if it was foreseeable that Boddie would be killed. Ah, there's the quagmire that scares the prosecutor. Was it foreseeable that Boddie would be killed? One thing we know for certain—T.C. did not foresee that Boddie would be killed. That's why T.C. tried to stop the killing. Ah, but the prosecutor will tell you that it does not matter what Mr. Simmons foresaw. It matters what a reasonable person would have foreseen. Well, T.C. Simmons may have been misguided, but he was truly a reasonable person. He proved how reasonable he was when he risked his own life to save Mr. Boddie. T.C. knew his cohorts well. He did not think, as well as he knew them, that they would ever kill a man. If it had been at all foreseeable that this would escalate into such a terrible murder, T.C. never would have gone along if only for his own safety sake."

I paused, lowered my voice and approached the jury box again, "Look, I know what T.C. did was reprehensible. He intended to hurt Mr. Boddie. He didn't report it to the police when he heard about Mr. Boddie being held against his will—though reporting it to the police back then may have been a waste of time. Anyway, he did some terrible things. *But he did not do the things he was charged with. All of those things revolve around the murder which he did not see coming and which he certainly did not do!*"

I felt I was connecting with the jury, so I paused so that my words could sink in more permanently. I just nodded at them for a while before continuing, "Yes, the prosecutor could have brought other charges but chose not to do so."

"Objection. That's not relevant, Your Honor!"

District Attorney Rabison had charged T.C. only with four charges related to the murder. He had not charged T.C. with an array of serious, but less important and less "sexy" charges such as those relating to a conspiracy to assault and batter Mr. Boddie, unlawfully holding Mr. Boddie, the actual batteries involved in chaining him up, and many other charges that T.C. had actually admitted committing.

I knew that Rabison was afraid that if even one juror was contemplating holding out, the other jurors might compromise their verdict by discarding the murder charges and convicting of the lesser offenses. The District Attorney had told the media before the trial that he did not seek indictments on the lesser offenses because he feared a possible jury compromise that would dishonor the memory of Mr. Boddie and result in a great injustice. I knew that was a bunch of crap. Rabison was certain that with the evidence he had, and his perceived public clamor for a guilty verdict, a jury forced to choose up or down would have to convict of murder. He knew that a compromise verdict on lesser offenses would be viewed publicly as a draw. Draws do not serve well as catapults to launch ambitious prosecutors' careers into orbit. Most prosecutors are not fueled solely by ambition. But "most" prosecutors were not prosecuting this case—Eddie Rabison was—and he would choke on a compromise verdict.

As defendants, we had the right to demand that the judge give the jury the option of convicting on the lesser included offenses, even though they were not indicted by the Grand Jury. Payton and I were ready to jump at that chance. We figured that a conviction on a lesser included offense was T.C.'s best chance. But T.C. had insisted that we not ask the Judge for a charge of any lesser offenses. He said they charged him with murder. He didn't commit murder. So he should be acquitted, and he would accept no other approach. I tried desperately to talk him out of his sui-cidal stand, that is, I tried to talk him out of it until I heard those FBI wiretap tapes. Once I knew he was guilty, I figured if the guy had the nerve to make what he called a principled all-or-nothing stand, then so be it. Either he or Rabison had to lose. It was a win-win proposition for me.

I then took a stab at unchartered territory again. "And don't forget, that even that beating he wanted to give to Mr. Boddie—whatever it was that he had planned—T.C. pulled out of it. He changed his mind. He didn't just change his mind and skedaddle out of there. He changed his mind and did something about it. He risked his life to save Mr. Boddie."

"Objection. That's been ruled on, Your Honor!"

I knew that Rabison was referring to my failed request to have the judge charge the jury that if they found that T.C. had withdrawn from any conspiracy he might have entered into, they could acquit him. "Withdrawal" defenses are very demanding, and the judge felt that, even crediting T.C.'s dubious testimony on the matter, his withdrawal was done far too late and after he passed over far too many chances for an earlier withdrawal which could have saved Mr. Boddie's life. The judge would not give a "withdrawal" charge to the jury. Payton was ecstatic with the ruling, because he thought the judge was dead wrong putting a great reversible issue in our back pocket. I was a lot more cynical. I didn't believe that there were three appellate judges in the entire state who would vote to reverse a conviction in such a high-profile, highly-charged case such as this one. Yet I also felt that the mere fact that the judge would not give a "withdrawal" charge did not prevent me from emphasizing the purported withdrawal to the jury under the guise of showing that the murder was not foreseeable. I turned out to be right.

"I'm going to overrule your objection, Mr. Rabison. Continue, Mr. Lipton."

I continued with my summation, telling the jurors that since I could not answer when Mr. Rabison finished his summation, they had to be especially vigilant as to what he was saying. They had to pose the questions, at least to themselves, that I was not able to pose. Then I made a last swipe at nullification to set up the key part of my summation, "And don't forget, if you don't like what you hear from Mr. Rabison—if you think what the evidence shows—that T.C. was a patsy to protect higher-ups—then you do what's right. The law is important, but what's right is often more important."

"Objection! He's calling for nullification again!"

I wondered what took him so long to get up.

"Sustained! Move on, Mr. Lipton."

Having put the rabbit in the hat, I proceeded to the heart of my summation: "You know, ladies and gentleman of the jury, a former Chief Judge of New York once made the often quoted statement that if a prosecutor wanted to, he could indict a ham sandwich. You see, everyone knows that a ham sandwich comes from pig, and a pig is the animal everyone loves to hate. It's dirty, and always rooting around in the mud. It's the trailer park white trash of the animal world. Now you notice that the Chief Judge did not say that a Grand Jury would indict a sirloin steak. You see, a sirloin steak is too classy, too well-thought-of to be mindlessly indicted by a Grand Jury."

My voice started rising ever so slightly, "Now we have a Grand Jury that has indicted a ham sandwich. T.C. Simmons is that ham sandwich. He's that trailer park white trash who is readily disposable, that pest to society, that blight on our communities. But you know what, ladies and gentleman, it turns out that all that stuff about the pig is a myth. A pig is really one of the cleanest animals, and it's a damn sight smarter than either a cow or a horse, but those people who want to protect those fancy sirloins don't want you to know the truth about the pig."

"Objection."

"Overruled. Continue Mr. Lipton, but let's get back to humans as soon as you can."

"Thank you Your Honor. I don't have to talk about pigs anymore, because I got T.C. Simmons to talk about, the low man on the totem pole of life, the easiest kind of guy to dump all of society's ills on."

I stopped talking for dramatic effect, starting screwing up my face as anger began to overcome me, or so I wanted it to appear. I stopped at the lawyer's table and faced the jurors.

"You know, in his opening statement to you, the prosecutor told you this case was about race, about a bigot who committed murder because of race."

I paused as if trying to hold in my anger. My voice suggested anger, but was modulated. "This case is not about race. We all know that there was a racial killing, a reprehensible racial killing, but this case is about class, about T.C.'s low, doormat class and Will Morgan's highly exalted, even worshiped class."

I brought my fist down hard on the table, almost startling the jurors out of their seats. Now I was almost screaming, "Why do you think the prosecutor spent so much time showing you what a great citizen Will Morgan was. Mayor for forty years, president of a lumber company—it seems that every year he was "citizen of the year," all of the charities, all of the things he has done for his community, people of all colors—a great, great man, a pillar of the community."

I spun over to T.C. and shouted at him, "Stand up, T.C."

I was still screaming, my arms flailing, my eyes ablaze. "This man—yes, he is a man, a human being, he is no pillar of the community. He is the doormat of the community. You think this case is about evidence? It's not about evidence—the evidence is on our side and the prosecutor knows it. This case is about the prosecutor telling you—dressing it up in pretty words, but basically telling you—'How can you believe a low life piece of white trash over the very symbol of Southern manhood and greatness!' That's what it amounts to, lynch the white trash scum!"

As my fist hit the table again, the prosecutor objected and the judge sustained the objection. And just in time. There is a time limit of five minutes for feigned moral indignation and my time was just about expiring. I stood staring at the ground for a few very pregnant seconds as if trying to collect myself, and then I turned to the jury and spoke in a very calm but shaky voice, "I'm sorry for losing control of myself. Please don't hold it against my client. He has enough unfair things being held against him."

I paced a few steps back and forward as if gathering my thoughts which, in a way, I was. As I paced I tried to glimpse the papers with my summation notes on them that I had tossed down as I launched into my moral indignation rant. I had forgotten where I wanted to go next, but then as I paced, I was able to glance at my notes on the podium. I turned to face the jurors.

"Look, ladies and gentlemen of the jury, I know it's not easy for you to face up to this. The easiest thing for you to do is to just drop all of this on the easy target, T.C. Because if you drop it on T.C., you don't have to look in the mirror when you render your verdict. And this is hard for me to say, and I wouldn't say it and risk offending some of you, if I didn't have faith that you would do your duty, no matter how difficult it is..."

I could see all of the jurors were staring at me with rapt attention. The white ones, the target of my remarks, were staring directly at me with frozen faces. I knew I was cooking. Time to put the sirloin steak on the griddle.

"The easy way out is to dump this all on T.C. You know you have all heard the term 'political correctness.' Means you can't make derogatory remarks or make jokes about blacks, or Jews, or Polish people, or Italians. Bet not one of you ever made the N word joke in public, right? But let me ask you this: How many of you have made derogatory remarks about poor whites, white trash in public? That's perfectly acceptable. Can't tell Polish jokes any more. But hey, even the President of the United States tells white trash jokes. It's still acceptable. Racism, oh, that was the fault of those white trash people. Lynchings—those damn trailer park people just can't control themselves. Fine, respectable men like Will Morgan would never engage in such mindless violence. Oh, they might have supported Jim Crow, but that was a cultural thing, not wanting to mix the races. But violence—oh, not someone like Will Morgan."

I looked down, breathed deeply and said, "I said you would

have to look in the mirror if you gave the right verdict in this case because you all know that if you convict a lowlife poor boy like T.C., you don't have to think of your own complicity in what went on way back then. Nobody identifies anyone in this courtroom with white trash, except for T.C. But if you let T.C. go, as the evidence shows should happen, than you are saying that Morgan did this, he was responsible for this—and if he was responsible for this, then in some way, we all were responsible for this."

I paused, put my hands up to my mouth, heaved in a big breath and let the deafening silence hang in the air for a moment. "You know, I'm not attacking anyone now. We all learn. Even men greater than any of us will ever be. In the first interview he gave after the Civil War, I mean The War Between the States, that great General, Robert E. Lee said, 'Thank the Lord slavery has been abolished.' They were all expecting him to defend that way of life he had just fought so hard and so long to maintain, and instead he says, he's glad it's gone. He did more than anyone else to help bring this nation back together. And Abe Lincoln—in 1860 he declared blacks should be free but never have the right to vote. And in his last speech in 1865 he said blacks...black men who could read or who had served in the military, should be able to vote. People grow and learn."

At that point, I dropped my head and stared at the floor for an instant. When I looked up, I put on the best anguished look I could muster.

"Look, I was no different. When Morgan was doing his dastardly deed, most Northerners were thinking they didn't have the prejudices those people in the South had, but they did. Too many of us, myself included, had beliefs then that we are deeply ashamed of today."

"Objection!"

"Mr. Lipton, please keep you personal experiences out of this."

"Yes, Judge. I will."

"All I meant to say was that people grow and learn. There's no shame in that. It's good that people do that. The good people of the South have outgrown their Jim Crow past. Hell, we wouldn't be having this trial if that weren't so. There was no penalty for murdering blacks forty years ago. And now this trial gives this jury the opportunity to show the world that the South has outgrown its slavery to class status. Darn it, T.C. Simmons is every bit the human being that Will Morgan is. No better no worse. They both made mistakes, had very mistaken views many years ago, but T.C. Simmons at least had enough humanity to realize that no matter how much prejudice and hate was in his heart, killing an innocent black man was wrong—while Will Morgan, a man with more opportunity in one day than T.C. Simmons had in his lifetime, couldn't figure out that your hate should stop where another man's nose begins.

"So Will Morgan commits the murder and now he comes in here, all arrogant and proud because he knows he could tell you that the moon is made of Swiss cheese and T.C. could say no it isn't, and you would believe Will Morgan. Not because the evidence supports him but because he is Will Morgan and my client is T.C. Simmons."

I was sweating profusely, and I wiped the sweat off my face with the back of my hand.

"Ladies and gentleman of the jury, when the prosecutor gets up here and tells you that Will Morgan is not the type of man who would commit a despicable act, just remember the White Citizens' Counsel—Good honest citizens, the lawyers, the doctors, the sheriffs of your communities, filled with Will Morgans, they were like puppeteers manipulating the characters like T.C. Simmons while they stayed above the fray. All of those people that have been convicted recently for Church bombings and murders done long ago, all of 'em white trash, not one Will Morgan among 'em."

I paused and fixed the whites in the jury with a menacing

stare.

"Do any of you think that the Will Morgans weren't behind any of that? The white trash has paid its dues, it's time for the "respectable" people to step up to the plate."

I went over to take a sip of water and let the jury swallow a bit before I moved on.

"Maybe what I'm doing is suicidal. Some New York lawyer lecturing a bunch of Southern folks about how bad they've been acting. But I wouldn't do it if I didn't have the faith in you to do the right thing."

I moved in a bit closer to the jury box.

"It's hard to be a juror some times. This is one of those times. But the jury system is the bedrock of this great country. It's the bedrock because there is nothing so solid, so great as a grass roots American jury. You know why we don't leave it up to the Establishment or so-called experts to render verdicts? You can see why in this case—they'll always come out for the big guy— the Will Morgans. And they'll always sink the T.C. Simmons."

I walked back over to T.C. I put my hands on his shoulders, tempted to strangle him in front of the jury. But I managed to suppress my real desires and continue.

"The only reason that a man like T.C. Simmons, a man who has little education, no money, and no social standing has a shot at justice is because of jurors like yourself. You have a power greater than Will Morgan, greater than the District Attorney, and, yes even greater than the judge. You and you alone have the power to render justice in this case. You have the power to do the right thing. It is hard to do, because the right thing in this case is the hard thing. Throwing away the evidence and going with Morgan is the easy thing, the comfortable thing. You can say you gave that black man vindication by making someone pay for his murder, and you'll get no one outraged over the fact that some lowlife was convicted. Maybe Will Morgan will even throw you a party."

"Objection!"

"I'll withdraw that, sorry, I guess I just ruined your shot at an after-trial party."

The jurors laughed, and I let them exhale a bit until I continued. "You don't have to please Will Morgan with your verdict. You don't have to please the exclusive country club people with your verdict. You don't even have to please me or the prosecutor or the judge with your verdict. All you have to please with your verdict is your God, What He demands is what the law of Georgia demands, the right verdict—and you all know what the right verdict is in this case. A message that the Will Morgans of this world can no longer use people like T.C. as scapegoats. Send a message that in this country a poor man gets equal consideration with a rich man when he is in the sacred halls of justice. Send a message that the powerful can no longer escape their responsibility for the violence they perpetrated against our brother black citizens years ago."

"Objection!"

I was startled by this objection, and it could not have come at a worse time. I was just moving into my peroration, and now, not only was the mood ruptured, but I might have to ditch my carefully crafted climax. I turned to look at the judge. I had never turned to the judge when the prior objections had been made. I wanted the judge to know that I thought this one was wrong, wrong, wrong, and I damn well knew that whatever the colorable justification Rabison had for objecting, the real reason he did it was to disrupt my final closing and, perhaps, throw me totally off balance.

The prosecutor had allowed greater technical violations of summation propriety to go without making a comment. There is an unstated rule among trial attorneys that unless it is necessary to protect the record or an adversary is going completely over the top, objections should be kept to an absolute minimum during summations and openings. Some obnoxious attorneys will object just to unravel an adversary, particularly if that adversary is inexperienced or lacks the ability to think fast and react quickly. But such attorneys soon become pariahs in the profession. This objection was made because I had clearly grabbed the jury, and Rabison wanted to break up the tempo, not allow me to leave them in a thrall.

The judge more than likely knew why the objection was made. But the law was the law, and, with apparent reluctance, the judge turned to face the jury.

"Ladies and gentlemen, your job is not to send a message to anybody. Your job is to decide the guilt or innocence of this person. I would tell you that if you want to send a message to go to Western Union except I am afraid that most of you wouldn't know what this old judge was talking about. But seriously, if you want to send a message, go to your elected representative, or write a letter to the editor, but here your job is to follow the law and resolve this case—whatever the consequences or rather, I should say, without regard to the consequences. Okay, Mr. Lipton, proceed."

As the judge spoke to the jury, my mind was moving at warp speed. I couldn't finish my list of messages to be sent by the jury. I could extemporize with a few more statements just so I could recreate the mood that had been interrupted by the objection. Or I could just end the summation now.

I turned and glared at Rabison, who looked more corpse-like than ever—the man who never ceases dying. He had attempted to grow a beard during the trial, but his scraggly countenance still had the pallor which embalmers try so hard to eliminate. My glare was intended to let the jury know I was angry at what he had done, and let them know that he had objected just to obstruct my summation. Then I turned back to the jury.

"Okay, then, if I can't ask you to send a message to anyone, I'll finish by restating a message that was sent to all of us. It is in the Bible. It is eloquent in its simplicity."

I paused, ran my eyes from one end of the jury box to other, catching the eye of each and every juror for an instant. "I want you to do what you and only you have the power to do in this case. As we are directed by the Bible, we must 'love justice, do mercy, and walk humbly with our God.'"

I let the silence hang for a moment.

"But whatever your verdict, on behalf of myself, Mr. Simkins and especially my client, T.C. Simmons, we thank you for giving us this opportunity to bring you the truth in this hall of justice. This could not happen in any other country. May God bless you, thank you."

I walked back to the lawyers' table. My back was to the jury, which turned out to be fortunate. The jurors did not see me glare at T.C. as he started to raise his arm to clasp my hand in congratulation for a job well done. I knew I had to hold the somber expression in front of the jury so they would not think that my emotion was practiced—which, of course, it was. I flashed my eyes in anger at T.C. and, thank goodness, he withdrew his hand and just bowed his head toward the floor. I exhaled a sigh of relief. T.C. was such a fool, I was only happy that he didn't jump up and high-five me, shouting, "Wowee, you really put one over on them!"

I sat ramrod straight in my chair staring out blankly into the ether until the jurors had exited the courtroom for a break before the prosecutor's summation. As soon as the last juror cleared the door, I slumped down in the chair, soaked with sweat and totally drained. Payton put his hand on my back and whispered in my ear, "Well done!" I just looked back at him and said right in front of T.C., "I don't know whether that's good or bad."

CHAPTER 39

A noted psychiatrist once said that a person can tolerate tragedy far more than he can tolerate uncertainty. Any trial lawyer knows how true that statement is. The time between the retirement of the jury and the verdict is the most brutal part of a trial. Even a criminal defendant becomes more distressed while waiting for a verdict than he does when faced with the certainty of a long incarceration after an adverse verdict. Once the human mind knows what it is confronting, it is an amazingly adaptable organ. It is the waiting and the uncertainty that burns little acid holes in your stomach.

I was standing in the hall talking to Payton when I saw the court officer approaching. Immediately my stomach went to mush and my knees weakened. Could this be the verdict? The court officer knew what I must have been thinking and waved me off.

"Just a note."

The Judge spoke, "Counsel, as you can read, the jury wants to know, even if they think that Morgan killed the victim, can they still convict T.C. of first or second degree murder for his being there?"

We all knew the answer to that one. My goodness, I had thought that either Morgan would go down, at least in the public eye or T.C. would go down, but I never dreamed that both would go down. I whispered to T.C.

"Want me to see if the D.A. still has that plea deal on the table?"

T.C. almost bit my head off. "Absolutely not. I am innocent. I would rather get the chair than plead guilty to something I didn't do. I wouldn't take a plea even if they let me walk out without jail time!"

What could be more irritating than a murderer riding a high

moral horse? I was tempted to belt him right then and there. Instead I just leaned over and hissed in his ear. "I've requested that The Bureau of Prisons provide you with an extra cell, one for you and one for your enormous set of balls."

"No plea bargain, period!"

I would have pressed the matter further, but in view of that note, I knew that the prosecutor would never accept a plea when fame and fortune were now within his grasp.

The judge called the jury in and responded to their note by telling them that they could convict T.C. of murder even if they found that Morgan did the killing. The jurors left to continue their deliberations leaving a gloating smile on the face of the District Attorney in their wake. When the jury returned with their verdict ten minutes later, they had two words for the prosecutor that would wipe the smile off his face. They were, "Not Guilty." On all counts.

As soon as the verdict was announced, the courtroom burst into applause. Even the black spectators rose to applaud. They would prefer no conviction at all rather than have a mere pawn absorb the guilt for the crimes committed by the King—and everyone knew, or thought they knew, that the King in this case was Will Morgan, and his Kingdom was the detritus of the "White Citizen's Council." The reporters rushed out to call in their story. T.C. put his head down and started sobbing. Payton put his arm around T.C. and hugged him tight. I wanted to vomit.

After the trial, the jurors assembled for a press conference to explain their verdict and answer some questions from the media. Most of the jurors agreed to the press conference in the hope that they could appease the media frenzy and reclaim their privacy. Other members of the jury agreed to the press conference because they feared that without it, the media interest in them might wane and their fifteen minutes of fame would come to an abrupt end. For one of the jurors, the purpose of the press conference was to pique the public interest to the point where his newly hired agent could nail down a good book or television movie-of-the-week deal.

Later, I watched a tape of the press conference as the jurors attempted to parse their verdict in the face of countless technical questions. Each juror who spoke held the common belief that the verdict was rendered according to the law as given to them by the judge. To me, it was obvious that, at bottom, what had fueled the verdict was the jurors' unanimous belief that Morgan had been the executioner of Boddie and the mover of the entire crime in all of its aspects. What apparently cinched a "not guilty" verdict, regardless of any evidence to the contrary, was the jurors' unanimous fury at the government for trying to "lynch" T.C. to protect Morgan and "the Big Boys." Those were the exact words of the Foreman. He actually talked about T.C., a racist white Klan member, being lynched. No matter what the jurors said about scrupulously following the law, I knew that I had won my nullification verdict. As an attorney, I could not help but be pleased with the victory. But as a sentient human being, I could not help but be sickened when I heard the jurors marvel at T.C.'s physical and moral courage, during those times, of risking his life to save a black man.

The part of the press conference that I found most amusing was when the Foreman answered a reporter's question regarding the last note the jury had sent out during their deliberations, the note that asked if T.C. "could be convicted on one of the murder counts even if they found that Morgan was the actual killer." When the jury was given a "yes" answer from the judge, we had all assumed the subsequent verdict rendered just a few minutes later would be "guilty."

During the press conference the Foreman explained that after the jurors had reached a unanimous verdict of "not guilty," he suggested that all the jurors remain silent for half an hour so each could meditate on his or her verdict just to make certain they were doing the right thing. Earlier in the deliberations, one of the jurors had insisted that he heard the judge say that they could *not* convict T.C. on a certain murder count if he was not the killer. All of the other jurors remembered the judge's charge to say exactly the opposite. The issue became moot when the jurors determined, or at least convinced themselves that they determined, that T.C. could not have foreseen the death of Boddie. But now, while they were meditating, they decided to send a note to the judge to clarify that point—merely out of curiosity.

I dissolved in laughter when I heard the explanation about the note. When the judge read that note out loud, I'd thought D.A. Rabison would reach orgasm right there in the courtroom. He practically had his bags packed ready to move into the governor's mansion. And, then, ten minutes later, his entire world went up in flames. Throughout the next few weeks, all of the pain I felt at seeing T.C.'s joy over the verdict was somewhat counterbalanced by the anguish I saw in Rabison's face as he rationalized away the verdict. Oh no, he would explain, he was not upset: "As a prosecutor, winning and losing was not important, doing justice was important." He did not agree with the verdict, but accepted and credited the good faith of the jurors. Yeah, right. He probably went to sleep every night envisioning inflicting an "Aaron Boddie" death on each one of those jurors who had just incinerated his career.

CHAPTER 40

Ijust wanted to leave, get back to Payton's office, and let this all sink in. I had fantasized about this very moment, getting a not guilty verdict, beating Morgan, the Establishment, everyone, proving that they couldn't step on T.C. just because he was disposable white trash. But in my fantasy I was freeing an innocent person. Now I knew better, and I knew that those cheering people didn't know better. I had to gather my thoughts. I just felt numb.

The judge officially released T.C. Rabison nodded his head, mumbled insincere congratulations and then disappeared out the door. I couldn't even look at him. I just muttered, "Thanks." I had dreamed of shoving this victory up his ass, acting in public like I did when I had just heard the first part of the tape and thought I had been vindicated. But as it turned out, he had been vindicated, only nobody knew it.

Payton and I linked arms and pushed through the well-wishers and out of the courthouse. We had to run interference for T.C., who followed closely behind our defensive blocking. As soon as we reached the court house steps, I realized that my thoughts about retreating to Payton's office were wishful ones. We ran smack into all manner of press: cameras, boom mikes and reporters shouting questions at us.

I noticed off to the left there was a small platform with a group of microphones looped together. District Attorney Rabison was talking into them, giving the usual bullshit prosecutor's line they always give when they lose a case. In a bland, cold voice he stated that their job was not to win or lose but to see that justice was done. And even though he disagreed with the verdict, the "people" had spoken and they had won, because that was how the system worked in America. He said that he accepted the jury verdict. That was big of him. I knew that the first thing he would

319

do when he got back in the sheltered confines of his office would be to curse the morons on the jury. When you are a defendant in a high-profile criminal case, it is a duel to the death with the prosecutor. He is pitting his career against your life, and there can be only one winner.

I also knew how much he wanted to win. In a high-profile case like this, T.C.'s scalp on his belt would have made his career. Only Marcia Clark and Christopher Darden of O.J. Simpson fame managed to parlay a defeat into prolonged fame and success. Defense counsel can become well-known and successful even by losing, as long as their client is famous or notorious. But prosecutors usually need to win to further their careers.

I tried to drag T.C. and Payton away from the podium, but the mob kept shoving us towards it. Boom mikes were hitting me in the head and reporters were shrieking questions at me, at T.C., and at Payton in the vain hopes that we would recognize them and select their question to answer on the fly, giving that local reporter his or her fifteen minutes of fame.

The wall of people finally stopped us next to the podium. One person stepped out and started to drag me to the platform. I virtually tripped onto the wooden box that had been placed in front of the stationary microphones. I knew they expected a comment from the "winning" lawyer, but I didn't want to say anything, not now, not until I had thought this thing out. I leaned into the microphones, and as I did so what seemed like hundreds of boom mikes descended from on high toward my head and a sea of arms holding microphones were thrust toward my face. I leaned into the microphones and said, "I don't think it is proper for me to speak now. This is T.C.'s victory. I think we should hear from him."

The crowd started chanting "T.C. T.C. T.C." I knew that T.C. could barely put two words together in coherent fashion, and I expected him to be mortified by my invitation. Indeed, I hoped he would be mortified by my invitation. Of course, what I said was true. It was his victory. It didn't belong to me, and those blockheads in the crowd had no way of knowing that it didn't belong to them either.

Payton and I virtually shoved T.C. onto the makeshift podium. As I did so, a reporter with a booming voice yelled at me over the crowd noise, "You must be thrilled with the verdict." I was seized by a sudden desire to turn to the man and let him know that "freeing a murdering bigot is not my idea of a thrill."

Fortunately, God has installed a trap door in every person's brain to block just such compulsive statements from escaping. Sometimes that trap door gets stuck in the open position, and that's when we end up getting ourselves in trouble. Luckily, this time the trap door swung shut just in time and my rash statement was swallowed—at least for the time being.

I looked eagerly at T.C.'s face for signs of mortification as he faced the cameras and microphones. I relished the moment as a small act of revenge for his betrayal. Except that it didn't occur. He started talking in a halting manner at first, but then as the cameras whirred and boom mikes descended, he became transformed before my very eyes, from a frightened, reclusive semi-literate sociopath into a confident, full-blown celebrity. The cameras had done in two minutes what it would have taken years of intensive therapy to accomplish.

"I...I... just want to thank this wonderful country and the jurors in my case."

He paused to put his head down and wipe away a tear that I could see did not even exist.

"But first, I want to thank my lawyers, Payton Simkins and Luke Lipton. They believed in me when no one else did. They knew what really happened, and they knew that justice would be done."

He was right about the first two statements. We had believed in him, and we did indeed know the real story. But we did not know that justice would prevail. Hearing that tape caused the truth to collide with our belief system. We knew that if justice had prevailed, T.C. would have been in big trouble. I had spent the first three weeks of the trial praying for justice. After hearing the tape I had spent the past agonizing week praying for a gross miscarriage of justice. It's one of the few times that my prayers had been answered.

"You know, everyone said I should plead guilty, that I didn't have a chance, that I was up against the big boys and all I was was white trash, with a Jewish lawyer from New York and a Negro lawyer from here. But I know this isn't the old days. This is the New South."

I couldn't believe what I was hearing. For two months I couldn't get T.C. to utter a sentence with a verb in it, and now here he was sounding like Martin Luther King.

"This verdict was God given. God has given me a mission in life to work to bring together all races—and I'm going to spend whatever years God grants me doing just that."

The thunderous applause that broke out suddenly went silent as a middle-aged black man elbowed his way next to T.C. For a moment, T.C. looked startled and frightened. The man, whom I now recognized, leaned into the microphone. "My name is Willis Pinkney. I was the foreman of the jury. I just wanted to come up here to thank this man. There weren't many white people who would put their lives on the line back then to save a black man. People like him is what gives me faith that black people will be able to make it in this country."

He leaned over and hugged T.C. I noticed an almost imperceptible jerk back when the black man first moved in on T.C. The old instincts kicking in. But then T.C. moved forward to embrace him, and the whole crowd embraced them both. There were so many camera flashes and television lights illuminating the scene that the sunshine on this cool clear day seemed diminished.

CHAPTER 41

T.C. went on and on, taking questions, giving answers, tears pouring out of the eyes of even hardened reporters. As he rambled on, the myth was growing right before my eyes. I knew I was in camera range, so I made certain to mirror the appropriate range of emotions as T.C. continued with his virtuoso plucking of the public's heartstrings.

I don't recall how we finally got T.C. away from those microphones. I remember police arriving in force to escort us through the crowd. The reporters followed us all the way to Payton's office, shouting questions at us as we walked. That night, I fully expected a boom mike to crash through my hotel room window followed with some brilliant cogent question such as, "Are you happy that you won?"

I had originally planned to go back to New York as soon as the trial was over, but I decided to stay another week in town when my wife informed me that there was even more of a media circus in New York. My old law firm was fielding an average of two hundred calls a day, everyone from well-wishers to people wanting me to endorse their products. I was tempted to sign on to the offer to do a commercial for some dog food. "Yup, without this Puppy Chow to give us energy each day, we never would have won the trial."

What I found most disconcerting was how many offers I received to appear as an expert on some radio or television show. No particular field, just an expert on anything and everything.

I was amazed at the array of issues people suddenly wanted me to comment on as an expert. When this country was founded, a polymath was considered to be a person like Jefferson: someone who had studied the philosophy of the Greeks in the original Greek, invented several useful products, become proficient in various sciences and still was able to shine as a diplomat, writer, and politician. Today, a polymath is anyone who has claimed his requisite few minutes of fame. I will never forget watching some reporter interview an athlete who had just set some kind of record. It was clear that the athlete was having difficulty even fighting his way through a subordinate clause. And then, out of nowhere, another reporter asked what this athlete thought about the first artificial heart, which had been implanted the previous day. The athlete was in favor. How courageous of him.

My wife said that my two grown children were ecstatic over the publicity. They were just starting out in their respective careers, one as a banker and the other as an entrepreneur. Now that their daddy was so famous for such a worthy cause, they had become instant successes. They were pleading with me to go on some of the talk shows or at least write an op-ed. piece for the *New York Times*. In fact the *New York Times* was just about the only newspaper that hadn't asked me to write a piece about the case. My former partner had assured me that, the *New York Times* being the *New York Times*, they would not ask me, but that if I wrote for them, publication would be guaranteed.

Neither my wife nor any of my friends could understand why I wasn't as excited as they were about the case. Actually, I knew they were not really excited about the case. I was quite certain they would have limped along in life had T.C. been convicted. What they were excited about was the publicity surrounding the case and its commercial possibilities for my career. As one of my former partners put it, "The trick is not getting the fifteen minutes of fame. The trick is leveraging that fifteen minutes into a lifetime of fame. And for that, you have to act quickly. America has a short attention span."

I was no idiot. In my wildest dreams, I could never envision this opportunity for myself. But this was not so simple—this required riding a tiger that I knew was really a rat with stripes. What would happen if this all became exposed? I'd still be connected with all of the talk shows, but this time I would be the subject of the new class of talking heads—the vilified subject.

The only consolation I really had during this explosion of publicity was that I truly felt bad about what had happened. T.C. had been and still was the scum the prosecutors had tried to depict him as being. The whole circus arising from my victory was built on a lie, and I just could not allow myself to leverage my life on a lie, an insidious lie. Even if God gave me a guarantee that this whole charade would never be unmasked, I would never want to ride the wave. I guess deep down I knew that when St. Peter started reviewing my book of life, he would be remarkably unimpressed with my fame. What I feared was that he would be remarkably angered by my duplicity if I hitched my life to a lie.

I knew there was a great deal of selfishness to my anger against T.C. Perhaps Payton was right—I was more upset that T.C. had fooled me than I was that he was fooling the country. But I was also furious about the iconization of T.C.

If the media had merely saluted the acquittal of an "innocent" man, it would not have bothered me so much. But now they'd transformed T.C. from an "innocent" man wrongly accused into a brilliant humanist, too long overlooked.

I had just seen some scholar on C-Span television talking about his brilliant book on the Whig party in America before an audience of eight people, only two of whom "rushed" the platform to buy his book at the conclusion of the fascinating talk. That same night, T.C. needed a police escort to cut his way through the mob flooding the high school auditorium, where T.C. had been a last-minute addition to a panel discussing the effects of the Civil War on white Southerners. The Whig scholar had spent twelve years combing through the most arcane primary sources for his work. T.C.'s resume consisted of having burned down a synagogue, killing a black man while a member of the Klan, and having had the good fortune to be on the receiving end of a gross miscarriage of justice. Now the crowd at the high school had to be content with getting their programs autographed. I knew that when T.C.'s inevitable book came out, they would settle for nothing less than a personal note on the fly page.

CHAPTER 42

"Please, hold all my calls. Mr. Lipton and I will be holed up in the conference room."

Payton shut the door to the conference room of his office. It had been one week since the verdict, and the publicity tsunami had only grown larger and more ferocious. The same media that only a month earlier had attempted to bury T.C. alive, had now simply brushed off the dirt, picked him up and placed him on a golden pedestal.

The media, in extolling the virtues of T.C., credited "the triumph of justice" to the exposing of Bummy Thornton's perjury. But here we were, more than a week after Bummy's testimony, and we still didn't know for sure whether Bummy Thornton's testimony had been true or not. I knew that no rational juror would have given Bummy's testimony any credibility after finding out there was a surreptitious pay-off for the testimony, but that did not necessarily mean that what looked to be the truth about his testimony was not the truth.

Payton was convinced that Bummy had been lying, that he had never been at the scene of the lynching. Payton was convinced that Morgan was so desperate to eliminate any possibility that he would not be believed in this potentially career-ending case that he went out and hired himself the perfect witness. Bummy Thornton, as the half-brother of Aaron Boddie, had the motive and the opportunity to try to find Aaron on the day of the murder. Also, there would be no discernible motive for Bummy to point the finger at T.C. unless it was T.C. who did the killing. To a man in Bummy's position, there probably wasn't a dime's worth of difference between Morgan and T.C. The stakes in this case were so high for Morgan that Payton was certain that if there was no witness like Bummy available, Morgan would have had to invent him. But since Bummy was available, all Morgan had to do was rehearse a story with him, then make it financially worthwhile for Bummy to take the stand and lie.

I thought, or maybe I hoped, that Bummy had been telling the truth about being at the murder scene and in describing what he saw. I thought that Bummy might have been, in many ways, the black T.C. Simmons, a man people always underestimated at their own peril. Maybe Bummy thought it was time to exact some reparations for all of the years the heel of Jim Crow had been planted firmly on his neck. And who better to exact the reparations from than Will Morgan, whose foot had been firmly planted in that Jim Crow shoe at the time of the lynching? I doubted that Bummy fully believed Morgan's story beyond what Bummy himself had been able to see that night, but I also doubted that Bummy much cared which of two equally repulsive redneck bigots, Morgan or T.C., actually took the fall for the lynching. The lynching could not be reversed, but Bummy could see to it that he exacted a good price for the testimony that Morgan so desperately needed. When I told the jury during my summation that Bummy Thornton's testimony had been bought and paid for, I may have been only halfright. The testimony may have been only paid for and not bought.

In the end, I stopped arguing with Payton about whether Bummy's testimony was true or not. In my mind, Bummy's testimony, at worst, may have been perjury suborned by Morgan in order to make certain that the truth won out at the trial. I felt that Morgan had received more than enough punishment for that transgression. But, of course, for Payton that wasn't enough. It was important for him to believe that Bummy was not there that night. If Bummy wasn't there that night, then the only evidence really discrediting T.C.'s story—other than Morgan's self-serving testimony—was the inadmissible evidence on that wiretap where T.C. ripped the hood off his own head. I supposed that believing Bummy was lying about being at the scene made Payton feel more comfortable with the verdict he was now so fully embracing.

Besides, I think that what bothered Payton most about a truthful Bummy Thornton testimony was not what it said about T.C.'s guilt, but what it said about Morgan's heroic, if belated, actions that night to save the life of Aaron Boddie. In Payton's eyes Morgan and his "respectable" ilk were responsible for that lynching, even if it was pawns like T.C. Simmons who actually carried it out. So I went on wondering if Bummy Thornton was telling the truth or not while Payton went on not caring whether he told the truth or not.

After the trial I tried to avoid reading the more over-the-top laudatory articles about T.C. What I studiously tried to read or view were the countless so-called legal experts dissecting the trial and vivisecting the trial attorneys. I found those analyses to be a great comic relief from the constant pressure I was under.

At first, the general consensus seemed to be that District Attorney Rabison had fastidiously and brilliantly woven a web of guilt from which T.C. Simmons' clearly outmatched attorneys would not be able to extricate him. By the time Bummy Thornton's testimony had been shredded the following morning on cross-examination, Payton and I had morphed into Clarence Darrow and District Attorney Rabison and his assistant District Attorneys had become the prosecution team in the O.J. Simpson trial.

The very same trial strategy and tactics that had been mercilessly lampooned by legal critics on radio and television shows midway through the trial looked more like a work of genius to these experts after the not guilty verdict was returned. I knew that if Payton and I and the Rabison prosecution team had done exactly the same things we did at trial, but the jury had rendered a different verdict, the District Attorney would be heading for his dream job of State Attorney General while Payton and I hid in shame in his office. Every trial tactic and legal decision is obvious when viewed through the unerring accuracy of a retroscope.

There was one column analyzing the trial that caused me some consternation in view of the ever-growing wave of adulation being heaped on the very unworthy T.C. Simmons. The Arlington-based columnist for the *Washington Post*, Michelle Garwood, had written that this trial proved the superiority of the adversary system of justice used in the United States over the inquisitorial system used in most other countries such as France. She noted that the inquisitorial system sounded much better since the "neutral" judge led his own investigators in an "objective" search for the truth. The adversarial system, on the other hand, was based on the less reasonable sounding presumption that the most biased people in the litigation, the parties themselves, were best suited for getting at the truth.

As Ms. Garwood put it, "Like Wagner's music, the adversarial system is much better than it sounds." Setting the adversarial hounds loose on the trail of any weakness in the other side's case was much more likely to unearth the truth than an inquisitorial "neutral" search for the truth.

Ms. Garwood correctly noted that in an inquisitorial system, Bummy Thornton's testimony would have ended on Friday when even the cynical journalists in the courtroom were convinced he was as straight and honest a witness as ever took the stand. Only a party fueled by adversarial zeal would have chased down that slight whiff of incredulity about the testimony that resulted in the pay-off bombshell during the cross-examination. Ms. Garwood concluded her column by stating that the truth unveiled by the crucible of adversarial investigation and cross-examination led the jury to its righteous and rightful verdict of acquittal.

The column caused me great concern because I knew Michelle Garwood was absolutely correct in her analysis of the superiority of our adversarial system of justice, but I also knew that no system is perfect, and the system had backfired in this case. Just as our great, inclusive tolerant country sometimes tosses up a T.C. Simmons, the adversarial system sometimes belches forth a hairball. This was not the case to use as the poster boy for the adversarial system.

We had uncovered the truth about Bummy Thornton's paid-for testimony, but that "truth" had only led the jury to an ultimate untruth—that T.C. was innocent of the crimes charged. But the more I wrestled with the column and what it meant, the more I thought that maybe the verdict represented a gross miscarriage of the justice system, but a kind of greater justice for society. If the better truth for the better good was that Morgan was the man behind the killing and that T.C. had been a kind of heroic figure at the lynching, then maybe the verdict was the righteous one, even if it was not the right one. We would not be the first nor the last people in this country to disseminate history as it should have been. And I was not certain that was completely bad, or even bad at all.

Payton and I were knee-deep in newspapers and magazines, all trumpeting the triumph of virtue over evil. The local newspaper had T.C.'s picture on the front page under a glaring headline that read "The Face of the New South?" Payton picked up that newspaper and flipped it over to me.

The Face of the New South. It seemed that every five minutes there was another face of the New South. A New South, and then an Improved New South and a Bigger and Better New South. It reminded me of the "New Nixon" they were always selling us back in the 1970s. In the end, it turned out that all of the "New" Nixons were just the repackaged Old Nixon. I was afraid that sometime in the future people would discover that T.C., as the Face of the New South, was really the Asshole of the Old South wrapped in alluring—and misleading—packaging.

"Hey, Luke, did you hear they're going to do a made for TV movie of this. I wonder who will play me?"

"Too bad Moms Mabley is dead. She'd have been perfect to play you Payton."

"Very funny, by the way, T.C. called yesterday, wants our advice on agents."

"The only agent he deserves is an FBI agent."

"Hey, cool down, Luke. This is wonderful, really wonderful."

"No, this is bullshit, really bullshit."

"Why is it bullshit? Look at this picture of T.C. with the black minister and the rabbi and the white priest—he really is bringing people together."

"It's bullshit because you and I know that he'd like to burn the rabbi, lynch the minister and castrate the priest on the grounds of Bob Jones University."

"So what?"

"What do you mean 'so what?' Don't you see we're dealing here with a myth?"

Payton smiled, "Like I said, so what? Myths are what made this country great."

"No, Payton, *truth* made this country great."

"You're dead wrong. This country would choke on the truth."

"What does that mean?"

"I don't mean that in a negative sense."

"Listen to you, you said 'this country would choke on the truth'. If that's not negative I'd hate to hear what you consider *to be* negative."

Payton walked over and plopped himself into a large chair with oversized pillows. He put his feet up on the coffee table in front of him. "What I mean is that myths are more fertile grounds for the growth of a happy society than the rocky soil of truth will ever be."

"You're going to have to pass that by me a bit more slowly."

"Well, do you think one person, black or white, is better off in this country because we now know the *truth* about Thomas Jefferson bedding an underage slave? Do you think one sports fanatic loves his sport even more now that we know that Mickey Mantle during his hey day was an alcoholic? Do you think the cause of human rights was furthered one iota because we now know that included in the "dream" that Martin Luther King spoke of may have been a dream about committing adultery? We should leave the myth of the greatness of these men alone. The myth was inspirational; the truth only destructive."

"So you think a country is better off if it is built on myths?"

"No, I didn't say that. There are good myths, and there are bad myths. This country is great because it was the first country in which the good myths prevailed."

"How so?"

"Well, in Europe they had the bad myth that Kings were chosen by God and that was very destructive. Communism was built on the bad myth that in order to free the people from the cruelties of capitalism, the individual had to surrender his freedom. At one time there were many nations built on the bad myth that gods needed human sacrifices to be appeased—thank goodness, Abraham replaced that with the good myth that the 'real' God did not want human sacrifice."

"You do believe in God, don't you, Payton?"

"It doesn't matter whether I believe in God or not. The *truth* may be that there is no God, but that's not what's important. What's important is who gets to control God. Is God used to support good myths or bad myths? You know those people who planted the bomb in the Church in Birmingham—the one that killed those little black girls—they were God-fearing people. The problem is that they had bought into the bad myth that God didn't like black people, that they were the spawn of Abraham's disfavored progeny. It's our job to persuade people that God wants all of His people to be treated equally. God has been used as the handmaiden to justify some of the worst atrocities committed in history. And He has also been used to support some of the most beneficent acts of mankind. The struggle over the soul of God has been mankind's real Armageddon."

"Maybe if God would spend less time rooting for various teams at sporting events, He would have time to attend to the important things in this world."

"Well, God works in mysterious ways."

"So does the United States Congress."

"So tell me something, Payton, how do you fight bad myths?"

"It's not easy. You know, bad myths are like bad mushrooms. You spend hours and hours picking them out of the ground, out of crevices, and salting the earth after you have pulled them out. You think you have totally eradicated them. And then the first rain comes and—boom—they're back again."

I laughed, but I also thought that the mushroom metaphor would be a good one to use before a jury if the appropriate issue arose. "I think I'll steal that mushroom metaphor from you."

"Why not, I stole it myself."

"From whom?"

"From Hitler. He used the mushroom metaphor to describe how hard it is to get rid of Jews. It's right there in *Mein Kampf*."

Payton leaned back in his chair and stared up at the ceiling.

"You know," he said, "there were some interesting things in *Mein Kampf*. Hitler ridiculed the Jews for spreading the pernicious and absurd myth that black people were the equals of white people."

"May I go out on a limb and assume that you think that is a good myth?"

"Hey, I never said that myths and truth don't ever intersect."

I started drumming my fingers on the table. I knew what Payton was getting at. We had argued constantly and vehemently the past few days about what was going on with the ever-growing myth of T.C.

I was becoming more and more outraged as T.C. plunged ever further into myth-making, organizing interracial groups for social betterment, receiving an award from a council of local black clerics, recounting time and again the importance of T.C.'s victory over the forces of disunity and racial strife.

I had felt more hurt than outraged when Payton began feeding the myth machine. In the last two days, he had appeared with T.C. on two national television talk shows and cheered the loudest when T.C. made the most absurd claims such as to his willingness to die for equality in this country.

I thought that Payton had swallowed the poison pill of public stardom. I had stayed out of the spotlight, and within a week I had become almost marginalized. When I walked outside with Payton, crowds chased him for autographs and pictures. I was left holding his coat while he posed for pictures with awestruck citizens. I accused him of being selfish, of perpetuating a lie to feed his own ego.

"I'm not being selfish," he said, "You're the one being selfish! You want to expose T.C. because you feel he betrayed you. You put all of your faith and all of your effort, put your career on the line because you were convinced you were supporting Gandhi and when it turned out you were supporting David Duke, you became bitter. And you became more bitter when you see Jewish groups giving him awards when you knew that he was so upset that there weren't Jewish kids in that synagogue he burnt down—a feeling he expressed not forty years ago, but less than one year ago. But Luke, you're just being self-indulgent, because it doesn't matter a damn who T.C. is—what matters is who people *think* he is. And they think he is Gandhi, and as long as they think that, he will continue to act like Gandhi. And damn it, if someone is going to build me a good house, I don't really care if secretly he wishes I was homeless as long as he builds me the goddamned house."

We both fell silent. I thought about what Payton had said. Was I being selfish? Was I willing to undermine this great thing that was happening just because I felt personally betrayed? And how much of my anger was really a fear of what would happen to me when this house of cards collapsed? Did it really matter to Holocaust survivors if they were rescued by people out of the goodness of their hearts or because some Jewish group was secretly paying them to do it? I didn't know. It's hard to search out your own feelings in the midst of the whirlwind. And when the wind dies down, it's often too late.

As we talked about the struggle for control of a country's myths and the need to harness revealed and unrevealable truths, my thoughts drifted back to that aphorism from my college biology class—ontogeny replicates phylogeny. The individual of a species mimics the development of the species as a whole. In the same way, I thought, individual families struggle for control of their own myths and truths much like that struggle occurs for the soul of the country itself.

Every family relies on its good myths every bit as much as the country does. I remembered that the one family picture that hung in our living room was that of my Uncle Mike, aka Micah, dressed in his World War II uniform. All I was told was that Uncle Mike had died during World War II, and all I knew was that he had since become deified in our household. Stories I was told and then retold to my friends about Uncle Mike gave me a kind of social status.

I remembered trying to pry more information from my parents about how and where Uncle Mike died, but my entreaties were met with silence. In those days people didn't talk about such things. Deified relatives were a matter of faith, not reason. The only further explanation about Uncle Mike I received was when my father stared wide-eyed into the blazing fireplace and muttered, "He took a bunch of 'em with him." And that was that.

Of course, once the seedling had been planted, my young imagination irrigated it and nurtured it until the myth of Uncle Mike had grown like the beanstalk. I told my friends that he had killed thirty Japs at Henderson field at Guadalcanal. When I went over to my friend Johnny's house and saw the famous Joe Rosenthal picture of the flag-raising at Iwo Jima framed on the wall, I was quick to point out that the guy at the base of the flag with his back to the camera was Uncle Mike. And when my friends asked me how Uncle Mike died, without skipping a beat I found myself describing how Uncle Mike parachuted into Hitler's Bavarian retreat, tossing hand grenades as he landed amidst a hail of bullets, slashing his way towards the cowering SS guards before ten of them brought him down. Before my gaped-mouthed friends could catch their breath, I added my father's words, "He took a bunch of 'em with him."

By the time I met up with some other friends the next week, I found that the myth of Uncle Mike had been enlarged by my first set of friends. By the time the Cold War had begun, my friends and I were discussing how Uncle Mike had died on a secret mission to poison Stalin's vodka. One wonderful thing about myths is that they are very adaptable to any new set of circumstances.

The strange thing about Uncle Mike was that after a while, I had a hard time separating the "truth" I knew, told by my parents, from the myth I had grown from their seedling. I didn't really know if it made any difference. Uncle Mike had died a hero, that much was definitely true. The actual details underlying that fact were only commentary.

I was so enthralled with the heroics of Uncle Mike that many years after I had become a lawyer in New York, I decided to obtain his war record through the Freedom of Information Act. I wanted to frame his official papers and send them to mom for a present. She could hang the documents right next to his picture.

It took me a long time to assemble the "commentary" to the heroics of Uncle Mike. I had to go beyond the Freedom of Information Act and use my contacts within the Defense Department to get the full story.

Uncle Mike had truly died "during World War II." During his last leave before being shipped overseas in 1943, he had gotten drunk and, in full uniform, crashed a purloined Army jeep and killed himself. Well, dad had said he died "during World War II." And dad was right about how Uncle Mike had "taken a bunch of 'em with him," too. Mike had crashed his jeep into a car that burst into flames, incinerating a young woman driver and her two children.

I didn't know how and whether to tell my mother about what I had discovered or, indeed, if she knew the whole truth. I decided to burn my documentation. If my mother did know the full details, then I would just be confronting her with my parents' lie to me. If she didn't know the full details, then what would I be accomplishing by destroying a comforting myth with the devastating truth? I sent her nothing. I told her nothing. I was even upset that I had found out the "truth" myself. Seek and Ye Shall Find. Unfortunately, I sought. I found. My life had been far richer when Uncle Mike was a hero.

Once, watching crowds of hysterical "groupies" mobbing T.C. after one of his speeches, I remarked to Payton how child-like they were. I told him, "They will believe anything." Payton just shrugged and said, "You know that, I know that, Goebbels knew that. My only hope is that they don't ever find out how duped they have been."

Parents teach their children that truth should always be the cynosure of their conduct. And what country leader, whether democrat or dictator, doesn't promise his "children" that truth will always be his navigator? Parents and dictators alike know that their children are desperate to perceive the most pernicious lies as truth. It's a given: myths will trample all over truth in a finger snap. And what is a myth but a lie? It can be a good lie or a bad lie. The struggle between the good lie and the bad lie is the true Manichean struggle that determines the direction of a family, a community, and, alas, even a country.

So Payton hoped that those people deifying T.C. never find out how duped they have been. He thought it was okay to lie to all of those "little children" out there mobbing and worshiping T.C. because it was for their own good. He believed that the truth should be husbanded for those who can handle it. But I still could not accept that it is ever better to create a "myth" than to talk the truth. My thoughts wandered back to Abe Lapinsky and Allan Kirk.

CHAPTER 43

W e left Payton's office to go to my hotel room. I was relieved to leave the office. I was completely exhausted from lack of sleep, from stress and from having to spend each recent entire day hip deep in a world gone mad for that bigoted fraud, T.C. Simmons.

I opened the hotel room door and Payton and I walked in. I had picked up the local newspaper which had been left in front of my hotel room door and now I tossed it on the bed. I turned back towards the door and saw Payton staring at a pearl-handled dagger that was lying on the table at the far end of the room.

"What the hell is that for? Now I know why you always get your cases settled."

I walked over and picked up the dagger and laid the blade of it flat in my hand. "I got that at a Civil War collectibles shop while you were arguing the suppression motion. It's the actual personal dagger of General Cleburne. It was taken off his body by a Union soldier after Cleburne was killed at the Battle of Franklyn. I bought it for my next door neighbor who's a big-time Civil War buff."

"Interesting stuff," Payton said, "but in two hours from now we have to be at a dinner sponsored by the Augusta Bar Association. You promised to come with me. Why don't you rest up for a bit. I'll pick you up at 8:00 o'clock."

"Sounds good. Hey, T.C. is in this hotel. I have his room number, why don't we bring him along. If he gets drunk enough, the real T.C. will come out, and then I won't have to be the one to expose him."

Payton smiled, "You're kidding, but I thought that would be a good idea. I called him and asked him to come but Master Simmons says he is too busy to see us tonight. He is receiving the

Brotherhood Award from the Episcopal Church in town."

All of a sudden, I felt I was right back in the miasma. I had forgotten how I'd been taken in by T.C.'s telling me of his religious salvation, about his membership in an integrated Episcopal Church. I asked Payton if he ever uncovered the truth about that part of T.C.'s life.

"As a matter of fact, I did—just yesterday when he told me about the Episcopalian award."

Payton shared T.C.'s religious awakening with me. It seems Payton asked T.C. why he joined that integrated Episcopalian Church five years before he could possibly know it would be valuable to him to say that he belonged to one of the few truly integrated churches in the South. T.C. had laughed and launched into an explanation that he gave with both pride and glee.

T.C. had little trouble finding crumby, low-paying, insecure jobs like pumping gas or working in the loading room of grocery stores, the kind he'd had all his life. Every time he tried to get a good job at some substantial company with security and benefits, the kind that could give you enough money to live on, he was always turned away. Those companies always asked the job applicants if they had ever been convicted of a crime. He figured that they would find out about the arson of the synagogue, so he put it down even though it was so long ago. That was enough to cause him not to be hired.

About six years before his current indictment, T.C. had applied for a job at a linen factory a few miles outside of Augusta, Georgia. It was a hard job with a lot of heavy lifting and the need for some training, but it paid very well, and T.C. wanted it badly. He wanted it so badly that he lied and did not put down his felony conviction on his application form. All T.C. put down was the three times back about ten years ago he got thrown in the drunk tank overnight, and he pleaded guilty to disorderly conduct. Carry Hall, the manager of the Plant, who was doing the hiring, complimented T.C. on his honesty for even putting down disorderly conduct convictions when they were not even considered "crimes" as asked for in the application. Whether it was due to T.C.'s honesty or his obvious eagerness to get working, he was given the job.

After one week on the job, T.C. was summoned to Mr. Hall's office. Mr. Hall handed T.C. his discharge notice and one week's pay, telling him only, "What made you think you could get away with lying about that arson you committed when you were in the Klan? Here's your pay, now get out of here, fast."

T.C. didn't even try to put up a defense. There would be no use in pleading that the arson and the Klan were so long ago. Some people are forgiven for what they have done in the past. T.C. Simmons was never forgiven for anything bad he had ever done.

The Sunday after being fired from the linen factory, T.C. was walking downtown past the First Episcopal Church. There was nothing unusual about T.C. walking past a church or even about his not being in church. Although he had been a Baptist growing up, T.C. was well acquainted with the First Episcopal Church because it was the only truly integrated church around. Long after the weekdays became integrated, Sundays remained segregated—both in the South and throughout the country. The First Episcopal Church had never interested T.C. until that Sunday when he saw Carry Hall, the hiring manager from the linen factory, leaving its services.

A plan immediately hatched in T.C.'s mind. He would join the church to show Mr. Hall what a changed man he had become. And it would be pretty hard for Carry Hall to turn down a fellow parishioner. So that Monday morning T.C. Simmons, wearing the only good pair of slacks he owned, knocked on the door of the rectory of the First Episcopal Church.

He was startled to see a black minister, but in his determination to pull off his scam he spent an hour pouring his heart out to the reverend. He told him everything about his terrible arson crime, his past membership in the Klan and his prior drinking problem. He sobbed when he admitted to the hateful bigoted feelings he used to have. He, of course, neglected to tell the kind minister that he still had those feelings.

The minister embraced T.C. Simmons, both literally and figuratively, with the open arms of true Christian love and forgiveness. He told him to come to the services next Sunday where he could introduce him to the other congregants.

The next Sunday, still dressed in the cleanest clothes he could find, T.C. came to services hoping to sit close enough to Carry Hall and his family to be noticed, and to progressively strike up a closer friendship each week. Hopefully, before too long, that job would be his again.

T.C. plopped himself down in the back row of the Church so he would be sure not to miss the Hall family coming in. But as the service wore on, he had still not seen Mr. Hall or his family. And before he knew it, T.C. was startled by the sound of rustling as the congregants rose to take the host at the front railing of the Church. Instinctively T.C. sprang forward, but when he approached the railing, he froze. Right in front of him and to his side were black men. The thought of taking the wafer with black men paralyzed T.C. He looked up and saw the Reverend staring at him. He hoped that his hesitancy would be taken for his Eucharistic inexperience. And then he felt a hand under his arm as the black man on his left guided him up to the rail, where T.C. finally took the wafer in his mouth. It was when he reached that part of T.C.'s story that Payton remarked to me,

"Of course, T.C. didn't mention to me that he tried to squirrel the wafer away in his cheek until he could spit it out at home. He didn't know how fast those things dissolve. Poor guy probably gargled for a month." We both laughed, and then Payton continued with T.C.'s story. After everyone who wanted to had taken communion, the minister came to the lectern and tapped on it to get the congregants' attention.

"I am very pleased to introduce a new member of our Congregation to you, a person who I am sure you will take into our family and treat like a brother. Please stand up Mr. Thomas Caleb Simmons, whom I am told wants to be called T.C. by his friends, and since we are his friends, we shall call him, T.C."

T.C. stood up and blushed a deep red. The Minister continued.

"I noticed that when brother Simmons went to get the wafer, he hesitated when he saw there were two black men going there with him. Now, there is nothing to be ashamed of T.C. At one time each one of us had that experience. Even our black congregants were not used to taking communion with white folks. And I am glad that happened because I have been forgetting to tell this Congregation about a very important story that relates to all of this."

T.C. initially felt like melting through the floor, but as all eyes turned towards him, he was faced only with smiles and friendly nods, even from the black congregants.

The Reverend continued.

"About half a year after the War Between the States had ended, the South lay in ruins, and the white people of the South were terrified of what would happen to them and fearful of what would happen to their way of life—a way of life, I am sad to say that included white supremacy."

He rocked back and forth on his heels as he spoke, adding drama to his speech.

"There was a First Episcopal Church but not the one here—this one was in Richmond, the former capital of the Confederacy. Richmond was in ruins, having been burned out by the fleeing Confederates. But the Church that day was packed, packed with the usual white congregation."

The Reverend stopped for a moment to look around the pews, making sure not one pair of eyes had lost contact with his. He continued.

"When it came time to take of the host, before any congregant could get to the front railing, a heretofore unobserved well dressed black man rushed to the front and reached the rail first. He knelt down to take the wafer in his mouth. But there was no wafer because the minister had frozen in place as had the entire congregation. For seconds that seemed to stretch forever nobody moved, nobody at all. The black man just stayed there kneeling, with his head bowed, waiting for a wafer that was not coming."

T.C. said that the Church was so quiet, he could hear his own heart beating.

"Nobody knew what would happen, but then, all of a sudden, an elderly, impeccably dressed white man, a man clearly of Old Virginia, walked up past the paralyzed congregants and knelt down next to the black man. And then one, and then two, and then the entire congregation followed. Soon the minister regained his composure and started distributing the wafer to congregant after congregant, starting with the black man and then going directly to that courageous, striking old gentleman."

The Reverend stopped, the point of the story being obvious. The congregation that had been enraptured by the spontaneous mini-sermon started buzzing amongst each other in reaction to the inspirational story. But suddenly, the Reverend tapped on the lectern again. He then tapped on his head, "I don't know what's wrong with my head. I keep forgetting important things all of the time. I must be getting older than I think. You see, I forgot to tell you a very important part of this story. You might have heard of that distinguished elderly Southern gentleman. His name was Robert E. Lee."

There was an audible collective gasp followed by complete silence until someone said, so that all could hear: "Is that true or just a homily?"

The reverend raised his hand skywards.

"I swear to the Savior Jesus that it was true. People can change. Good people can change. And when you get to know T.C., you will hear how another good person has changed."

T.C. was delighted at his embrace by the congregation but upset that he had not seen Mr. Hall that week. Nor did he see him the next week or the week after that. Finally, in exasperation, he called on the Reverend and asked him what had happened to Carry Hall. As it turned out, Carry Hall had been divorced and had remarried a Methodist about two months earlier. The time T.C. had seen him in Church was his farewell visit to the congregation. He was now attending the First Methodist Church across town. But why, the Reverend wanted to know did T.C. want to know about Carry Hall?

T.C. lied to the Reverend when he told him that another congregant happened to mention to T.C. that Carry Hall was a member of the congregation. T.C. did not want anyone to know that he joined the congregation just so he could network himself with Mr. Hall. Now his entire plan lay in ruins. T.C. was distraught, so much so that in a torrent of words he told the Reverend about his rejection from the job at the linen factory when Carry Hall found out about the arson conviction and the past membership in the Klan.

The Reverend smiled and said, "I should have told that story about Robert E. Lee while the Halls were still attending Church. But, anyway, why don't you come back here Tuesday, and I will see what I can do. Carry is still a good friend of mine, and he of all people should know about redemption—he had a brother who was once in the Klan, and that brother was one of the founders of this interracial Church."

T.C. said he felt like he had been born again. And born again he was that Tuesday, when the Reverend told him to report for work at the linen factory on Monday of the next week. T.C. had the job of his dreams, and it remained the job of his dreams until the factory owner shipped most of the jobs to cheaper labor overseas, and T.C. was among the most junior employees who got laid off. And that was where T.C. ended his explanation of why he had joined the First Episcopal Church.

But Payton had one other question to ask of T.C.

"Hey, T.C. I could understand why you joined that Church to get that job in the linen factory. But why did you stay in the Church after you were laid off?"

Payton told me that he fully expected T.C. to answer that it was part of his plan to stay there so he could use the minister for references or to get another job if he ever needed him. What worked for the linen factory could work for some other job. But that is not what T.C. answered. He dropped his head and mumbled to Payton, "I stayed... I stayed because they treated me better than anyone treated me in my life."

At that point in recounting the story, Payton turned to me and said,

"You know Luke, when T.C. was telling me that story, he was so proud of how he snookered in that Church just so he could get back at his tormentors and get what he felt he deserved, and he felt nothing of these people doing all of this stuff for him while I knew he despised them and everything they stood for. I really wanted to strangle him. I thought you were right all along. We've got to expose this bigoted bastard."

I looked at Payton, "And why didn't you do it? Strangle him, I mean. Exposing him takes too long."

Payton breathed in an audible intake of air. "You know, I hate to admit it, but I really felt sorry for that bastard. It must have tormented him to be so attracted to those very people he most despised. All his life he was an outcast trying to fit in by hating other outcasts of society, and then those people embraced him and he couldn't shake that hate. You know, he talked with pride of how cunning he had been fooling people who thought him too dumb to fool anybody, but then when he mumbled how good they treated him, well, I just think it must have tormented the guy."

I had been holding a pencil, and now, in exasperation, I had flipped it up in the air.

"Payton, I never will understand you. You're willing to give a bigoted murderer like T.C. the benefit of every doubt and even when there is no doubt, but you won't give Morgan the slightest break, even when you find out what he really did that night."

Payton shook his head. "I will never give Morgan or his like a break. My parents may have been fooled into thinking that the mindless jackassess like T.C. Simmons parading around in their ridiculous sheets were their real enemies, but I know that my real enemy has always been behind the curtain, out of sight, controlling things."

I'd had this argument with Payton so many times that I didn't have the energy or desire to start up with it again. So I just let the topic drop. Besides, the narrative of T.C.'s religious epiphany did little to relieve the exhaustion that was enveloping me. Payton saw me fighting to keep awake and said, "I think you really need a nap. I'll see you in about two hours."

Payton walked out of the room closing the door behind him. I threw myself on the bed without removing any of my clothes or turning down the dust cover. I had intended to set the alarm clock, but an exhausted sleep enveloped me as soon as my head hit the pillow.

As quickly as I fell asleep, I awoke, startled by something. It was as if someone had grabbed and shaken me awake. I blinked to clear my vision. The room was deadly silent. I looked over at the clock. Damn. I had only been asleep for twenty minutes. My hand reached down and gathered up the newspaper that had been lying on the bed next to me. I stared at the picture of T.C., standing there in a new suit, holding a black baby in one massive arm and a white baby in the other.

I would have thought that the anger I felt toward T.C. would have abated by now—that I somehow would have become accustomed to it. But that was not the case. Perhaps it was my fatigue or my inability to sleep. Maybe it was something about that picture. Whatever the reason, I began to seethe with a renewed anger, and suddenly I knew what I had to do.

I tore off the top page of the note pad which the hotel had thoughtfully placed near the phone and on which I had written T.C.'s room number. I crumpled up the paper, stuck it back in my pocket, got out of bed and headed for T.C.'s room.

I looked around the hall to make sure that it was empty. Then I pounded on T.C.'s door until I heard the lock unlatch and the door opened slightly to the length of the security chain. T.C.'s eye, looking for all the world like the eye of the Cyclops, pressed up against the space between the chain and the door.

"What are you doing here? Why didn't you call first? You know I got a lot...."

"Just open the damn door, I have to talk to you."

T.C. undid the chain and opened the door. I quickly pushed past him to get into his room and out of the hallway before I was seen. The first thing I noticed when I came into the room was a beautiful new, and very expensive looking tuxedo hanging on the knob of the dresser. "Nice threads," I said, "There must be a hell of an overcharge if you don't get it back to the rental place by midnight."

I could hear the contempt in his voice. "It ain't rented. It's just one of the tuxedos I own. My agent includes a new tuxedo sometime as part of what they give me to speak somewhere. I don't ask for money or anything else from those people what gives me awards and such."

I noticed for the first time that T.C. was wearing a pair of torn and graying old underpants which were far too tight. His growing stomach hung over the top of the limp elastic waist band.

"Hey, T.C. why not have your agent demand a new pair of underpants next time?"

"And why don't you mind your own fucking business? I don't need no new underwear. People don't see my drawers. They only get to see my nice new tuxedos. I did get me some new overalls 'cept they already look old when you buy 'em because my agent said the overalls is good because it makes me look like I don't have very much. You know, like you told those jury folk— only when I get an award or some honor I got to wear a tuxedo."

The bastard had to remind me of my role in creating this Frankenstein. I looked back at the spanking new tuxedo and then to the old pair of underpants. I knew which was the real T.C. It was the one hidden from the public. The one that the public would never see. They thought they were seeing the spiffy new T.C. Simmons. But I knew that underneath it all, closest to his loins if not his heart, it was the same old dirty, filthy, disgusting stink-to-the-heavens T.C. Simmons.

"I want to talk to you, T.C."

T.C. brushed past me and, with his back turned to me, started running his hands over the sateen collar of the tuxedo. "Seems like all the talkin' you come here to do is about my clothes. If you got something else to say—say it."

I snapped my mouth shut on what I really wanted to say, but I found a few sarcastic words fighting their way free nonetheless. "Gee, T.C., I can't tell you how much I appreciate your giving me some of your valuable time."

My words either went through or over T.C.'s empty head. He responded, "That's okay, just talk fast 'cause I got to git."

I hesitated a bit to see if he would turn around to face me while I talked, but he just went on running his hands over various parts of the tuxedo. "Since I don't have much time either, I'll give it you fast. I want permission from you to talk about anything and everything concerning your case. I don't really need your permission. You've been talking about so many things that we lawyers call privileged, that I'm not sure there is any privilege left to protect, but there are some things I'd like to say that I don't think you would want to hear."

T.C. did not seem to react to what I was saying. He was busy holding up a pre-tied bow tie to his neck. He didn't even turn around and his voice came back very calm and matter-of-fact.

"I don't know what you mean with this privilege stuff, but you can say whatever the hell you want. They ain't gonna believe you any more than they believed Will Morgan, and he was the goddamned Mayor. If'n they didn't believe him, you think they're going to believe a New York Jew lawyer?"

For the first time my voice flared. "Look, you wouldn't be walking around free if I hadn't come down here. I created you, you son of a bitch."

T.C. squatted down to check the sateen seam and cuffs on his tuxedo pants. "I don't know why you Jews always have to take credit for everyone's makin' it."

I interrupted him partly to keep myself under control. "Well, I'll need you to sign some papers that says you waive the attorney-client privilege. I'll explain what it means before you sign."

"You don't got to explain nothin'. I told you I don't really give a damn what you have to say. Just send the papers to my agent and if he says I can sign 'em, I'll sign 'em."

I stood there feeling my face flush red with anger. T.C. stood bent over, running his hands up and down the crease of the pants. His massive body seemed to fill the room. I gulped in some air to steady my nerves. I knew I had to act, and act fast.

I withdrew the Cleburne dagger that I had slipped into my belt. I had bought the dagger for my neighbor, but now I thought it very appropriate that T.C. should be done in with this dagger from a Confederate general. It was a way of cleansing the dagger once used to further bigotry and hatred—poetic redemption—having the same dagger exterminate at least one vestige of bigotry and hatred.

I planted my feet firmly, perfectly spaced for balance, and raised the dagger above my head. This was going to be truly a case of if you aim for the king, you had better kill him. I knew if I missed or lost my nerve, T.C. could break me like a matchstick.

He had straightened up and was now fingering the buttonhole in the tuxedo jacket. His back was still facing me. I picked a spot about two-thirds up his spine. I wanted to be certain that if I didn't kill him with one blow, I would at least hit his spinal area and incapacitate him. I leaned slightly forward to start my momentum, then froze when he started talking again. "Fund-raiser tonight is for a pickaninny orphanage. I ain't even chargin' them nothin' except for this tuxedo. A good friend of mine onc't said, 'pickaninnies got to eat too.'"

My hand was so tight around the hilt of the dagger that my palm and fingers were turning as white as the ivory handle. But I didn't move forward. It wasn't that I was frightened —it's just that it suddenly occurred to me that I couldn't do it this way. To stab him in the back was cowardly. It was the way of the Klan. The way T.C. would have done it. I wanted him to know what was coming.

"Turn around T.C.!" I backed up about two steps as T.C. turned around. I pulled the dagger down to my chest level, aiming the point right towards his mid-section in case he charged me. He stared at the dagger and blinked, as if trying to put what he was seeing in context.

I suddenly felt strong and full of resolve. I bit off my words in anger. "That's right, you bigot. I'm not going to let you get away with this crap any longer. I made you, and I'm going unmake you. When they find your body, they'll think one of your friends in the Klan did it because of all of your 'great work' for minorities. Don't you think it appropriate that you should give your life for civil rights, T.C.? They'll call you the white Martin Luther King at your funeral."

T.C. just looked me straight in the eye, without any visible expression and with no sign of fear.

"You ain't gonna do nothin' because you don't got the guts to do it. You never had the guts to do nothin'. When we was kids you always shot your mouth off about Demarest and his buddies. Only when the time came, I was there and you wasn't. Jews like you was always good at making speeches like the one you just made, but you never had the guts to fight."

For what was a moment and seemed like an eternity, we both stood glaring at each other. When he finally moved toward me, I drew the dagger back over my shoulder and braced myself for the impact. But I froze. Not completely, but for an instant. Maybe he was right, maybe I didn't have the guts. Whatever the reason, I hesitated for just a moment and, as the saying goes, he who hesitates is lost, and I lost.

My split-second indecision allowed T.C. to catch my arm as I was bringing it down. He stopped my forward motion, knocking the dagger high up into the air, over my shoulder and onto the bed. He held me motionless for a second and then picked me up off the ground like I was a sack of feathers and hurled me several feet into the wall. I no sooner hit the ground than he picked me up and hurled me once again into the wall, shaking the room and sending several pictures crashing to the floor. It was all happening so fast I was feeling neither fright nor pain.

I was sprawled on the ground and saw him looming over me. He put his face directly over mine and muttered, "You fuckin' kike. You ain't gonna kill me like your kind killed Jesus."

His untethered hatred seemed to ignite new strength and determination in me. I leaped up and tried to bring my knee hard into his groin. But before I could make contact, his massive hands caught my leg and he flipped me over on my back and put his hands around my throat. His massive torso shook like a quaking mountain as he alternately grinned and laughed. He was an animal in his element. He had run his prey to ground, and now he was going in for the kill.

"Now, you sonofabitch, I'm gonna' choke the life out of you—I'm going to do to you what I should have done to you back at Clarks Hill Dam when you tricked me."

Despite the fact that he was about to strangle me, I still felt the energy of my hatred for him, an energy undiminished by fear. In the split second before he did me in, I reached up to the bed and grabbed the dagger. I didn't have the time or option to direct it with any accuracy so I simply swiped it toward his face but I felt it make contact. His grip on my throat loosened and he let go with a wail of pain.

I looked up and saw him with his hands to his face, bellowing and walking around in a circle, blood pouring from between his fingers. He slowly crumbled and fell to his knees still howling.

"I can't see. I can't see! I'm blind. I'm blind."

I didn't know how much damage I had done, but I was satisfied that my aimless blow had apparently blinded him. I could not reconcile my sense of satisfaction with my normal aversion to inflicting physical harm on anyone. But T.C. was not "anyone." At this moment he symbolized everything I loathed—and I'm certain that my role in helping him achieve this status made me hate him, and myself, even more.

My preoccupation was interrupted by a banging on the door.

"What's going on in there? Open up the door."

The loud noises must have attracted hotel security. T.C. had slumped to the floor and curled himself into a fetal ball, continuing his wailing and bleeding.

There was the thumping on the door again. "Open up. Now!"

I knew I had to do something fast. I bent down and tried to haul T.C. to his feet. He stumbled, started to collapse, but then caught himself and stood steady, his body streaked with blood and tears, his antique underpants ripped completely across the back.

"I'm gonna tell them that you did this to me," he slobbered.

The door shook with the continued pounding.

"Open the fucking door!"

T.C. reached out his free arm toward the door lock. I stood right behind him, staring into his massive back. In that very instant, I realized there was nothing I could think of that would save me, no myth persuasive enough that I could weave on the spot. I was finished. This was my last chance to end what I had begun.

"Hold it one second, T.C." I said.

He stopped, his hand on the lock, his back to me. I still had the dagger in my hand and I plunged it into his back as hard and as deep as I could. I could feel the knife penetrate flesh and muscle and scrape against bone.

I expected to hear the same kind of scream from him as when I had cut his eye, but instead all I heard was a sudden gasp and then he pitched forward, attempted to raise himself up and then rolled onto his back. The voice from the other side of the door was now loud and angry.

"Hey what the hell going on in there? Open up in thirty seconds, or I'm coming in."

I looked down on the floor where T.C. was lying, blood pouring from his wounded eye. His other eye stared serenely at the ceiling. His lips were moving, but his voice was so soft I couldn't hear him. I bent down and put my ear near his lips.

"I can't move. I can't feel my legs. Please, please help me..."

T.C. grabbed my free hand and squeezed it pleadingly. I looked at his frightened and desperate face, but his mouth was twisted into an angry grimace. I imagined that this was the same kind of grimace that this same face wore that fateful night when Aaron Boddie was incinerated. The voice from the other side of the door sounded off again.

"You've got fifteen seconds!"

I leaned over T.C. and whispered in his ear. "Can you hear me?"

He nodded his head yes. Holding his hand tight as if to reassure him, I leaned down and whispered in his ear. "T.C. You won't have to worry about not feeling your legs because soon you won't feel anything. You're going to be burning in hell. And I just want you to know that you are going to die at the hand of a Jew. And you're going to die in the same way you thought black people should die. I'm gonna castrate you."

The door shuddered as the fist on the other side slammed against it again and again.

I looked up at the door. Then I looked into T.C.'s one good eye. I could see that he was terrified. I felt great pleasure in that. I pulled my left hand out of his hand and reached down and pulled down his old scraggly underpants. I took his testicles tightly in my hands and started hacking away at his scrotum with the dagger. I expected to hear T.C. scream. The longer I waited for that scream, the more frantically I hacked away at his testicles. Faster, harder, my heart was racing—I felt a surge of energy coursing through my body.

"If you don't open up right now I'm going to break the fucking door down!"

T.C. had managed to elevate his head slightly, just enough to see what I was doing. I was angry, furious, that he didn't seem to be feeling the pain. I was no longer satisfied just to see his face etched with horror. I wanted to know that he was suffering excruciating pain.

I pulled the dagger back and stabbed its point deep into his groin. I withdrew it and plunged it in again, with more anger and barbarity. The third time I plunged the blade in, I felt T.C.'s body jerk, and then he was still. I stood up, dripping with gore and stared down at the huge bloody carcass at my feet. He looked like a butchered bull. My body felt like it had been run over by a Mack truck, but I never felt better in my life. I had won many legal battles, but never had I accomplished such perfect justice. I felt liberated.

*   *   *

"O.K. Lipton, wake up, if you don't open the door I'm going to call security to do it."

I had awakened from nightmares hard before, but never so

hard as from this one. My body was shaking, and I could feel that my suit was soaked with perspiration. I sat up ramrod straight in the bed and kept muttering the usual post nightmare mantra,

"It didn't happen. It didn't happen. It's not true. It didn't happen."

I was so consumed with trying to calm myself down that it took a while for me to respond to Payton's insistent voice and pounding on the hotel door.

"Open the damn door, Luke. Wake up. Open the damn door."

I jumped out of bed and opened the door to a frantic Payton. "I'm sorry, I just conked out, I fell asleep without setting the alarm clock."

"For God's sake, Luke, I've been pounding on your door for over fifteen minutes. I thought you had died. You know we're due at the Augusta Bar Association meeting downstairs at 8:30—it's already 8:15."

"O.K., O.K., so we'll be a little late. What are you worried about? Afraid your adoring acolytes will be deprived of a few minutes of your reflected T.C. glory?

"Now don't start with me, Luke. Keeping 'the good T.C's' myth alive requires our continued support and reinforcement. Remember, we were the handmaidens of his ascension. We must show continued delight in his, and our, vindication."

I shaved while listening to Payton's continuing T.C. bullshit. If I were using a straight razor instead of a Gillette Sensor safety razor, I swear I would have cut his throat right then and there.

"Remember that copy of the FBI tape you gave me?" I asked him. "I think I'll play it for those cracker lawyers. That will raise the hair on their red necks."

"Very funny," Payton responded, not laughing, "If I were you, I would get rid of that tape."

"Get rid of it? If my memory serves me, you were the one suggested I send it to the *Augusta Gazette* so the whole world would know what a fraud T.C. really is."

"That was then."

"Oh sure, that was before you decided that the power and the glory of T.C. is more important than the virtues of truth and justice."

Just then I nicked myself releasing a rivulet of blood. Seeing the blood reminded me of my nightmare. I did not find the reminder repulsive. Strangely enough, rather than a sense of revulsion, I remembered the feeling of liberation my execution of T.C. had brought.

Payton handed me a Kleenex to staunch the bleeding. "Luke, please listen to me. As hard as it is for you to stomach, T.C. is doing more for race relations and rebuilding the esteem of the South than an army of preachers or politicians. Do yourself a favor. Leave it alone."

CHAPTER 44

Texas Guinan, in making the point that there is a sameness to all parts of this great country, once said: "Stick a pin in a map of the United States, and what do you have? Bridgeport." There is the same universality to Bar Association dinners. Whether in Texas, Minnesota, or New York—in big cities or small counties— Bar Association dinners are the same. Most years, the Augusta Bar Association was no exception.

Seated at the dais (sometimes mispronounced as di-as) is the local clergyman who will deliver the benediction and closing prayer. Also on the dais are the most important judges of the region, the officers of the Bar Association, the Guest of Honor (often another one of the more important Judges of the region) and some old fellow who is there because he's simply outlived most of the other members of the Association. Because this elderly fellow has no official office or title, he is often referred to euphemistically as "The Dean" of the Bar Association.

Various awards are made either before or after the dinner— always to lawyers or law firms who did more than their share in fulfilling community obligations expected of lawyers. Other awards are given to those members who survived long enough to be rewarded for their amount of years of membership—fifty year medals, forty year medals, etc. and then there is usually a presentation of that year's "Gold Medal" to some lawyer who had worked tirelessly in the thorny legal vineyards hoping one day to receive his Bar Association's coveted "Gold Medal." After the announcements of the schedule of other bar activities to be held during the forthcoming year, the newly elected officers are named and the proceedings are closed with a prayer from the local clergyman.

That was the agenda for most years, but this year the

Augusta Bar Association annual dinner was unique. The entire program was given over to the toasting and praising of two honored guests. Me and Payton. When we walked into the hotel ballroom we both received a standing ovation. Even the "Dean" stood to applaud us.

We were escorted to the center of the dais to a continuing ovation. I found myself waiving at the audience as if I were in a ticker tape parade—the gesture brought even more applause. We were finally able to sit down, and when the room quieted down, the man who appeared to be the President of the Bar Association began to speak.

"As members of the bar we pride ourselves as being custodians of the 'Rule of Law.' But tragically, in times past we've seen this 'Rule of Law' subverted by those who have nurtured bigotry and hatred. Even more tragic has been the complicity of some of our brethren at the bar who have allowed this to happen. In times past, to our shame, there have been lawyers as legislators, judges, and community leaders, who have been handmaidens of the devil by remaining blind to injustice and silent when their voices should have been heard."

"Tonight we honor two men whose voices *were* heard—not only here in Augusta, but all over the world. Two lawyers who, in their commitment to justice, said 'No!' 'No' to those who would persecute a white man simply because he was poor. 'No' to those who would attempt to legally lynch a white man who attempted to save a black man at the risk of his own life. 'No' to the perpetuation of the myth that the South is a swamp where bigotry, hatred, and racism still breed.

"Luke Lipton and our own Payton Simkins defended T.C. Simmons. In so doing they also defended the dignity of our profession and the 'Rule of Law.' We are honored beyond measure that you have ennobled us this evening with your presence. May God bless you both as you have blessed us."

The crowd jumped to its feet—audience and dais alike—all

applauding and "Hear, hear-ing" me and Payton. We both remained modestly seated for a few moments, and then Payton leaned over to me and said, "Hear that, Luke—think about what I said about the damage the truth would do. Think about it, Luke. And let's stand up."

CHAPTER 45

I did think about what Payton said. I was still thinking about it as I rode in the taxi to the airport for my plane flight home. And thinking about T.C. and the mythology surrounding him, I thought back to my youth when Davy Crockett was my hero—the Disney Davy Crockett that is—a man who went down fighting for freedom against those evil Mexicans.

Although I was in college when I fully realized the truth, I was still devastated. Old Davy was an admirable person, driven out of his congressional seat largely because he had the courage to speak out against President Andrew Jackson's homicidal expulsion of Indians from Georgia. But good old Davy Crockett was fighting at the Alamo for the slave powers in this country. They wanted slavery extended into Texas, and Mexico would have none of that. Mexico had abolished slavery.

Ten years after Davy Crockett died fighting at the Alamo for the freedom to have slavery, a young congressman named Lincoln and an American solider named Grant would determine the Mexican War to be a blatant act of aggression meant only to further the slave interests in this country. But do I want to give back Texas to Mexico? No. Are the Texans of all ancestry better off being part of the United States? Absolutely, that's the reason so many Mexicans risk their lives to sneak into the United States illegally. So, if the ultimate defeat of the Mexicans achieved that positive result, then maybe I would have been better off sticking with the Disney Davy Crockett.

But accepting the mythological Davy Crockett still didn't quiet my troubled mind about the mythological T.C. So far, I had played it as neutrally as possible. I had refused all personal appearances and comments on the trial and its meaning or, rather, on the meaning of its growing myth. The *New York Times* even referred to me by what they called the most astonishing oxymoron of our age, "the silent lawyer."

Most of the media mistook my silence for praiseworthy modesty and even wrote editorials praising my "humility." But appearing in editorials doesn't bring you fame or public adoration. That comes from appearing on television and being interviewed on radio during drive time, something which Payton and T.C. had made into an oft-repeated art form. Payton even seemed to have vaulted over that fifteen-minute chasm. He told me he had just signed to do his own series on the Fox Cable channel called *Justice In America*. I felt a disturbing unease when I heard that. I felt most uneasy because of how uneasy I felt when I heard it. Oscar Wilde once said, "For true happiness, not only must you succeed, but your friends must fail." Well, my friend was succeeding, and I was jealous.

My family was furious with me for missing the boat. The calls for my appearances had already tapered off. Now most of the calls to my home or old office were queries as to how Payton or T.C. could be contacted. Payton will end up in a grave with a huge kiosk over it detailing his fame and accomplishments. My tombstone will be so small, the word "principles" won't even fit on it.

What would it do to my career, my family, should all of this explode? What if some enterprising journalist uncovered the truth, or someone leaks those wiretap tapes to some television station? My family was so excited with the publicity—even bemoaning the fact that my reticence deprived them of more. If there was an explosion of truth, the thunder of bad publicity would keep them from leaving the house. Oh sure, I would argue that I had a lawyer's obligation to keep quiet and that I did not profit from the "myth." "Lipton should have come forward with the *truth!*" all of those sideline pundits would shriek.

Payton and T.C. would at least have a full bank account and scrapbook when all of this came tumbling down. I would have the worst of both worlds: no sharing in the benefits, completely shar-ing in the deficits, and the shame.

I leaned toward the driver: "Could you stop at that post office for a moment please? I'll be right out."

I left the cab, slipped on my driving gloves and went into the post office. I bought a reinforced mailing envelope and wrote down the address of the *Augusta Gazette*, which I had been car-rying in my wallet. I then bought four self-stick stamps and placed them on the envelope. I slipped the copy of the FBI wiretap tape that Payton had given me into the envelope.

I stood for a while looking at the mail slot. I knew if I was going to mail this damaging tape to the newspaper, it should be mailed from here rather than from the airport at the same time as I was scheduled to be there for my flight back to New York. I trust-ed the newspaper to protect its sources, but I didn't want to take any chances.

I knew that mailing the tape would not be as good a pro-phylactic move as my coming forward with the truth. But if I had chosen that course, I would have gotten into a pissing match with T.C. and Payton, those two formidable media icons, who would deny everything. This tape was the only irrefutable evidence. I could never use it directly to support myself, because I had no lawful right to have the tape in the first place. This anonymous mailing was the only way to liberate the truth.

I thought of the Biblical admonition that "The Truth will set you free." Tell that to some guy who has just confessed to a dou-ble homicide!

I was standing in front of the mail drop, just holding out the envelope and staring, lost in my thoughts. This was it. Do it or not. Now or never. All I had to do was to let go, and it would be over—T.C. would be undone, and the crap he had been dumping on the public would stop. I didn't notice the woman next to me scanning the address on my package.

"The *Augusta Gazette*? I hope it's a bomb. Those Commie

bastards ought to be run out of this country."

I instinctively pulled the envelope back and stuffed it into my pocket. I forced a small laugh.

"Oh no, it's just an idea for a story I was going to submit. But it needs more work."

I don't know why that brief encounter disturbed me so much. I didn't think it was some mystical omen cautioning me not to mail the package, but it really shook me up. I walked out of the Post Office with the tape in the envelope tucked securely in my coat pocket.

I arrived at the airport, subjected myself to the enhanced security check, and walked to my flight gate. I sat in one of the theater-like seats designed to keep the passengers in relative comfort while waiting for their flight to be called and boarded. The envelope in my pocket pressed against my hip, reminding me that there was more for me to do before I left for New York. And then I thought of Wiley Post.

Whenever I spoke to an incoming class of attorneys at my old law firm, I gave them the "Wiley Post" lecture. I told them about the 1930s newsreel clip of the then-renowned pilot Wiley Post. He is seen sitting at the controls of a seaplane with the famous humorist Will Rogers smiling over his right shoulder. Wiley has a huge grin on his face and is waving at the camera. Those who see the film know that the flight will end in the death of both passengers. In watching the film, the viewer's instinct is to yell to the two smiling passengers: "Don't go! Don't go!" There is a feeling that if you could stop the film, you could save those two valuable lives.

I would turn to the new attorneys and tell them to make sure that they think of repercussions before they act. I would tell them, before taking an action that might have adverse consequences, always think "Wiley Post. Wiley Post." I told them if President Clinton had thought "Wiley Post" when Monica Lewinsky first walked into his office wearing that blue dress, he never would have been impeached. He should have acted when he still had time to abort his take-off.

I really did think the Wiley Post thing worked because it once saved my career. I was sitting in the office with a partner from my firm talking to an adversary attorney. I was beginning to tell that lawyer things that could have cost my firm its biggest client and me my job. As I talked, my partner whispered to me, "Wiley Post. Wiley Post." I hesitated for only a moment then continued to ramble on. Finally, my partner's voice became more insistent: "Luke, you're on the runway!" I said a few more words. This time his whisper was louder and harsher. "Soon it will be impossible to abort the takeoff safely." That finally got through, and my job was saved.

Now here I was thinking Wiley Post again. I knew I might never have the chance to right the T.C. wrong again. A short distance from where I was seated I spotted a trashcan. Next to it was a mailbox. Those were my two choices, and there was nothing behind the curtain. I knew I should think this through before take-off. I should think this out calmly and not act on emotion—as if I hadn't thought about it enough.

And then, seemingly, there was another mysterious omen. I heard T.C.'s name being mentioned on an overhead airport television set. I looked up and saw the President of the United States with his arm around T.C., saying to the reporters surrounding them:

"This man is what this country is all about. In one dramatic moment he demonstrated that the instinct of brotherly love can eclipse lessons of hatred and even fear of death. He has given us a whole new definition of courage, tolerance, and compassionate understanding. That's why I have chosen him to chair a committee that I have just established by executive order: "The National Council for Interracial Concerns."

I thought I was going to pass out. The President of the United States of America. At least T.C. had enough sense to keep his big mouth shut. Wrong. When I looked back at the television set, there was the station anchorwoman interviewing T.C. He was wearing one of those tee-shirts depicting a black hand grasping a white hand.

"What I have always wondered is, why did you join the Klan in the first place??

"To get revenge."

"To get revenge?"

T.C. took a deep breath. I thought, this was going to be some whopper coming up. I couldn't wait to hear this answer.

"Actually, the full story will be in my book, but, well, I..."

"Come on, you can tell us just the outline of what happened."

"Well you see, there was this Jewish family I knew. Back then the people in this town hated Jews real bad. One day some Klan fellows burn a cross on their lawn, only the fire gets out of control. I was walking by and I knowed one of the kids in that family, so I run into the burning house and helped save the family by taking them out one at a time out the house."

"That's real heroism, they must have been quite grateful to you."

"Well, they was, but the Klan wasn't. They beat me pretty severe, one Klansman even stabbed me he was so mad. You want to see the scar?"

Without waiting for an answer T.C. pulled down his shirt to reveal his shoulder scar. I thought "You jackass!" T.C. had testified at trial that he had gotten that scar when he tried to save Boddie's life. T.C. either needs more scars or fewer stories. I wondered if anyone would pick up on that. I wondered if anyone would care.

"Oh my, that is some vicious scar. But I still don't understand how that incident got you to join the Klan?"

"Well, that boy in that family asked me what could he do to pay me back for saving him and his family's lives and that's when

I got the idea. I told him that I wanted him to be blood brothers with me. You know, we cut each others' fingers and mixed our blood. We done that. And then I went out and convinced the Klan that I had changed my Jewish life-saving ways and wanted to join up. What I really had in my head was that now that I had Jewish blood in me, I would become a member of the Klan. That's what I call revenge."

"Did they ever get suspicious of you?"

"No, back then they wanted to grow the Klan so they let me join up. After I got in I told them all that I had inside information that there was a Jew in the Klan or someone with Jew blood—which was true—drove 'em all nuts."

At that point, I thought the interviewer would fall off her chair she was laughing so hard.

"So what happened?"

"They even accused the Grand Cyclops of being a secret Jew, it was crazy, man. And you know, every time they burned a cross, I held up my Jewish finger, you know, to like put a curse on them."

"Mr. Simmons..."

"Please call me T.C."

"T.C. I know how dangerous the Klan was in those days—for you to not only save a Jewish family from their terror, but also to hold the Klan up to ridicule in so courageous a way—well, all I can say is that I wish there were more men of your valor and nobility. I don't think our audience can truly appreciate what courage it took to do something like that back then."

I couldn't believe what I was seeing and hearing. I wondered if Payton would categorize this bullshit as a "good myth." What if I called the television station and shared the real *truth* with that swooning anchor—that T.C. had threatened to kill me after we exchanged blood and he found out that I was Jewish. But if called, what good would it do other than to make me feel good. And that burning cross crap. The only reason T.C. would have run into our house if someone was burning a cross on our lawn would be to get another match.

That interview really both bothered and scared me. T.C. appeared to be totally out of control. Obviously his "good" myth-making knew no bounds. Soon he would be saying that Jesse Jackson could not possibly have cradled Martin Luther King's body in his arms, because T.C. was cradling Dr. King's body after the shooting. And it wouldn't be too much longer until he started explaining the scar on his back as an injury he received during the Vietnam War while parachuting into Hanoi to take out Ho Chi Minh.

I looked up just as T.C.'s interview was finishing.

"I just want to say, T.C., I just want to tell my audience that your humility and humanity demonstrate that there are those good people who never let fame go to their heads."

"Hey," T.C. responded with an 'aw shucks' smile, "I'm the same person I always was."

"Anyway, T.C.," The anchor closed with a smile, "you are what the very best of America is all about."

"No, he's not!" I shouted out loud. I was furious now. I again slipped on my gloves and pulled the envelope containing the tape out of my pocket. I was walking toward the mail box sitting next to the trash can. "Wiley Post, Wiley Post" kept pounding in my head. "Fuck you, Wiley Post!" my head kept answering.

I stared at the mailbox. "You're on the runway again Luke." That voice again. My hand was shaking. Just drop it in.

My mind was racing faster than Wiley Post's engine. T.C. was totally out of control. There was so much hot air in that balloon now, that when it burst, the concussion would kill everyone in sight, including me. And damn you, Payton, the truth is important, it's essential. If this country really does choke on the truth, then it deserves to die.

"Excuse me, if you are not using the mailbox, may I borrow it for a moment?"

I turned to see a visibly irritated person apparently waiting to mail something. I did a double take because he looked almost *exactly* like T.C., except he was wearing a suit, not overalls. I must have been staring at him a little too intently.

"Is there something wrong?"

"Well, you just look like somebody."

"I know. I know. Everyone mistakes me for that hayseed who seems to have monopolized the media. I have given up even denying that I'm him, because people won't believe me. I've had to give out five autographs just since I've been in this airport."

"But that's not being truthful—don't you think it's kind of dishonest pretending to be someone you're not?"

"What the hell—there's no harm in it. It doesn't hurt me and it makes them happy."

"Yes, I understand, a *good* myth."

"Excuse me, mister, but I think you are making a bigger thing out of this than it deserves. I'm just grateful I don't look like some notorious murderer." He said this with a good-natured smile. He mailed his envelope and went on his way.

If he only knew. Actually, he looked *exactly* like a murderer. A very famous, almost worshiped murderer. My mind was racing, and remembering—remembering Abe Lapinsky, and Senator Kirk and all the other false "heroes" I had encountered on my way to this moment.

As I stood in front of the trashcan on the one side and the mailbox on the other, I realized I had come to the moment of truth. I could either drop the envelope in the mailbox and unmask one of the greatest frauds in recent memory, or I could take the tape out of the envelope and, after mangling it, drop it into the trash can, thereby consigning the truth about T.C. to the dustbin of history.

CHAPTER 46

Okay, the mailbox represented the truth. Mail the envelope and the truth will be splashed across the headlines of every newspaper in the country. The best argument for the truth was that telling it is always the right thing to do. Of course, there could be adverse consequences. I might not be able to continue living the lifestyle I lived now, but at least I'd be able to live with myself. Anyone can always rationalize not telling the truth—but I've always thought that lying, even an understandable lie, is inevitably the first step down a slippery slope that leads right to hell.

On the practical side, revealing the truth would save me a lot of sleepless nights. After all, I was not the only holder of the truth. Law enforcement people knew, Payton knew, hey, even T.C. knew. They all had motives to conceal the truth, but people's positions in life and their consciences have a way of changing dramatically. The first person out with the truth would be a hero of sorts. Everyone else would be considered a hateful human being who helped perpetrate or at least cover up a terribly destructive hoax. If I told the truth, some people—even my family—would be disappointed that I, out of Princeton and Harvard, could have been duped by the likes of a T.C.—but as unpleasant as that might turn out to be, it would be better to be thought a dupe than an accomplice to a terrible fraud.

My concern that someone might leak the contents of the tape or a copy of the tape itself did not include a great concern that Rabison would be the one who did the leaking. Rabison was an immoral crass opportunist, but he was not stupid. It was precisely because he would have the opportunity and motive to leak the tape after the acquittal of T.C. that he would be the last person to do so. I knew Rabison would have cut off his right arm to get a conviction of T.C. Simmons. But once the irrevocable verdict of acquittal was rendered, I thought the chances were minuscule that Rabison would cut off his left arm to accomplish at most the recapture of some of Morgan's reputation.

The last thing Rabison wanted was to be the focus of a ferocious court-ordered FBI investigation into the unauthorized dissemination of those tapes. If the dissemination of those tapes somehow compromised whatever the bigger investigation was about, Rabison would never emerge from under the cloak of suspicion. His career would be ruined, all of which, of course, was another practical reason for my leaking the tape to the newspapers. I might be able to kill two rats with one tape, T.C. and Rabison.

No, Rabison wouldn't reveal the tapes, and there was no doubt in my mind that if the truth was going to come out eventually, it would be best that I be the one to reveal it. Nixon and Clinton learned the hard way that the cover-up often buries you deeper than that which you are trying to hide. Besides, it's not too bad being seen as a courageous person of conscience. I would be exchanging my perceived role as the national hero who saved T.C. to become the national icon who brought forth the truth. It sounds so perfect that one would think it a Hollywood script. And why not? I started to wonder who would play me in the movie, and then I saw one of the newly vigilant airport security personnel staring at me, wondering why I was smiling at a mailbox. That snapped me back to Wiley Post.

Another damned good reason to tell the truth would be so that lowlife T.C. would get what was coming to him instead of what was being given to him. If I didn't clip his venal wings, it would rip my insides out every time I saw him on some national talk show or in some media profile spouting his love for all of mankind. I didn't know if I could live with myself if I didn't unmask the face of evil.

Okay, Mr. Mailbox, so much for you. My eyes shifted to the

trashcan, the death of the truth and the perpetration of the myth. It occurred to me that those who say that telling the truth is an imperative are really shoveling garbage. If the truthful way was always the right way, why don't we hear people saying, "My, but you look ugly today."

I greatly doubted that Raoul Wallenberg was burning in hell because he lied to the Nazis to save the lives of thousands of Jews from Hitler's concentration camps. Similarly, I highly doubted that the Dutch informer who truthfully told the Gestapo where Ann Frank's family was hiding punched his ticket to heaven by his act of truth telling.

The one verity always pounded into me from my youth was to always to tell the truth. The illustrative story that every child of my generation memorized was that of George Washington and the cherry tree. The moral of the story was to never tell a lie. But then it turned out that the very story meant to teach the lesson of the value of truth telling was itself a lie! Parson Weems made up the entire story of Washington and the cherry tree. The fact was that if George Washington did cut down one of his father's prized cherry trees, you can bet when his old man appeared and hovered over his son clutching a studded belt, little George blamed it all on one of the slaves. That really made a point for the garbage can.

What difference did it make that the story of George and the cherry tree is a lie? It made me and my little friends tell far more truths than we would have told without it, so the story served a good purpose of showing the importance of truth telling even if it had to lie to do so. To be fair—there was no saintly T.C., but look at how much good it was doing for so many people, and, indeed, for this country, that people think T.C. is a modern-day saint.

If I revealed the truth about T.C., I would put a poison arrow in the quiver of every group I had detested throughout my life. The black racists would be able to say that this proved that every white person, no matter how free of racism he seems, was deep down a racist bigot. And the real hard-core white racists would be overjoyed at the racial friction an unmasking of T.C. would provoke.

And who knows what the truth means anyway? Truth cannot really be sifted out through the flawed gauze of human intelligence. Only God knows the real truth, the important truth. I should leave truth to God and do my best to sell the best myths possible here on Earth.

Practically, if I unmasked T.C., I could also unhorse myself. Right now I was basking in his reflected glow, but if I unmasked him I might well be blistered by the flames of his destruction. Who's to say that people would appreciate my telling the truth? The truth is scant armor when facing an army of believers. The landscape of this country is littered with the bodies of dead messengers.

My mind swirled with the competing arguments. Like a trained trial attorney, I had managed to convince myself of the righteousness of each mutually exclusive argument. I had taken out my yellow pad, drawn up the pros and cons and reached total paralysis. So I decided to toss away the yellow pad and follow my heart rather than my head.

I heard the announcement of the final boarding for my flight. I had do something—or I could do nothing and just take the envelope with me and delay my decision. But I decided to act. I would go where fate or some Divine source led me. I approached midway between the mailbox and the trashcan and stood for a moment when suddenly, miraculously, I felt as if some guiding spirit directed my hand to the correct destination. Maybe that wasn't the fact—maybe it wasn't a guiding spirit, but rather my own unconscious desire. Whatever it was, I went where it took me. In an instant it was done.

EPILOGUE

As the plane took to the sky, I stared down at the ground, my eyes fixed on the airport terminal where I had just made the most momentous decision of my life. But had I made the right decision? I always told new associates at the law firm that once they did a thorough Wiley Post they should never second-guess their decision. But here I was violating my own rule.

As thoughts tumbled through my mind, I suddenly realized why Wiley Post had failed me now. In the past, acting as a good professional attorney, I had always been concerned about making the most rational choice. Now, for one of the very few times in my life, I was more concerned with making the right choice. The rule of reason, which had tethered me to a world controlled by rational thought, had been frayed and then finally snapped.

The night before I left Augusta had been a restless one for me. To help pass the sleepless night, I found myself reading the Gideon Bible that was in the hotel night table. I opened it up to a page at random, and by sheer coincidence (or perhaps it wasn't a sheer coincidence at all) the page had fallen open on the story of Jacob and Esau: how Jacob deceived his father Isaac in order to inherit the birthright which rightly belonged to his brother Esau. It became clear to me that what is right, whether the truth or the good myth, was not at all clear even to God. There is no question that mankind benefited more from the treachery of Jacob than it suffered from his deliberate suppression of the truth.

Now, on the plane, as a diversion and to rest my reeling mind, I pulled my Blackberry hand computer from my pocket and started scanning my messages. My wife had sent me just a partial list of the countless people offering me inducements to get hold of T.C. or Payton with proposals for advertisements, movies, books, paid speeches, television appearances and virtually any other kind of commercial exploitation known to mankind and some even heretofore unknown. There were also countless pleas for T.C. to help various charities. The messages were full of bombast and desperation, and I assumed they tried to contact me only after being rejected or ignored by T.C.'s manager and agent and Payton's people at his law firm.

As I scrolled through the messages, the few that weren't filtered by my wife were the ones from people who knew how to reach my Blackberry, mostly my former colleagues from Morton and Philips. Their messages were filled with flattering praise for what I had done and the celebrity I had achieved. Each gushing sentence they wrote oozed uncontrollable envy. I'd had the guts to leave the diamond-studded monastery and leap blindly into the unknown. My colleagues were certainly burning with jealousy, but there was no chance that any of them would follow me out the door because it was irrational to leave a secure, obscenely well paid job merely to attempt to inject some excitement into an often dreary and enervating existence. Being a partner at a Wall Street firm was an offer that no one, particularly a person with a family and a high-maintenance lifestyle, could afford to refuse. The yellow pad solution would not allow for it.

The most interesting message on the Blackberry from my wife involved a request for my appearance. I, the one dubbed by the *New York Times* as the "silent attorney," was still getting some offers, but word seemed to have gotten around that I was not available as bait for the media feeding frenzy. One newspaper theorized that with all of the money I must have earned at Morton and Philips, I didn't need any more money and didn't want any attention. One columnist praised me for being a vanishing breed whose only reward needed was a job well done. I only wished the motives for my silence were that noble.

The offer that interested me was the belated offer to be one of the three speakers at the dedication next month of the Senator

Allan Kirk FBI Building in Manhattan. For months, it had been planned that there would be two speakers at the dedication, the President of the United States and a revered Republican congressman from Long Island. At one point, they had wanted as a "common man" speaker, the worker whose life the public was told Senator Kirk saved from the elephant at the cost of his own life. But the poor young man must have been so traumatized by his near death experience that he could never seem to remember exactly how it was that Senator Kirk saved his life. He was prepped, rehearsed and well compensated, but he couldn't keep the story straight.

I had been added as a third speaker when my sudden sun flare of fame rose so high that it obliterated the fact that I hardly knew Senator Kirk. I wondered what my former colleague, Senator Kirk's close friend, Lou Howard, felt when he heard that I was offered a speaking role at the dedication while he was not. I also wondered if I would accept the invitation.

I tried to sleep, but I could not. The doubts about what I had done at the airport took hold of me with an awakening and disturbing vengeance. I went over and over the checklist of the arguments pro and con for what I had finally decided to do. I wondered where the road not taken would have led. Had I made the right choice? Maybe both roads were culs-de-sac. Maybe either decision would have led to disaster or maybe either decision would have worked out well. But I couldn't convince myself of that. I couldn't convince myself that the decision I made didn't make all the difference, one way or the other.

I perused the inside of the airplane, looking for a sign other than the one that was presently warning passengers to keep their seat belts fastened. I saw nothing of interest in front of me; so I turned to my right and started looking behind me. My eyes were immediately drawn to the seat across the aisle, one row behind me. Seated there was a nun in a flowing black habit. Her eyes were closed and her head was bowed. Her lips were moving in silent conversation while her right hand clutched a large cross that hung from her neck. Her fingers seemed to caress the cross in perfect cadence with the movement of her lips. Every so often her lips would become still as if she was listening to an answer and when her lips stopped moving her hand would stop fidgeting with the cross, and would, instead, grab it tightly. Then her lips would move again, and her fingers would also again begin playing up and down the cross.

When I was young and knew everything there was to know, I always marveled at the stupidity of people who believed in a God who was obviously created by man in his own image. I would also become infuriated with the arrogance of those who thought that, if there was a God, He would have nothing better to do with His time than to listen to them prattle on about their petty little problems. But this sudden need I had for faith had loosened the death grip reason had on my soul. I regretted that I did not have a better relationship with God whether or not He really existed. I did not stare at the nun with scorn or pity. I stared at her with envy.

I learned at my mother's knee that it was not polite to stare, but I could not wrest my eyes from that nun. I knew she was talking to God because one did not see such a beatific look on a woman's face when she was talking on a cell phone. I wondered what she was talking to God about. Was she praying for her own safety on this flight? Or was she praying for others, for the poor and downtrodden? Of maybe she wasn't asking God *for* anything. Maybe she was just expressing her faith *in* God rather than asking Him for favors. One thing I knew for certain was that she had a pipeline Upstairs that was unavailable to me. I thought for a moment that maybe I should lean over and nudge her and ask,

"Excuse me, but would it be too much of an imposition for you to ask Him if the passenger in seat 6A did the right thing with the tape?"

I refrained from following my impulse, but the little laugh

that escaped my lips apparently disturbed the nun's reverie. She picked up her head and looked directly at me. Our stares met, neither of us either smiling or frowning. For a few short seconds our eyes remained locked in the embrace of the curious, and confused. I wanted to pull my gaze away, but my stare was frozen in place. I noticed after a few moments that her gaze narrowed as if she was looking directly into my soul. She held that piercing glare for only a few moments until it was overcome by a broad smile that gradually enveloped her face.

But it was not the smile that sent what felt like jolts of electricity ripping through my body. It was what accompanied that smile. I could not be certain, but I think I saw the slightest, almost imperceptible, wink of her right eye. I realize that a more objective, a more rational person might have seen that almost imperceptible wink as a mere tic or even an acknowledgment of our eyes having met. But, I was no longer a man of reason. I was a man of faith, and, as such, I chose to see much more in that slight wink from the nun. After the initial explosion of excitement upon perceiving that sign, my body relaxed, and I became fully at ease with myself for the first time since I had made my choice with that tape.

Reflexively, my head dropped towards my chest. I found myself gently clasping my hands together in prayer, something I hadn't even done when my physician thought I might have a cancerous lesion on my lung. I couldn't even remember any prayer to recite, so I just softly muttered the only prayer I thought appropriate for this miraculous occasion.

"Thank you, Lord."